Ao Haru Ride

The scent of air after rain...
In the light around us, I felt your heartbeat.

10

IO SAKISAKA

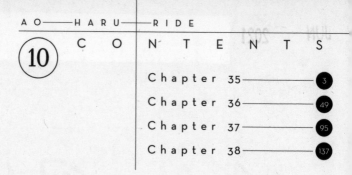

STORY
THUS
FAR

Futaba Yoshioka was quiet and awkward around boys in junior high, but she's taken on a tomboy persona in high school. It's there that she once again meets her first love, Tanaka (now Kou Mabuchi), and falls for him again.

When Futaba can't let go of her feelings for Kou after being rejected, she agrees to go out with Toma Kikuchi, who says he'll accept her even if she still cares about Kou. Meanwhile, Kou realizes he's spent time with Yui out of guilt and attempts to separate himself from her, but Yui won't let him. Kou's frustrations mount when he learns that Futaba and Toma are dating, but by then it's too late. Now boyfriend and girlfriend, Futaba and Toma share a kiss...

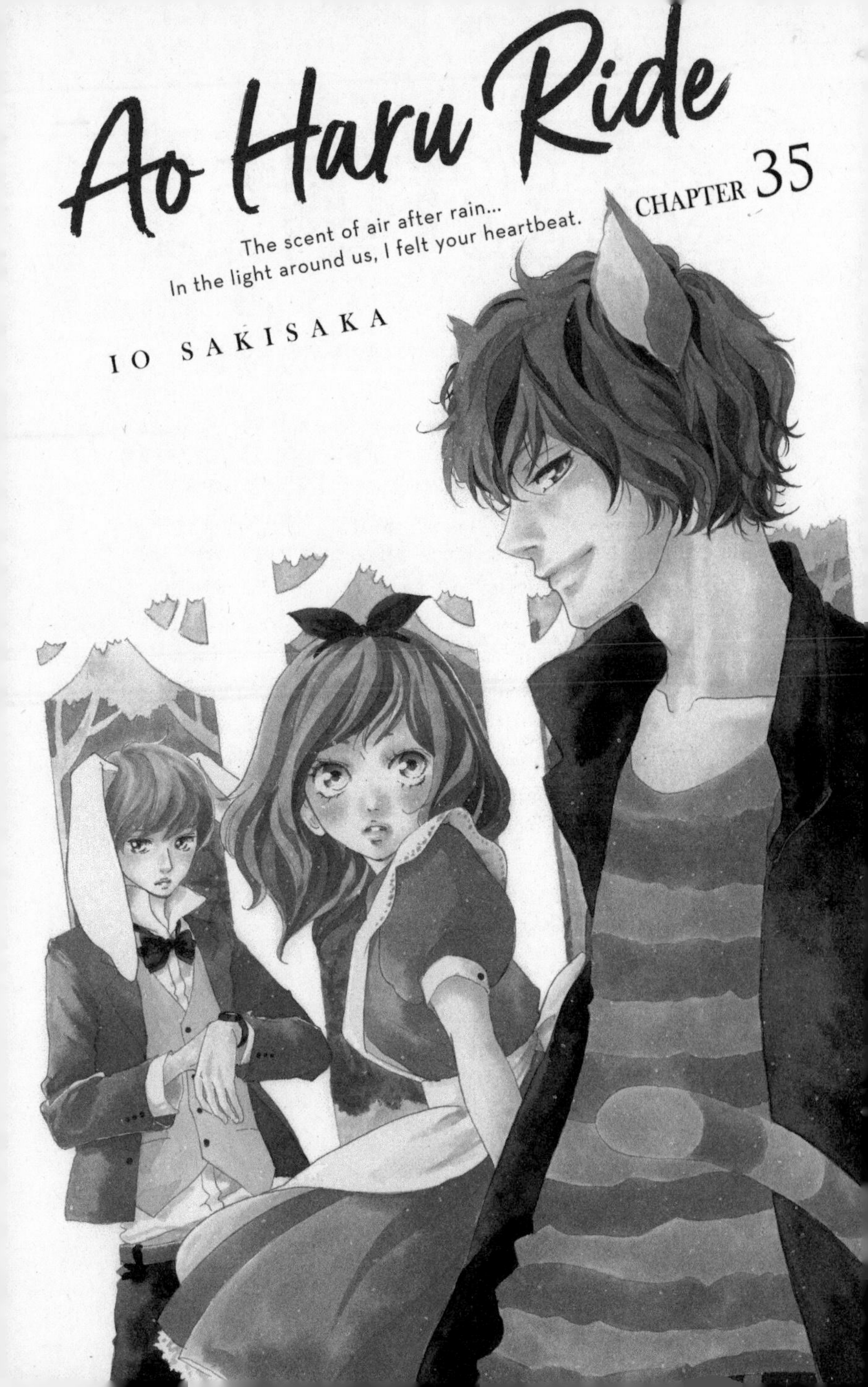
Ao Haru Ride
CHAPTER 35
The scent of air after rain...
In the light around us, I felt your heartbeat.
IO SAKISAKA

GREETINGS

Hi! I'm Io Sakisaka. Thank you for picking up a copy of
Ao Haru Ride volume 10!

The other day, as I was working on the plot for *Ao Haru Ride*,
I was surprised to find the story come to me without much
effort. I could complete it in one go. I was thrilled, and I said
to myself, "This is great! People are going to love it! Yes!"
But...it was just a dream. I woke up completely shocked—how
could it have been a dream?! When I thought back to the plot
that I wrote in my dream, it was an incoherent mess. I was
unbelievably disappointed. It felt like a sick joke. To think all
my joy and elation was nothing more than an illusion. This
happened just as I was up against a plot deadline, so the
disappointment was severe. Please don't ever make me see
my dreams in my dreams again. Okay?

Volume 10 is the result of diligent work, all done while awake.
I hope you'll enjoy it through to the end!

 Io Sakisaka

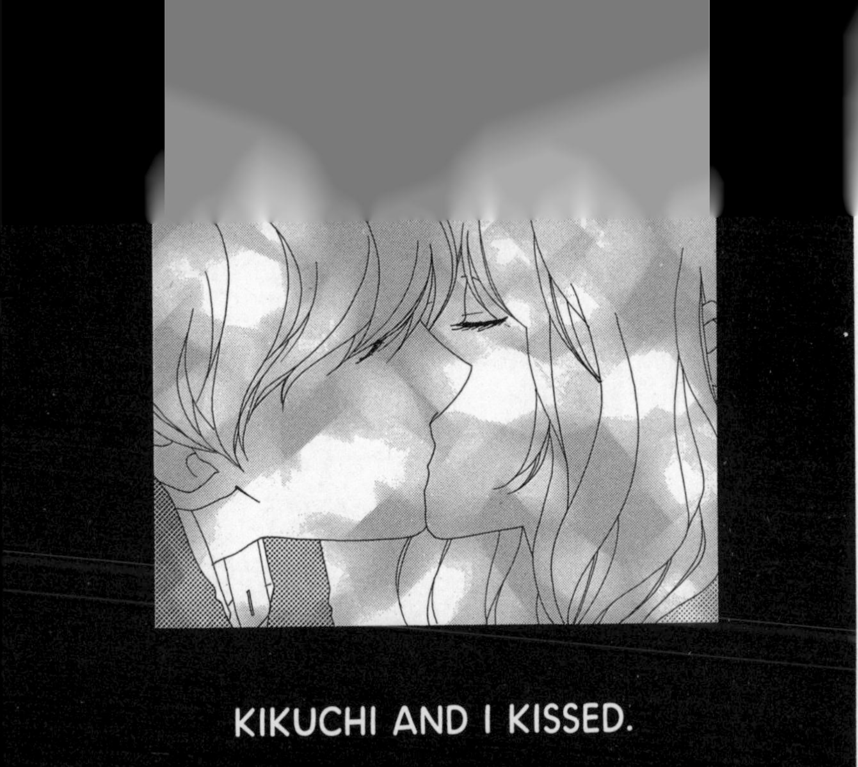
KIKUCHI AND I KISSED.

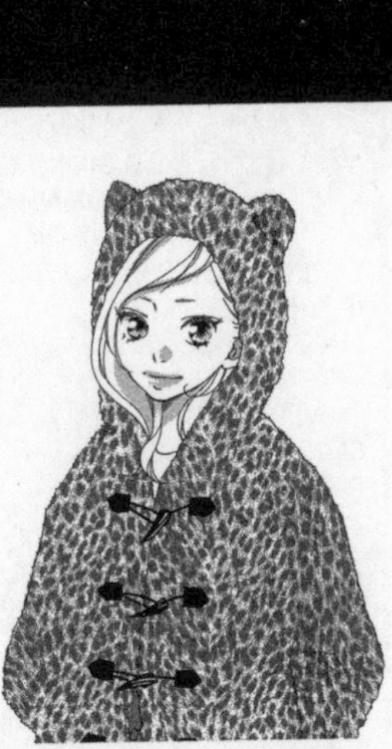

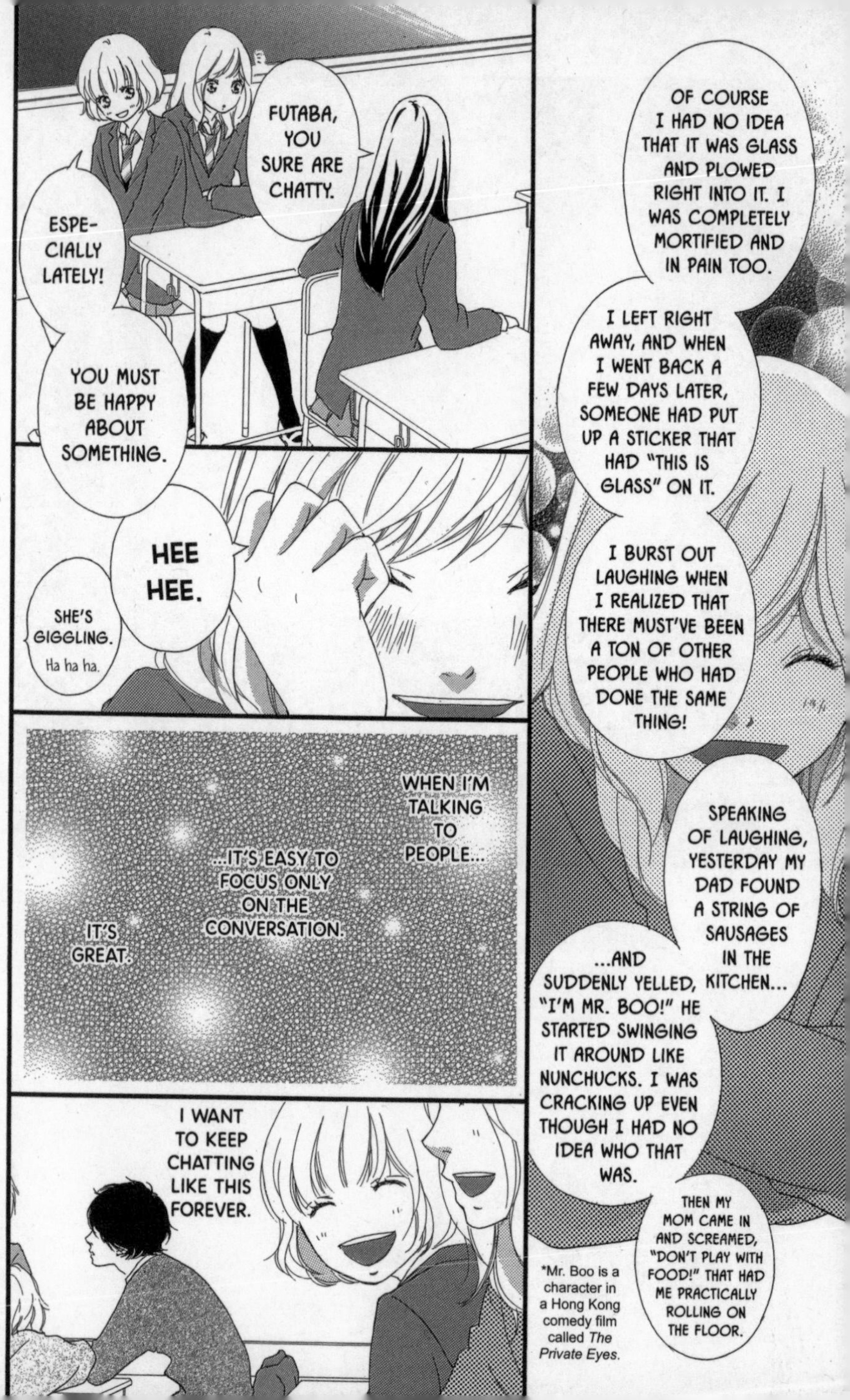
OF COURSE I HAD NO IDEA THAT IT WAS GLASS AND PLOWED RIGHT INTO IT. I WAS COMPLETELY MORTIFIED AND IN PAIN TOO.
I LEFT RIGHT AWAY, AND WHEN I WENT BACK A FEW DAYS LATER, SOMEONE HAD PUT UP A STICKER THAT HAD "THIS IS GLASS" ON IT.
I BURST OUT LAUGHING WHEN I REALIZED THAT THERE MUST'VE BEEN A TON OF OTHER PEOPLE WHO HAD DONE THE SAME THING!
SPEAKING OF LAUGHING, YESTERDAY MY DAD FOUND A STRING OF SAUSAGES IN THE KITCHEN...
...AND SUDDENLY YELLED, "I'M MR. BOO!" HE STARTED SWINGING IT AROUND LIKE NUNCHUCKS. I WAS CRACKING UP EVEN THOUGH I HAD NO IDEA WHO THAT WAS.
THEN MY MOM CAME IN AND SCREAMED, "DON'T PLAY WITH FOOD!" THAT HAD ME PRACTICALLY ROLLING ON THE FLOOR.
*Mr. Boo is a character in a Hong Kong comedy film called *The Private Eyes*.
FUTABA, YOU SURE ARE CHATTY.
ESPE-CIALLY LATELY!
YOU MUST BE HAPPY ABOUT SOMETHING.
HEE HEE.
SHE'S GIGGLING.
Ha ha ha.
WHEN I'M TALKING TO PEOPLE...
...IT'S EASY TO FOCUS ONLY ON THE CONVERSATION.
IT'S GREAT.
I WANT TO KEEP CHATTING LIKE THIS FOREVER.

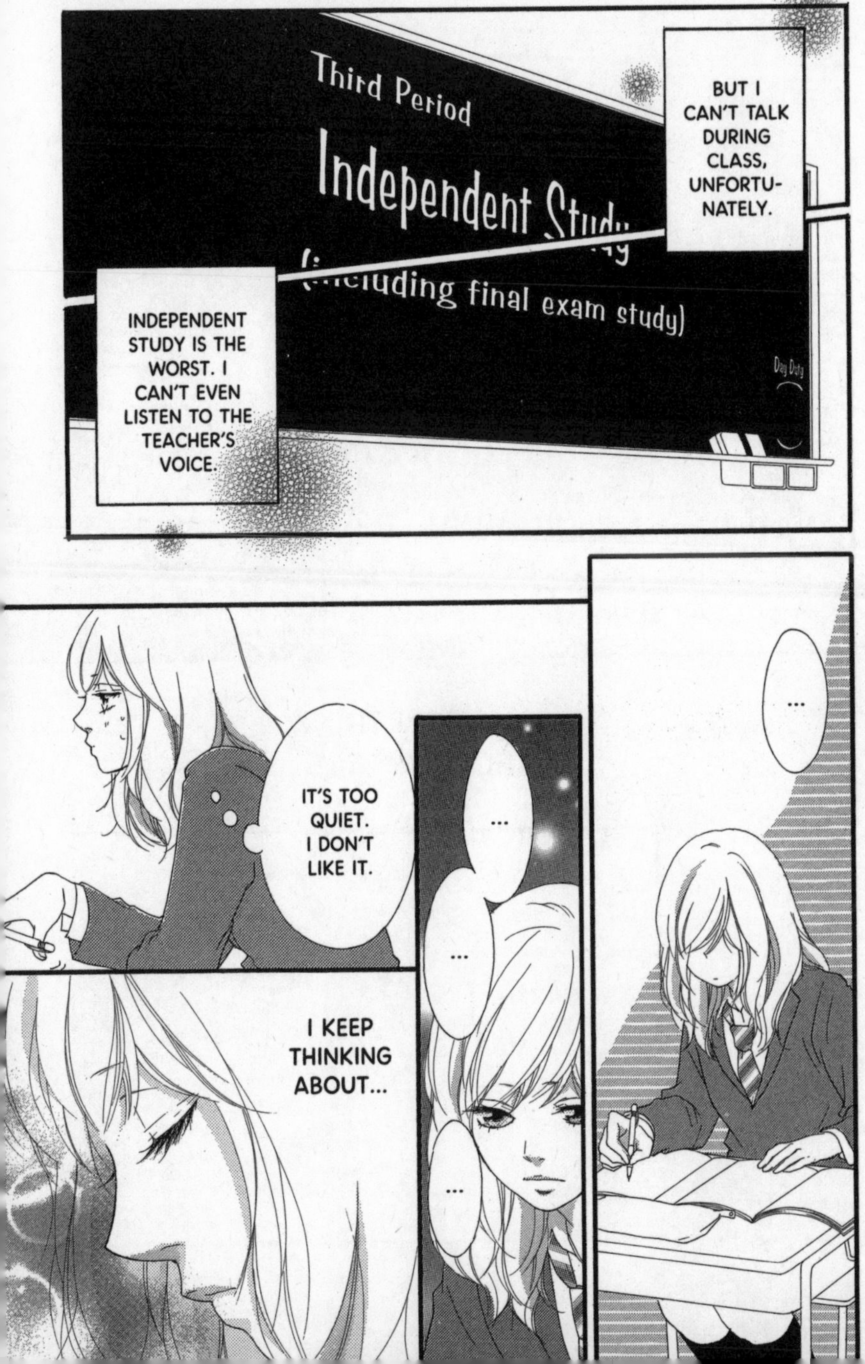

BUT I CAN'T TALK DURING CLASS, UNFORTUNATELY.
Third Period
Independent
final exam study)
Day Duty
INDEPENDENT STUDY IS THE WORST. I CAN'T EVEN LISTEN TO THE TEACHER'S VOICE.
...
...
...
...
IT'S TOO QUIET. I DON'T LIKE IT.
I KEEP THINKING ABOUT...

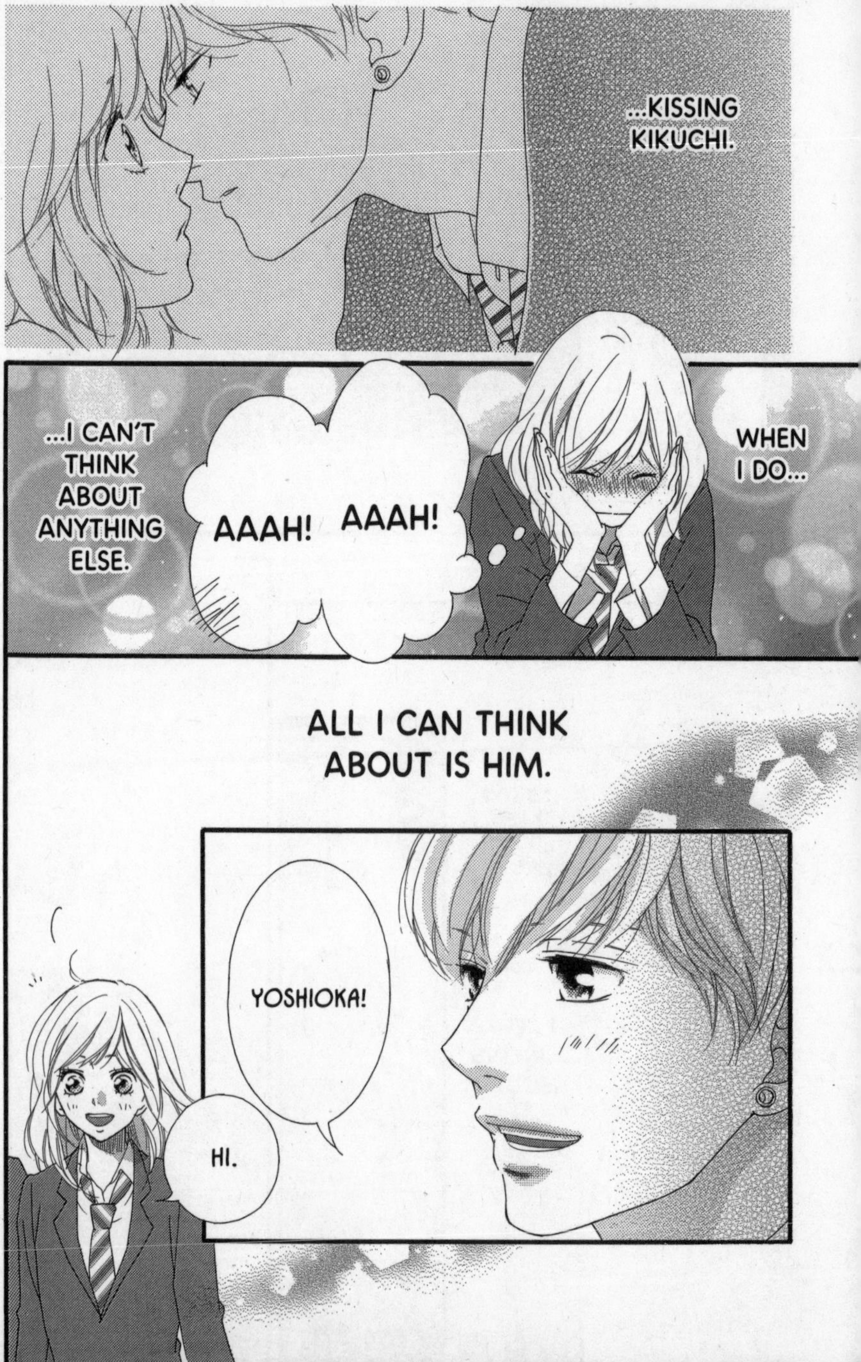
...KISSING KIKUCHI.
WHEN I DO...
AAAH! AAAH!
...I CAN'T THINK ABOUT ANYTHING ELSE.
ALL I CAN THINK ABOUT IS HIM.
YOSHIOKA!
HI.

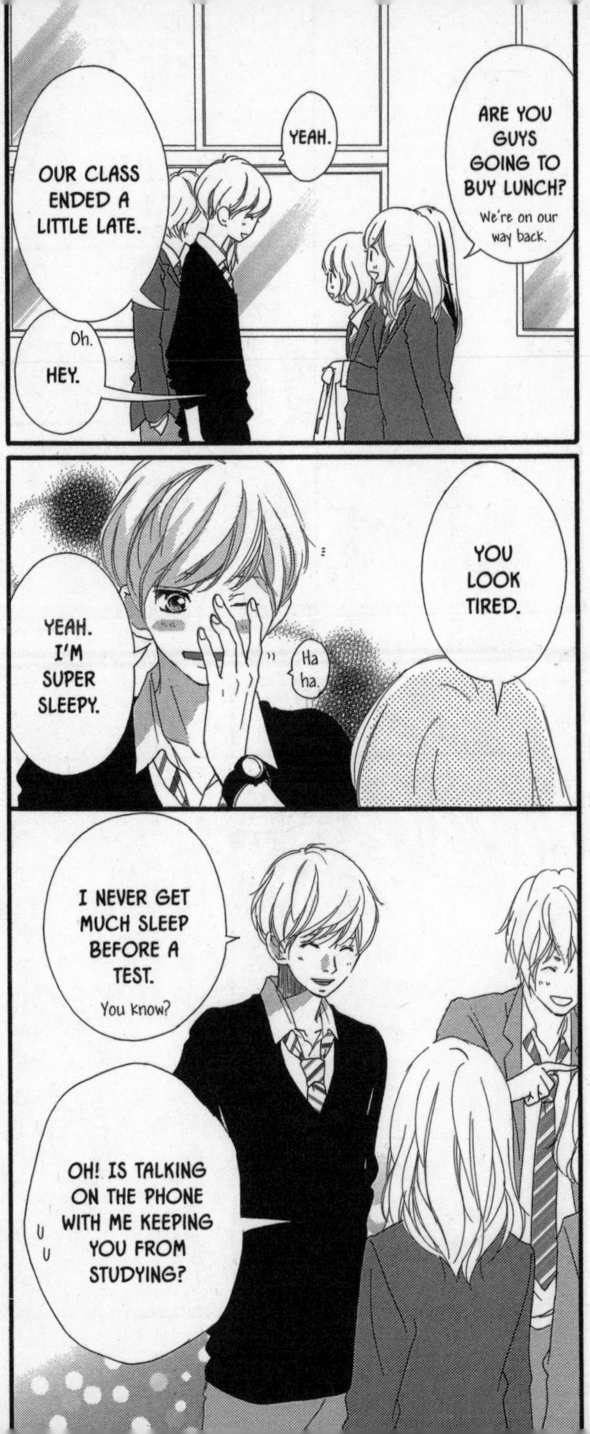
ARE YOU GUYS GOING TO BUY LUNCH?
We're on our way back.
YEAH.
OUR CLASS ENDED A LITTLE LATE.
Oh.
HEY.
YOU LOOK TIRED.
Ha ha.
YEAH. I'M SUPER SLEEPY.
I NEVER GET MUCH SLEEP BEFORE A TEST.
You know?
OH! IS TALKING ON THE PHONE WITH ME KEEPING YOU FROM STUDYING?

I have an older sister. It's rare that we call or email each other, and lately we haven't been able to get together much either. Our relationship appears so indifferent that an outsider might think that we don't get along, but that isn't the case. We both really care about each another. (At least I think we do.) Since our relationship is like that, I didn't bother to say anything to her when *Ao Haru Ride* was chosen to become an anime. But after my sister heard the news somehow—and this was probably the first time ever—she wrote me a very long congratulatory email. It made me cry. I was overjoyed. My heart was so full when I pictured her writing me this long letter. Even now, whenever I'm feeling down, I will go back and read that email. Thanks, Sis. I'm going to keep doing my best.

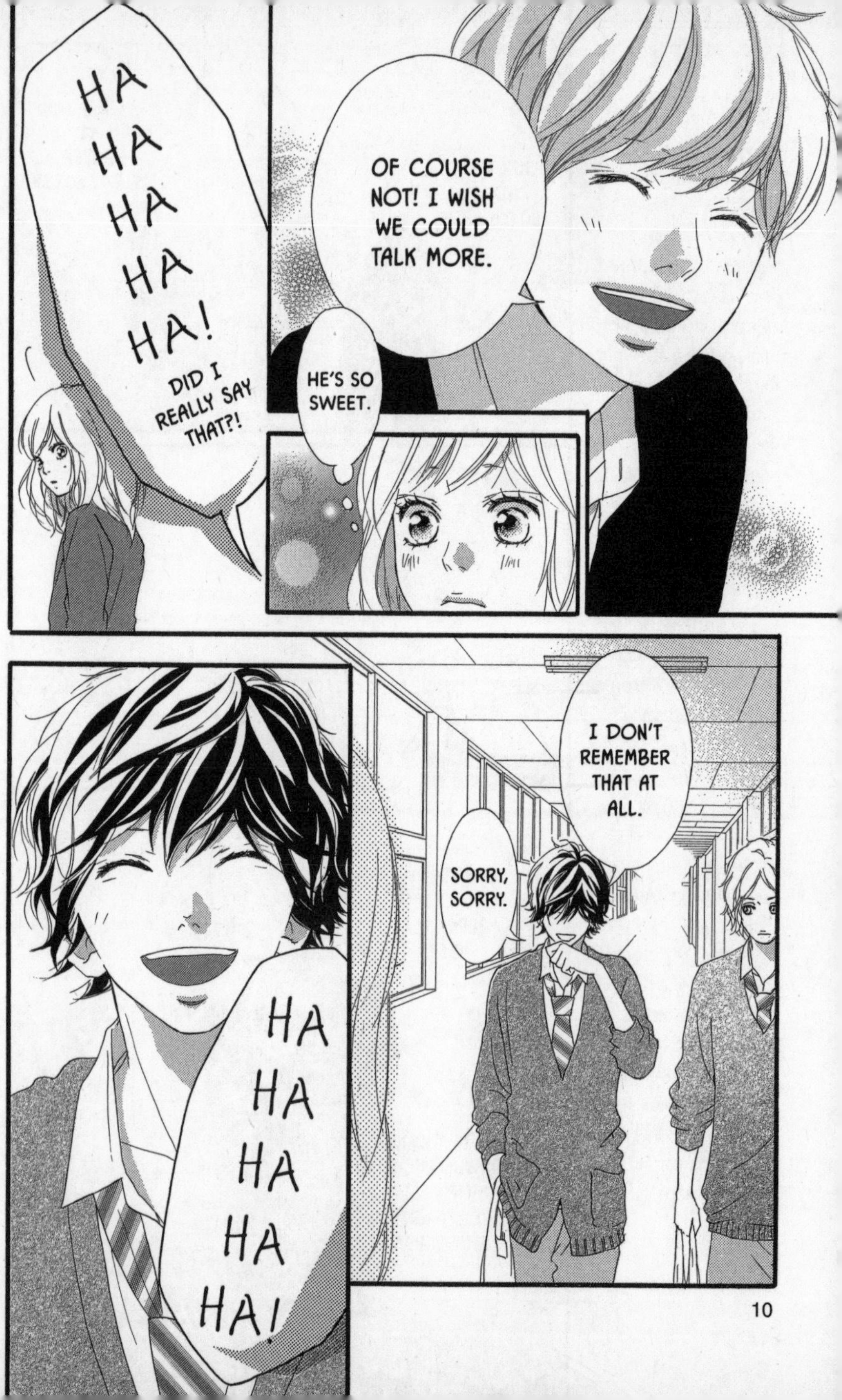
OF COURSE NOT! I WISH WE COULD TALK MORE.
HE'S SO SWEET.
HA HA HA HA HA!
DID I REALLY SAY THAT?!
I DON'T REMEMBER THAT AT ALL.
SORRY, SORRY.
HA HA HA HA HA!

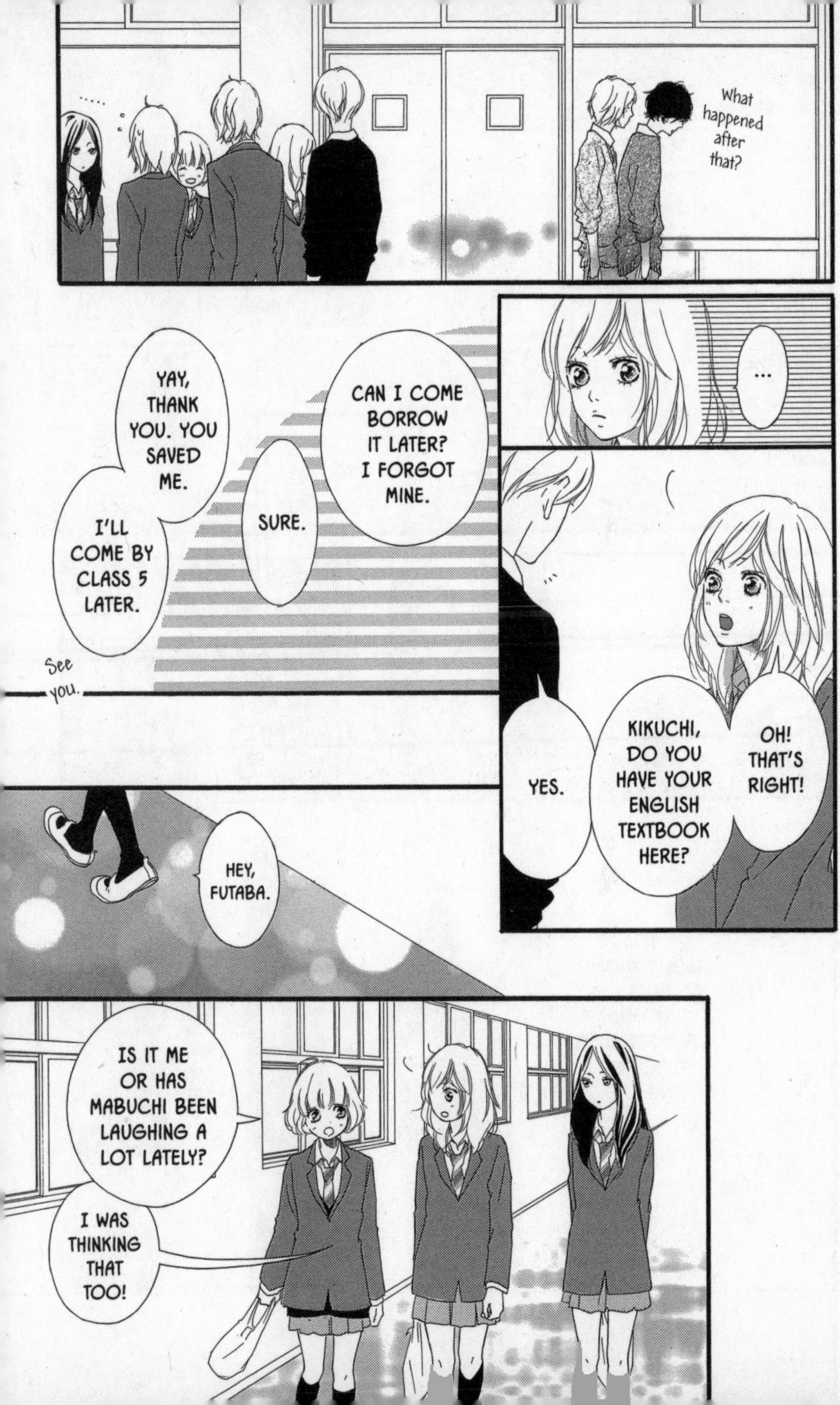
What happened after that?
.....
...
OH! THAT'S RIGHT!
KIKUCHI, DO YOU HAVE YOUR ENGLISH TEXTBOOK HERE?
YES.
CAN I COME BORROW IT LATER? I FORGOT MINE.
SURE.
YAY, THANK YOU. YOU SAVED ME.
I'LL COME BY CLASS 5 LATER.
See you.
HEY, FUTABA.
IS IT ME OR HAS MABUCHI BEEN LAUGHING A LOT LATELY?
I WAS THINKING THAT TOO!

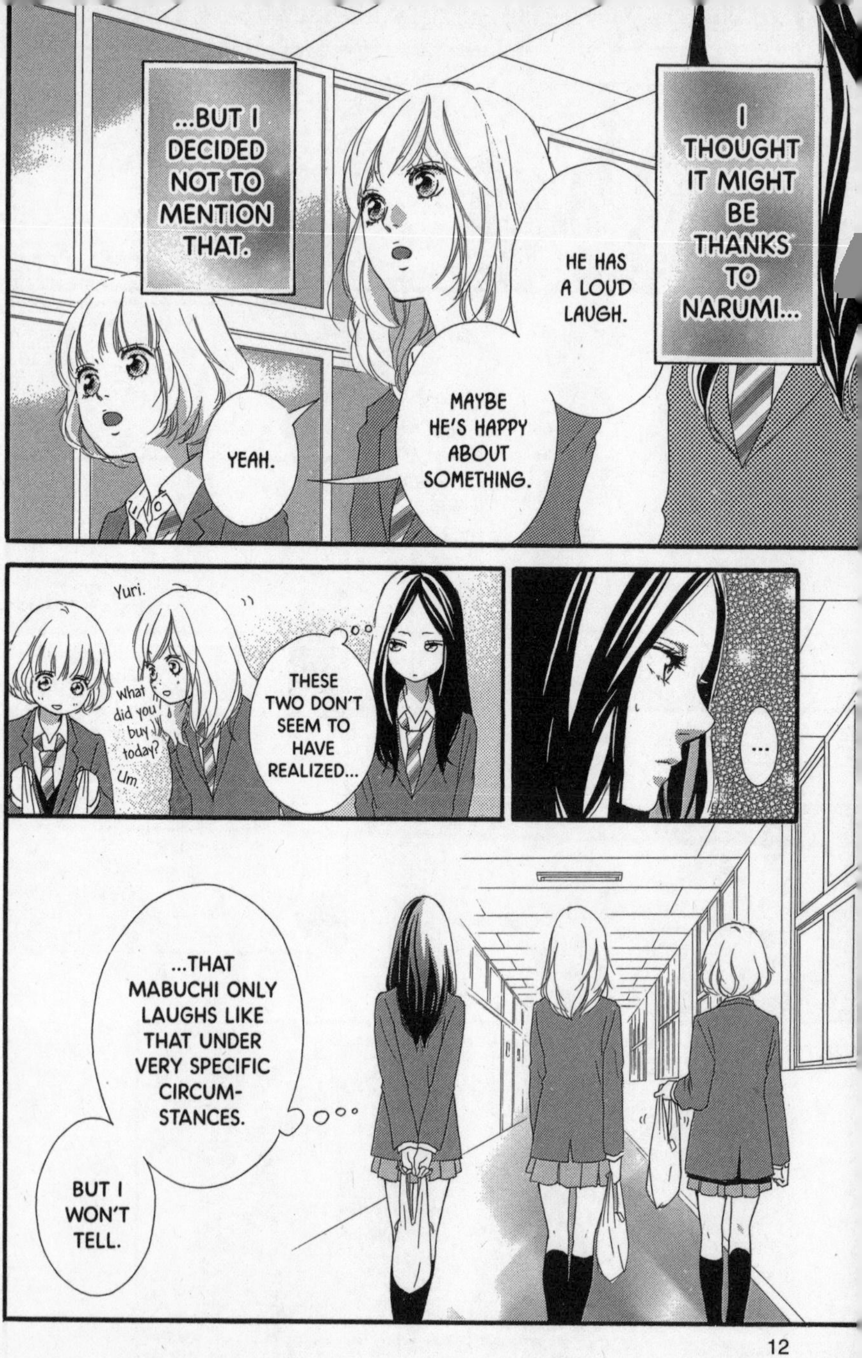
I THOUGHT IT MIGHT BE THANKS TO NARUMI...
HE HAS A LOUD LAUGH.
MAYBE HE'S HAPPY ABOUT SOMETHING.
YEAH.
...BUT I DECIDED NOT TO MENTION THAT.
...
THESE TWO DON'T SEEM TO HAVE REALIZED...
Yuri.
What did you buy today?
Um.
...THAT MABUCHI ONLY LAUGHS LIKE THAT UNDER VERY SPECIFIC CIRCUM-STANCES.
BUT I WON'T TELL.

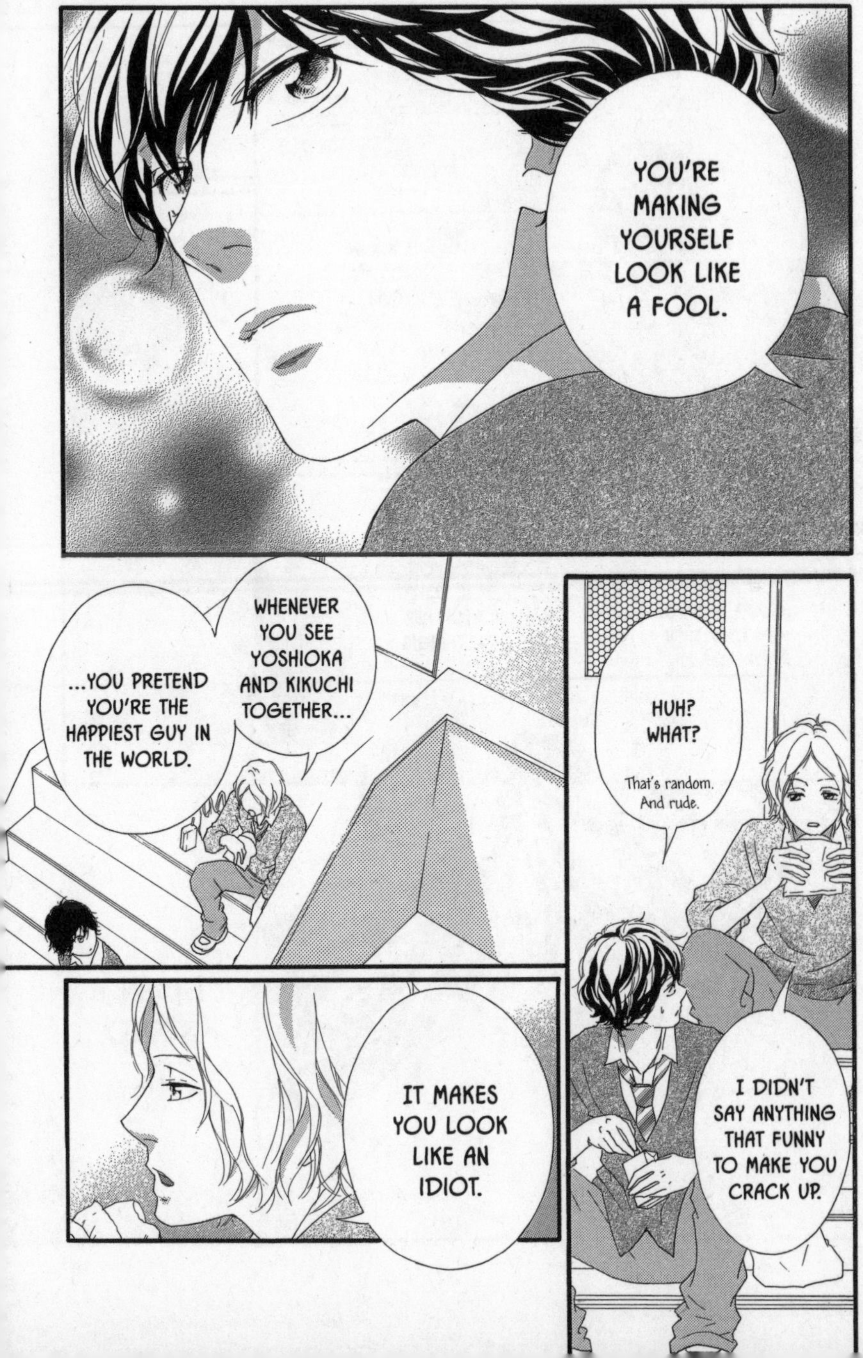
YOU'RE MAKING YOURSELF LOOK LIKE A FOOL.
HUH? WHAT?
That's random. And rude.
I DIDN'T SAY ANYTHING THAT FUNNY TO MAKE YOU CRACK UP.
WHENEVER YOU SEE YOSHIOKA AND KIKUCHI TOGETHER...
...YOU PRETEND YOU'RE THE HAPPIEST GUY IN THE WORLD.
IT MAKES YOU LOOK LIKE AN IDIOT.

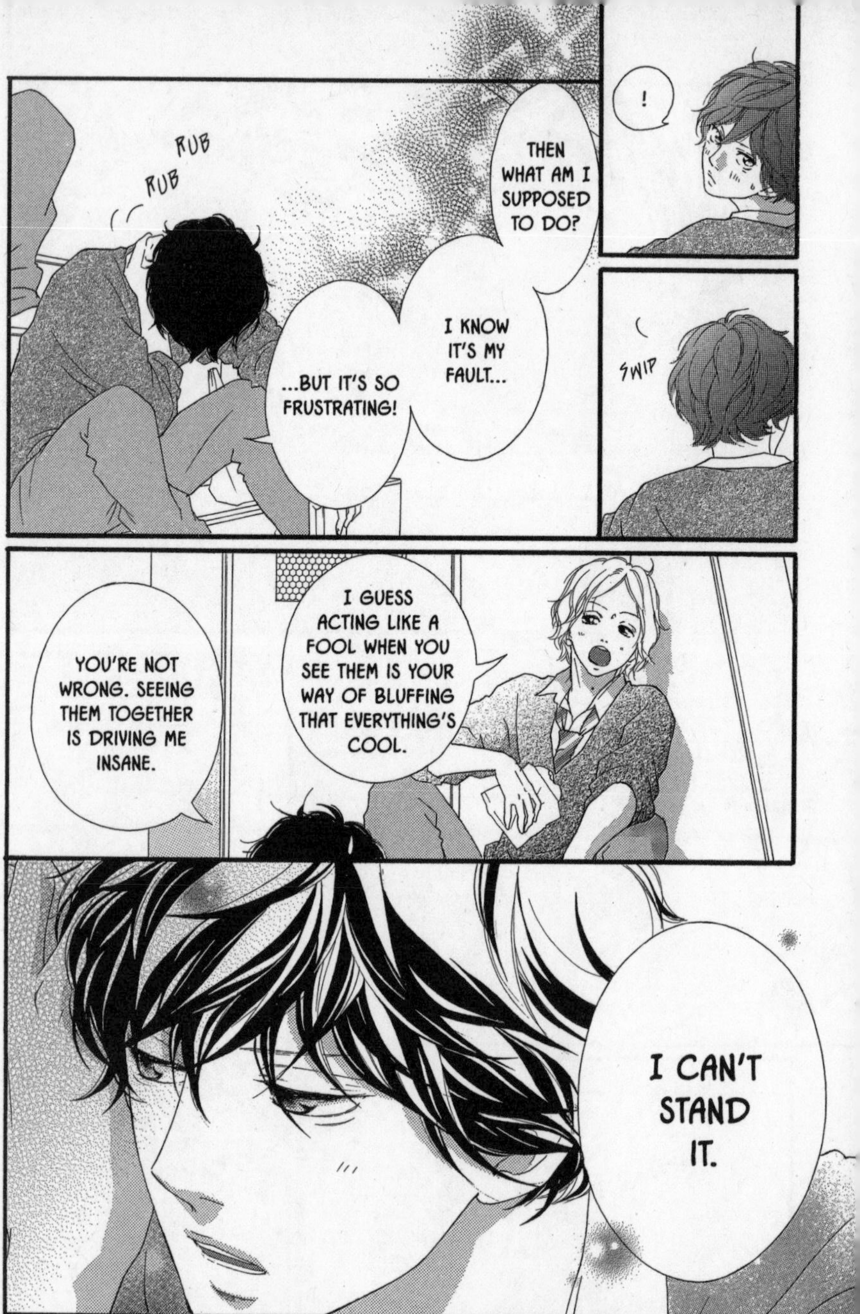
!
SWIP
THEN WHAT AM I SUPPOSED TO DO?
RUB RUB
I KNOW IT'S MY FAULT...
...BUT IT'S SO FRUSTRATING!
I GUESS ACTING LIKE A FOOL WHEN YOU SEE THEM IS YOUR WAY OF BLUFFING THAT EVERYTHING'S COOL.
YOU'RE NOT WRONG. SEEING THEM TOGETHER IS DRIVING ME INSANE.
I CAN'T STAND IT.

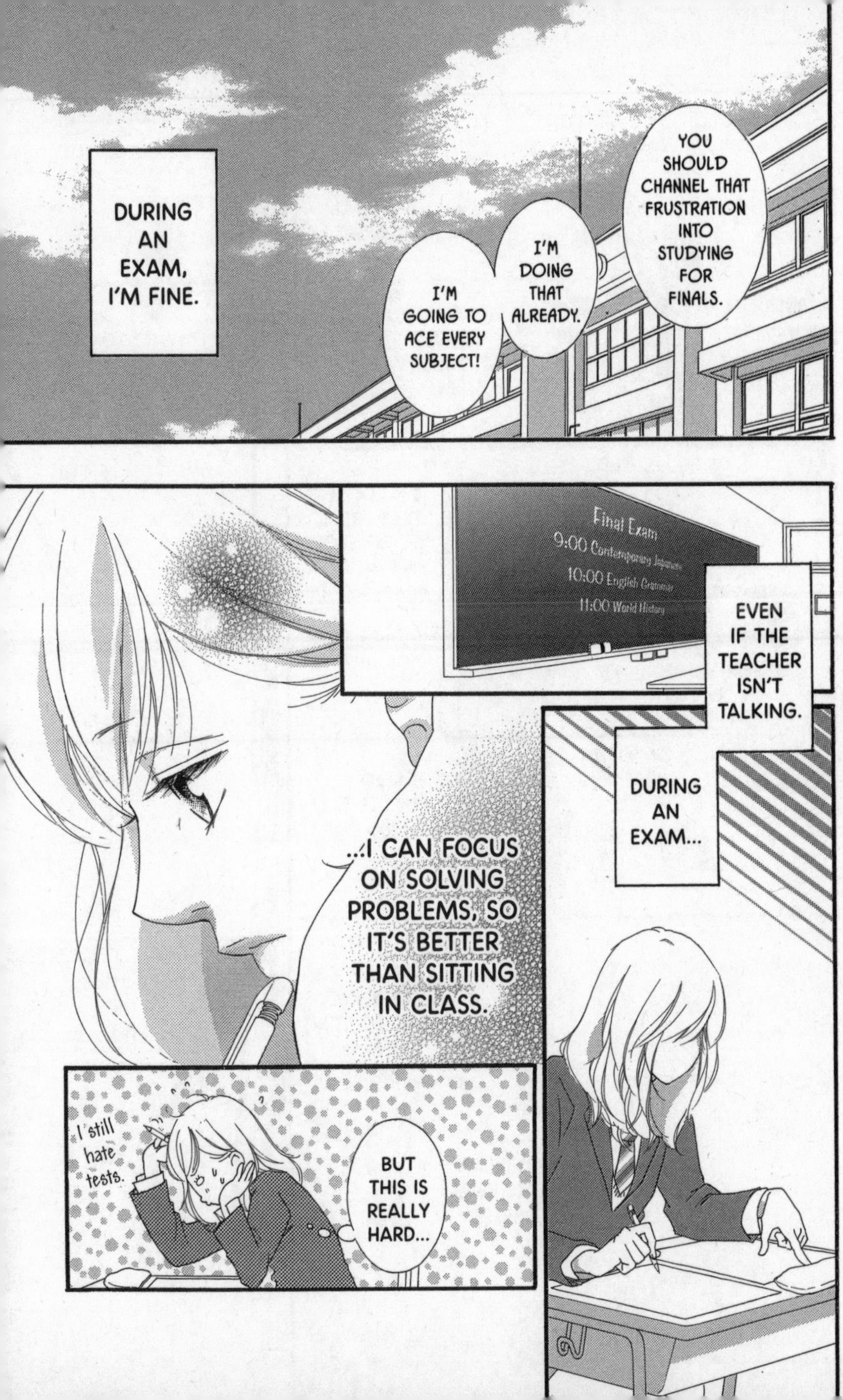

YOU SHOULD CHANNEL THAT FRUSTRATION INTO STUDYING FOR FINALS.
I'M DOING THAT ALREADY.
I'M GOING TO ACE EVERY SUBJECT!
DURING AN EXAM, I'M FINE.
Final Exam
9:00 Contemporary Japanese
10:00 English Grammar
11:00 World History
EVEN IF THE TEACHER ISN'T TALKING.
DURING AN EXAM...
...I CAN FOCUS ON SOLVING PROBLEMS, SO IT'S BETTER THAN SITTING IN CLASS.
BUT THIS IS REALLY HARD...
I still hate tests.

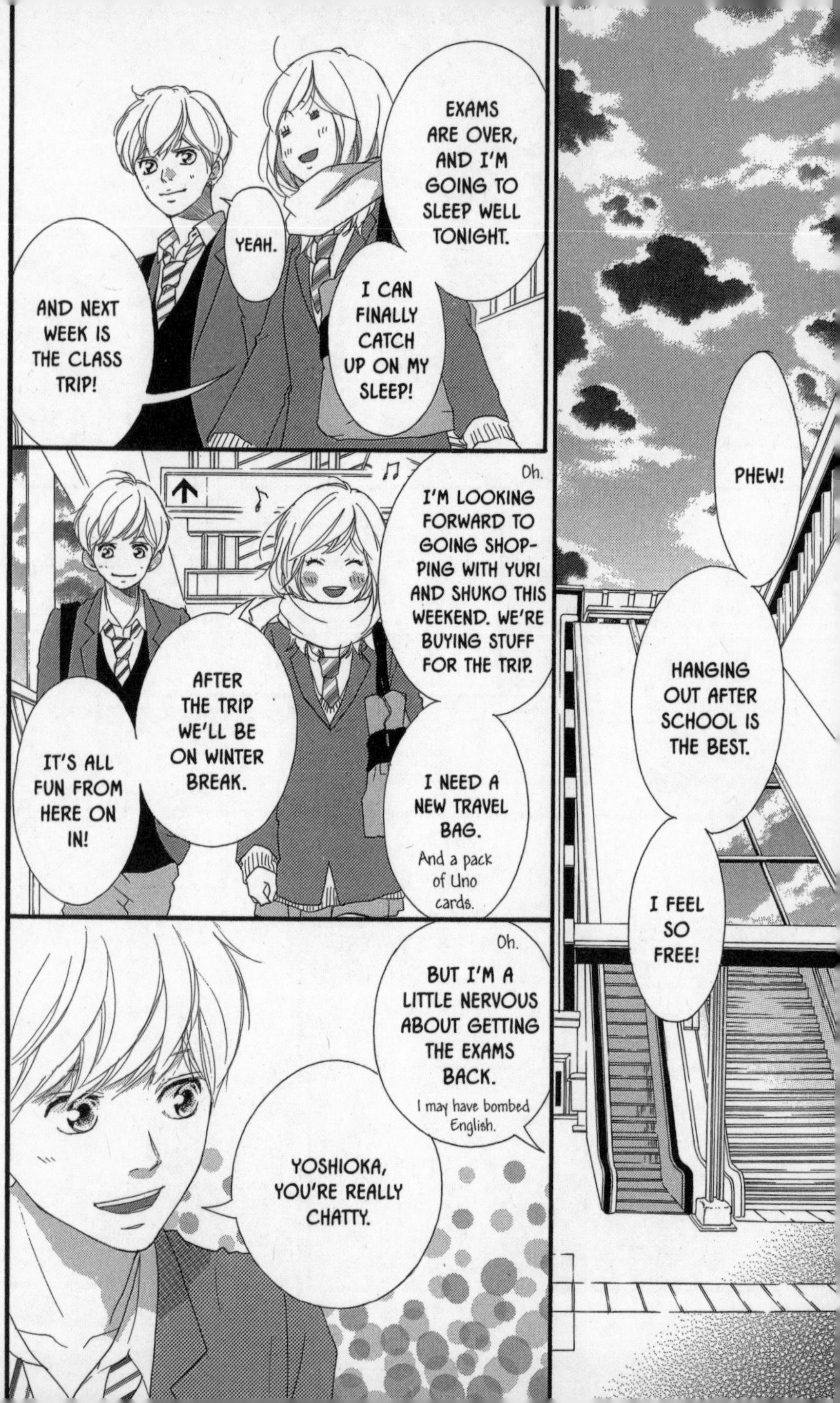
PHEW!
HANGING OUT AFTER SCHOOL IS THE BEST.
I FEEL SO FREE!
EXAMS ARE OVER, AND I'M GOING TO SLEEP WELL TONIGHT.
I CAN FINALLY CATCH UP ON MY SLEEP!
YEAH.
AND NEXT WEEK IS THE CLASS TRIP!
Oh.
I'M LOOKING FORWARD TO GOING SHOPPING WITH YURI AND SHUKO THIS WEEKEND. WE'RE BUYING STUFF FOR THE TRIP.
I NEED A NEW TRAVEL BAG.
And a pack of Uno cards.
AFTER THE TRIP WE'LL BE ON WINTER BREAK.
IT'S ALL FUN FROM HERE ON IN!
Oh.
BUT I'M A LITTLE NERVOUS ABOUT GETTING THE EXAMS BACK.
I may have bombed English.
YOSHIOKA, YOU'RE REALLY CHATTY.

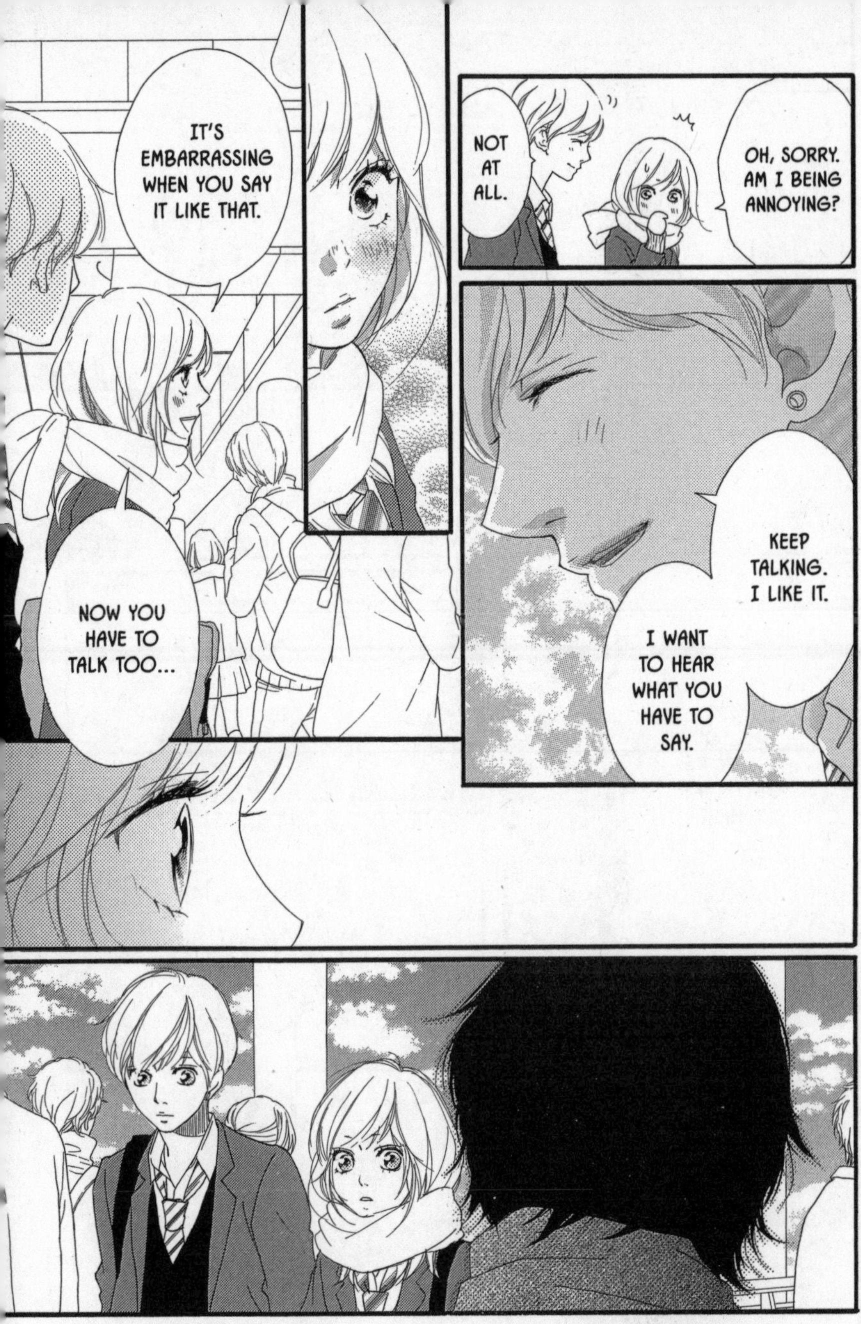
OH, SORRY. AM I BEING ANNOYING?
NOT AT ALL.
KEEP TALKING. I LIKE IT.
I WANT TO HEAR WHAT YOU HAVE TO SAY.
IT'S EMBARRASSING WHEN YOU SAY IT LIKE THAT.
NOW YOU HAVE TO TALK TOO...

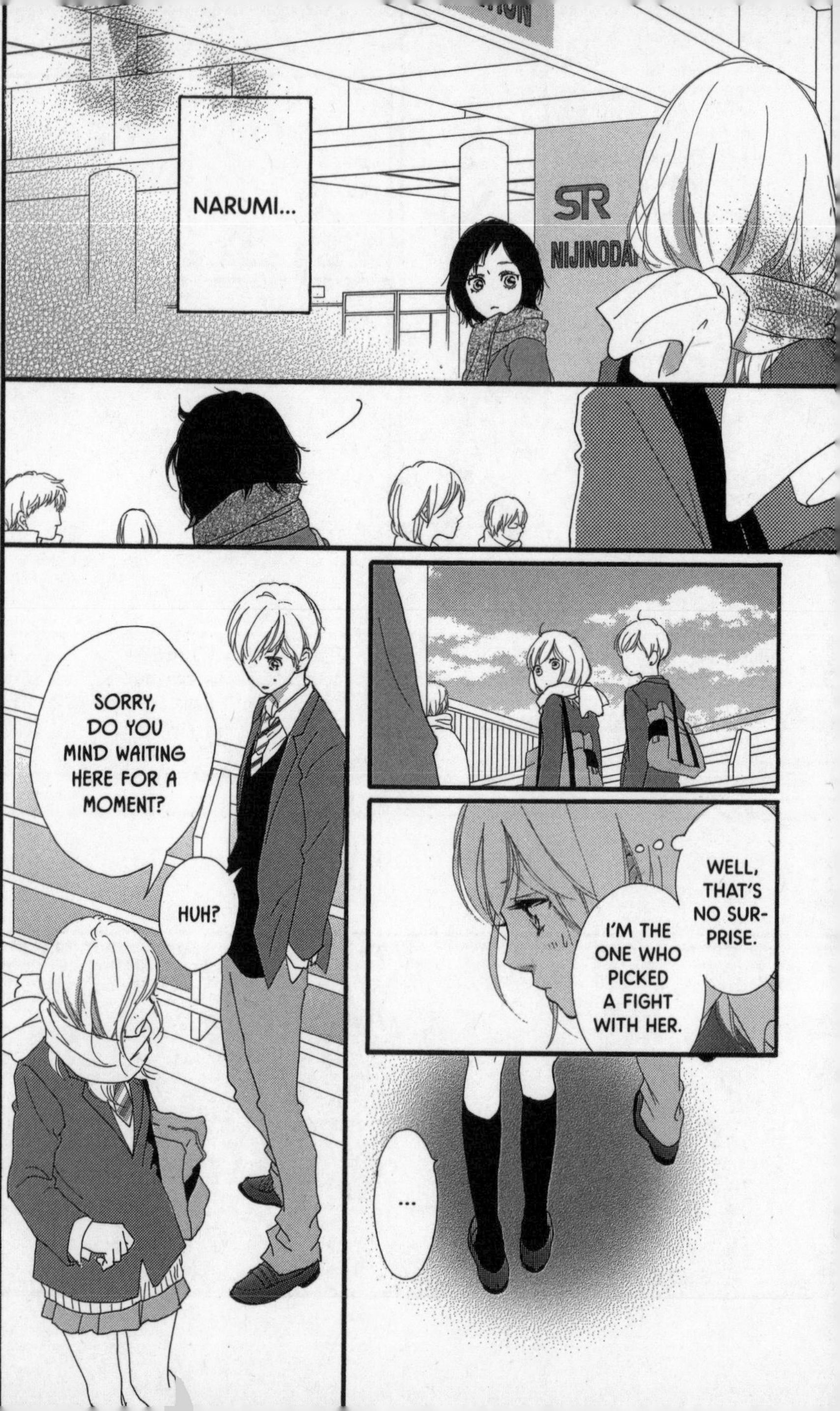
NARUMI...
SR
WELL, THAT'S NO SUR-PRISE.
I'M THE ONE WHO PICKED A FIGHT WITH HER.
...
SORRY, DO YOU MIND WAITING HERE FOR A MOMENT?
HUH?

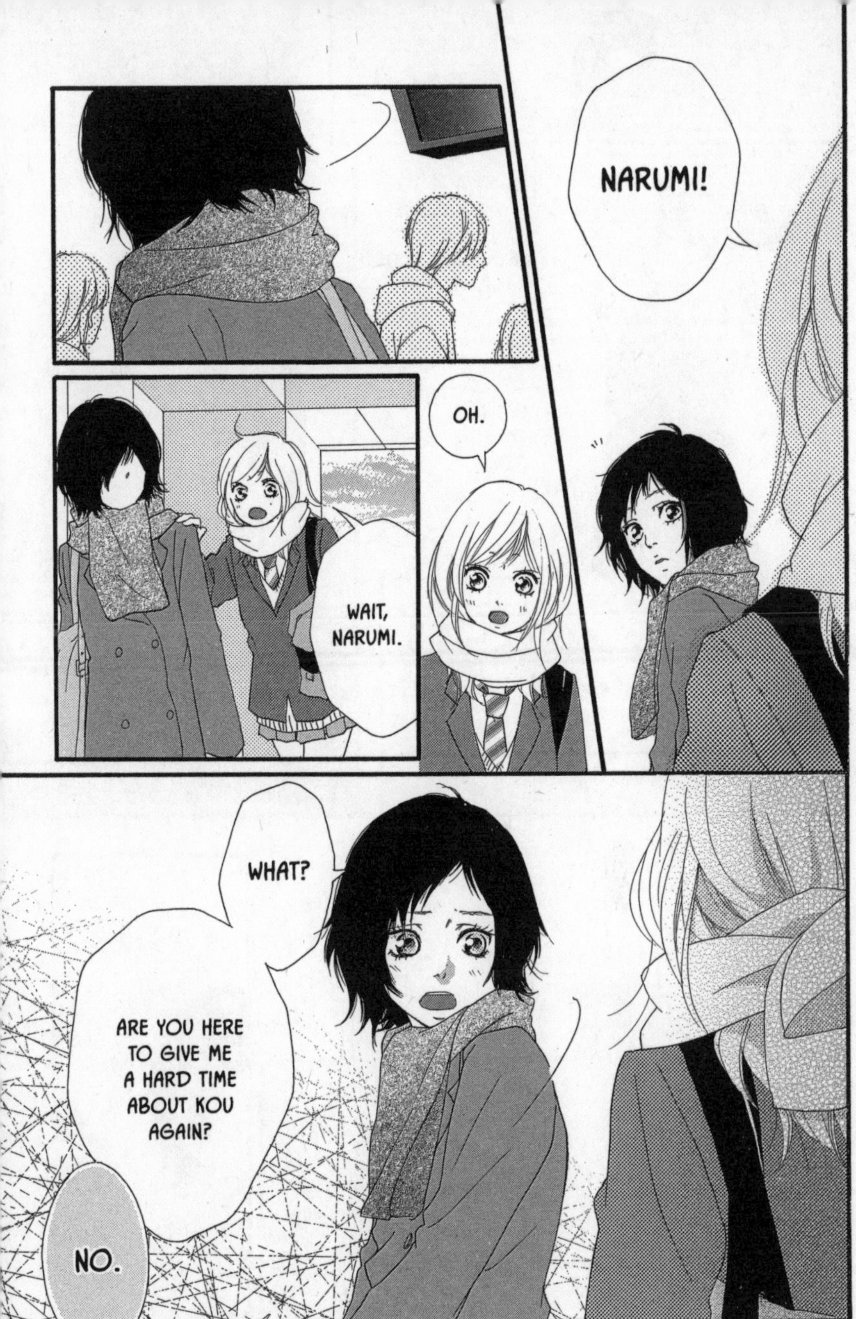
NARUMI!
WAIT, NARUMI.
OH.
WHAT?
ARE YOU HERE TO GIVE ME A HARD TIME ABOUT KOU AGAIN?
NO.

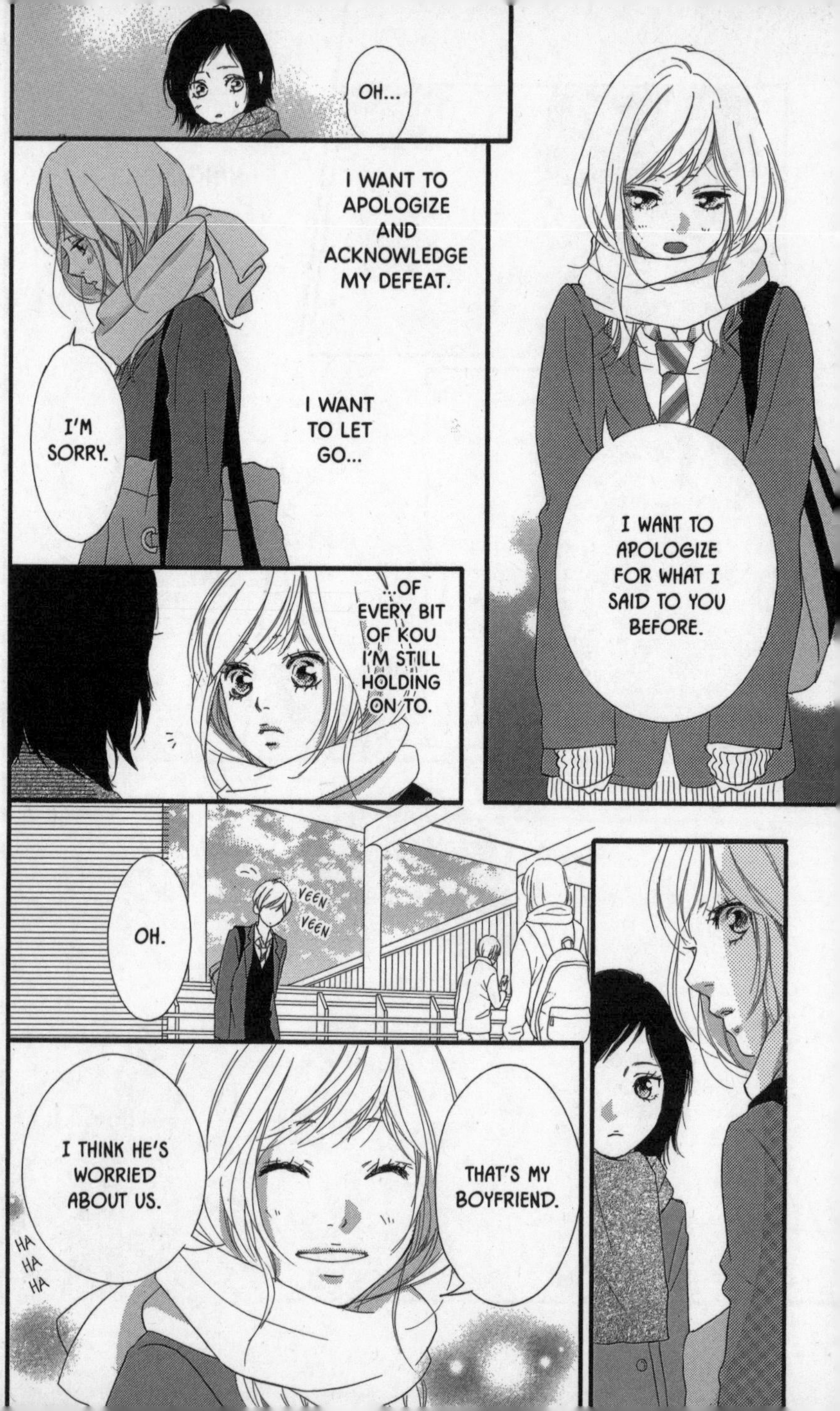
I WANT TO APOLOGIZE FOR WHAT I SAID TO YOU BEFORE.
OH...
I WANT TO APOLOGIZE AND ACKNOWLEDGE MY DEFEAT.
I WANT TO LET GO...
I'M SORRY.
...OF EVERY BIT OF KOU I'M STILL HOLDING ON TO.
VEEN VEEN
OH.
THAT'S MY BOYFRIEND.
I THINK HE'S WORRIED ABOUT US.
HA HA HA

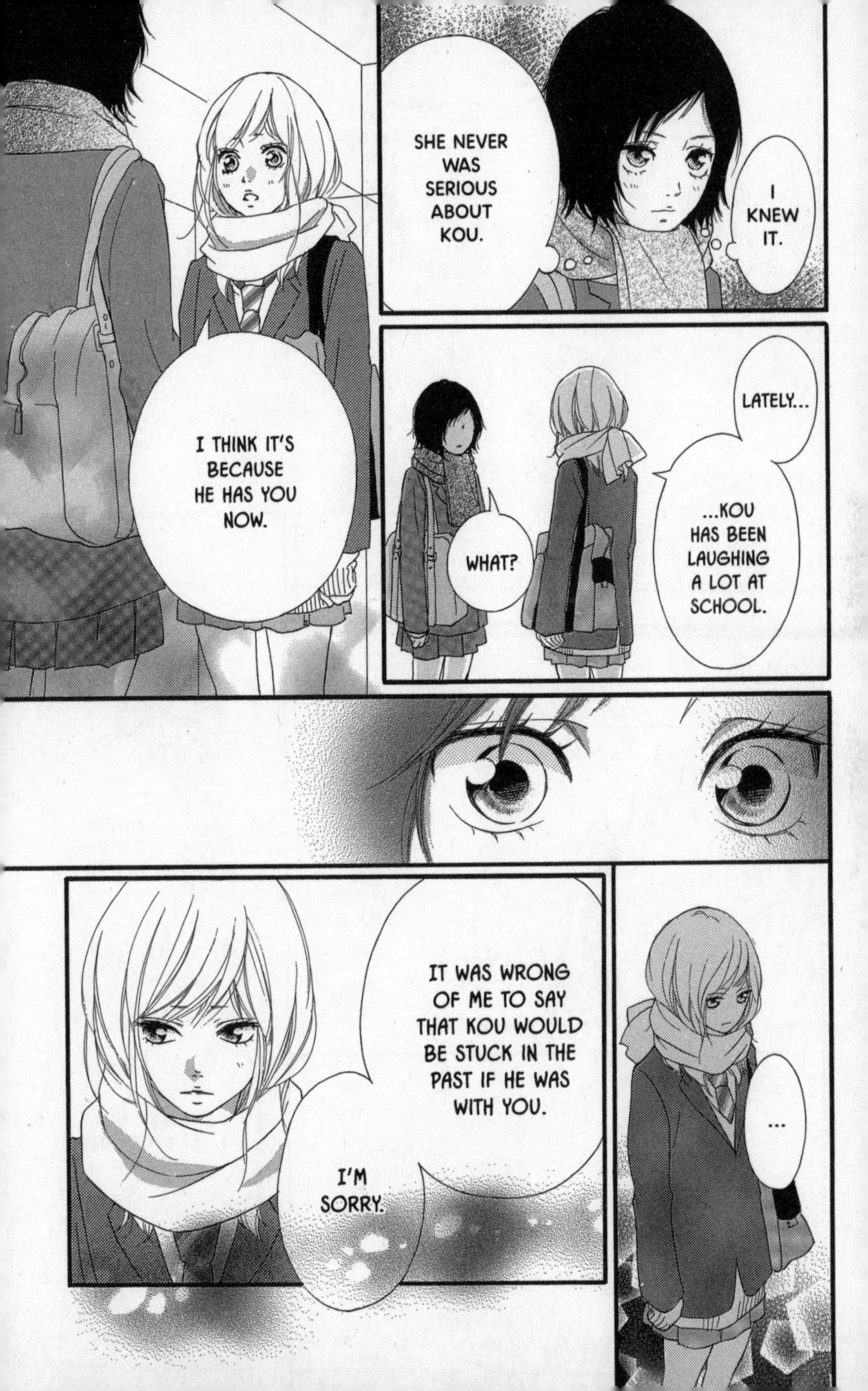
I KNEW IT.
SHE NEVER WAS SERIOUS ABOUT KOU.
LATELY...
...KOU HAS BEEN LAUGHING A LOT AT SCHOOL.
WHAT?
I THINK IT'S BECAUSE HE HAS YOU NOW.
...
IT WAS WRONG OF ME TO SAY THAT KOU WOULD BE STUCK IN THE PAST IF HE WAS WITH YOU.
I'M SORRY.

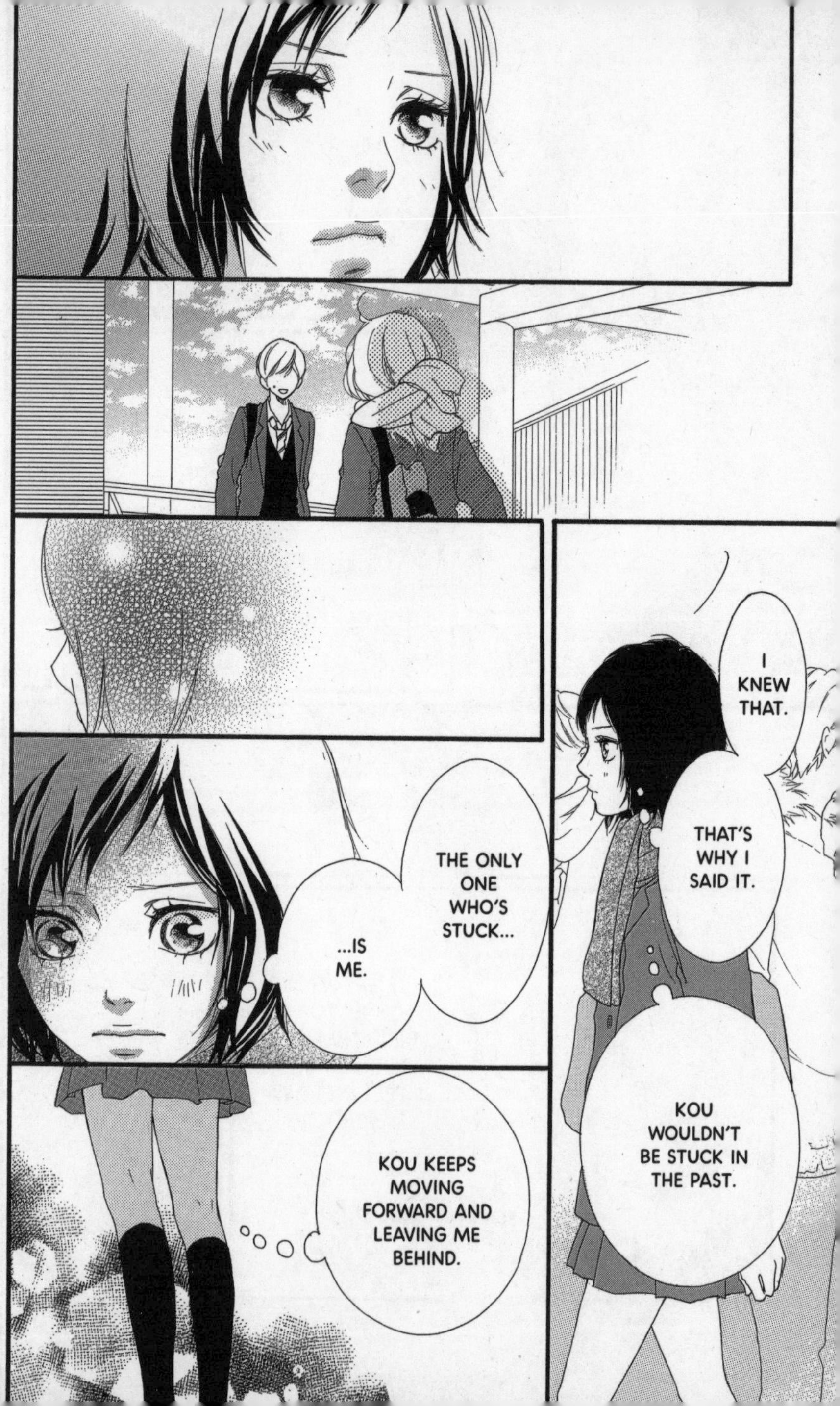
I KNEW THAT.
THAT'S WHY I SAID IT.
KOU WOULDN'T BE STUCK IN THE PAST.
THE ONLY ONE WHO'S STUCK...
...IS ME.
KOU KEEPS MOVING FORWARD AND LEAVING ME BEHIND.

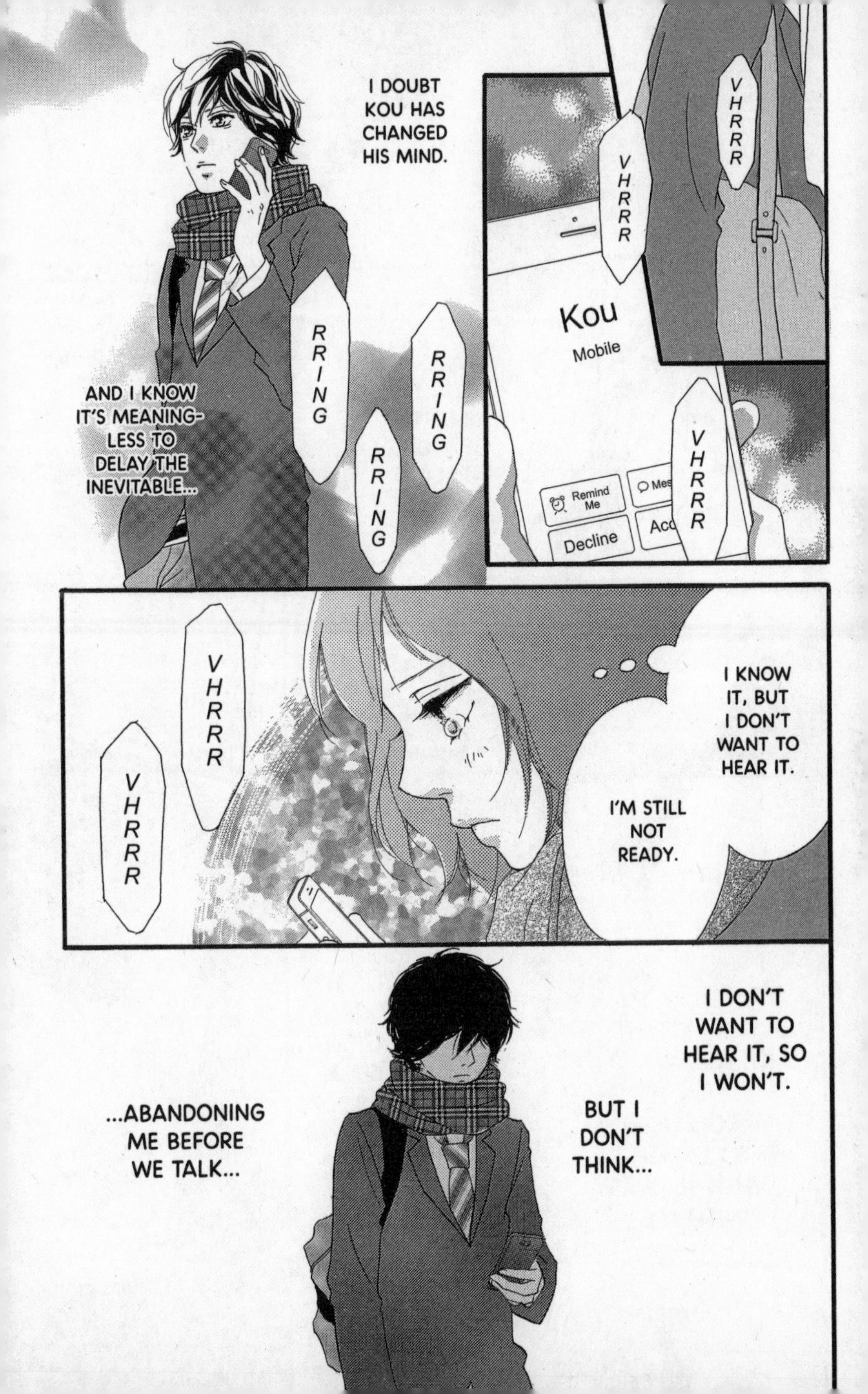
VHRRR
VHRRR
Kou
Mobile
Remind Me
Mes
Decline
Acc
VHRRR
I DOUBT KOU HAS CHANGED HIS MIND.
RRING
RRING
RRING
AND I KNOW IT'S MEANING-LESS TO DELAY THE INEVITABLE...
I KNOW IT, BUT I DON'T WANT TO HEAR IT.
I'M STILL NOT READY.
VHRRR
VHRRR
I DON'T WANT TO HEAR IT, SO I WON'T.
BUT I DON'T THINK...
...ABANDONING ME BEFORE WE TALK...

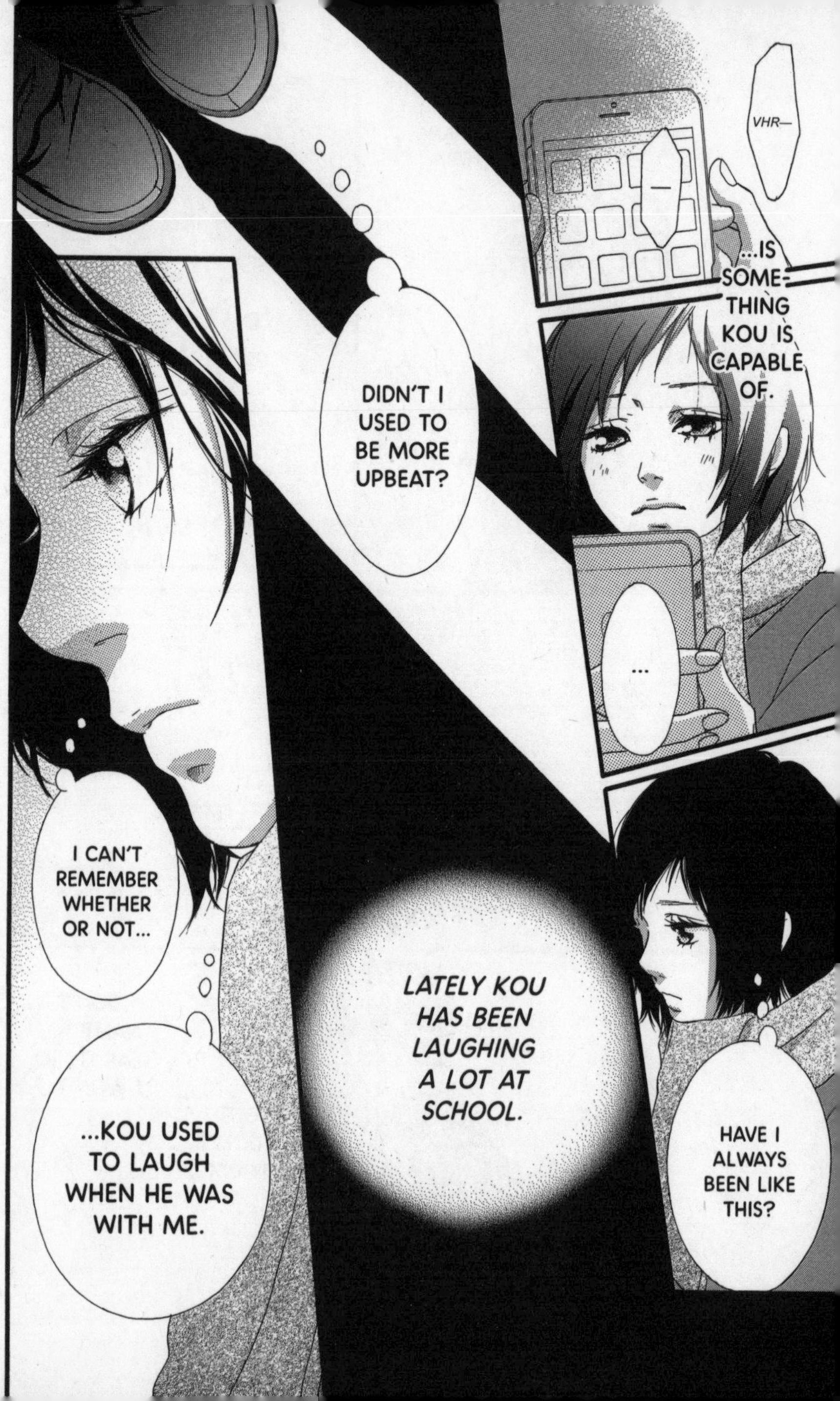
VHR—
—
...IS SOMETHING KOU IS CAPABLE OF.
...
HAVE I ALWAYS BEEN LIKE THIS?
DIDN'T I USED TO BE MORE UPBEAT?
LATELY KOU HAS BEEN LAUGHING A LOT AT SCHOOL.
I CAN'T REMEMBER WHETHER OR NOT...
...KOU USED TO LAUGH WHEN HE WAS WITH ME.

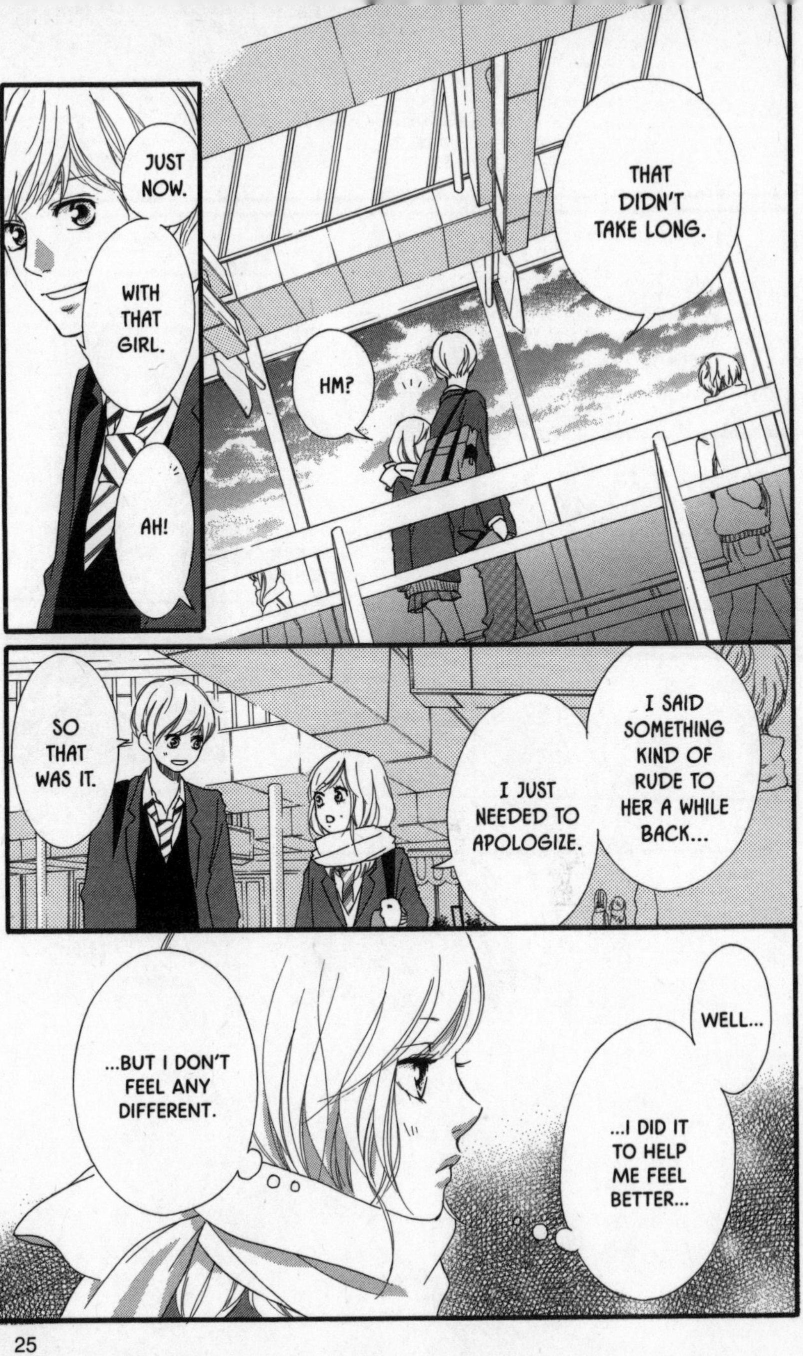
THAT DIDN'T TAKE LONG.
HM?
JUST NOW.
WITH THAT GIRL.
AH!
I SAID SOMETHING KIND OF RUDE TO HER A WHILE BACK...
I JUST NEEDED TO APOLOGIZE.
SO THAT WAS IT.
WELL...
...I DID IT TO HELP ME FEEL BETTER...
...BUT I DON'T FEEL ANY DIFFERENT.

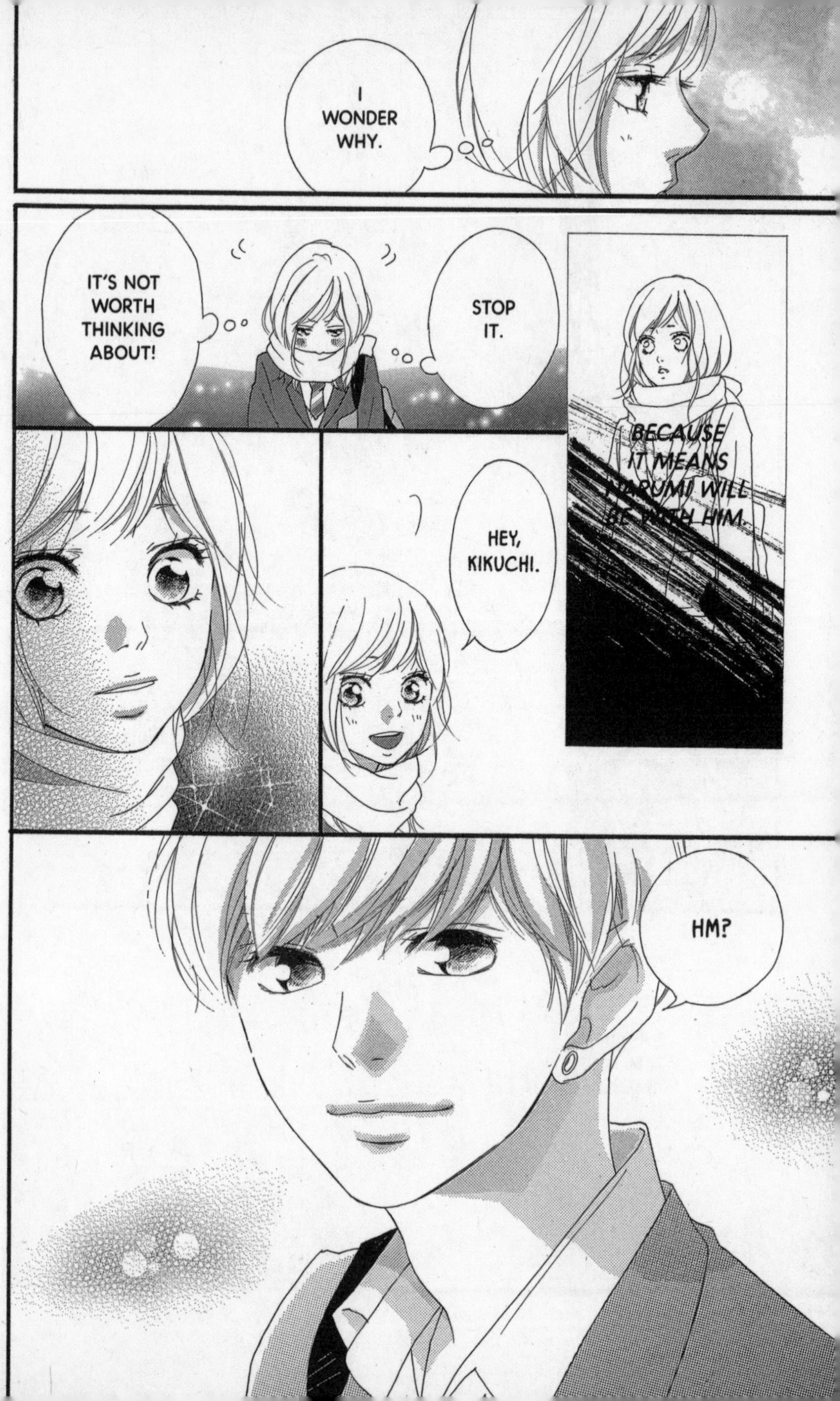
I WONDER WHY.
BECAUSE IT MEANS NARUMI WILL BE WITH HIM.
STOP IT.
IT'S NOT WORTH THINKING ABOUT!
HEY, KIKUCHI.
HM?

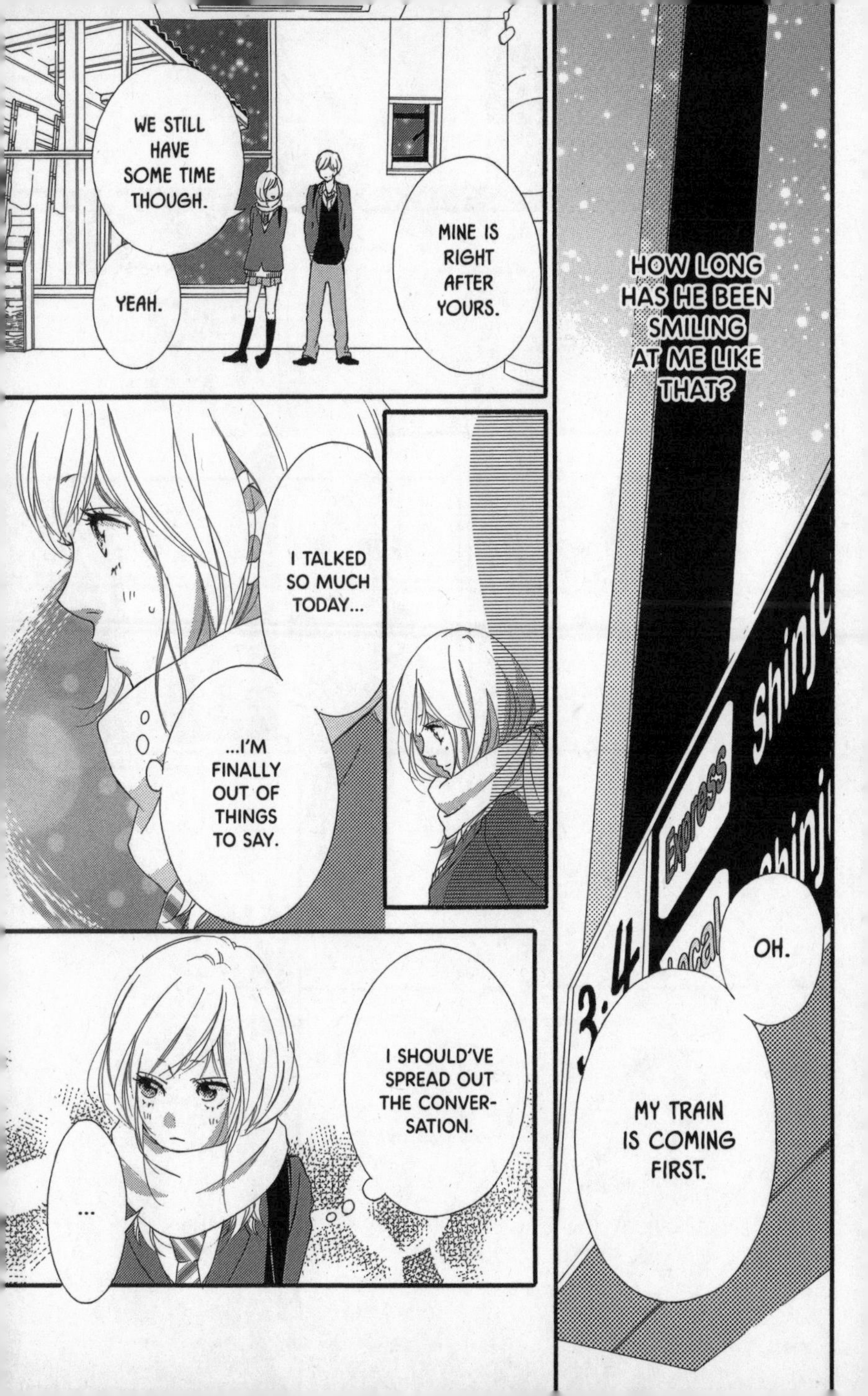
HOW LONG HAS HE BEEN SMILING AT ME LIKE THAT?
Express
OH.
MY TRAIN IS COMING FIRST.
MINE IS RIGHT AFTER YOURS.
WE STILL HAVE SOME TIME THOUGH.
YEAH.
I TALKED SO MUCH TODAY...
...I'M FINALLY OUT OF THINGS TO SAY.
I SHOULD'VE SPREAD OUT THE CONVER-SATION.
...

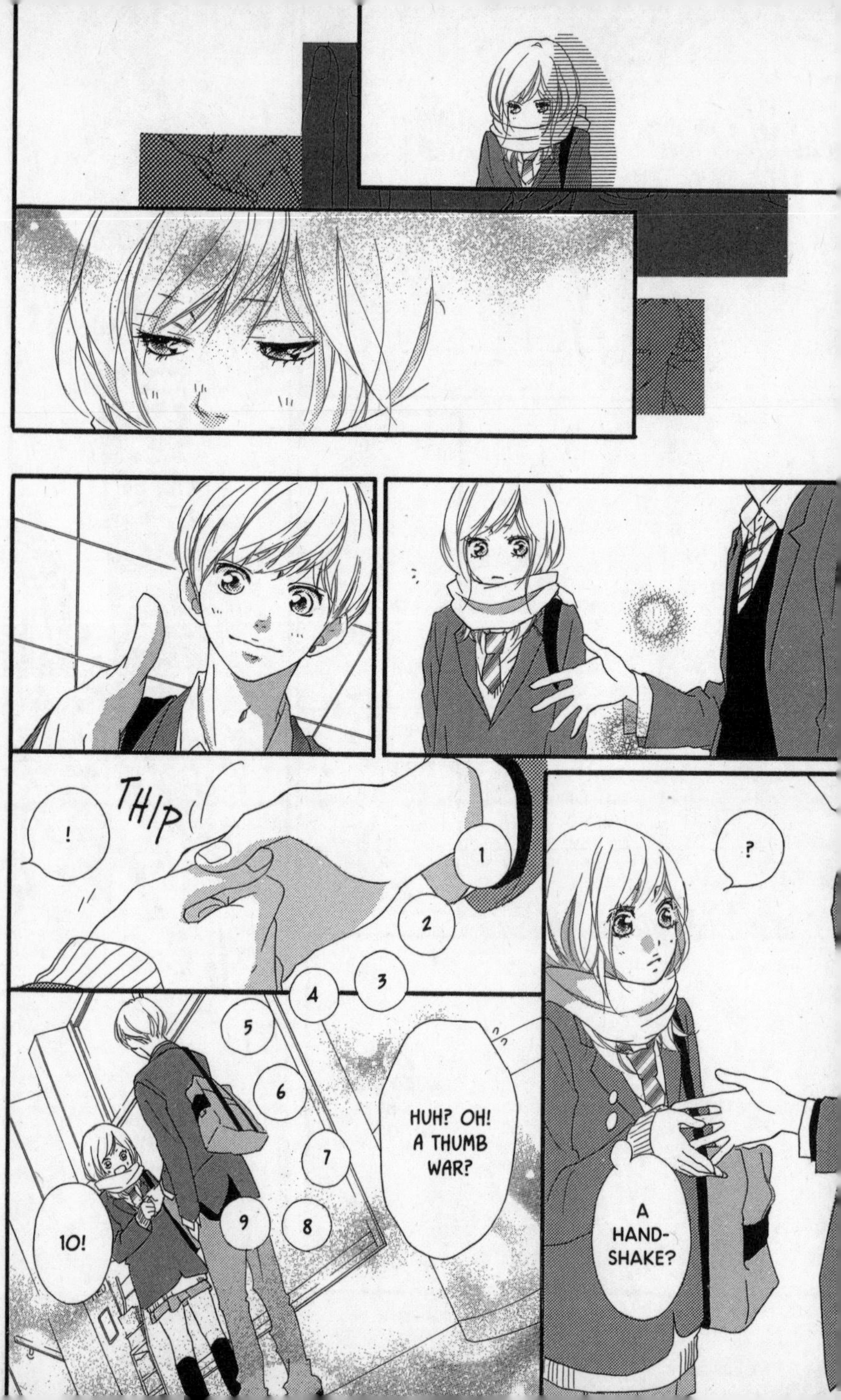
?
A HAND-SHAKE?
THIP
!
1
2
3
4
HUH? OH! A THUMB WAR?
5
6
7
8
9
10!

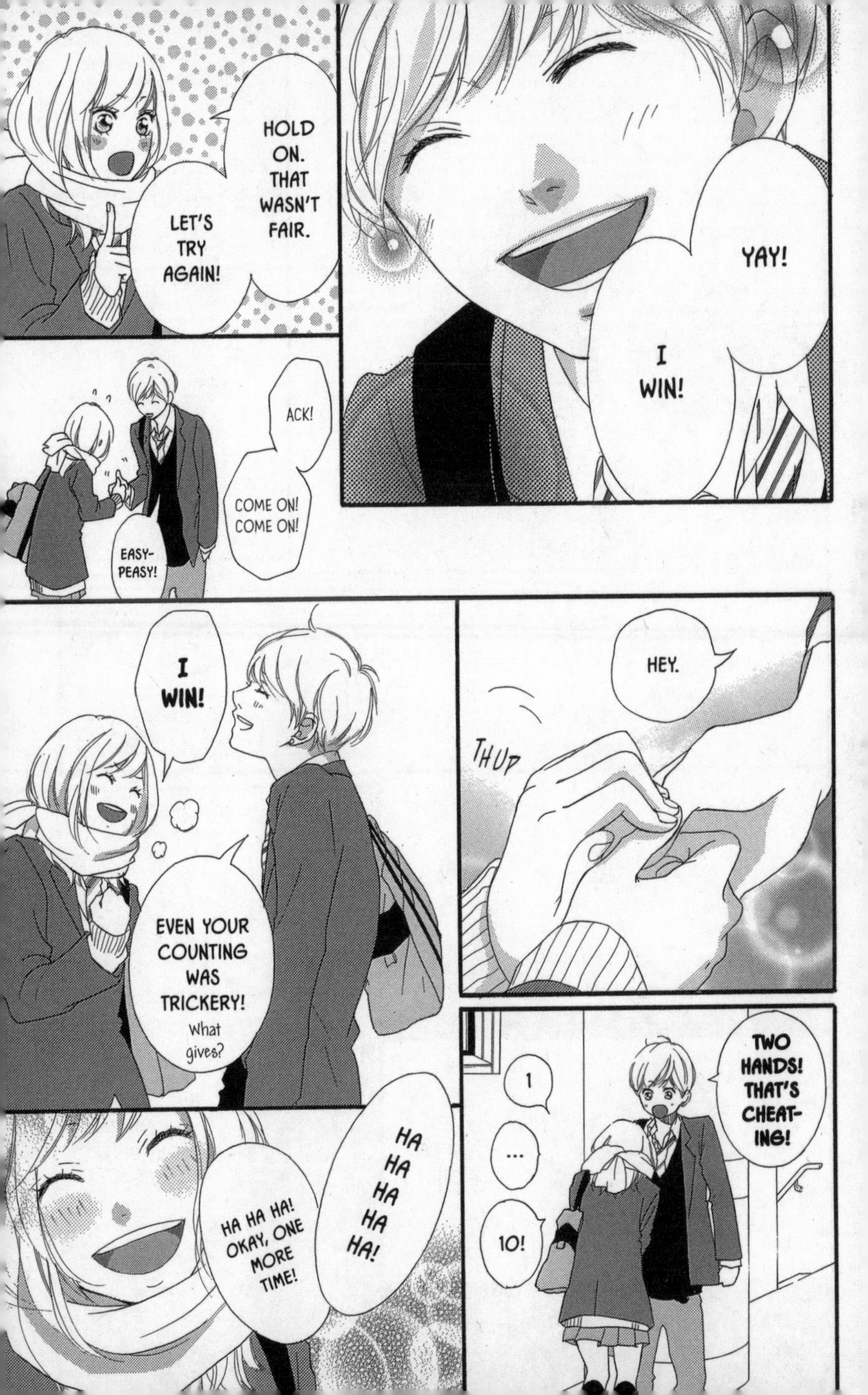
YAY!
I WIN!
HOLD ON. THAT WASN'T FAIR.
LET'S TRY AGAIN!
ACK!
COME ON! COME ON!
EASY-PEASY!
HEY.
THUP
1
...
10!
TWO HANDS! THAT'S CHEAT-ING!
I WIN!
EVEN YOUR COUNTING WAS TRICKERY! What gives?
HA HA HA HA HA HA!
HA HA HA! OKAY, ONE MORE TIME!

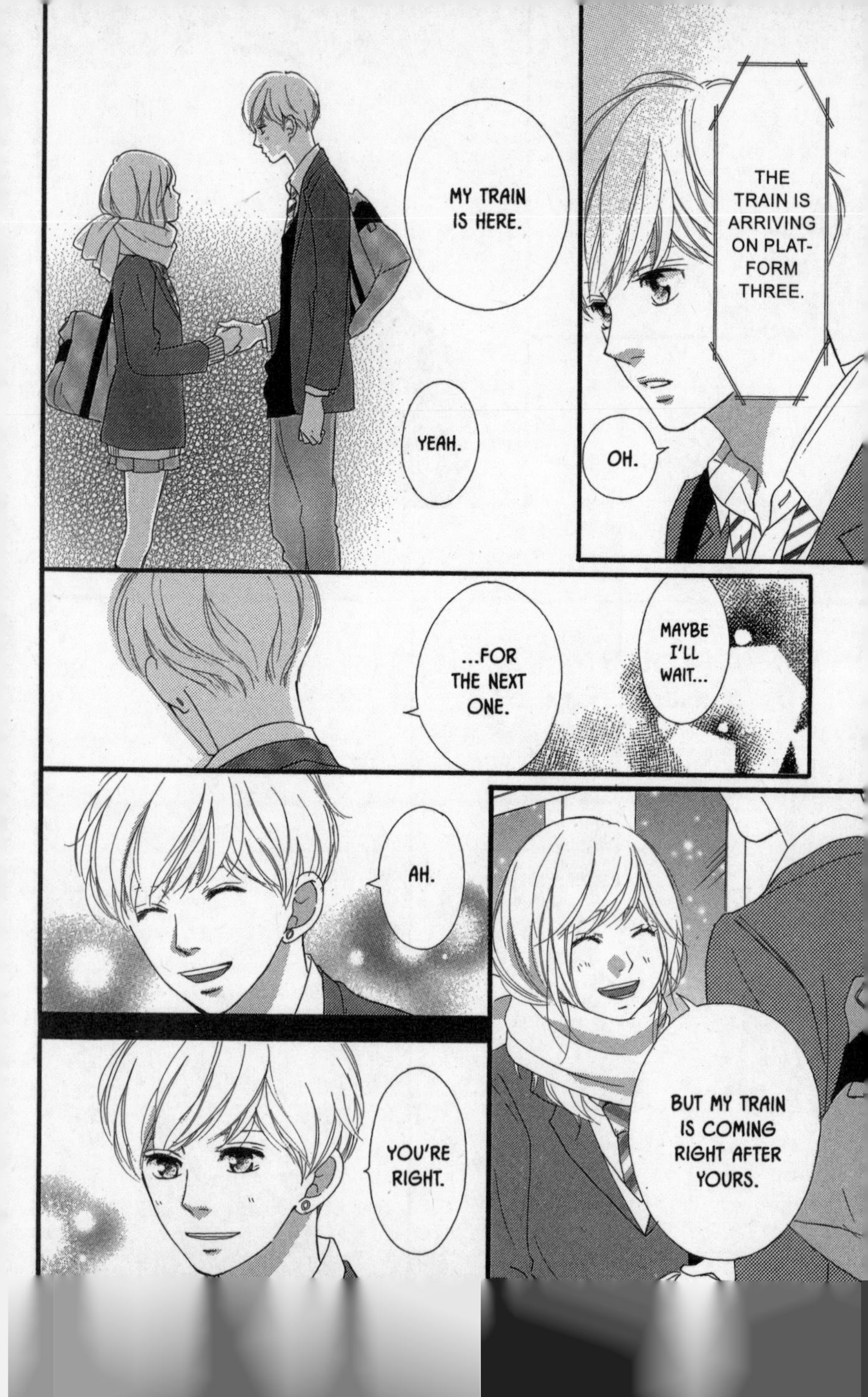
THE TRAIN IS ARRIVING ON PLAT-FORM THREE.
OH.
MY TRAIN IS HERE.
YEAH.
MAYBE I'LL WAIT...
...FOR THE NEXT ONE.
BUT MY TRAIN IS COMING RIGHT AFTER YOURS.
AH.
YOU'RE RIGHT.

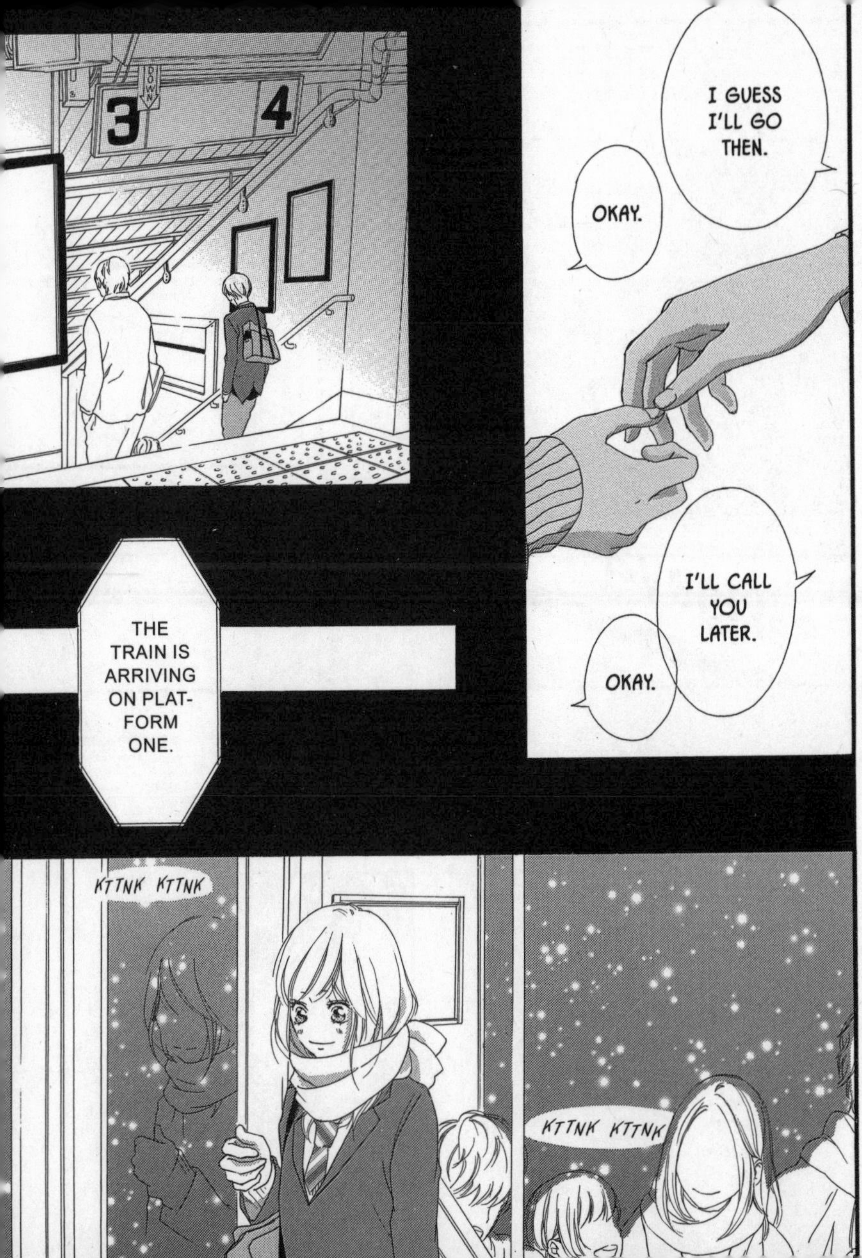
I GUESS I'LL GO THEN.
OKAY.
I'LL CALL YOU LATER.
OKAY.
3
4
DOWN
THE TRAIN IS ARRIVING ON PLAT-FORM ONE.
KTTNK KTTNK
KTTNK KTTNK

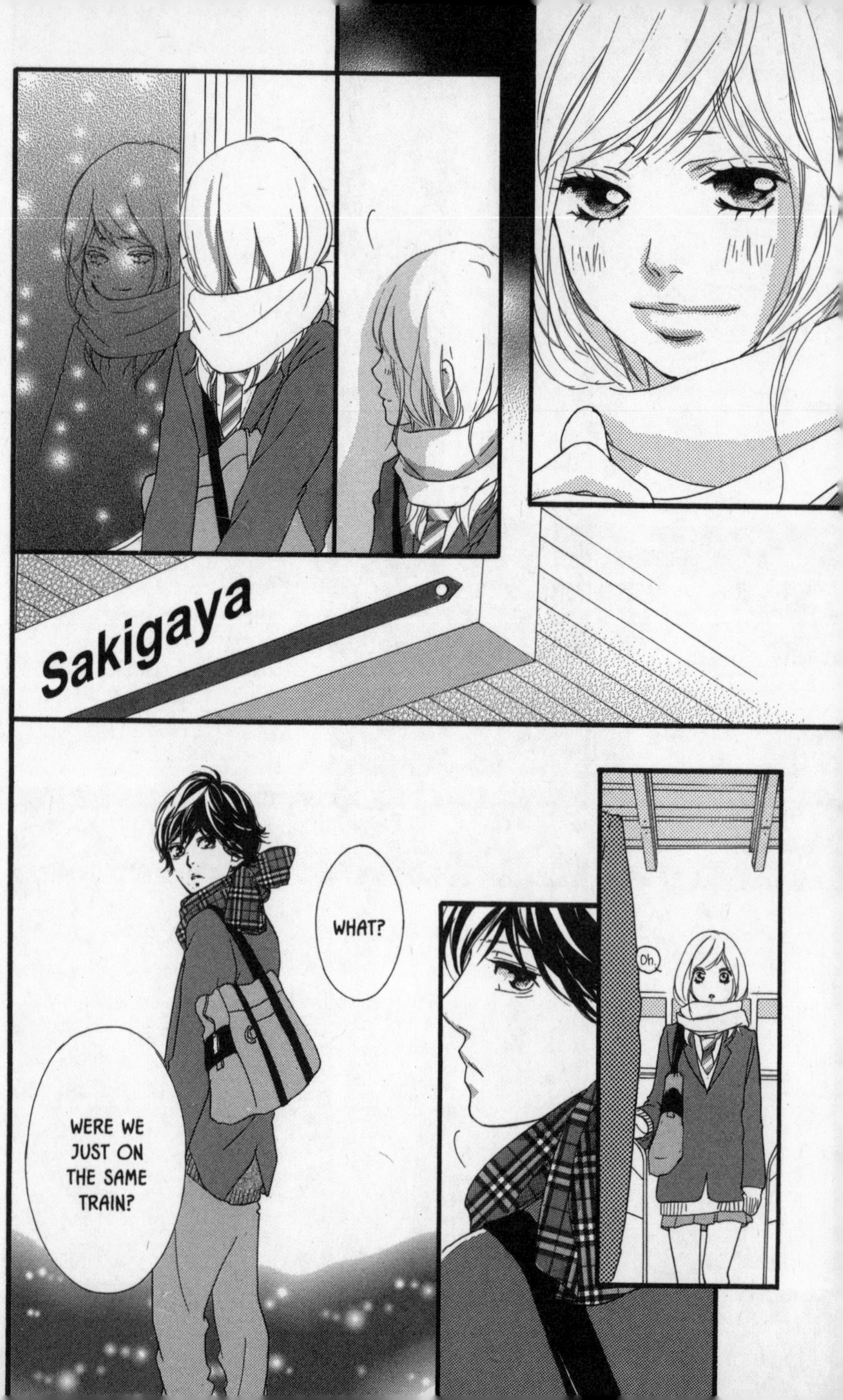
Sakigaya
Oh.
WHAT?
WERE WE JUST ON THE SAME TRAIN?

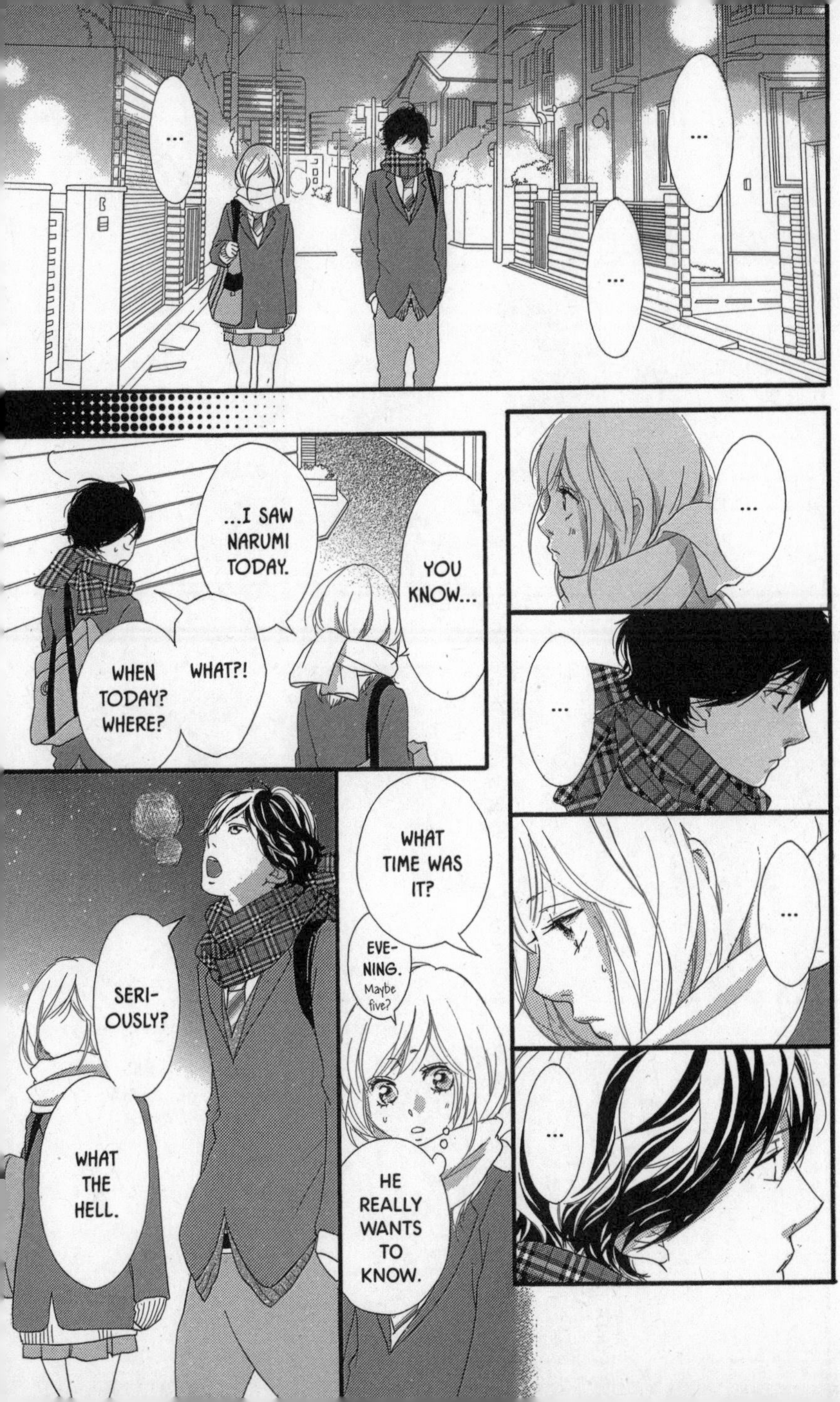
...
...
...
...
...
...
...
YOU KNOW...
...I SAW NARUMI TODAY.
WHAT?!
WHEN TODAY? WHERE?
WHAT TIME WAS IT?
EVE-NING.
Maybe five?
HE REALLY WANTS TO KNOW.
SERI-OUSLY?
WHAT THE HELL.

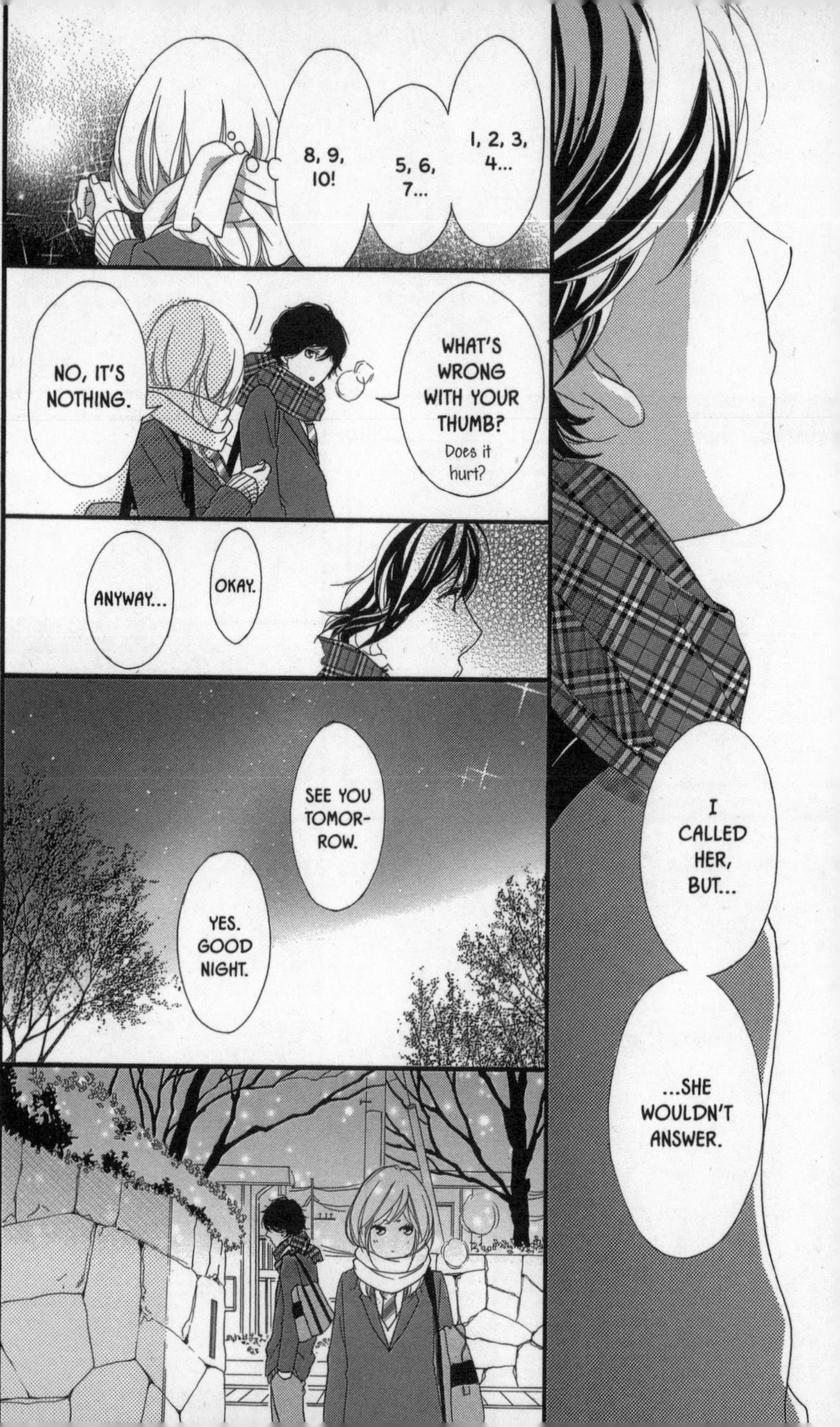
I CALLED HER, BUT...
...SHE WOULDN'T ANSWER.
1, 2, 3, 4...
5, 6, 7...
8, 9, 10!
WHAT'S WRONG WITH YOUR THUMB? Does it hurt?
NO, IT'S NOTHING.
OKAY.
ANYWAY...
SEE YOU TOMORROW.
YES. GOOD NIGHT.

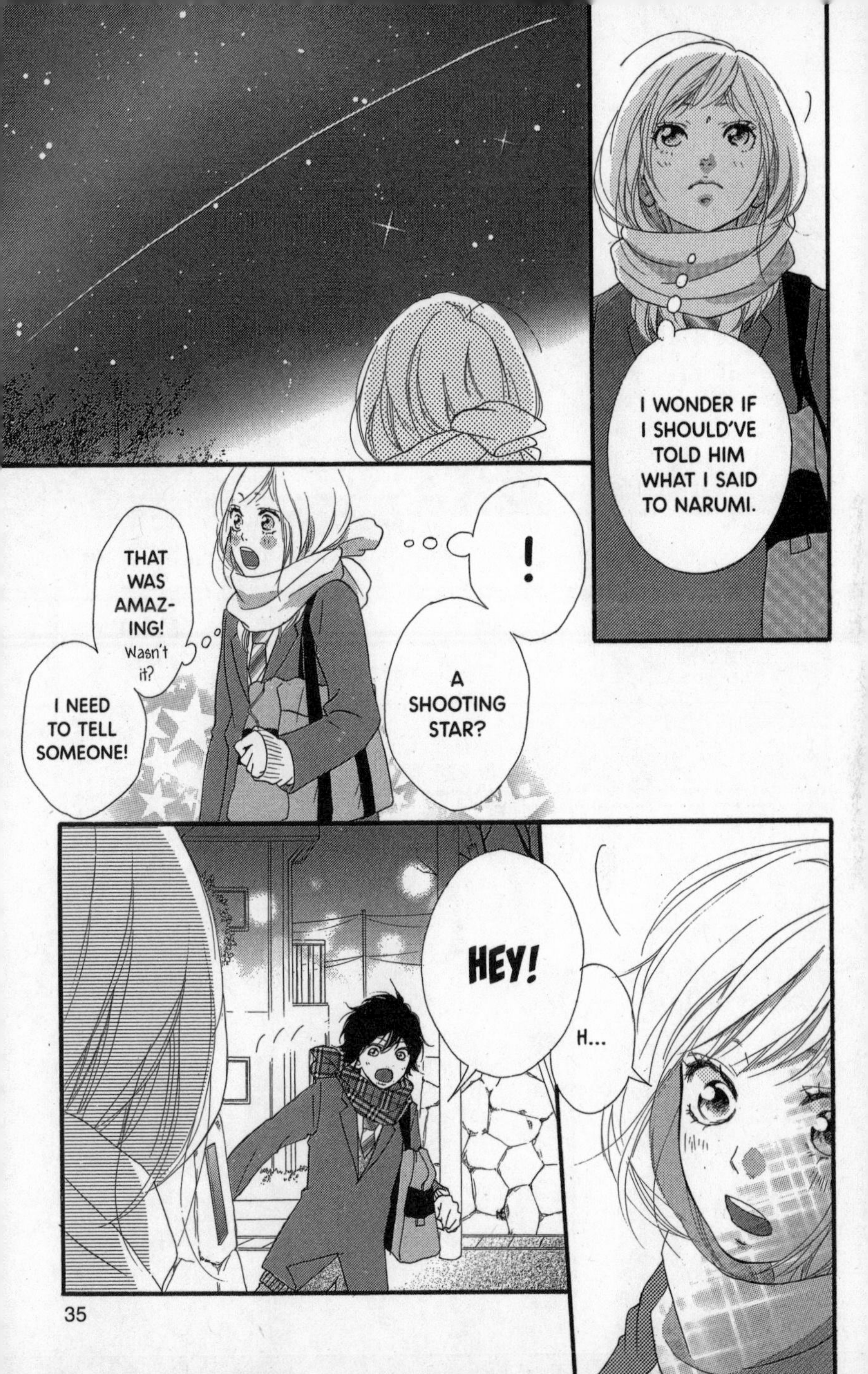
I WONDER IF I SHOULD'VE TOLD HIM WHAT I SAID TO NARUMI.
!
A SHOOTING STAR?
THAT WAS AMAZ-ING!
Wasn't it?
I NEED TO TELL SOMEONE!
H...
HEY!

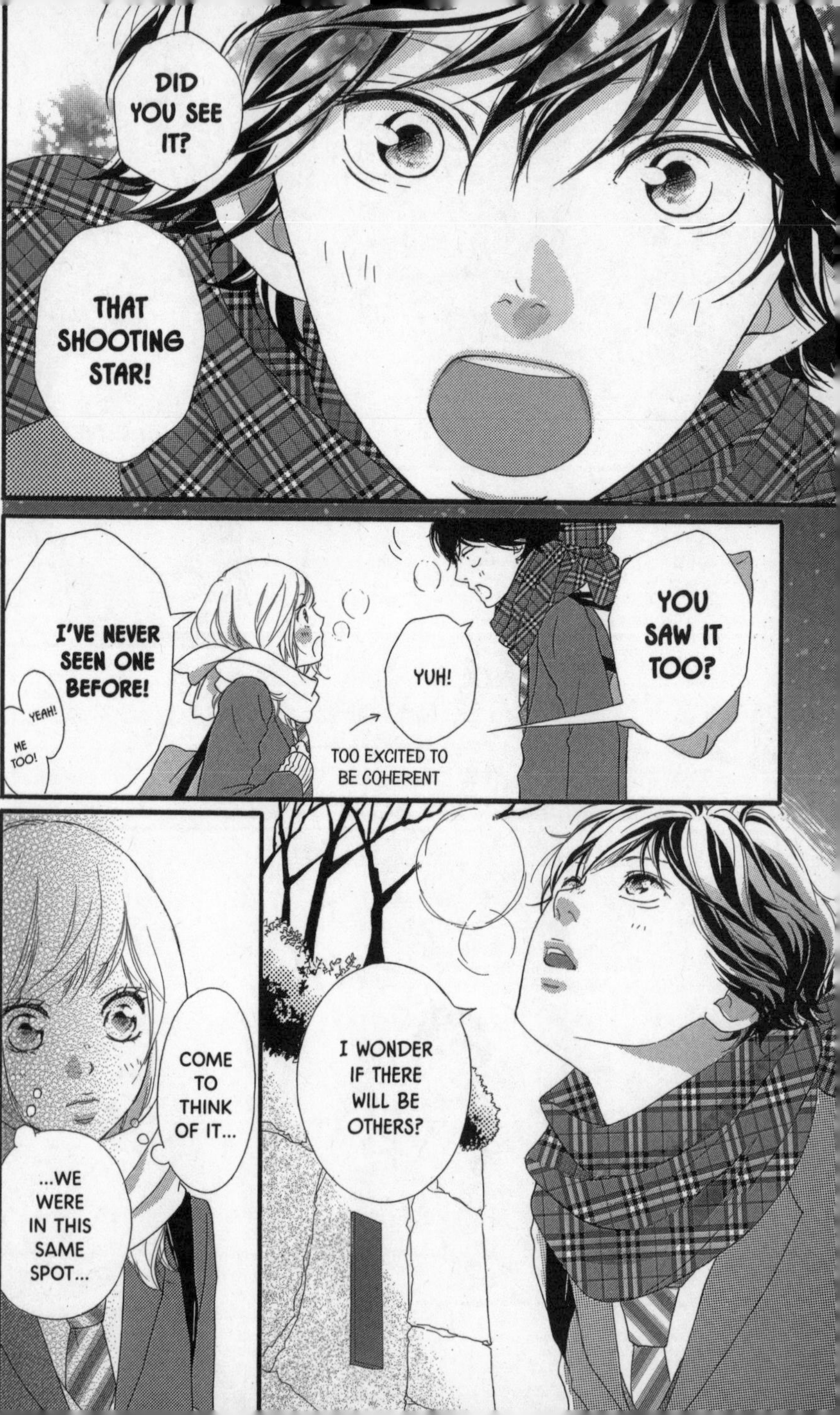
DID YOU SEE IT?
THAT SHOOTING STAR!
YOU SAW IT TOO?
YUH!
TOO EXCITED TO BE COHERENT
I'VE NEVER SEEN ONE BEFORE!
YEAH! ME TOO!
I WONDER IF THERE WILL BE OTHERS?
COME TO THINK OF IT...
...WE WERE IN THIS SAME SPOT...

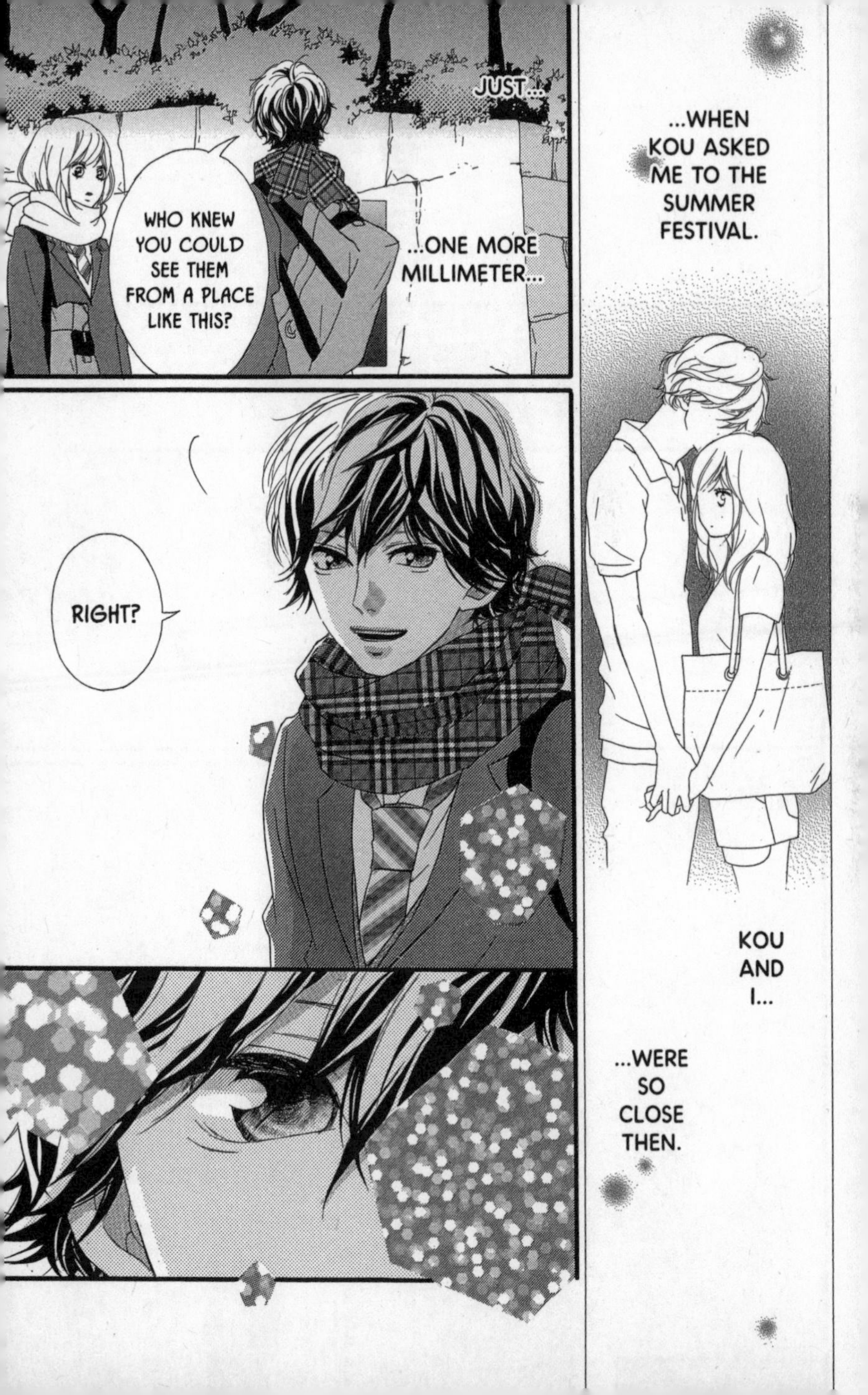
...WHEN KOU ASKED ME TO THE SUMMER FESTIVAL.
KOU AND I...
...WERE SO CLOSE THEN.
JUST...
...ONE MORE MILLIMETER...
WHO KNEW YOU COULD SEE THEM FROM A PLACE LIKE THIS?
RIGHT?

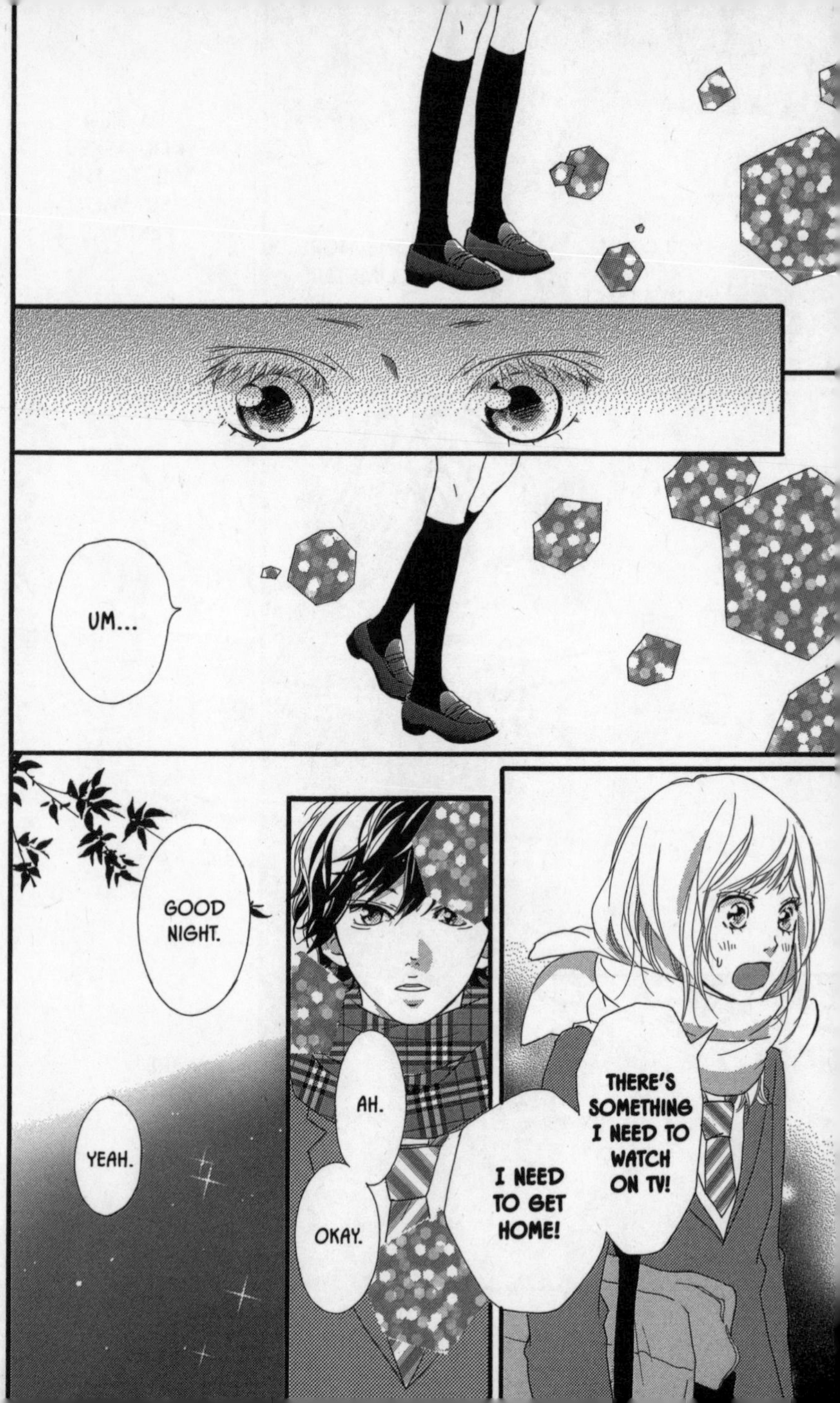
UM...
THERE'S SOMETHING I NEED TO WATCH ON TV!
I NEED TO GET HOME!
AH.
OKAY.
GOOD NIGHT.
YEAH.

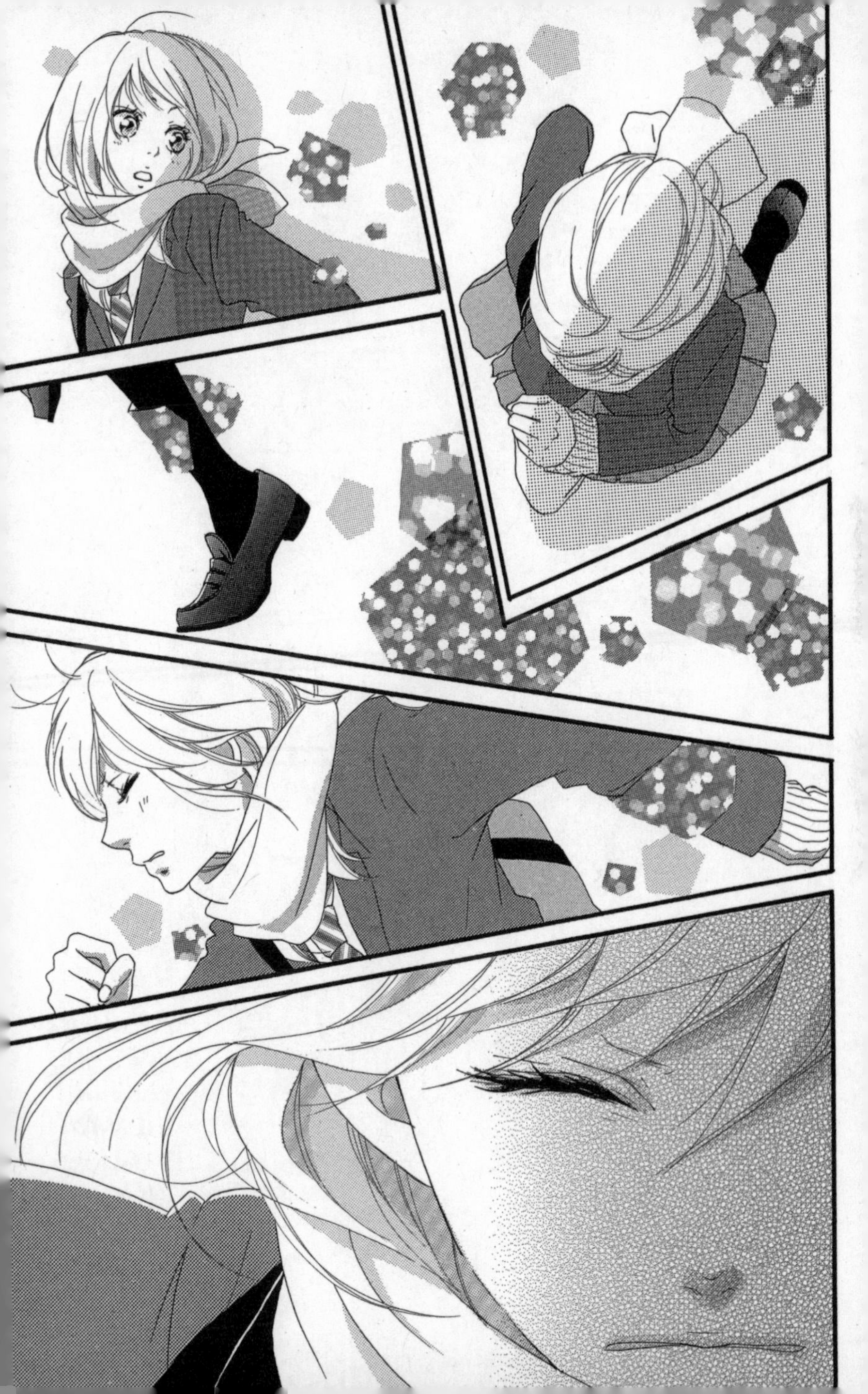

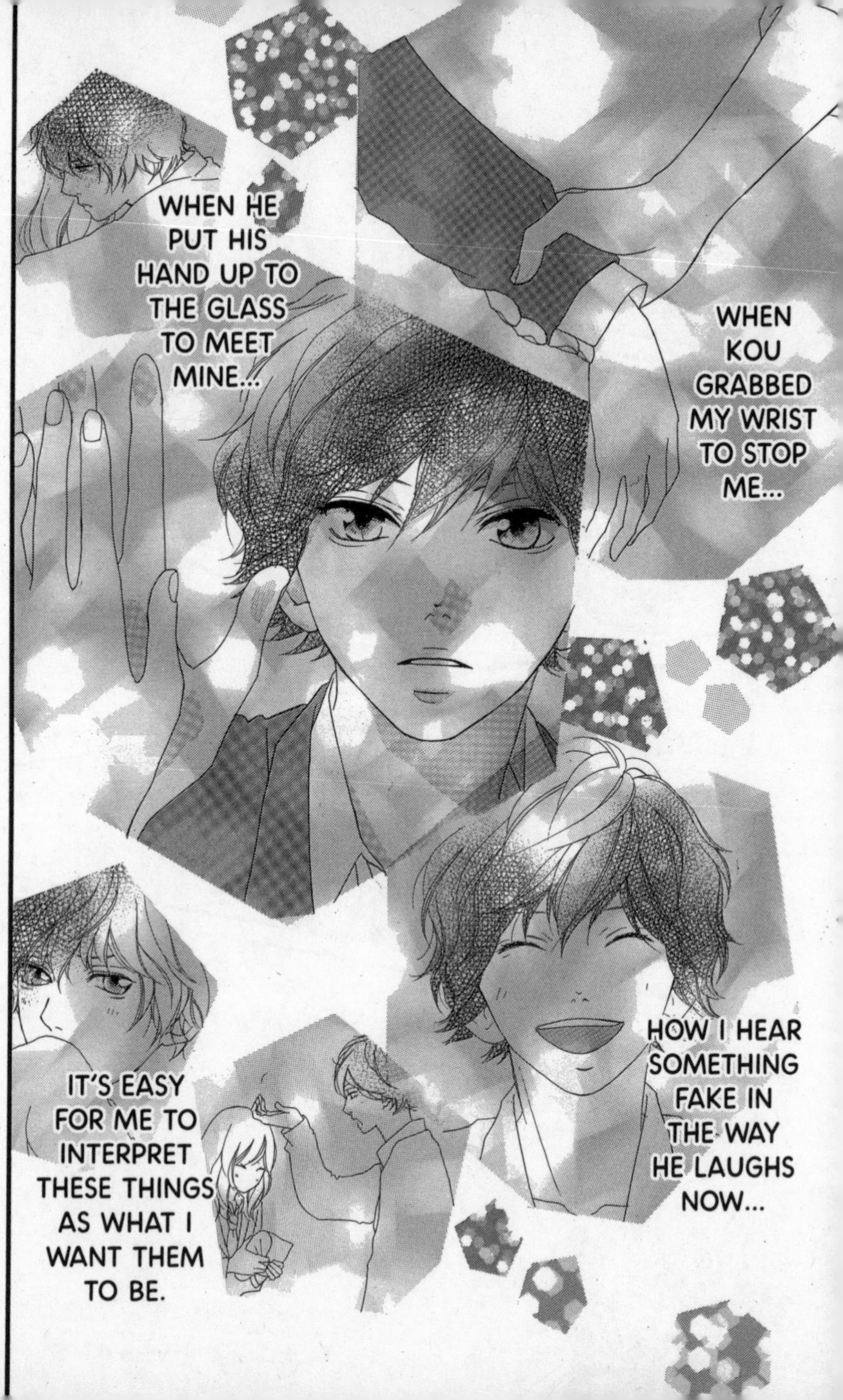
WHEN KOU GRABBED MY WRIST TO STOP ME...
WHEN HE PUT HIS HAND UP TO THE GLASS TO MEET MINE...
HOW I HEAR SOMETHING FAKE IN THE WAY HE LAUGHS NOW...
IT'S EASY FOR ME TO INTERPRET THESE THINGS AS WHAT I WANT THEM TO BE.

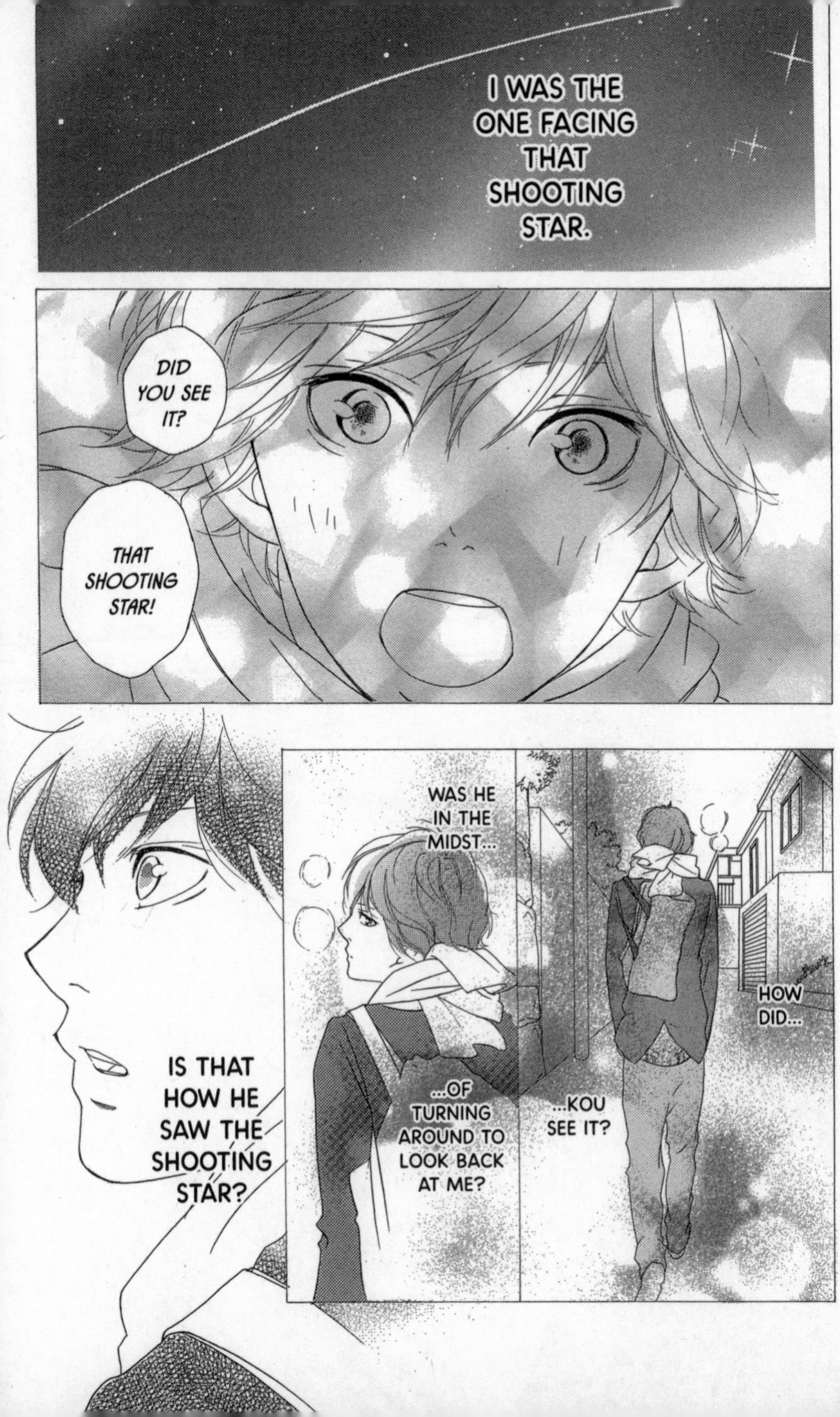
I WAS THE ONE FACING THAT SHOOTING STAR.
DID YOU SEE IT?
THAT SHOOTING STAR!
HOW DID...
...KOU SEE IT?
WAS HE IN THE MIDST...
...OF TURNING AROUND TO LOOK BACK AT ME?
IS THAT HOW HE SAW THE SHOOTING STAR?

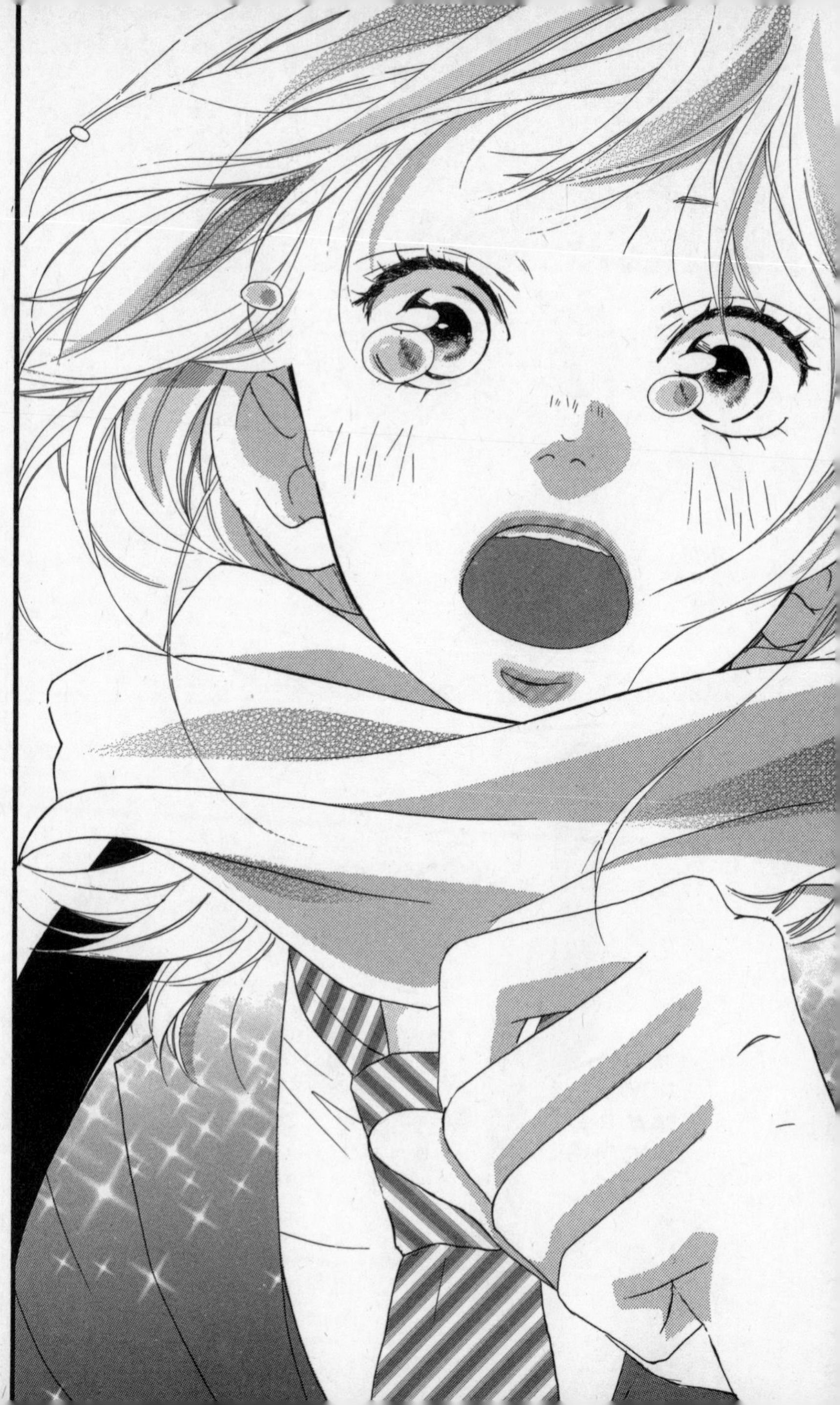

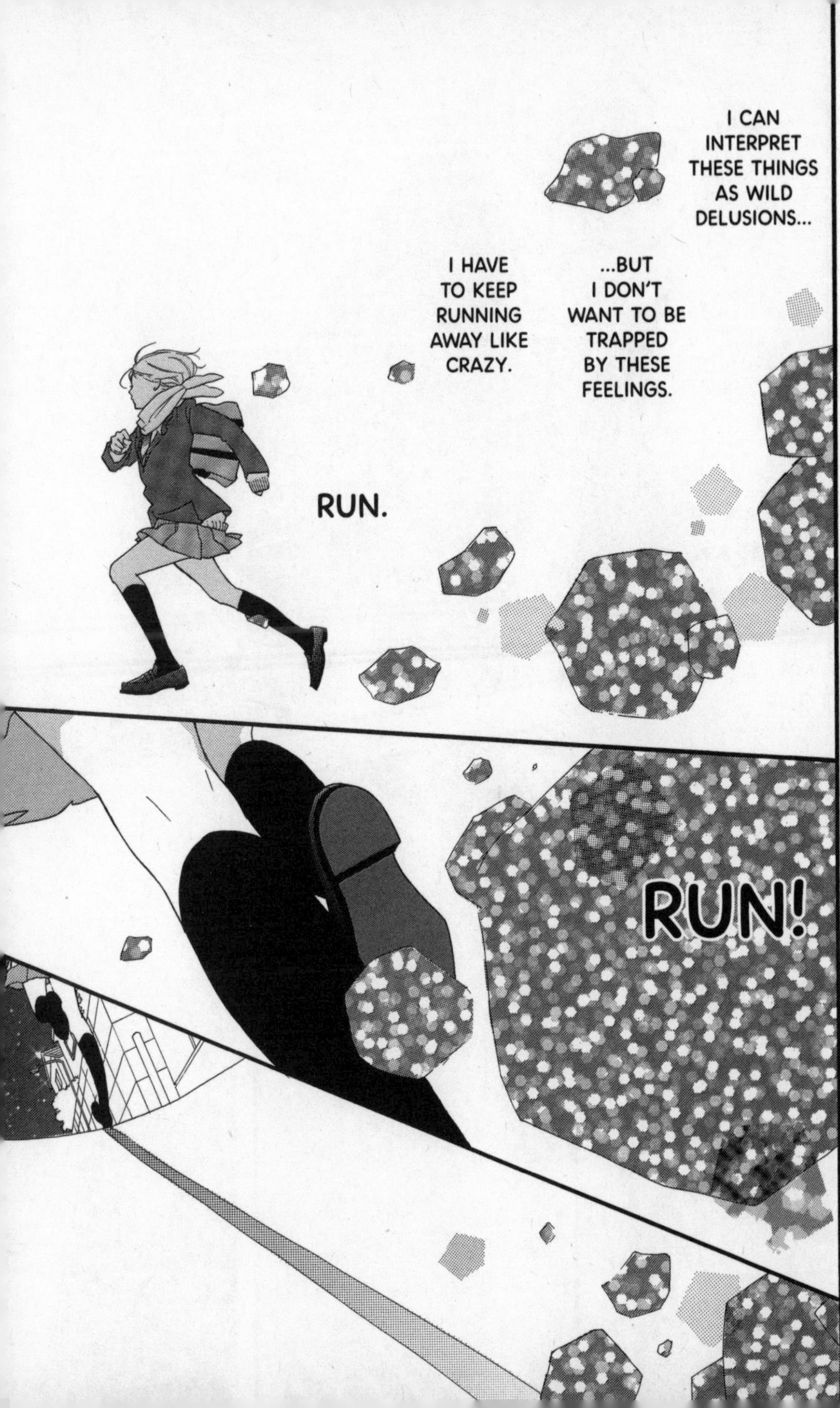
I CAN INTERPRET THESE THINGS AS WILD DELUSIONS...
...BUT I DON'T WANT TO BE TRAPPED BY THESE FEELINGS.
I HAVE TO KEEP RUNNING AWAY LIKE CRAZY.
RUN.
RUN!

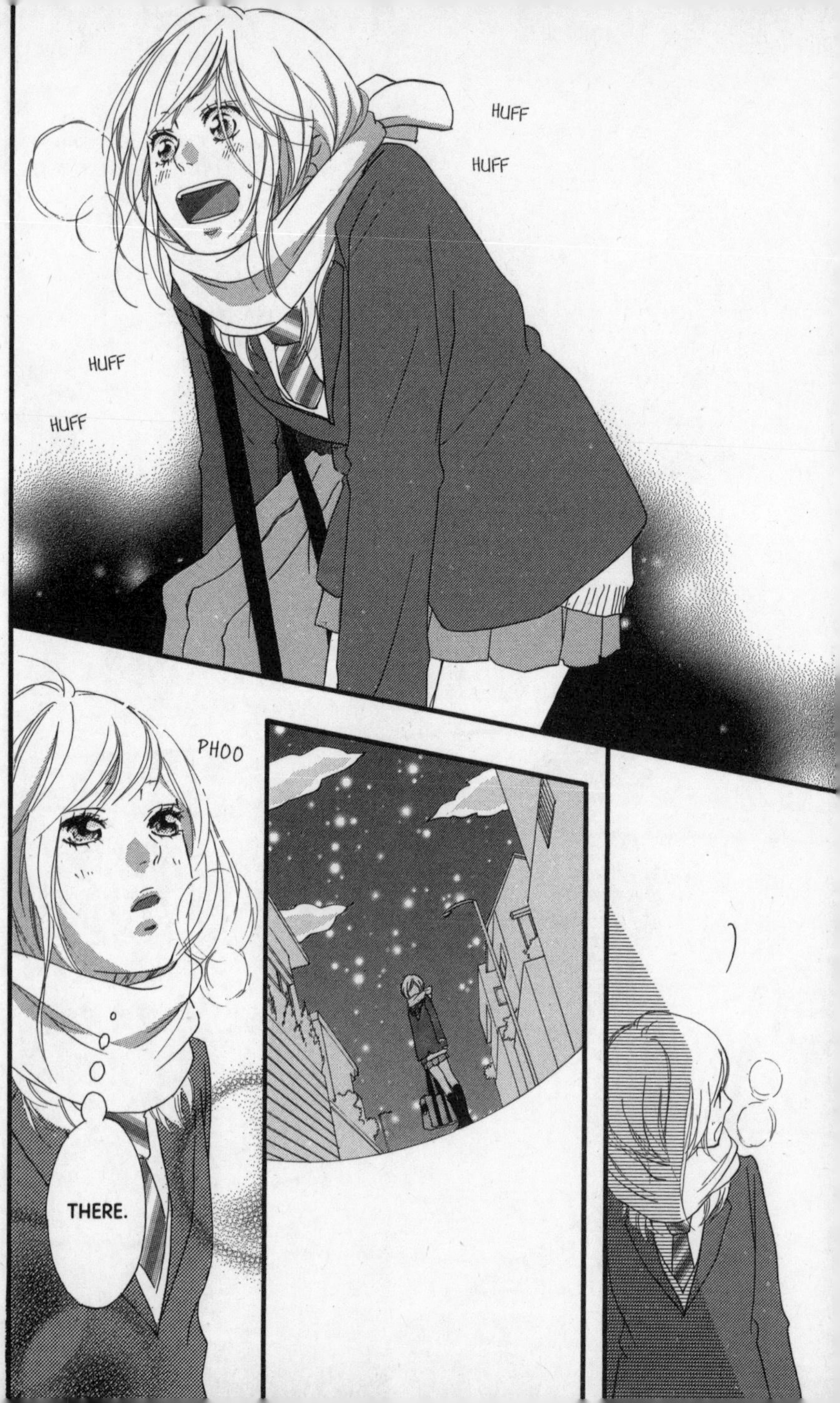
HUFF
HUFF
HUFF
HUFF
PHOO
THERE.

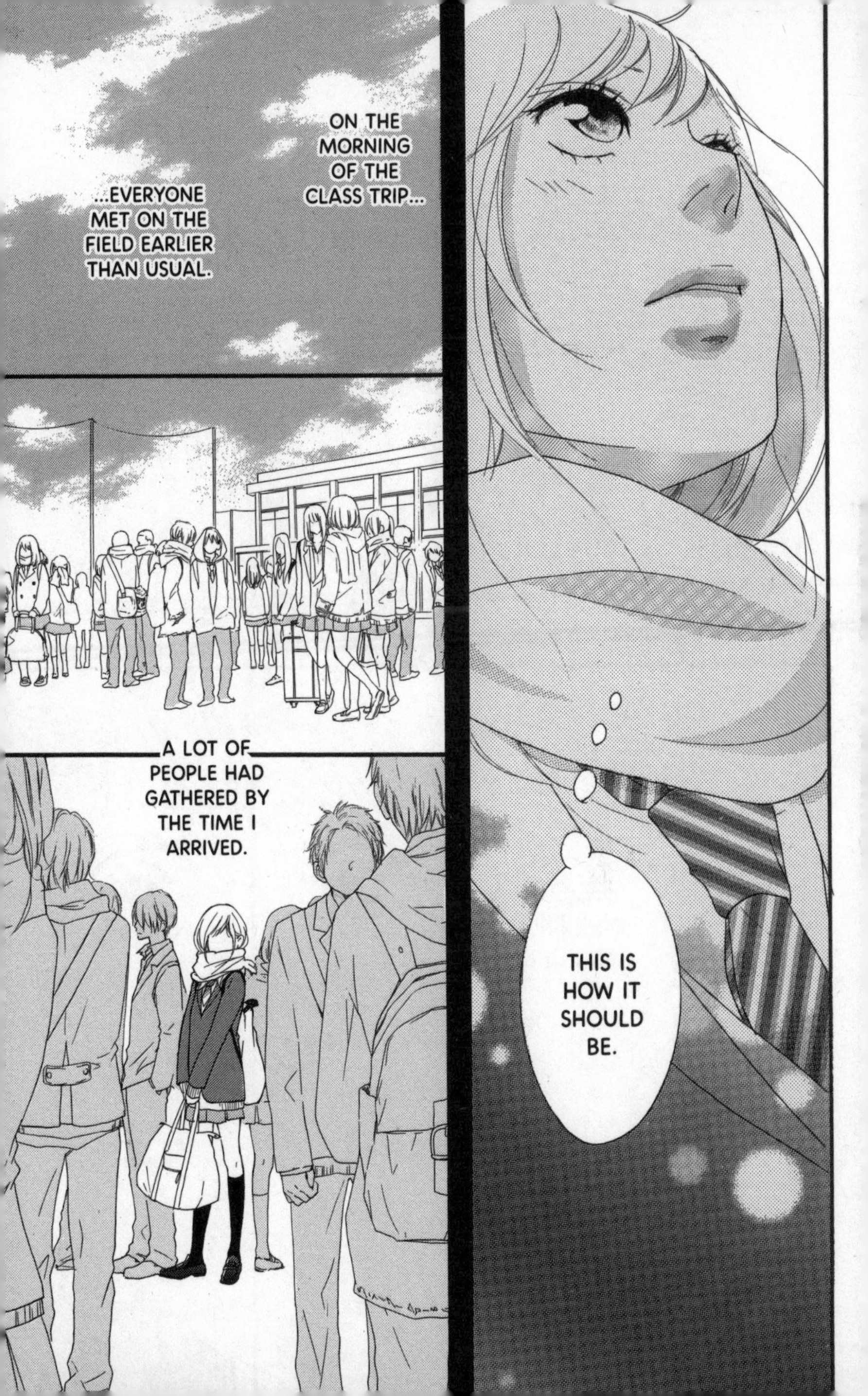
THIS IS HOW IT SHOULD BE.
ON THE MORNING OF THE CLASS TRIP...
...EVERYONE MET ON THE FIELD EARLIER THAN USUAL.
A LOT OF PEOPLE HAD GATHERED BY THE TIME I ARRIVED.

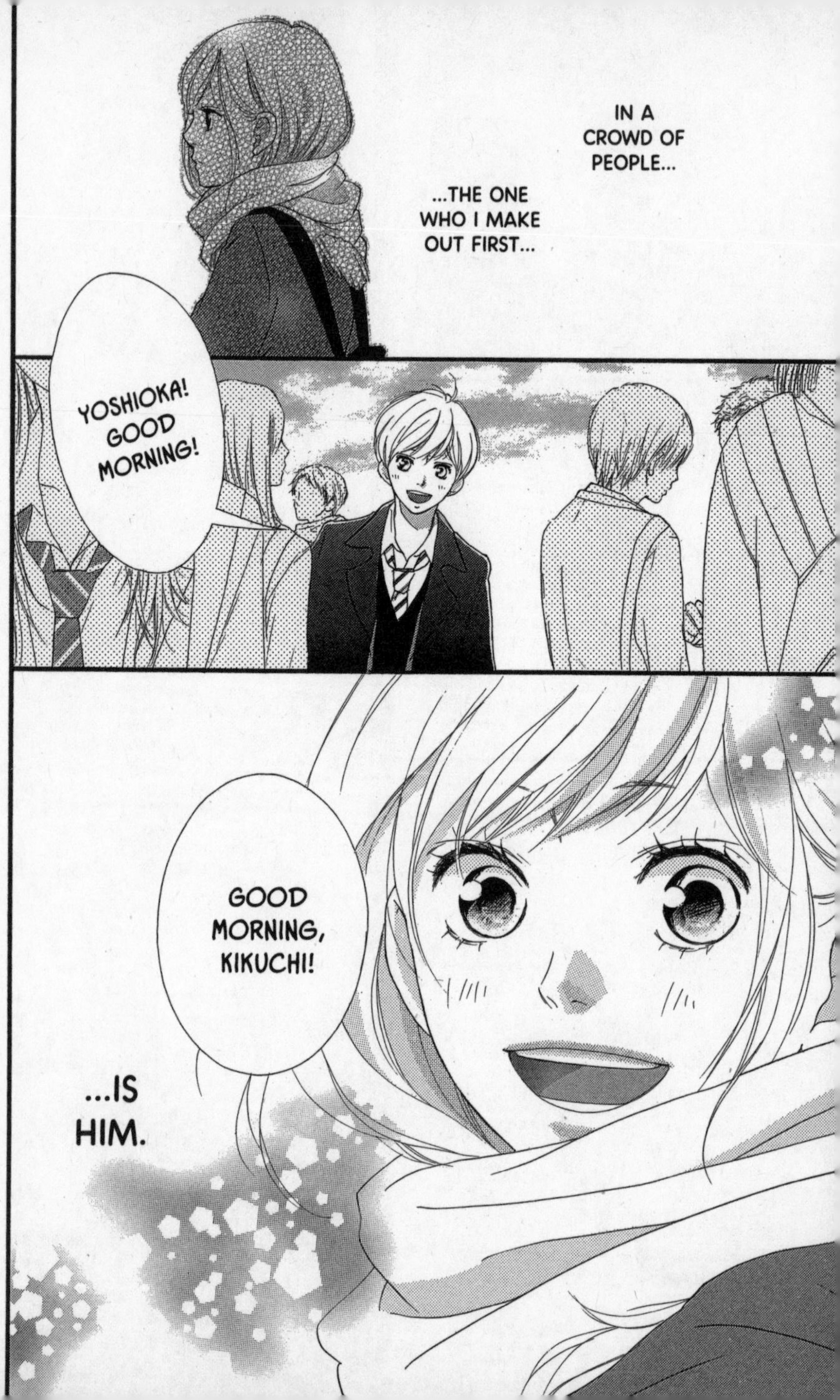
IN A CROWD OF PEOPLE...
...THE ONE WHO I MAKE OUT FIRST...
YOSHIOKA! GOOD MORNING!
GOOD MORNING, KIKUCHI!
...IS HIM.

The scent of air after rain...
In the light around us,
I felt your heartbeat.

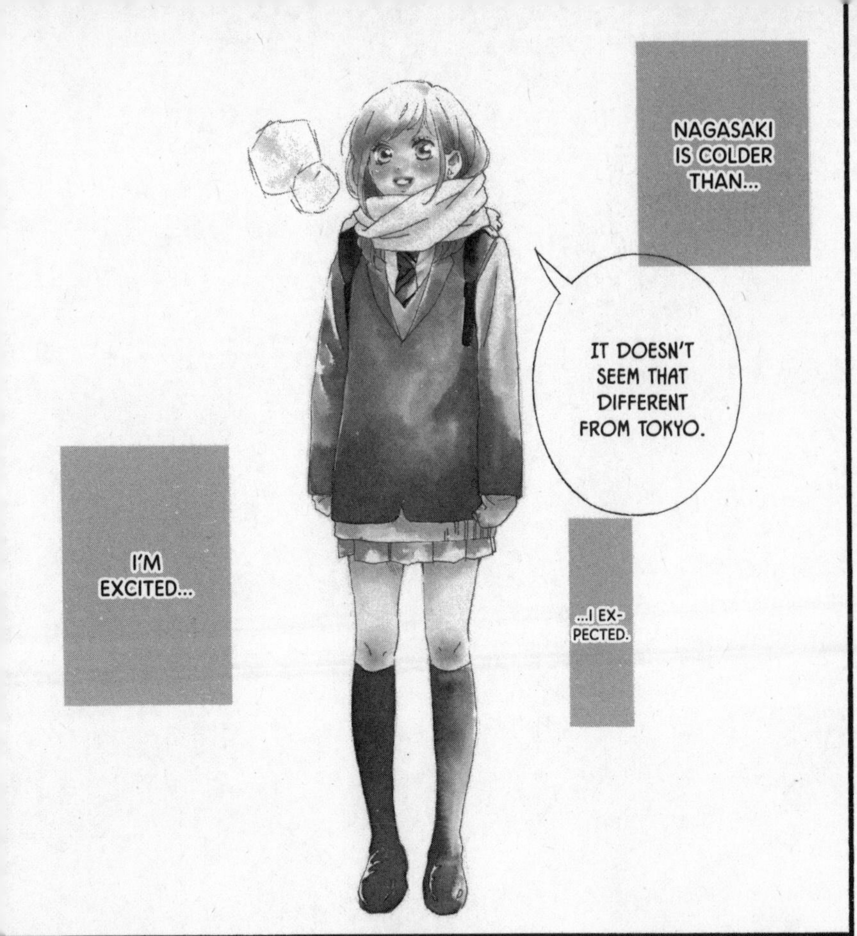
NAGASAKI IS COLDER THAN...
IT DOESN'T SEEM THAT DIFFERENT FROM TOKYO.
...I EX-PECTED.
I'M EXCITED...
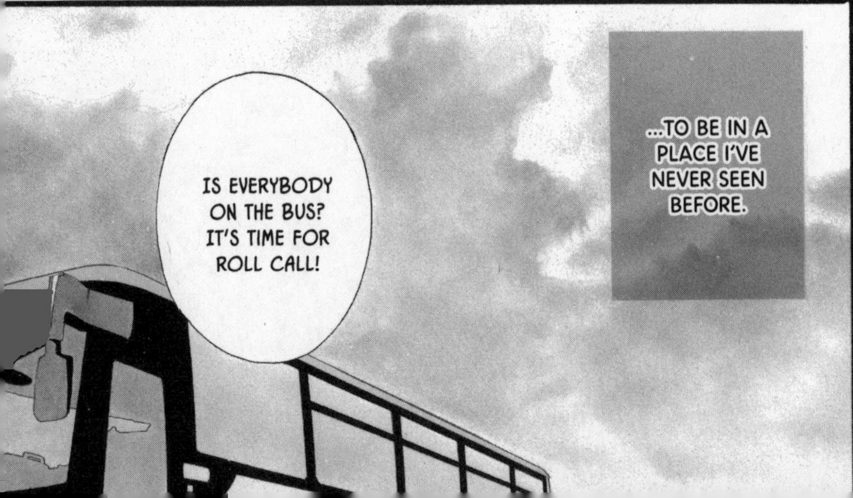
...TO BE IN A PLACE I'VE NEVER SEEN BEFORE.
IS EVERYBODY ON THE BUS? IT'S TIME FOR ROLL CALL!

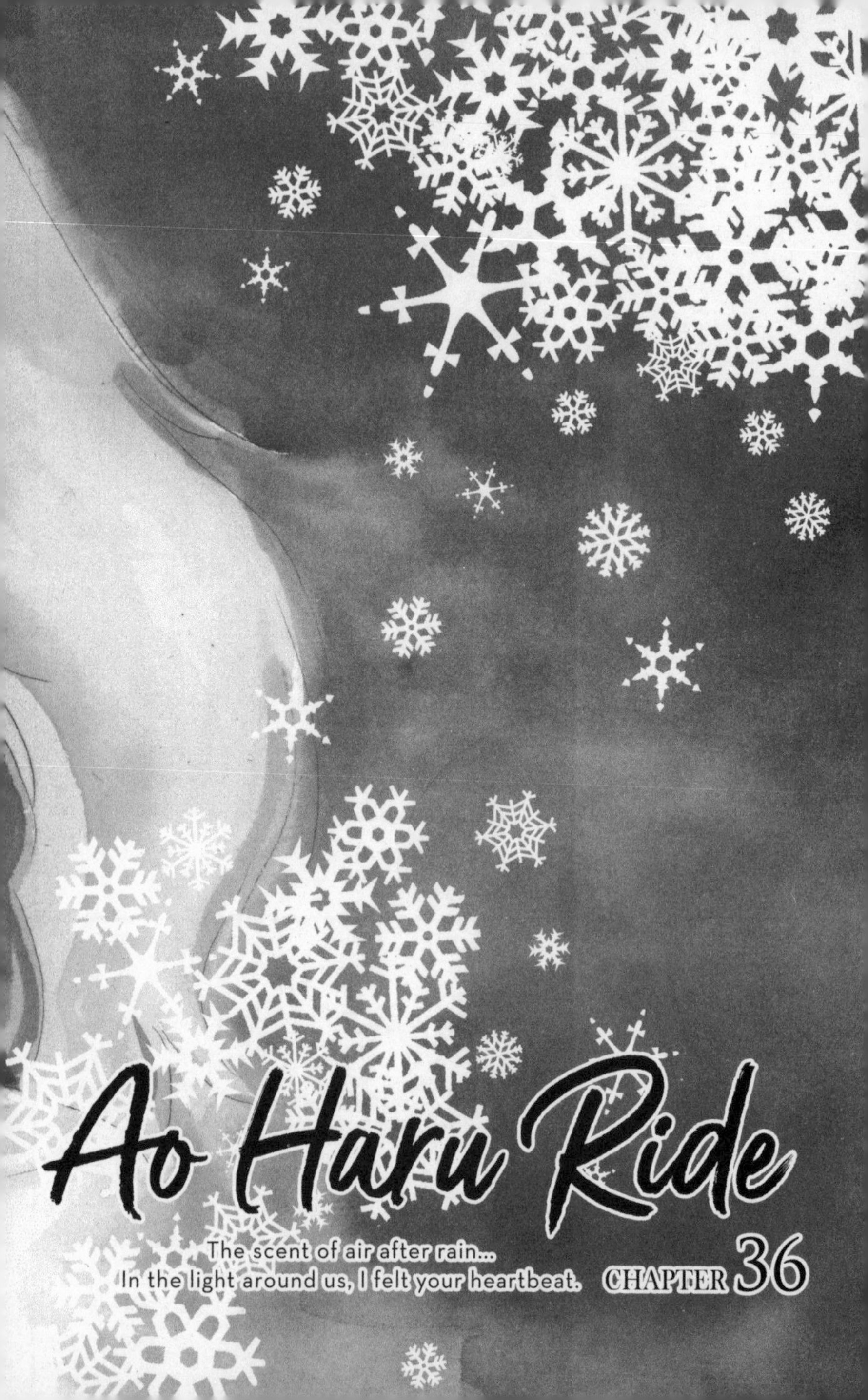
Ao Haru Ride
The scent of air after rain...
In the light around us, I felt your heartbeat.
CHAPTER 36

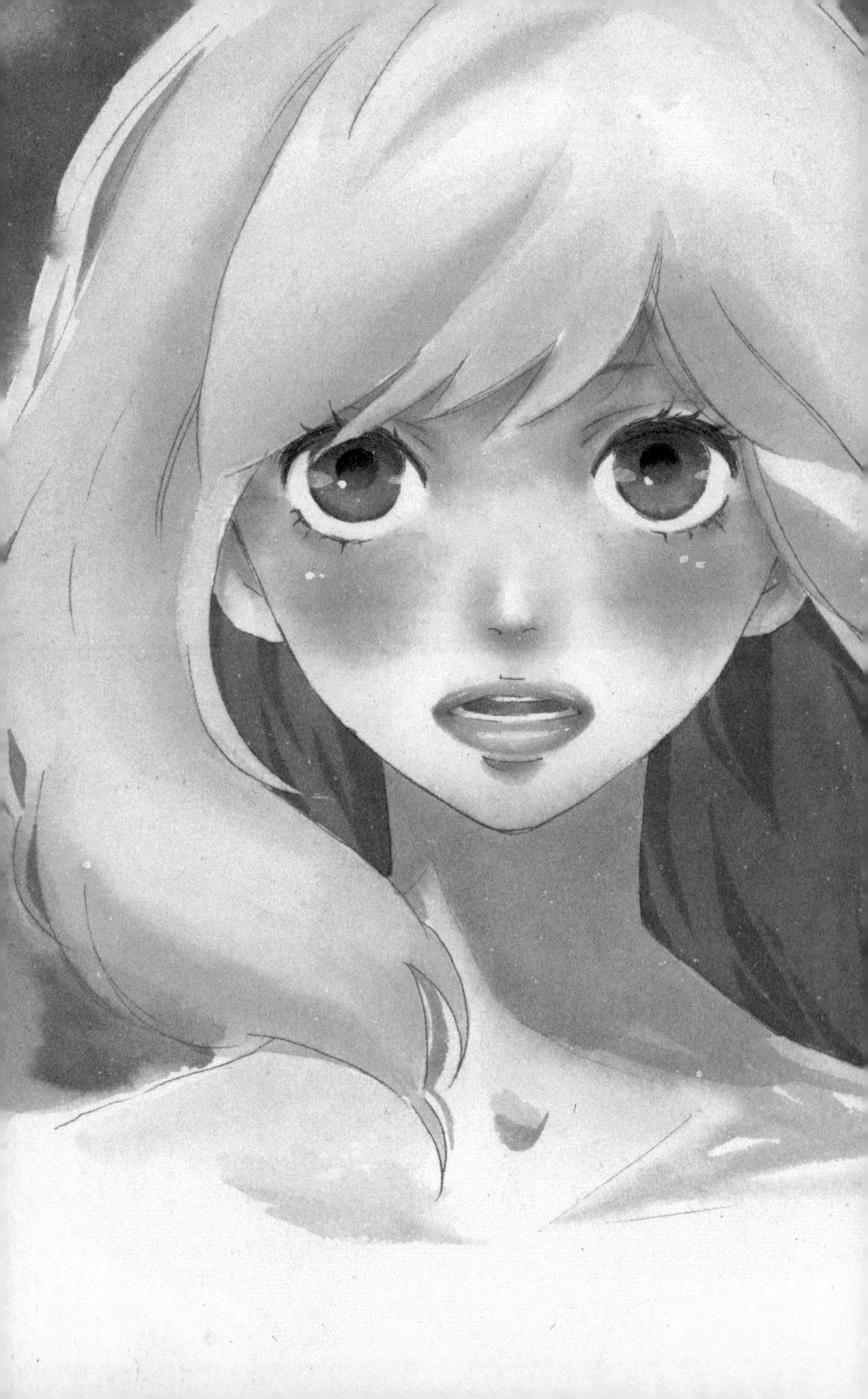

The scent of air after rain...
In the light around us,
I felt your heartbeat.

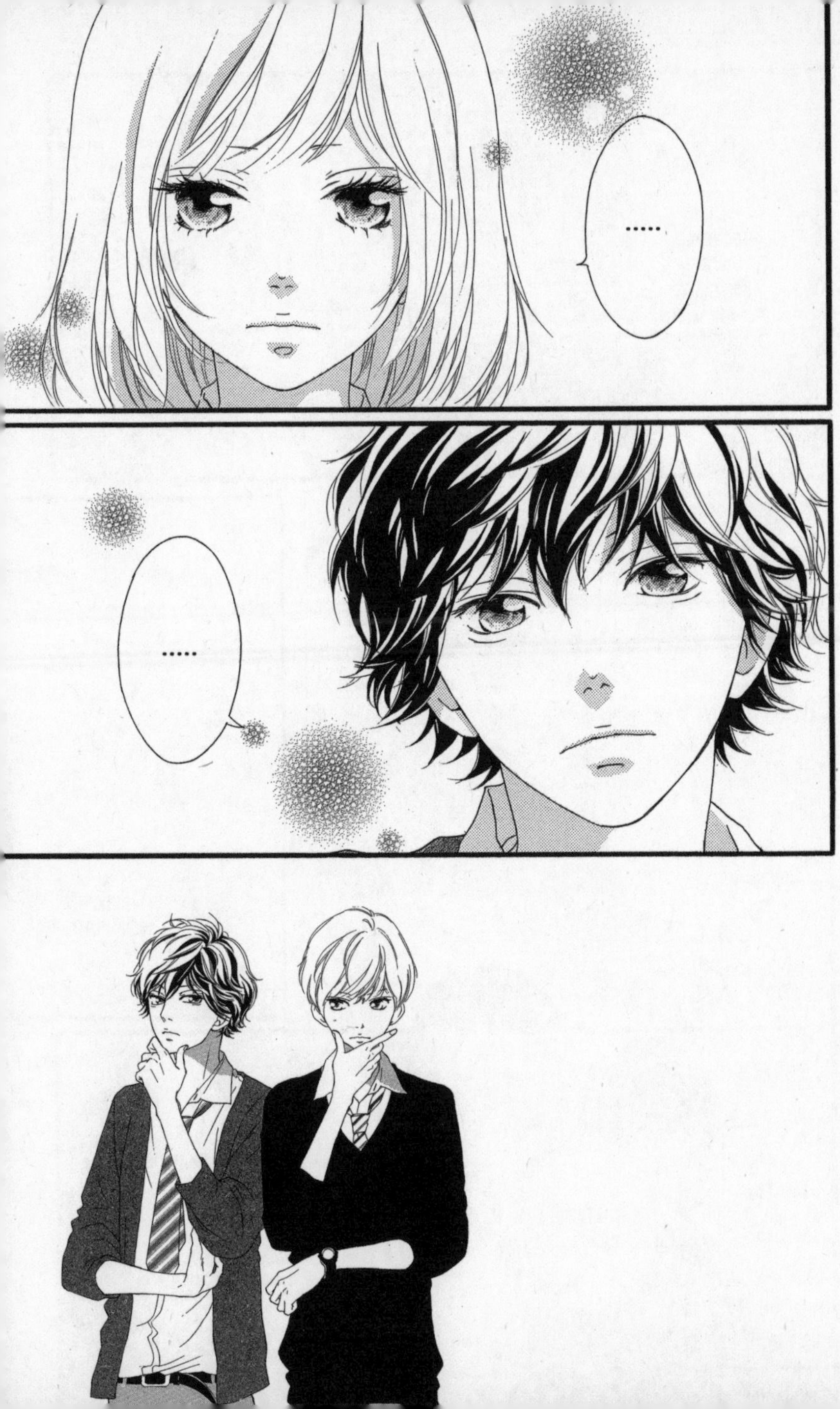
......
......

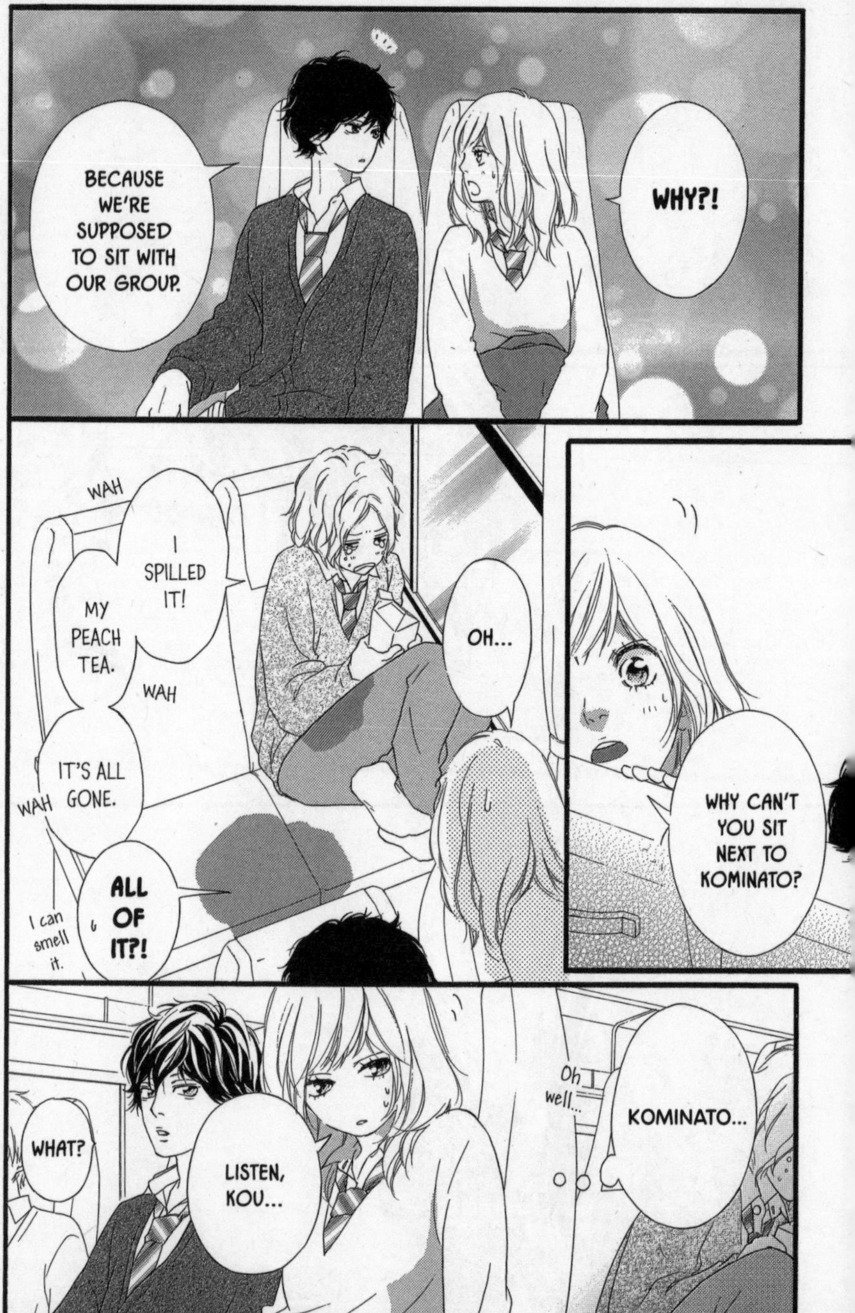
WHY?!
BECAUSE WE'RE SUPPOSED TO SIT WITH OUR GROUP.
WHY CAN'T YOU SIT NEXT TO KOMINATO?
OH...
I SPILLED IT!
WAH
MY PEACH TEA.
WAH
IT'S ALL GONE.
WAH
ALL OF IT?!
I can smell it.
KOMINATO...
Oh well...
LISTEN, KOU...
WHAT?

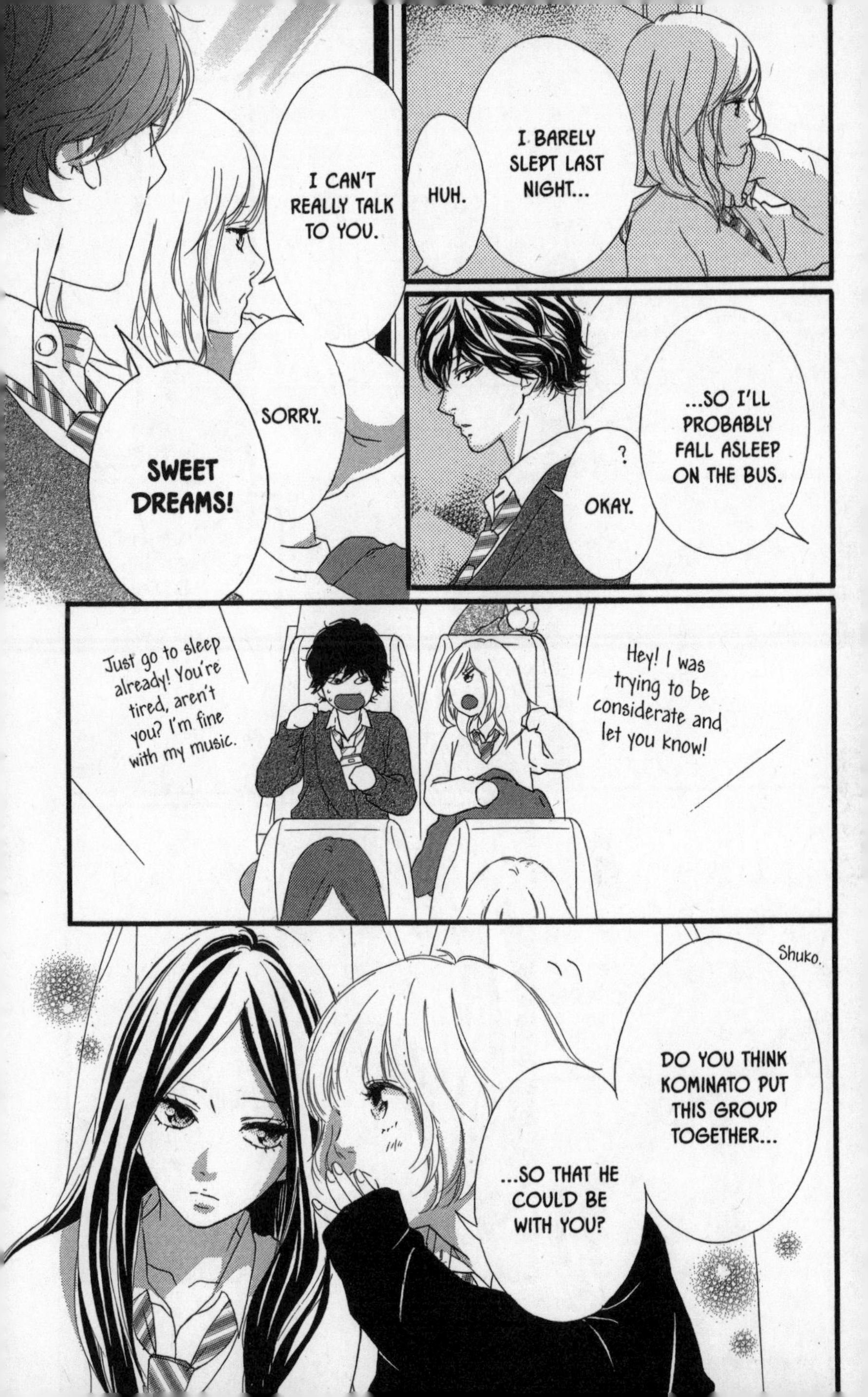
I BARELY SLEPT LAST NIGHT...
HUH.
...SO I'LL PROBABLY FALL ASLEEP ON THE BUS.
? OKAY.
I CAN'T REALLY TALK TO YOU.
SORRY.
SWEET DREAMS!
Hey! I was trying to be considerate and let you know!
Just go to sleep already! You're tired, aren't you? I'm fine with my music.
Shuko.
DO YOU THINK KOMINATO PUT THIS GROUP TOGETHER...
...SO THAT HE COULD BE WITH YOU?

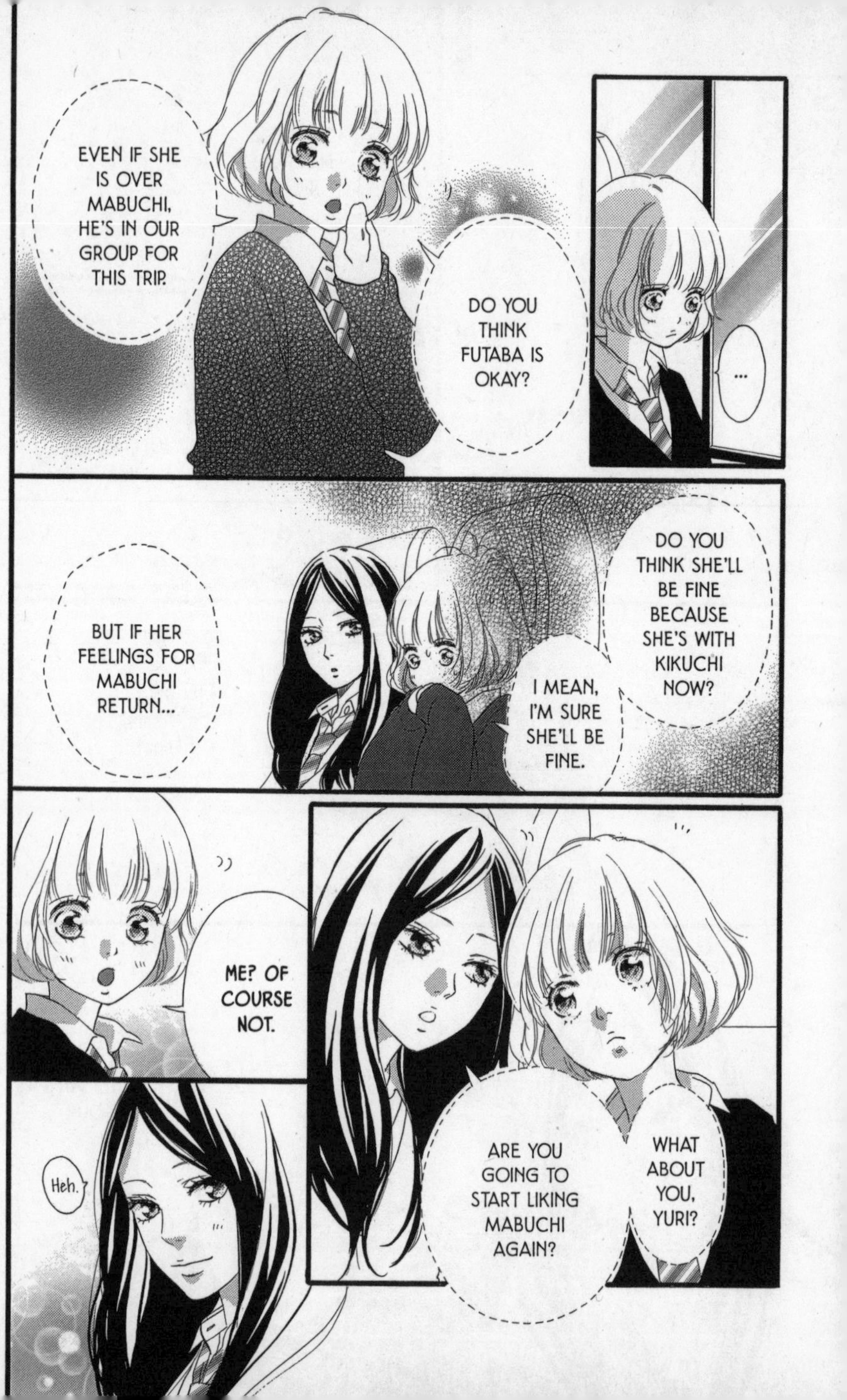
...
EVEN IF SHE IS OVER MABUCHI, HE'S IN OUR GROUP FOR THIS TRIP.
DO YOU THINK FUTABA IS OKAY?
DO YOU THINK SHE'LL BE FINE BECAUSE SHE'S WITH KIKUCHI NOW?
I MEAN, I'M SURE SHE'LL BE FINE.
BUT IF HER FEELINGS FOR MABUCHI RETURN...
WHAT ABOUT YOU, YURI?
ARE YOU GOING TO START LIKING MABUCHI AGAIN?
ME? OF COURSE NOT.
Heh.

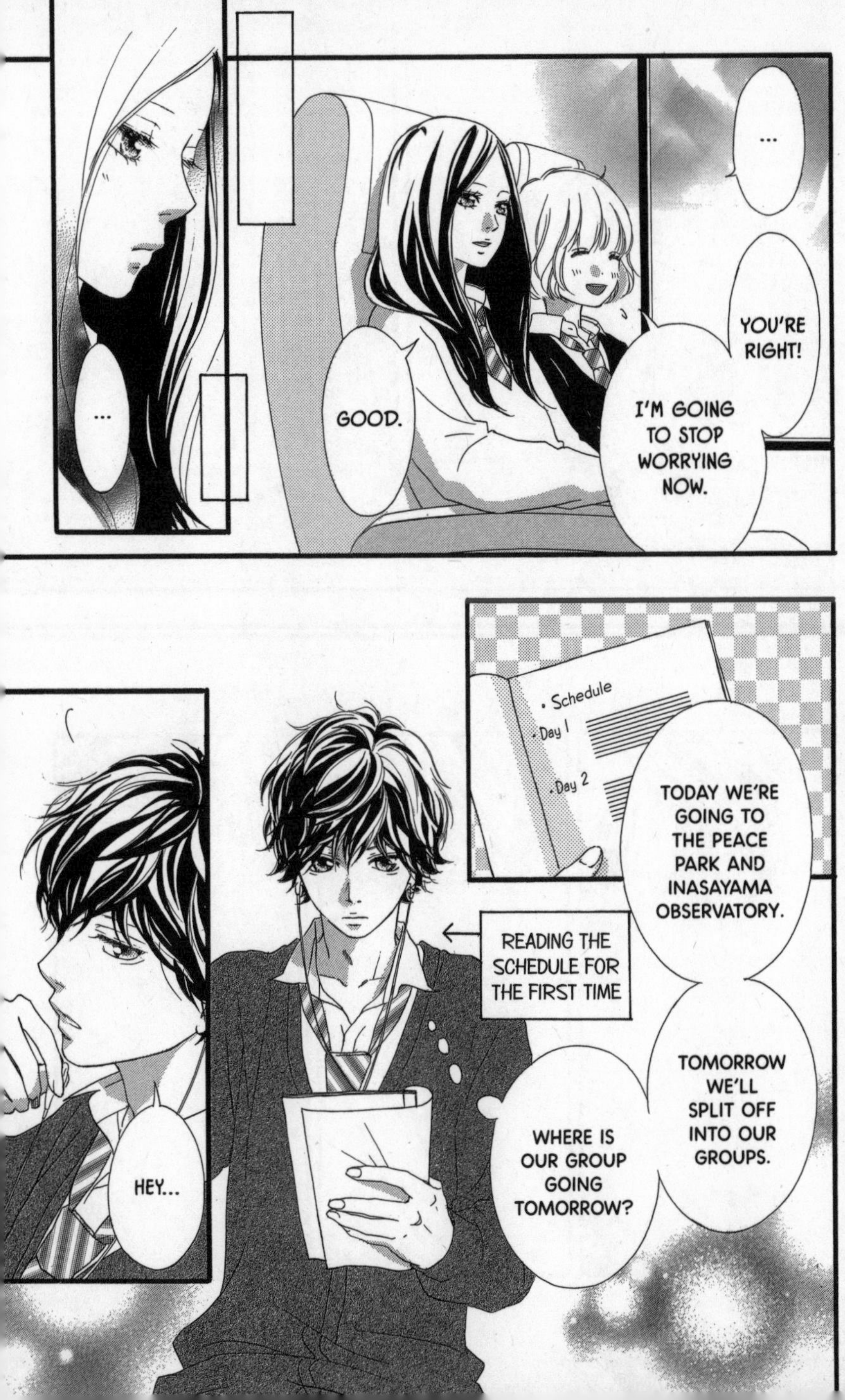
...
YOU'RE RIGHT!
I'M GOING TO STOP WORRYING NOW.
GOOD.
...
• Schedule
• Day 1
• Day 2
TODAY WE'RE GOING TO THE PEACE PARK AND INASAYAMA OBSERVATORY.
TOMORROW WE'LL SPLIT OFF INTO OUR GROUPS.
READING THE SCHEDULE FOR THE FIRST TIME
WHERE IS OUR GROUP GOING TOMORROW?
HEY...

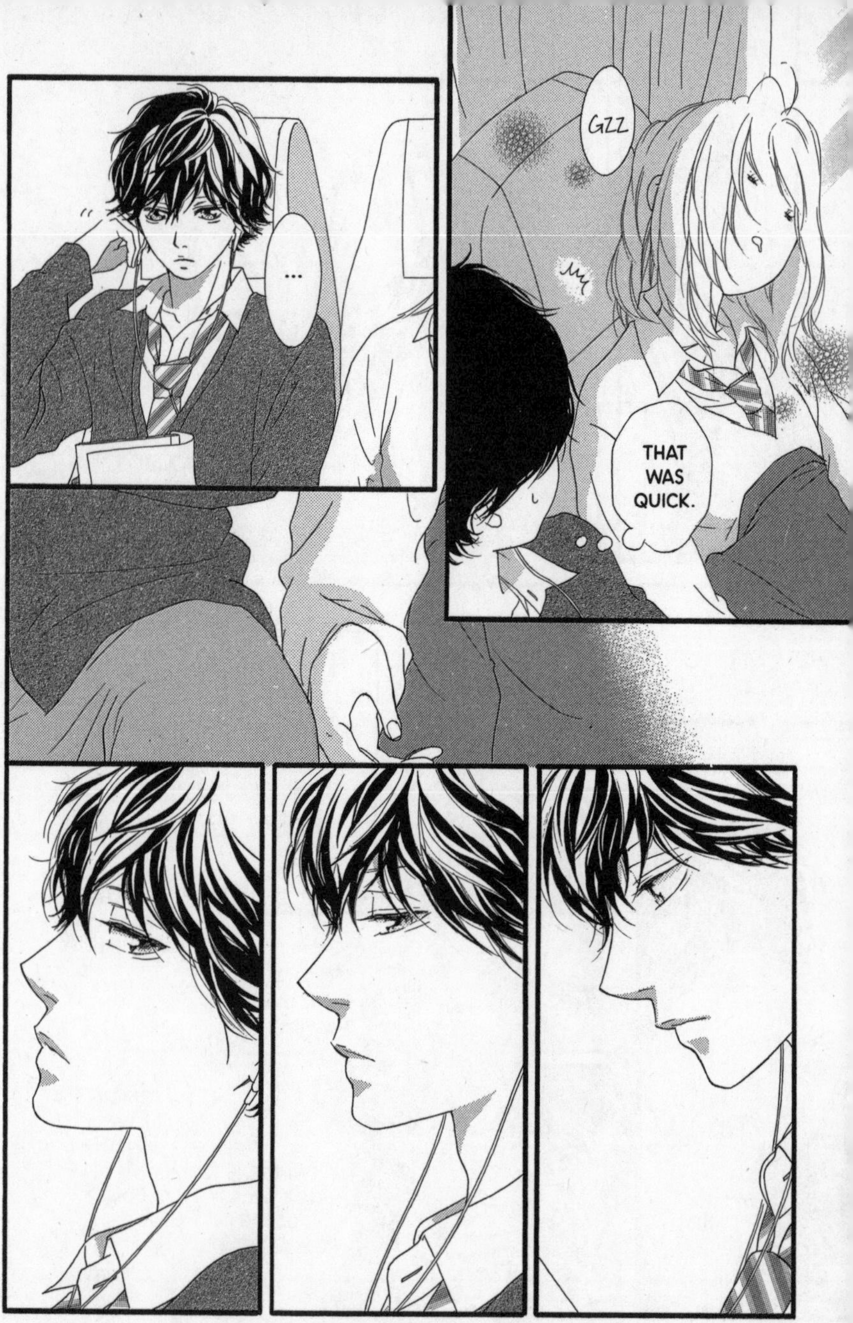
GZZ
THAT WAS QUICK.
...

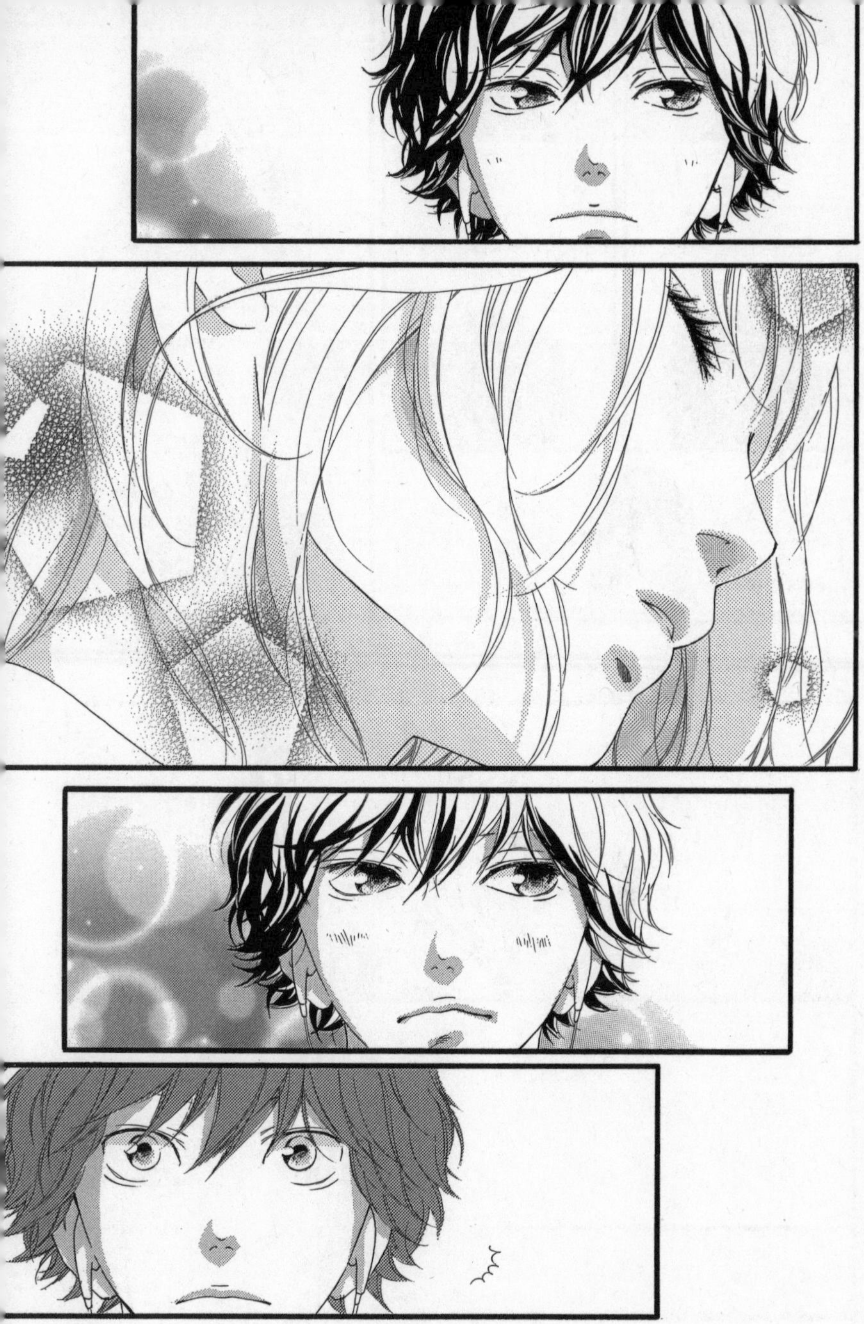

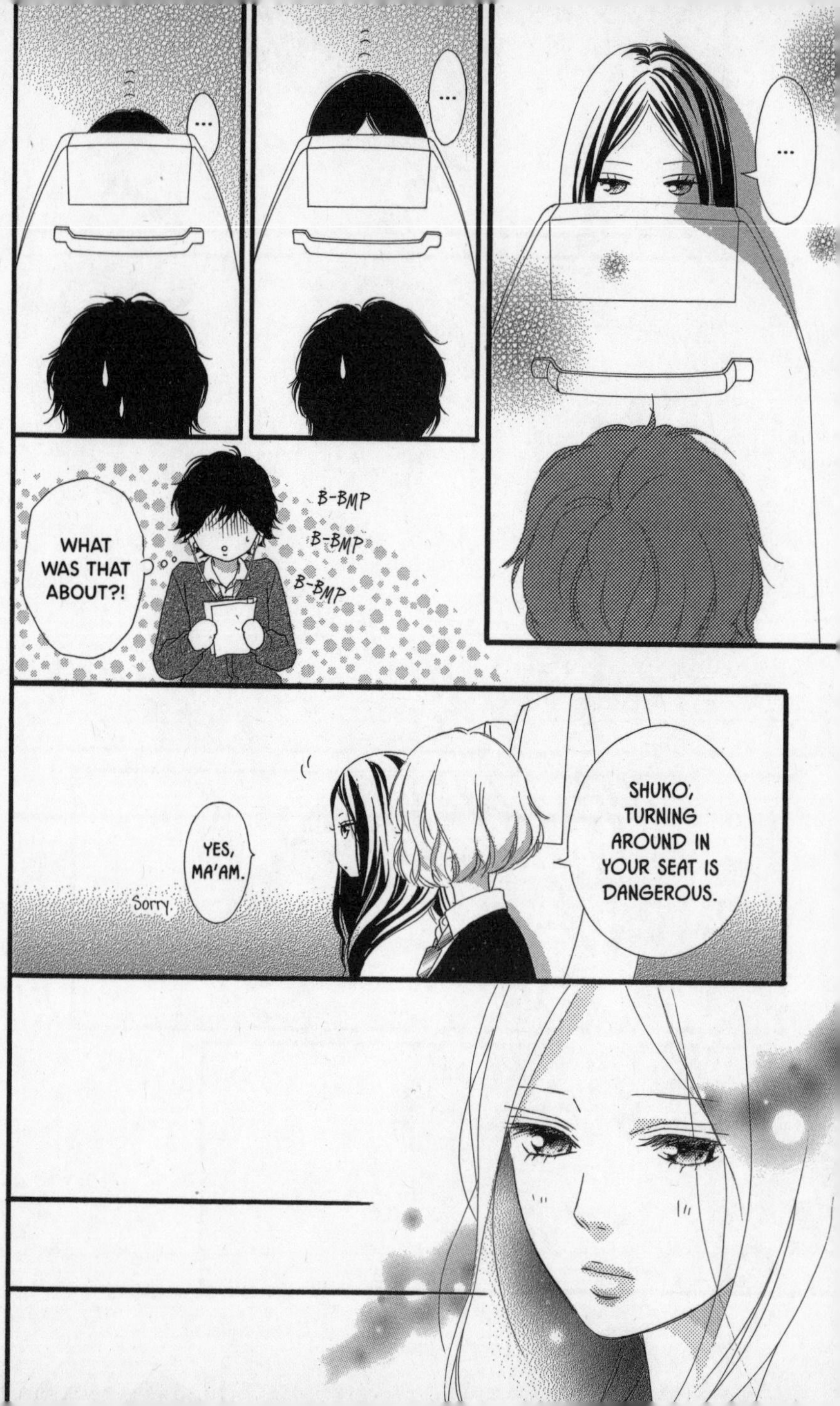
...
...
...
WHAT WAS THAT ABOUT?!
B-BMP
B-BMP
B-BMP
SHUKO, TURNING AROUND IN YOUR SEAT IS DANGEROUS.
YES, MA'AM.
Sorry.

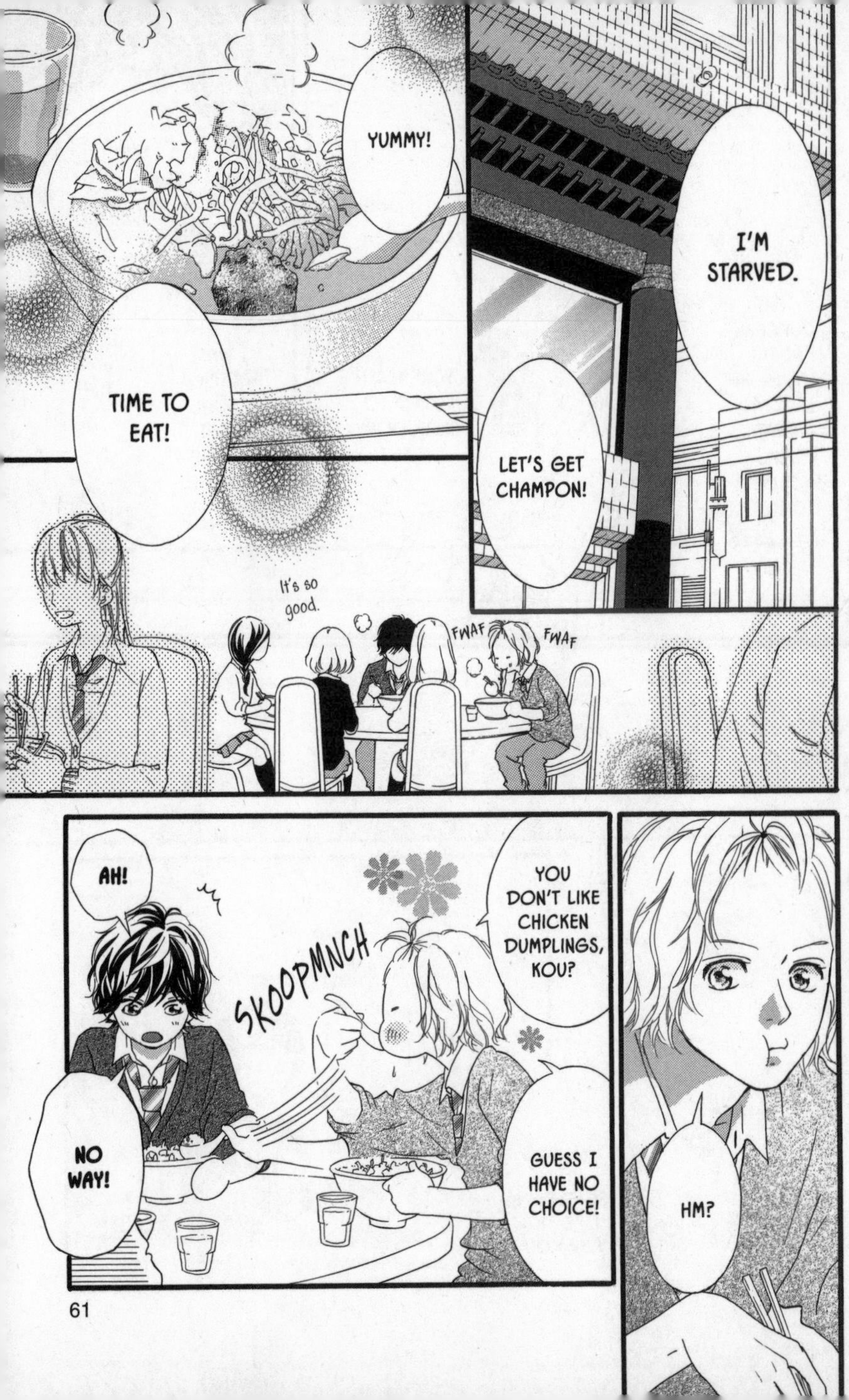
I'M STARVED.
LET'S GET CHAMPON!
YUMMY!
TIME TO EAT!
FWAF
FWAF
It's so good.
HM?
YOU DON'T LIKE CHICKEN DUMPLINGS, KOU?
GUESS I HAVE NO CHOICE!
SKOOPMNCH
AH!
NO WAY!

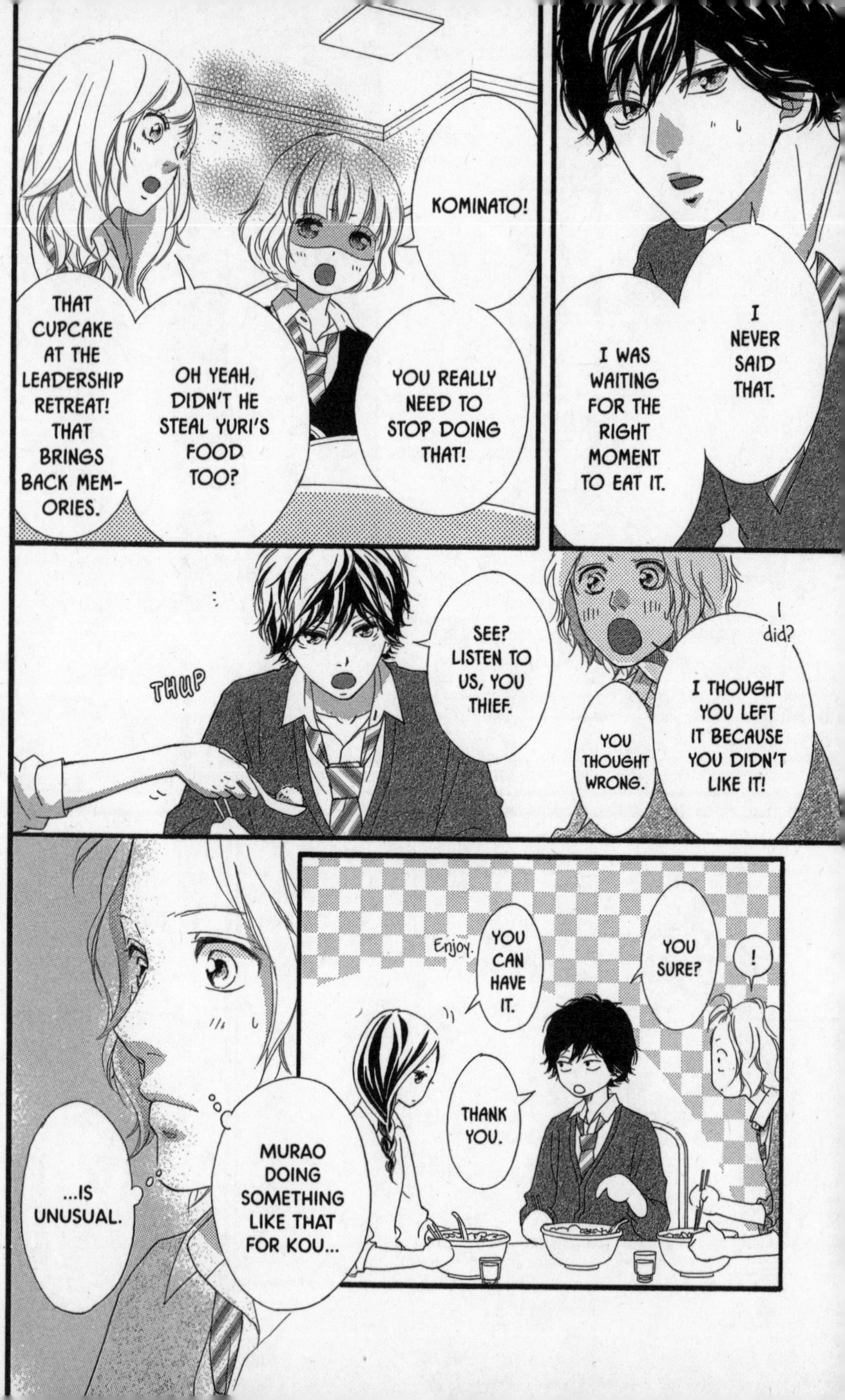
I NEVER SAID THAT.
I WAS WAITING FOR THE RIGHT MOMENT TO EAT IT.
KOMINATO!
YOU REALLY NEED TO STOP DOING THAT!
OH YEAH, DIDN'T HE STEAL YURI'S FOOD TOO?
THAT CUPCAKE AT THE LEADERSHIP RETREAT! THAT BRINGS BACK MEM-ORIES.
I did?
I THOUGHT YOU LEFT IT BECAUSE YOU DIDN'T LIKE IT!
YOU THOUGHT WRONG.
SEE? LISTEN TO US, YOU THIEF.
THUP
!
YOU SURE?
YOU CAN HAVE IT.
Enjoy.
THANK YOU.
MURAO DOING SOMETHING LIKE THAT FOR KOU...
...IS UNUSUAL.

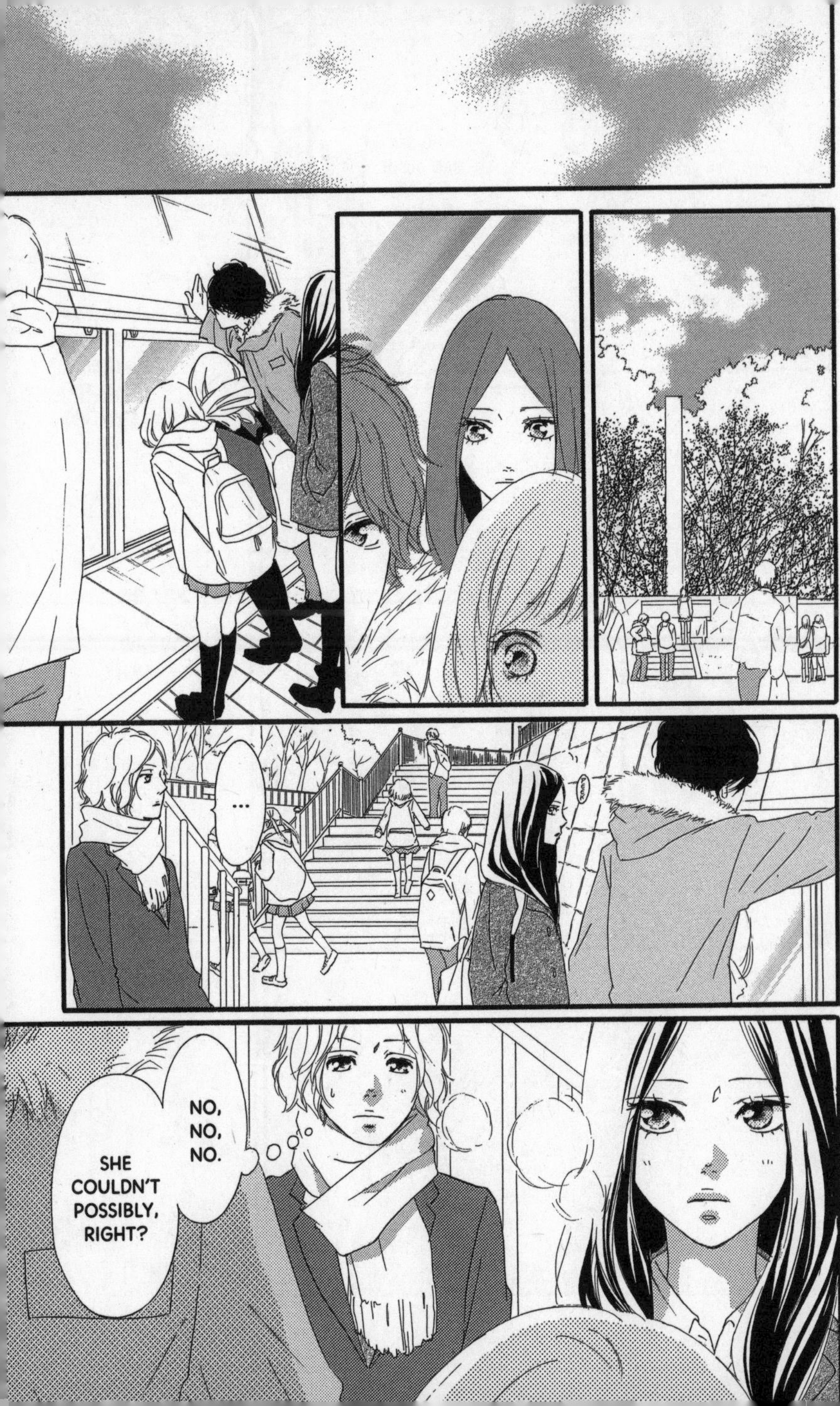
PEEK
...
NO, NO, NO.
SHE COULDN'T POSSIBLY, RIGHT?

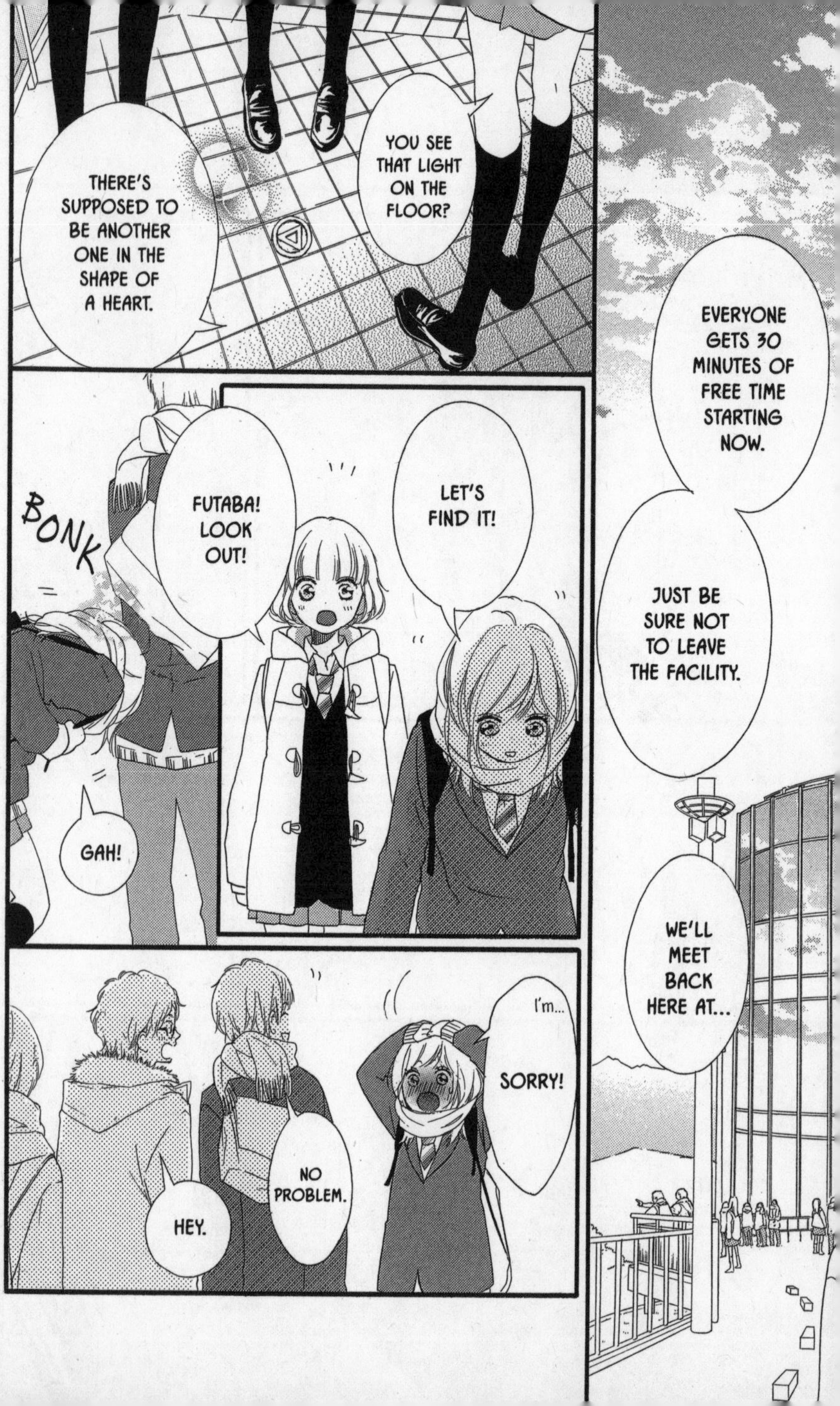
EVERYONE GETS 30 MINUTES OF FREE TIME STARTING NOW.
JUST BE SURE NOT TO LEAVE THE FACILITY.
WE'LL MEET BACK HERE AT...
YOU SEE THAT LIGHT ON THE FLOOR?
THERE'S SUPPOSED TO BE ANOTHER ONE IN THE SHAPE OF A HEART.
LET'S FIND IT!
FUTABA! LOOK OUT!
BONK
GAH!
I'm...
SORRY!
NO PROBLEM.
HEY.

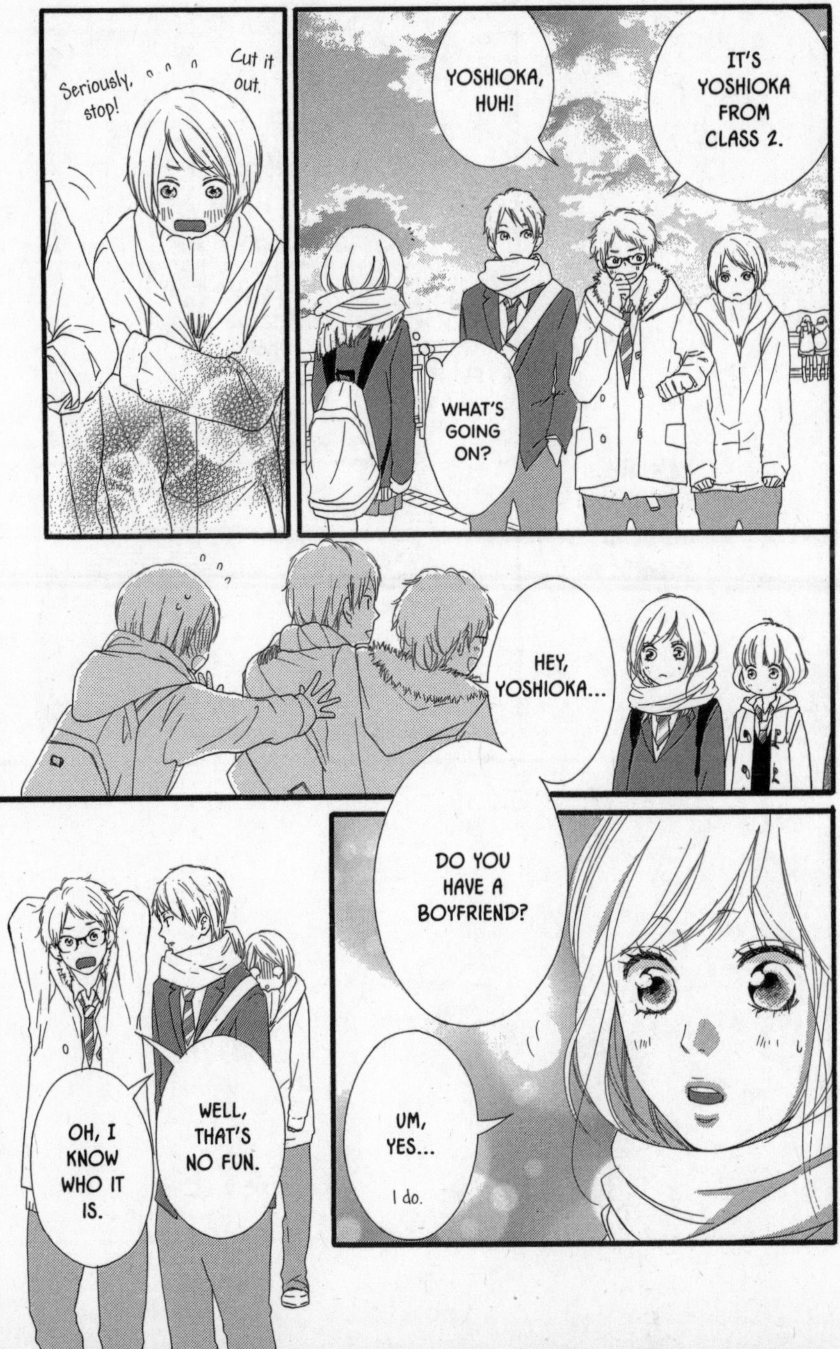
IT'S YOSHIOKA FROM CLASS 2.
YOSHIOKA, HUH!
WHAT'S GOING ON?
Cut it out.
Seriously, stop!
HEY, YOSHIOKA...
DO YOU HAVE A BOYFRIEND?
UM, YES...
I do.
WELL, THAT'S NO FUN.
OH, I KNOW WHO IT IS.

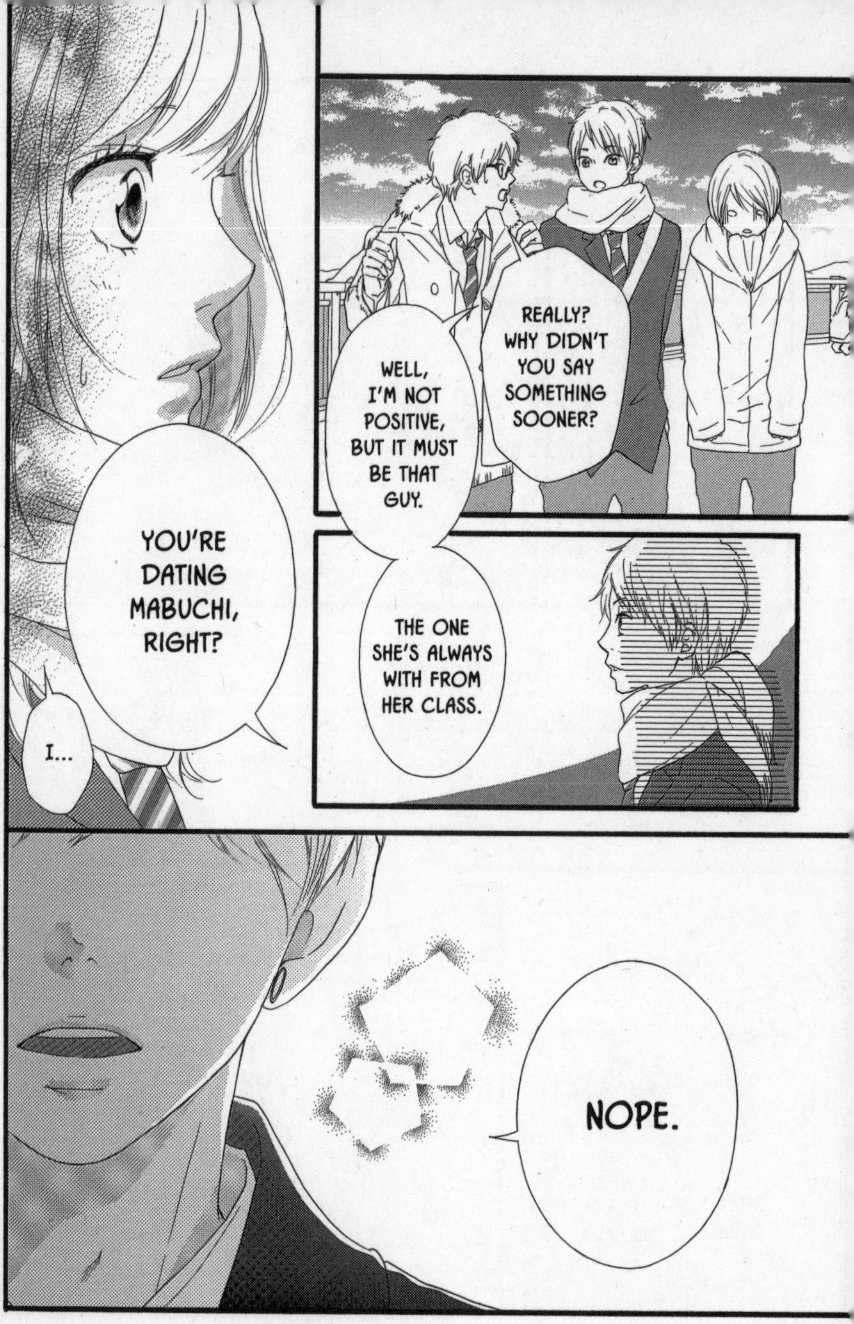
REALLY? WHY DIDN'T YOU SAY SOMETHING SOONER?
WELL, I'M NOT POSITIVE, BUT IT MUST BE THAT GUY.
THE ONE SHE'S ALWAYS WITH FROM HER CLASS.
YOU'RE DATING MABUCHI, RIGHT?
I...
NOPE.

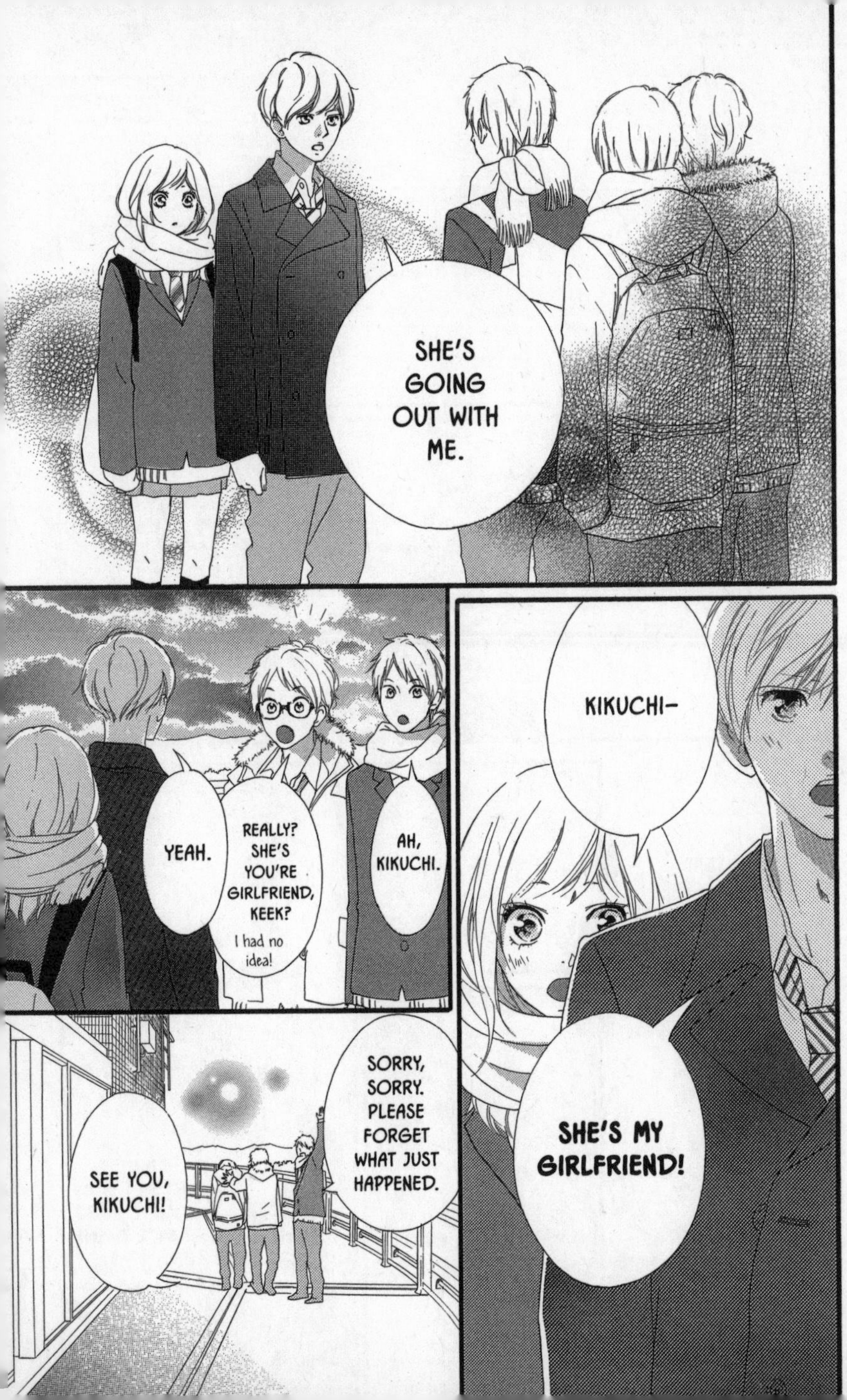
SHE'S GOING OUT WITH ME.
KIKUCHI-
SHE'S MY GIRLFRIEND!
AH, KIKUCHI.
REALLY? SHE'S YOU'RE GIRLFRIEND, KEEK?
I had no idea!
YEAH.
SORRY, SORRY. PLEASE FORGET WHAT JUST HAPPENED.
SEE YOU, KIKUCHI!

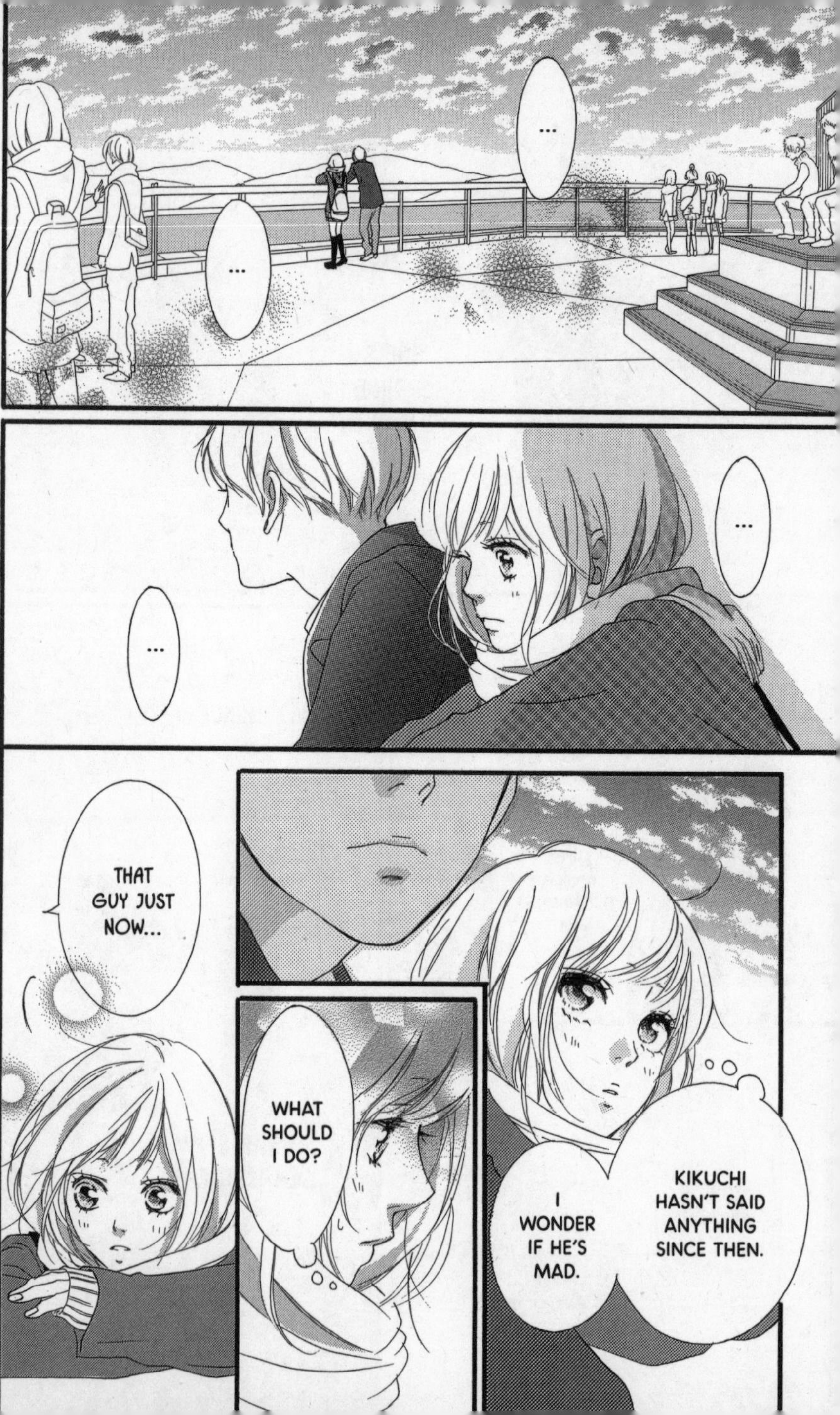
...
...
...
...
KIKUCHI HASN'T SAID ANYTHING SINCE THEN.
I WONDER IF HE'S MAD.
WHAT SHOULD I DO?
THAT GUY JUST NOW...

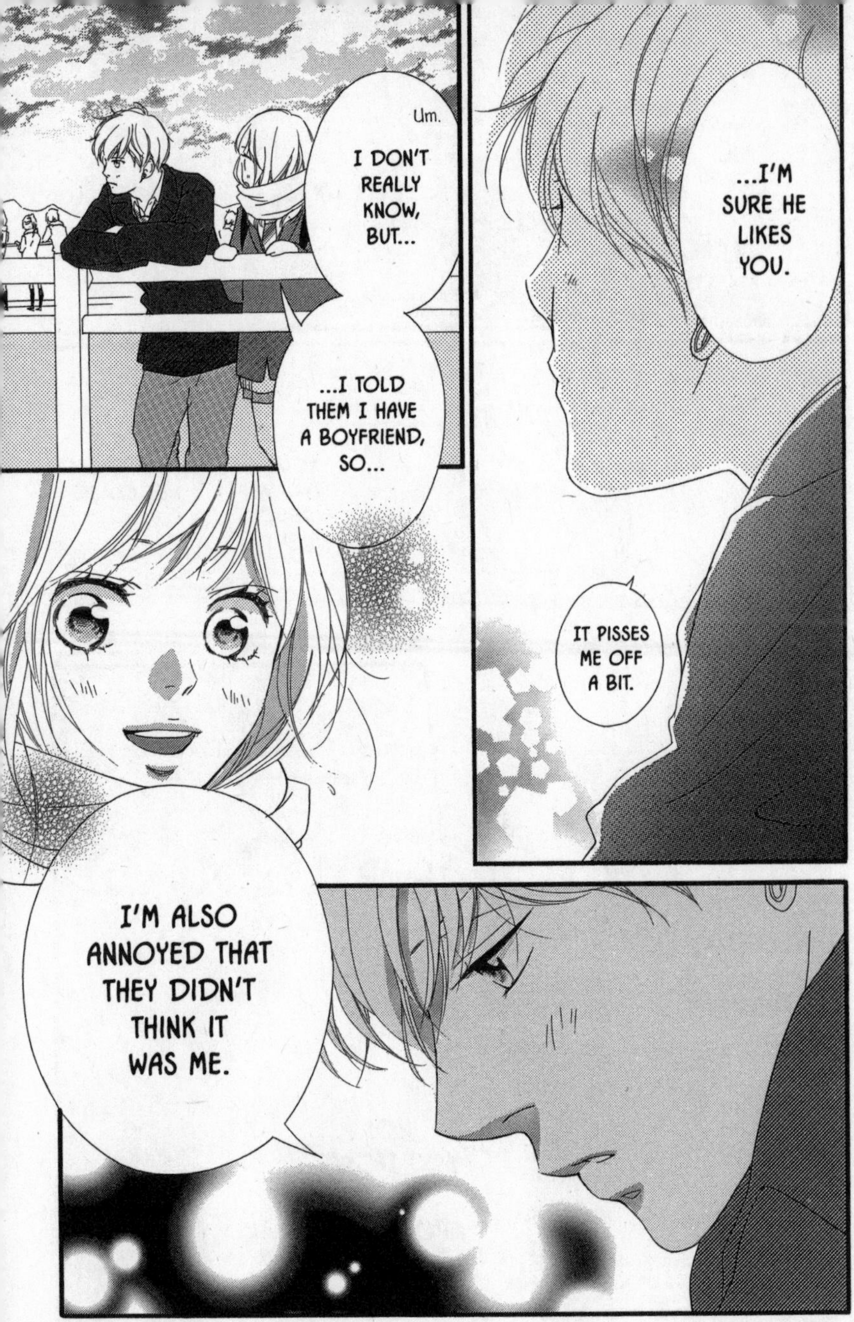

...I'M SURE HE LIKES YOU.
IT PISSES ME OFF A BIT.
Um.
I DON'T REALLY KNOW, BUT...
...I TOLD THEM I HAVE A BOYFRIEND, SO...
I'M ALSO ANNOYED THAT THEY DIDN'T THINK IT WAS ME.

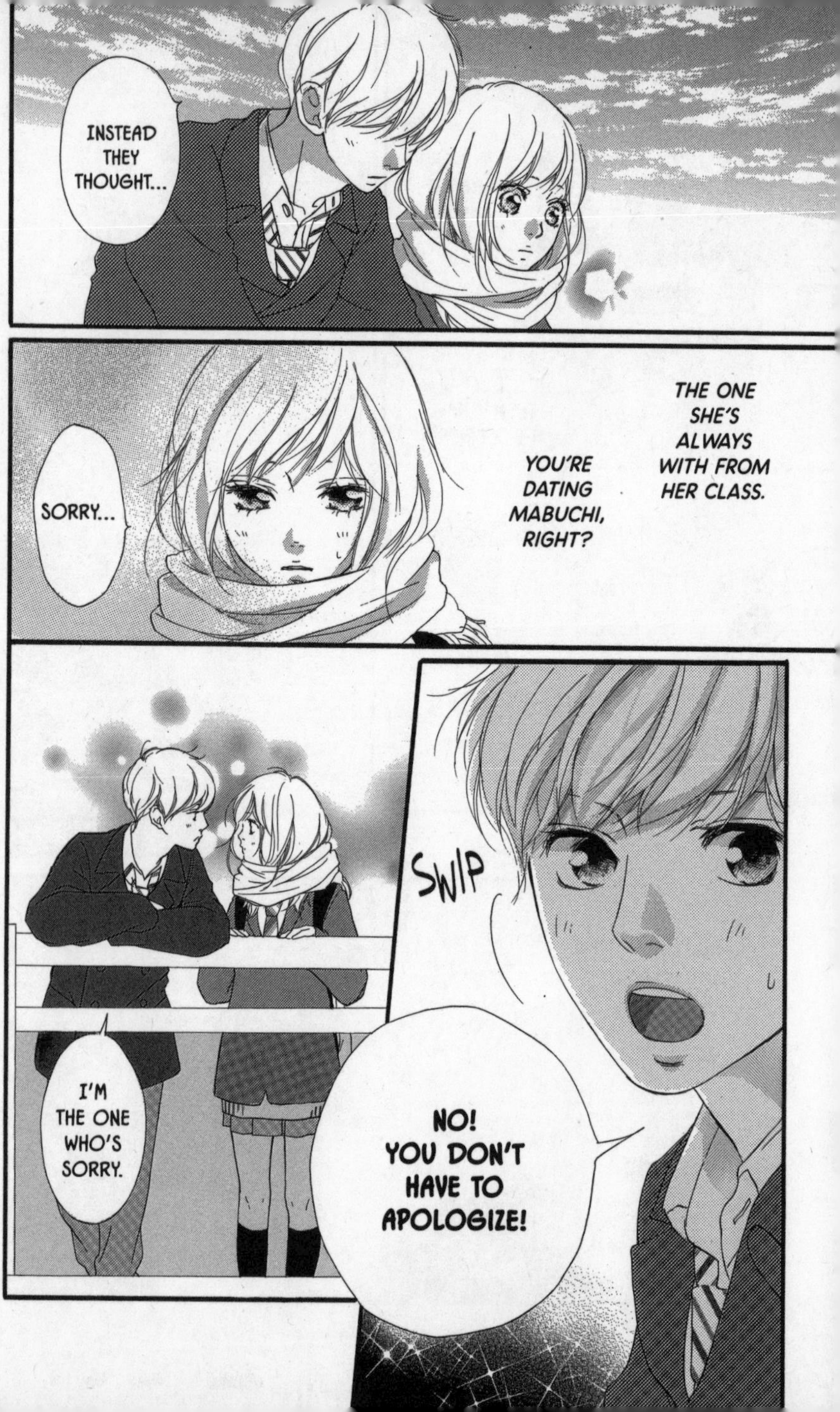
INSTEAD THEY THOUGHT...
THE ONE SHE'S ALWAYS WITH FROM HER CLASS.
YOU'RE DATING MABUCHI, RIGHT?
SORRY...
SWIP
NO! YOU DON'T HAVE TO APOLOGIZE!
I'M THE ONE WHO'S SORRY.

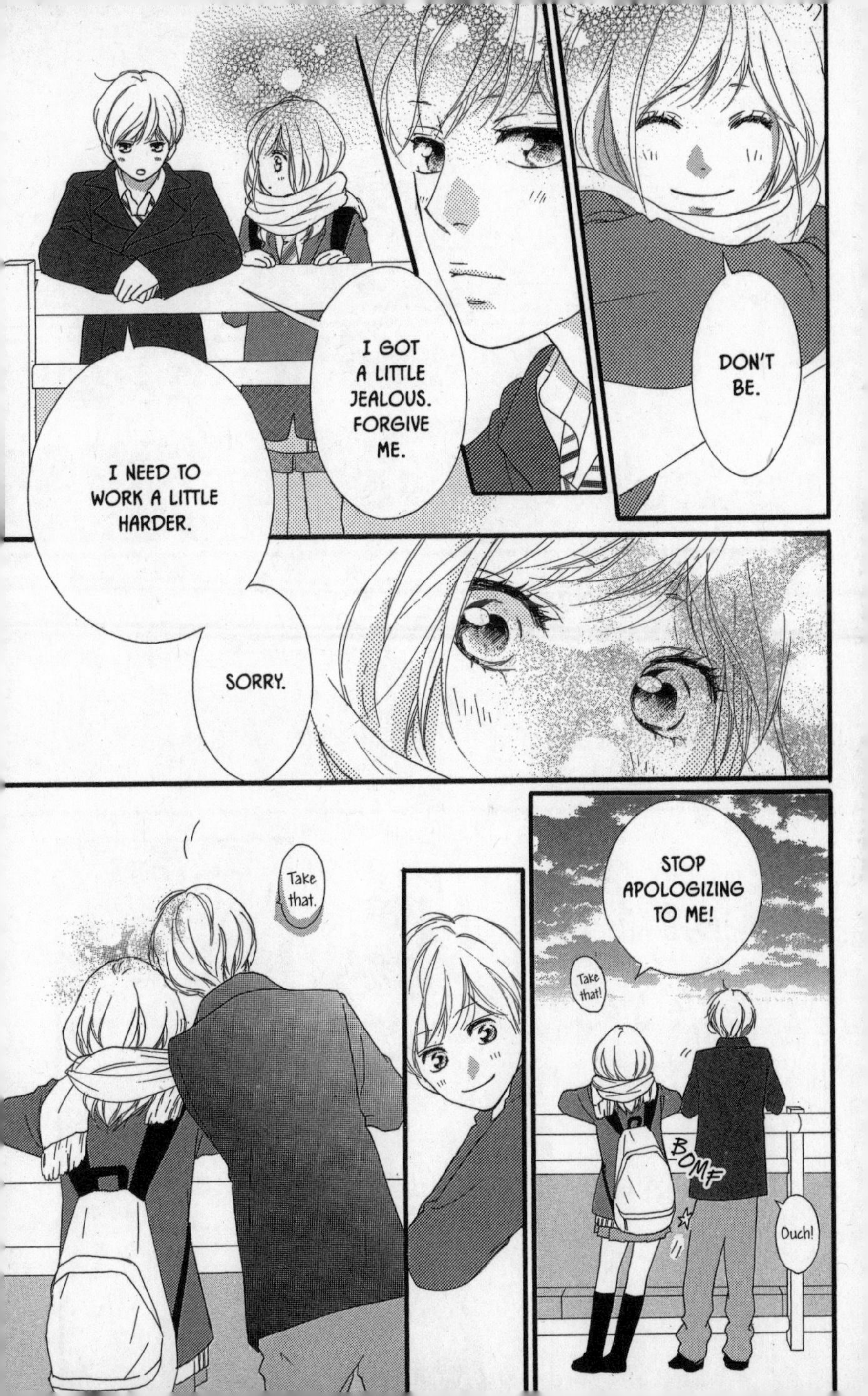
DON'T BE.
I GOT A LITTLE JEALOUS. FORGIVE ME.
I NEED TO WORK A LITTLE HARDER.
SORRY.
STOP APOLOGIZING TO ME!
Take that!
BOMF
Ouch!
Take that.

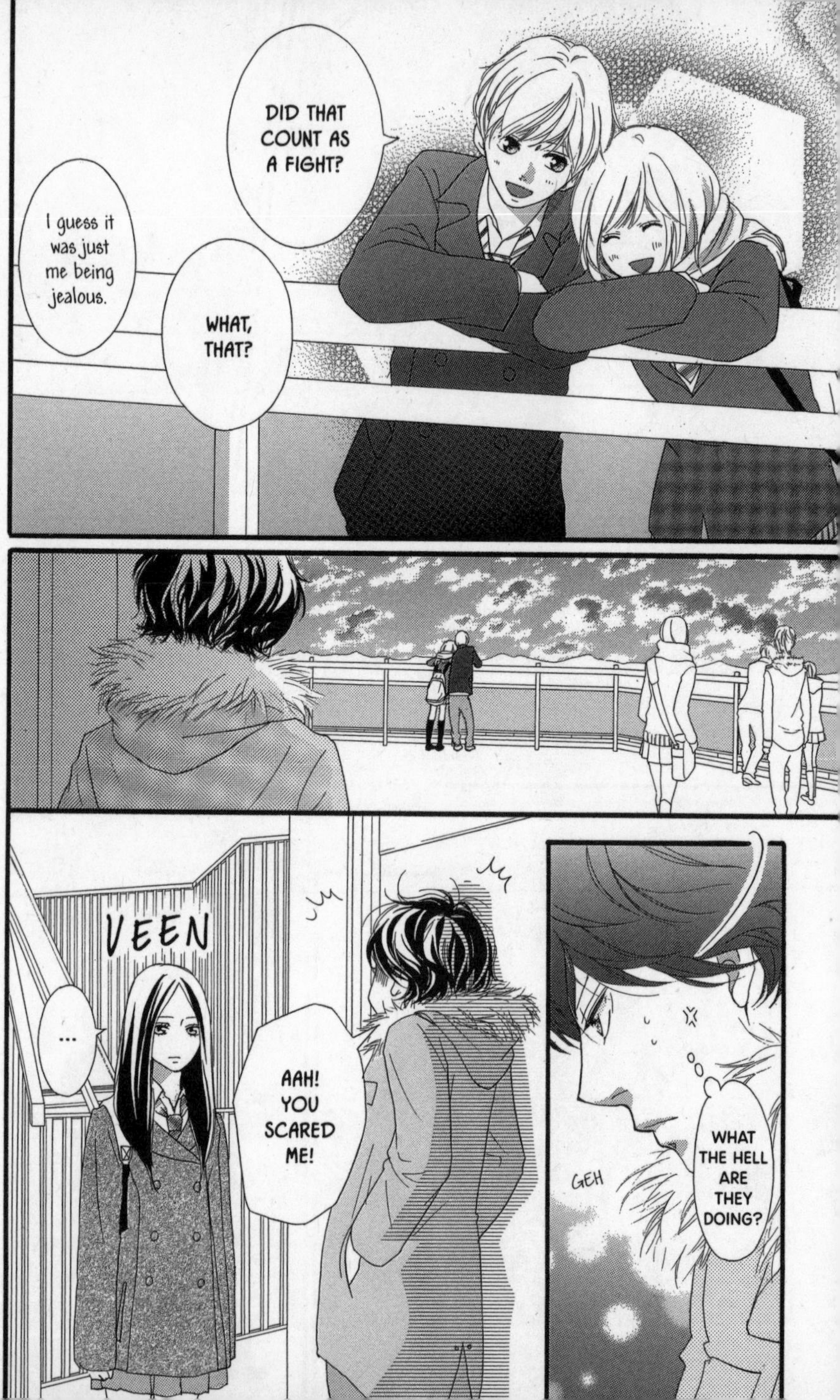
DID THAT COUNT AS A FIGHT?
WHAT, THAT?
I guess it was just me being jealous.
WHAT THE HELL ARE THEY DOING?
GEH
AAH! YOU SCARED ME!
VEEN
...

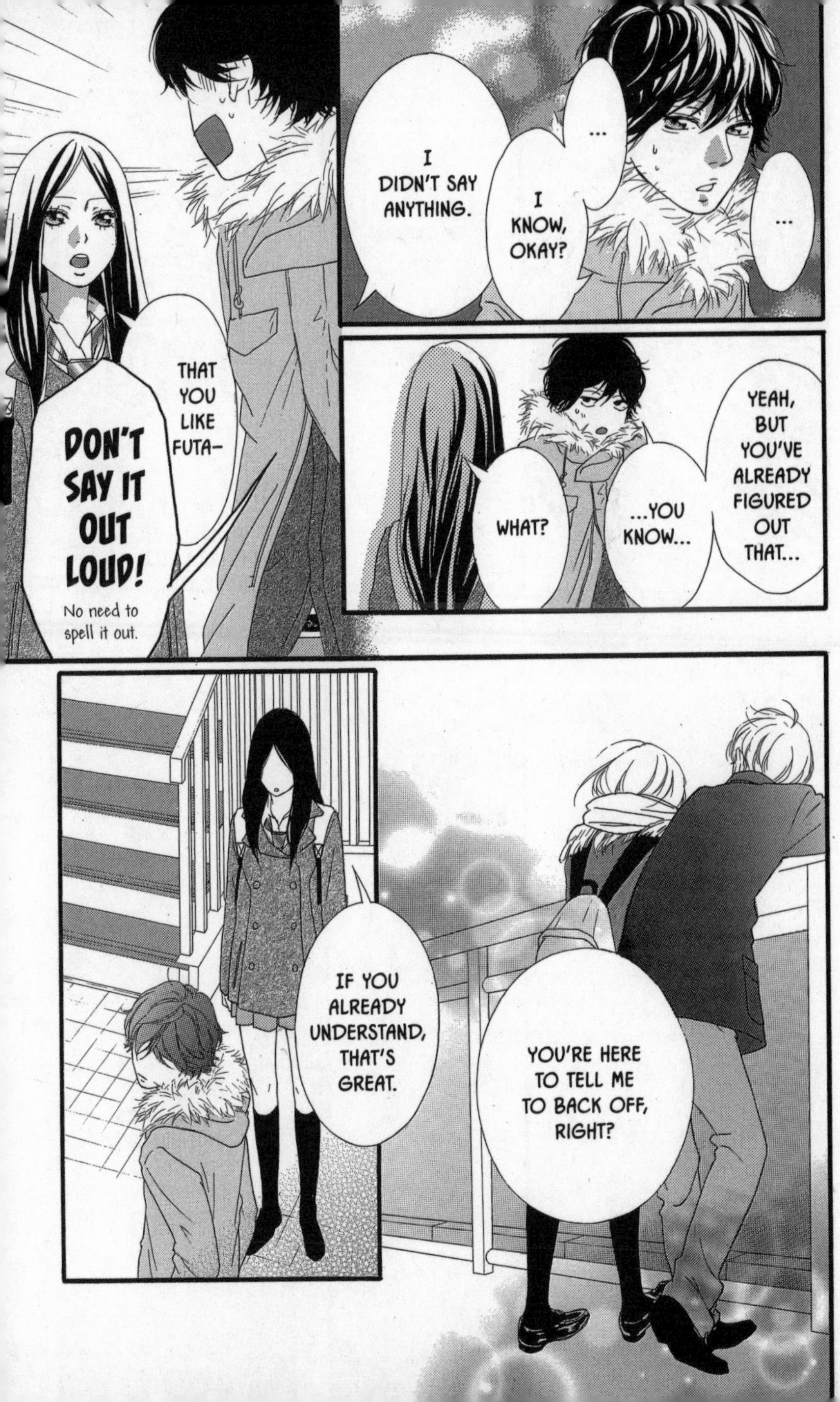
...
...
I KNOW, OKAY?
I DIDN'T SAY ANYTHING.
YEAH, BUT YOU'VE ALREADY FIGURED OUT THAT...
...YOU KNOW...
WHAT?
THAT YOU LIKE FUTA—
DON'T SAY IT OUT LOUD!
No need to spell it out.
YOU'RE HERE TO TELL ME TO BACK OFF, RIGHT?
IF YOU ALREADY UNDERSTAND, THAT'S GREAT.

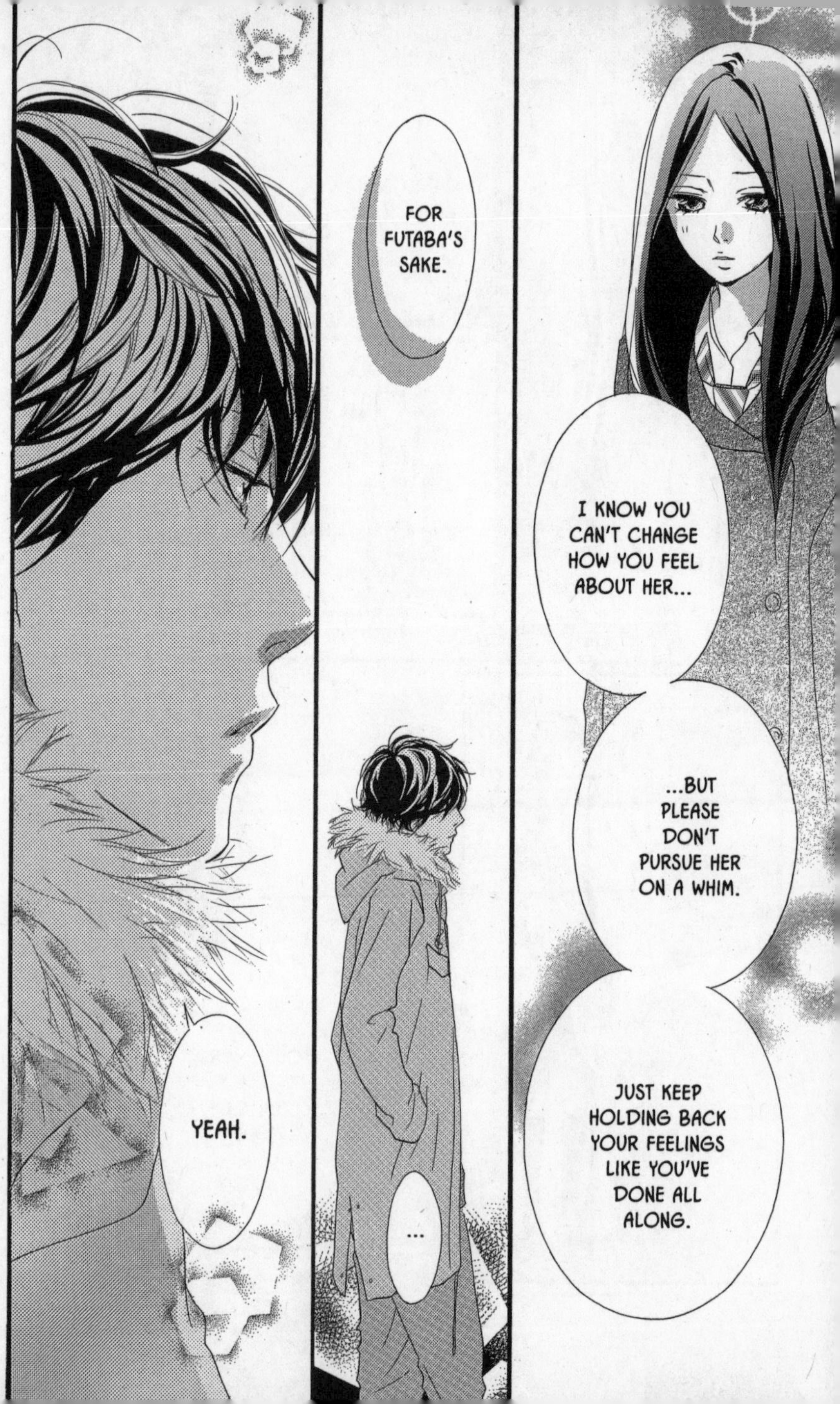
I KNOW YOU CAN'T CHANGE HOW YOU FEEL ABOUT HER...
...BUT PLEASE DON'T PURSUE HER ON A WHIM.
JUST KEEP HOLDING BACK YOUR FEELINGS LIKE YOU'VE DONE ALL ALONG.
FOR FUTABA'S SAKE.
...
YEAH.

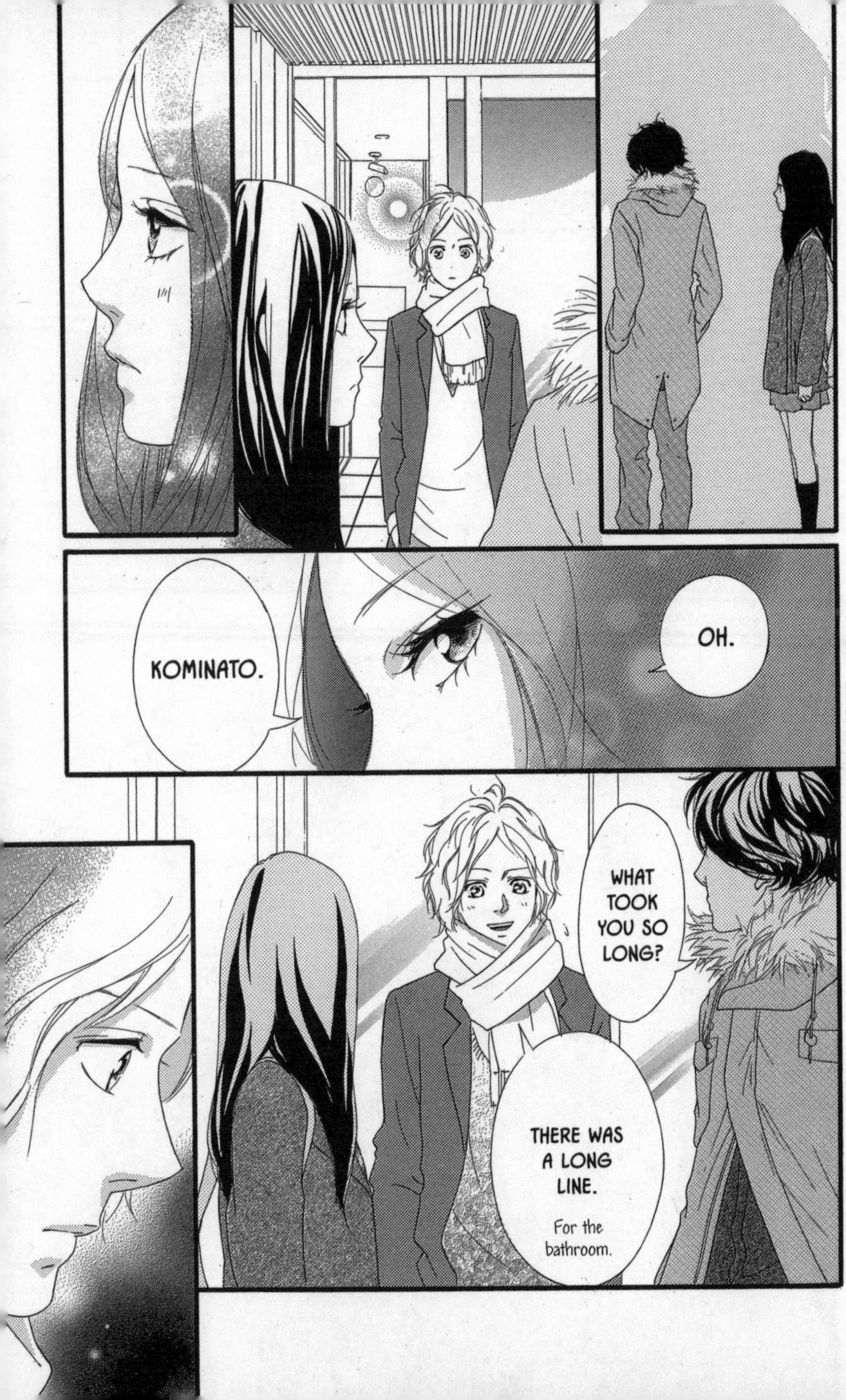
OH.
KOMINATO.
WHAT TOOK YOU SO LONG?
THERE WAS A LONG LINE.
For the bathroom.

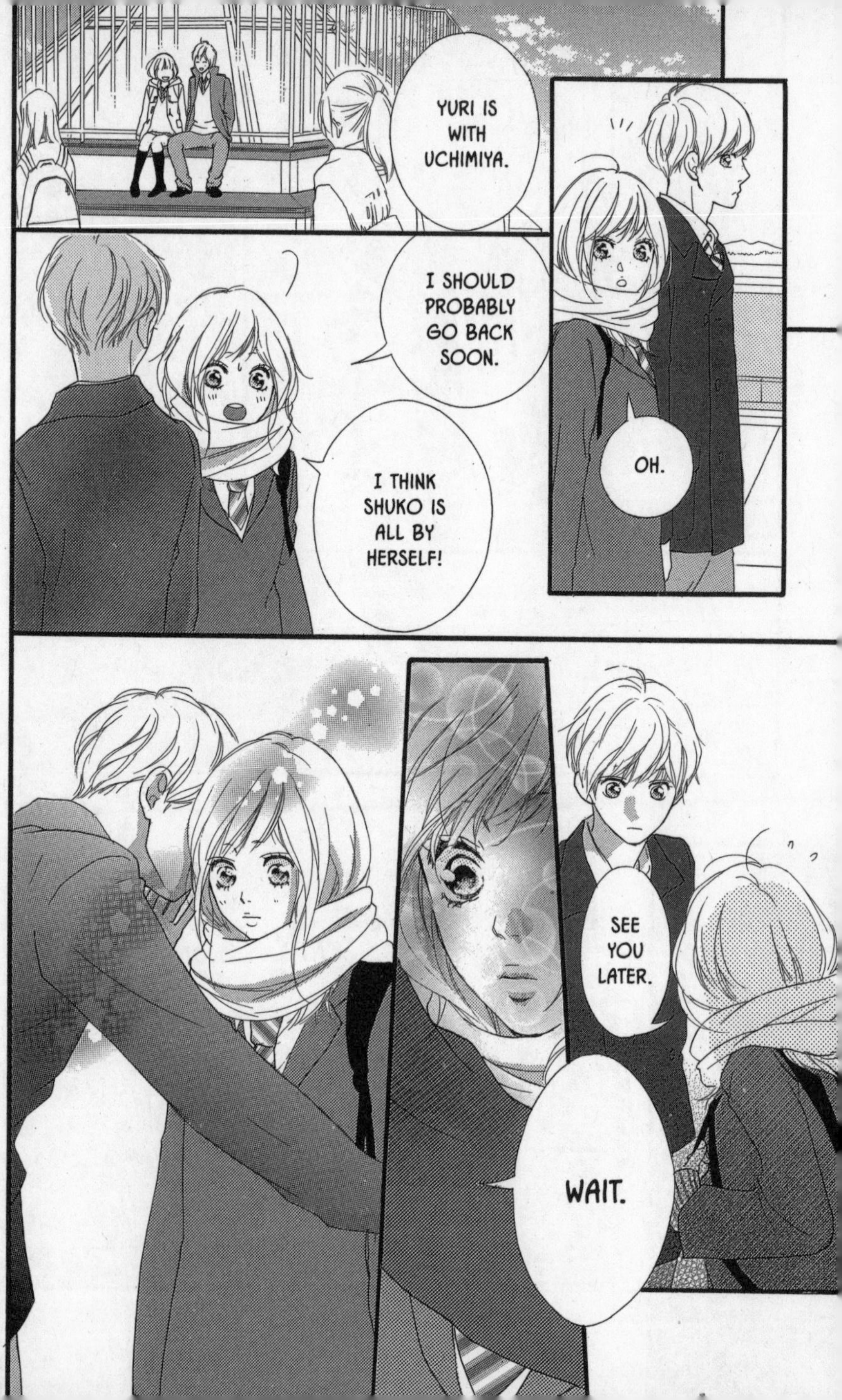
YURI IS WITH UCHIMIYA.
OH.
I SHOULD PROBABLY GO BACK SOON.
I THINK SHUKO IS ALL BY HERSELF!
SEE YOU LATER.
WAIT.

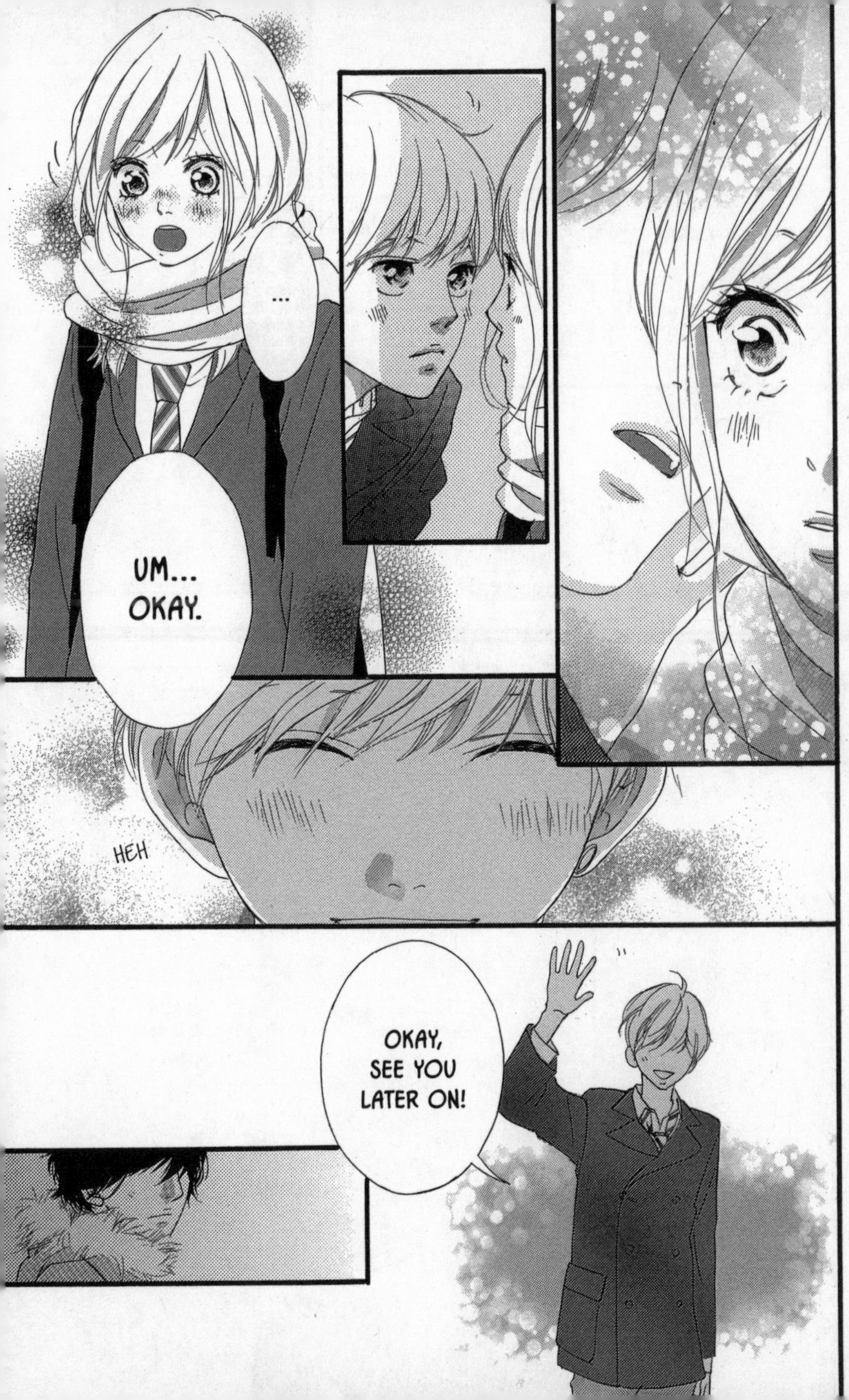
...
UM... OKAY.
HEH
OKAY, SEE YOU LATER ON!

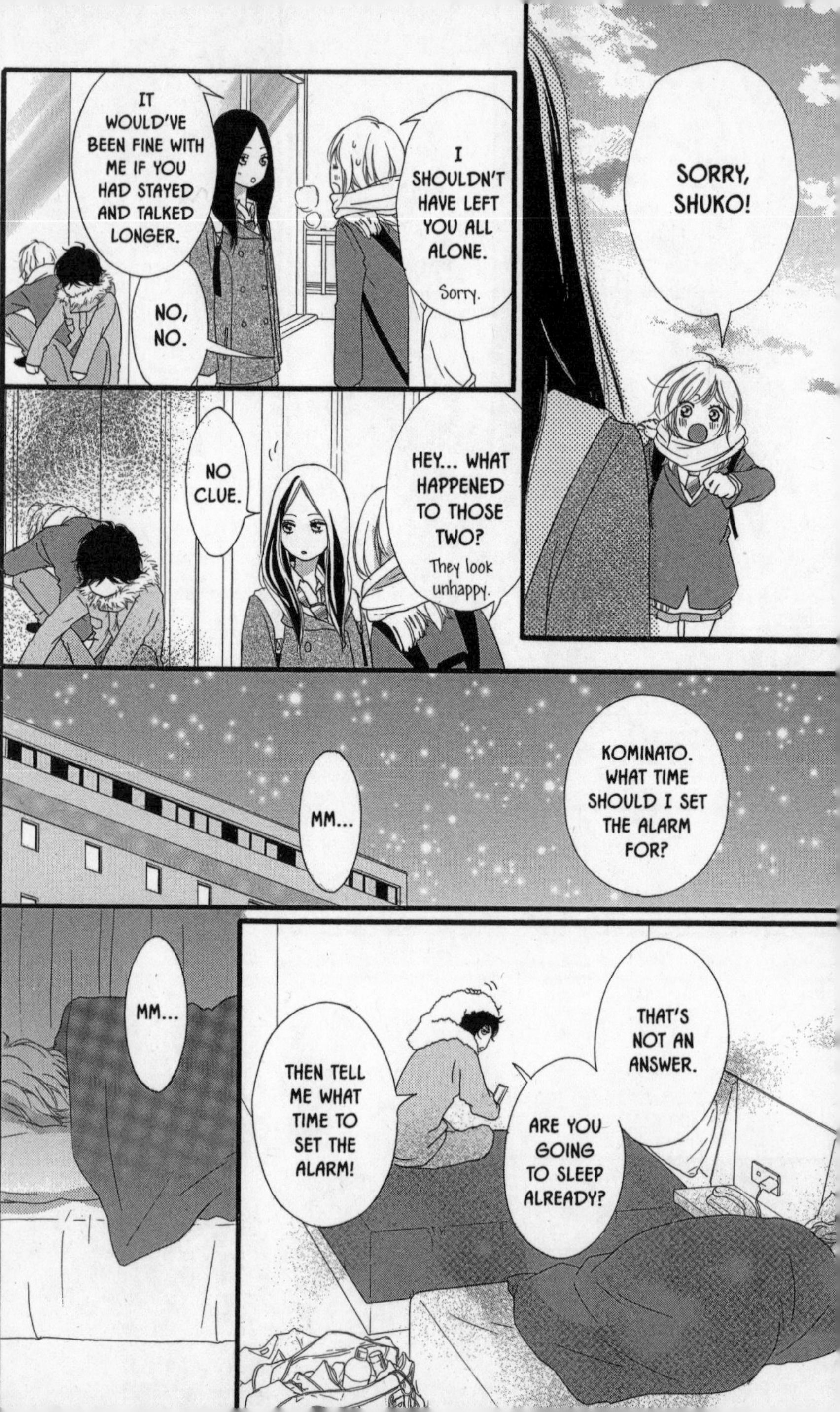
SORRY, SHUKO!
I SHOULDN'T HAVE LEFT YOU ALL ALONE.
Sorry.
IT WOULD'VE BEEN FINE WITH ME IF YOU HAD STAYED AND TALKED LONGER.
NO, NO.
HEY... WHAT HAPPENED TO THOSE TWO?
They look unhappy.
NO CLUE.
KOMINATO. WHAT TIME SHOULD I SET THE ALARM FOR?
MM...
THAT'S NOT AN ANSWER.
ARE YOU GOING TO SLEEP ALREADY?
THEN TELL ME WHAT TIME TO SET THE ALARM!
MM...

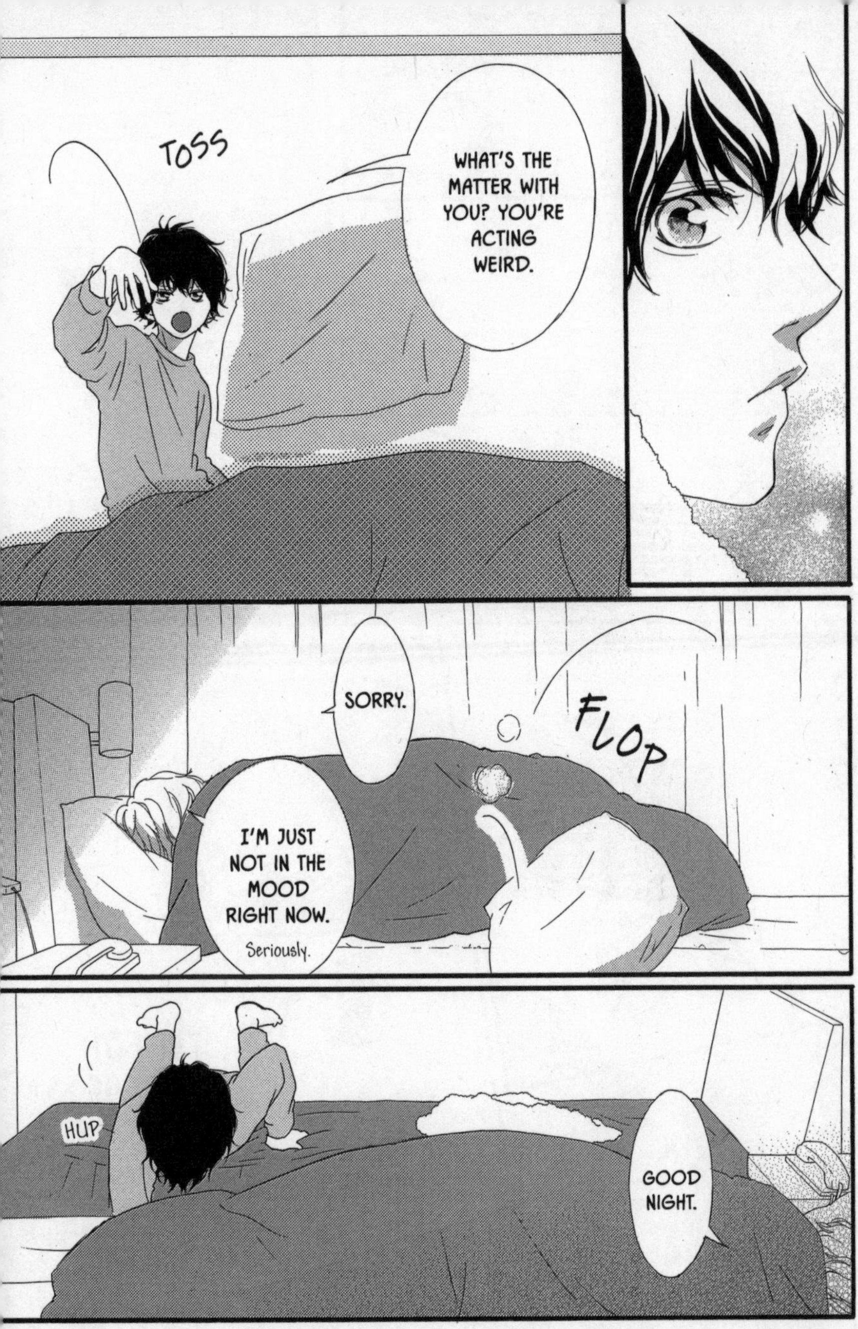
WHAT'S THE MATTER WITH YOU? YOU'RE ACTING WEIRD.
TOSS
FLOP
SORRY.
I'M JUST NOT IN THE MOOD RIGHT NOW.
Seriously.
GOOD NIGHT.
HUP

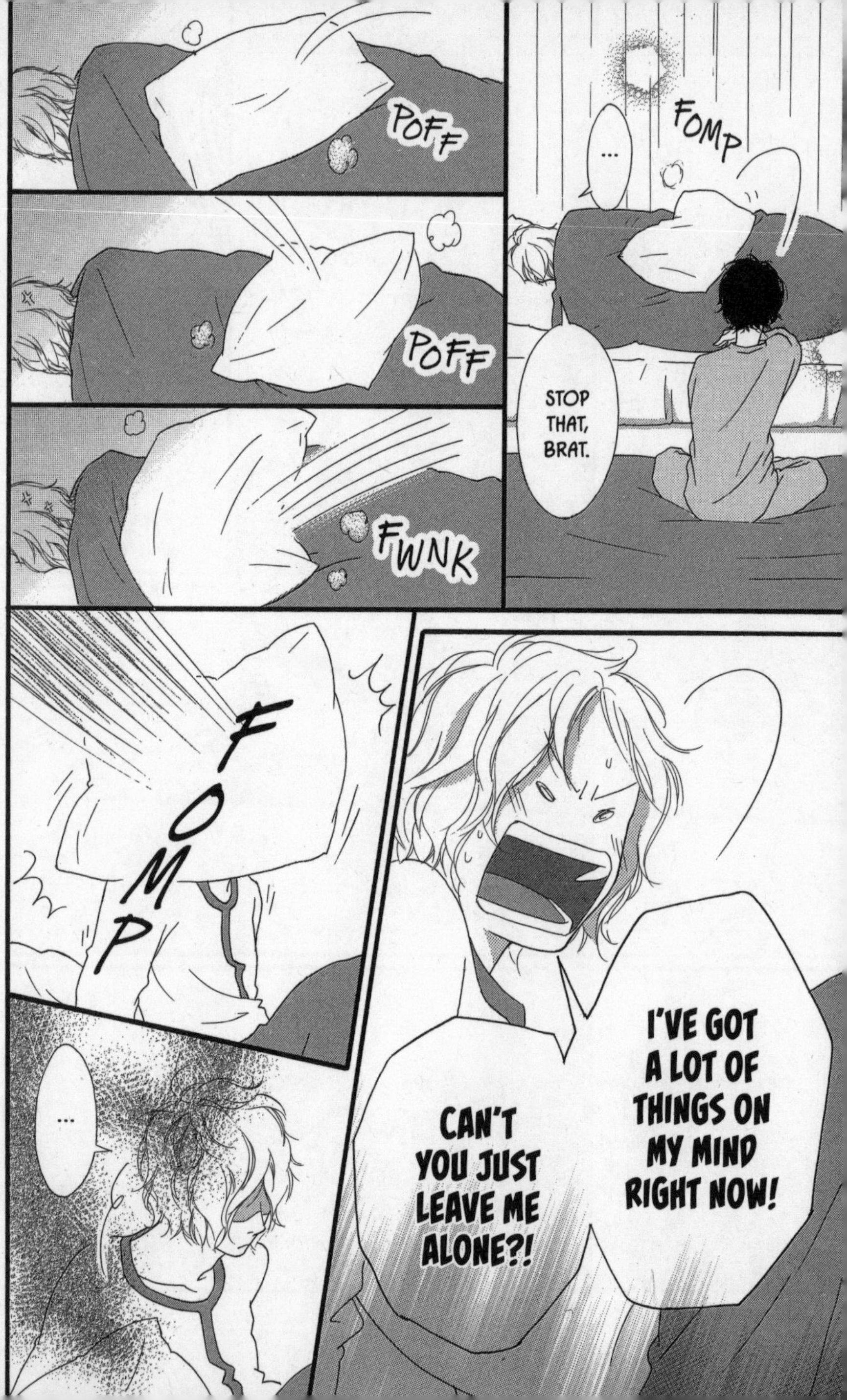
FOMP
...
STOP THAT, BRAT.
POFF
POFF
FWNK
I'VE GOT A LOT OF THINGS ON MY MIND RIGHT NOW!
CAN'T YOU JUST LEAVE ME ALONE?!
FOMP
...

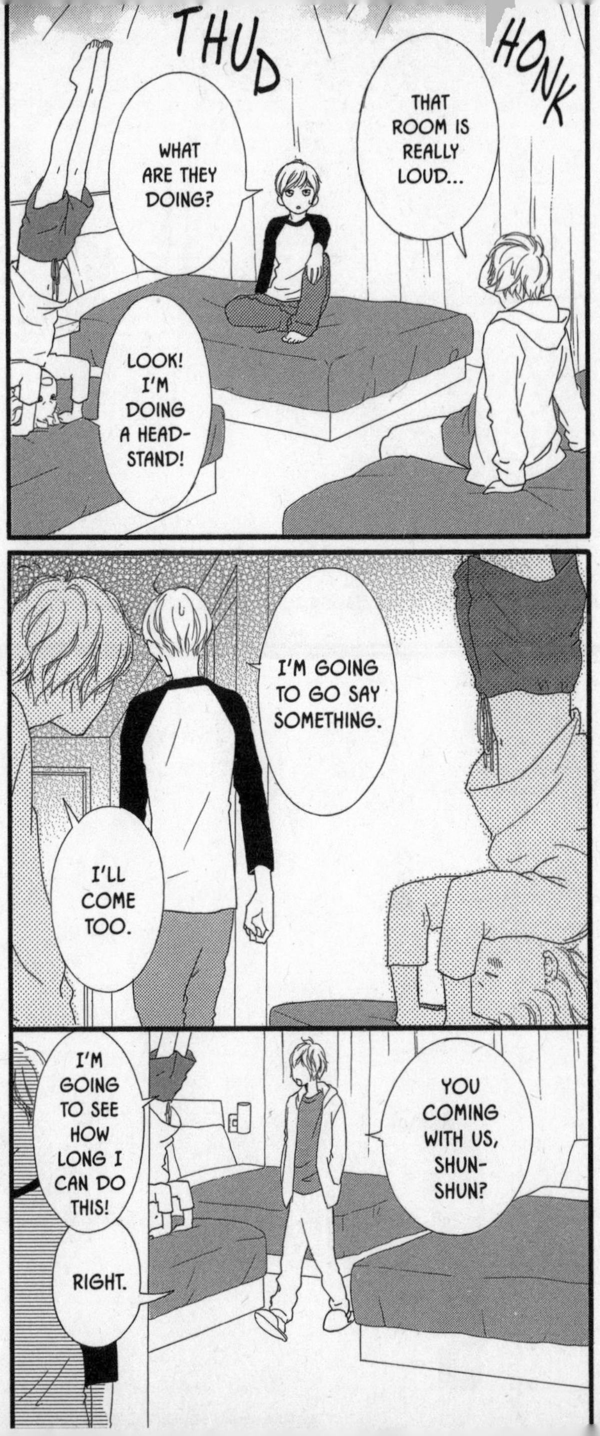
HONK
THUD
THAT ROOM IS REALLY LOUD...
WHAT ARE THEY DOING?
LOOK! I'M DOING A HEAD-STAND!
I'M GOING TO GO SAY SOMETHING.
I'LL COME TOO.
YOU COMING WITH US, SHUN-SHUN?
I'M GOING TO SEE HOW LONG I CAN DO THIS!
RIGHT.

The class trip to Nagasaki starts in this volume. To prepare for it, I got to go to Nagasaki to take photos! In the blazing hot summer, my editor and I went to Nagasaki and snapped photos all over the city, ate champon, shuddered at the size of the local cicadas, bought castella cake, sweated a ton and came back home. Thanks to that visit, I felt ready to work on the class trip story right away. But the story leading up to the class trip ended up being longer than I expected, and I didn't actually start writing about the class trip until winter. So why on earth did we go to Nagasaki in that heat? I imagine this is what my editor thought, and to be honest, I thought it too. Sorry. Now this is going to sound like I am just trying to change the subject, but—wow—the grape mochi that we had there was so good! I fell in love with it.

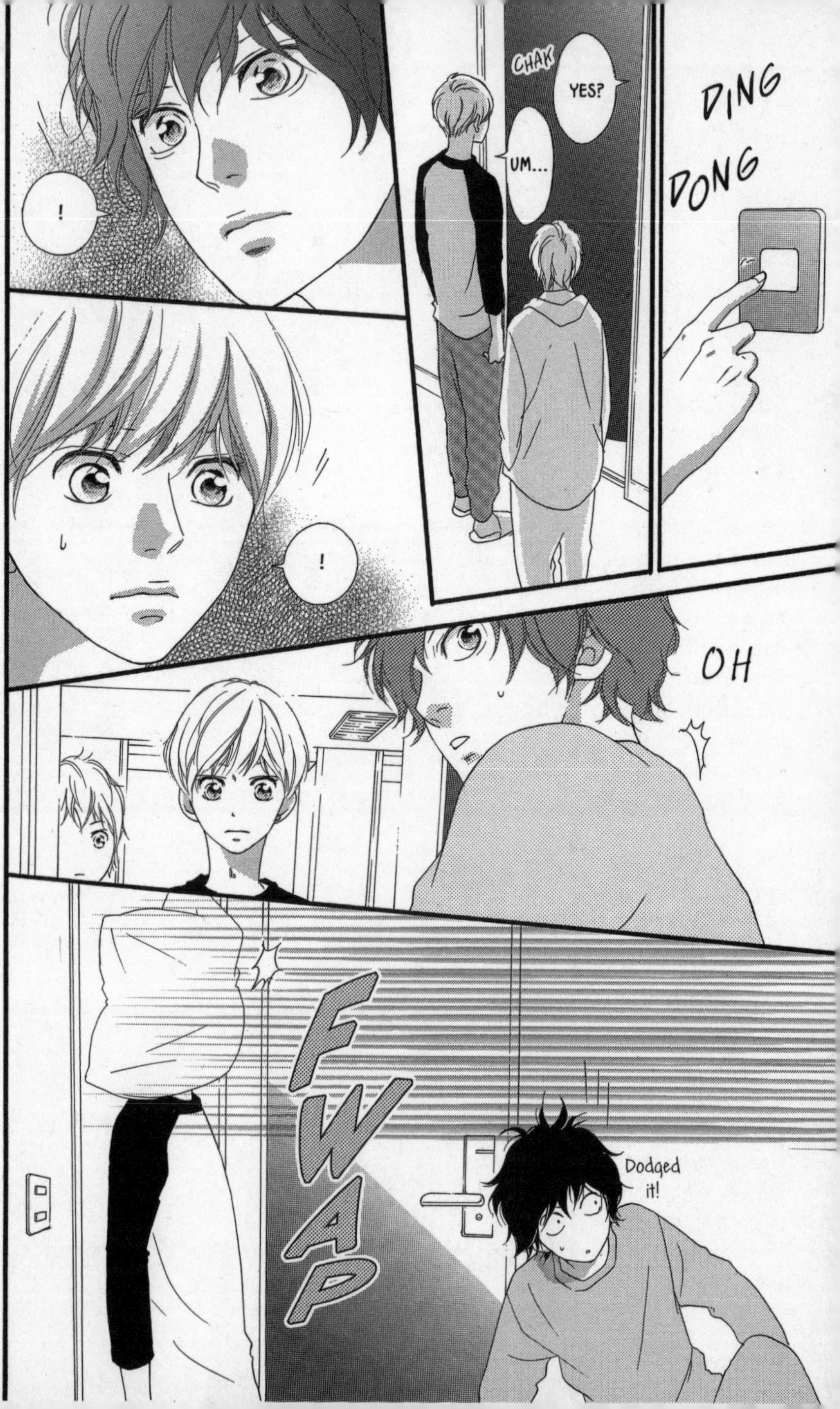
DING
DONG
CHAK
YES?
UM...
!
!
OH
FWAP
Dodged it!

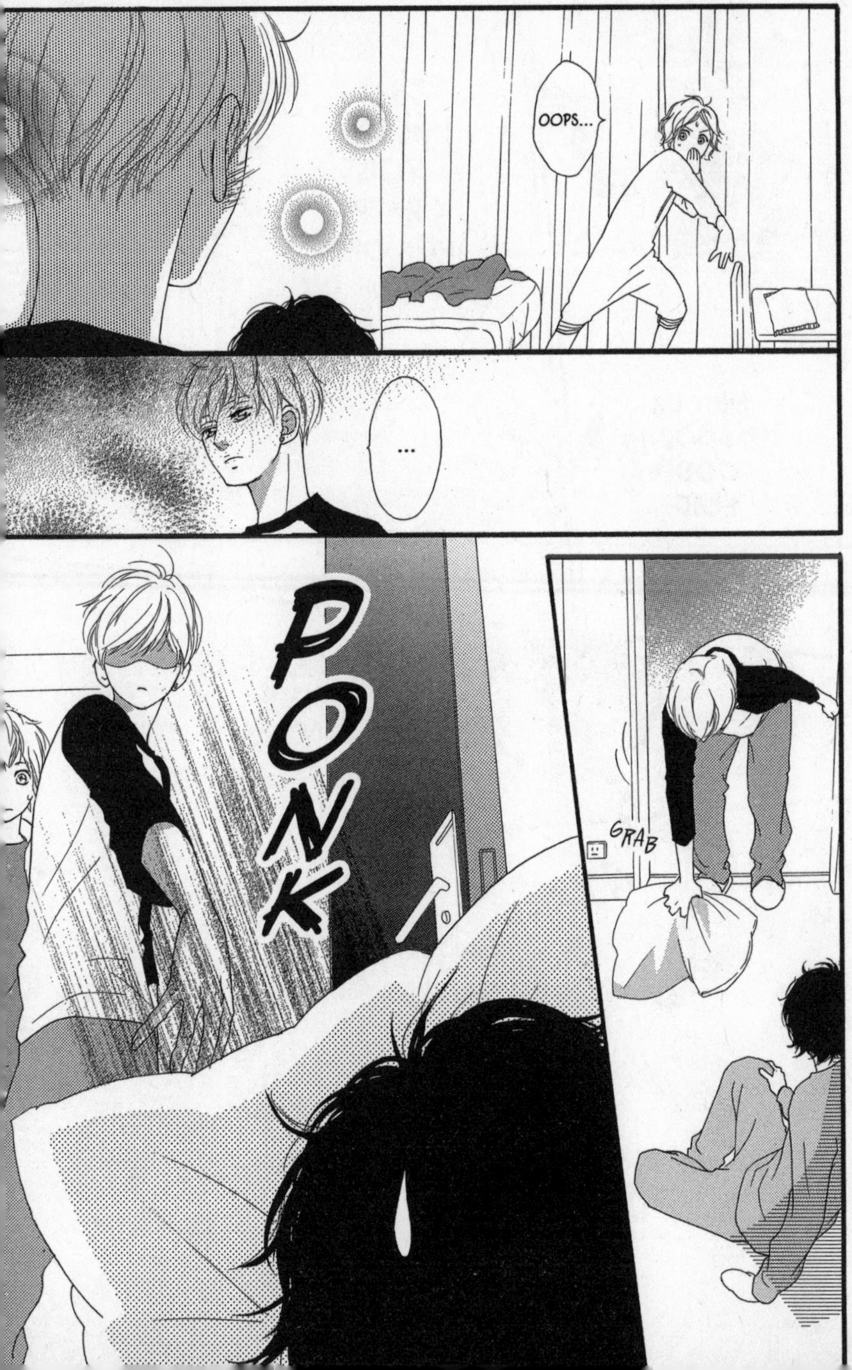
OOPS...
...
GRAB
PONK

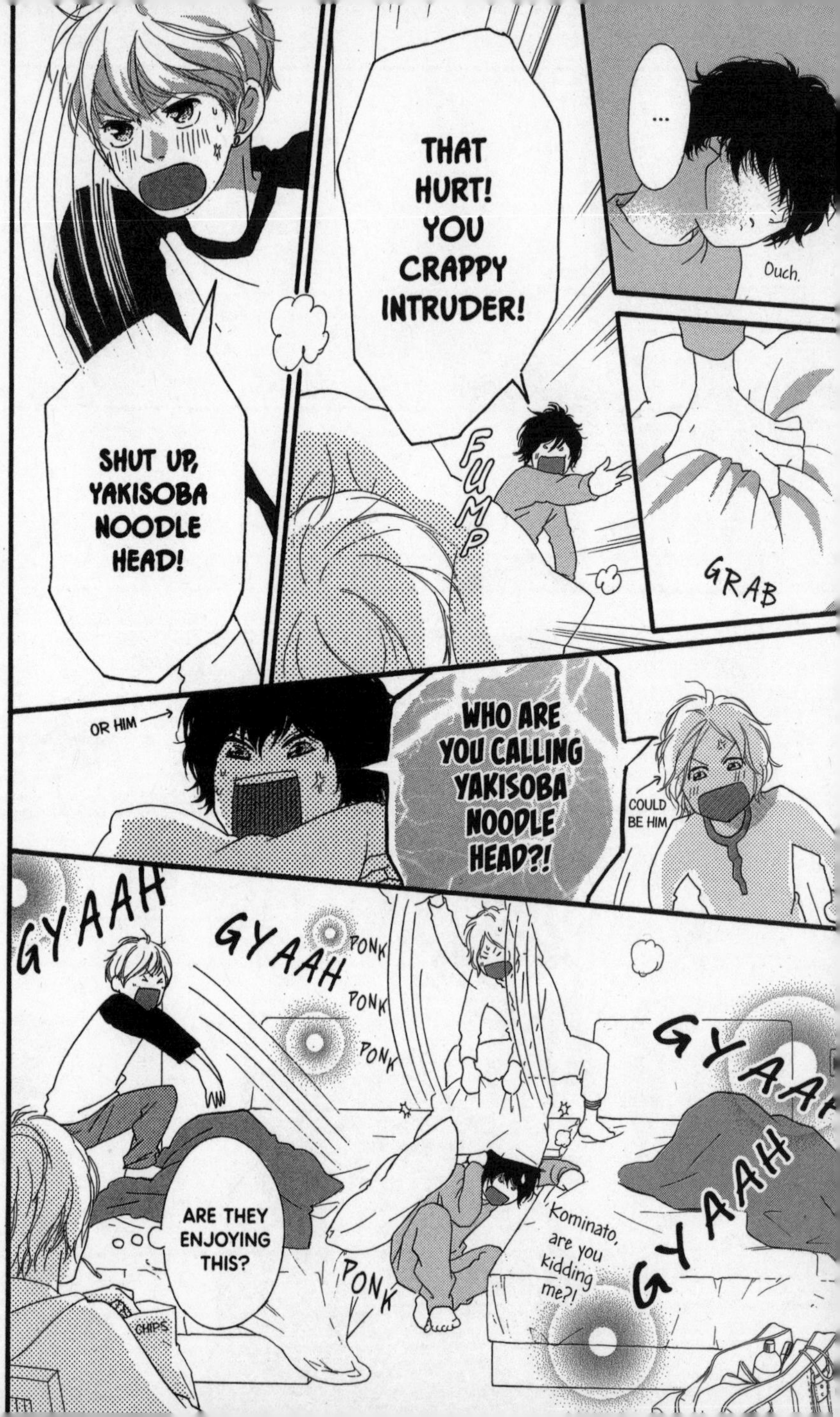
...
Ouch.
GRAB
THAT HURT! YOU CRAPPY INTRUDER!
FUMP
SHUT UP, YAKISOBA NOODLE HEAD!
COULD BE HIM
WHO ARE YOU CALLING YAKISOBA NOODLE HEAD?!
OR HIM
GYAAH
GYAAH
Kominato, are you kidding me?!
PONK
PONK
PONK
GYAAH
GYAAH
ARE THEY ENJOYING THIS?
PONK
CHIPS

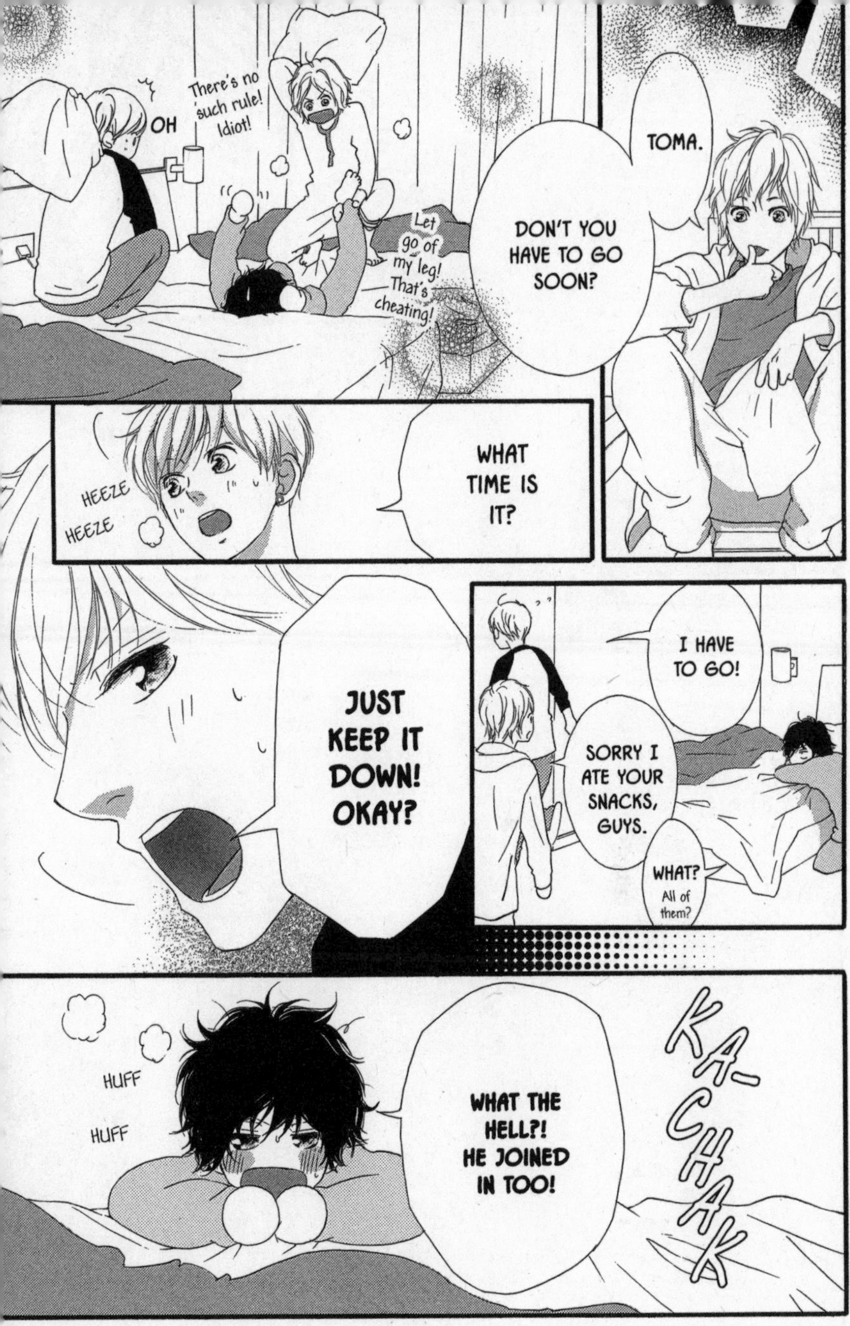

TOMA.
DON'T YOU HAVE TO GO SOON?
There's no such rule! Idiot!
OH
Let go of my leg! That's cheating!
WHAT TIME IS IT?
HEEZE HEEZE
I HAVE TO GO!
SORRY I ATE YOUR SNACKS, GUYS.
WHAT? All of them?
JUST KEEP IT DOWN! OKAY?
KA-CHAK
WHAT THE HELL?! HE JOINED IN TOO!
HUFF HUFF

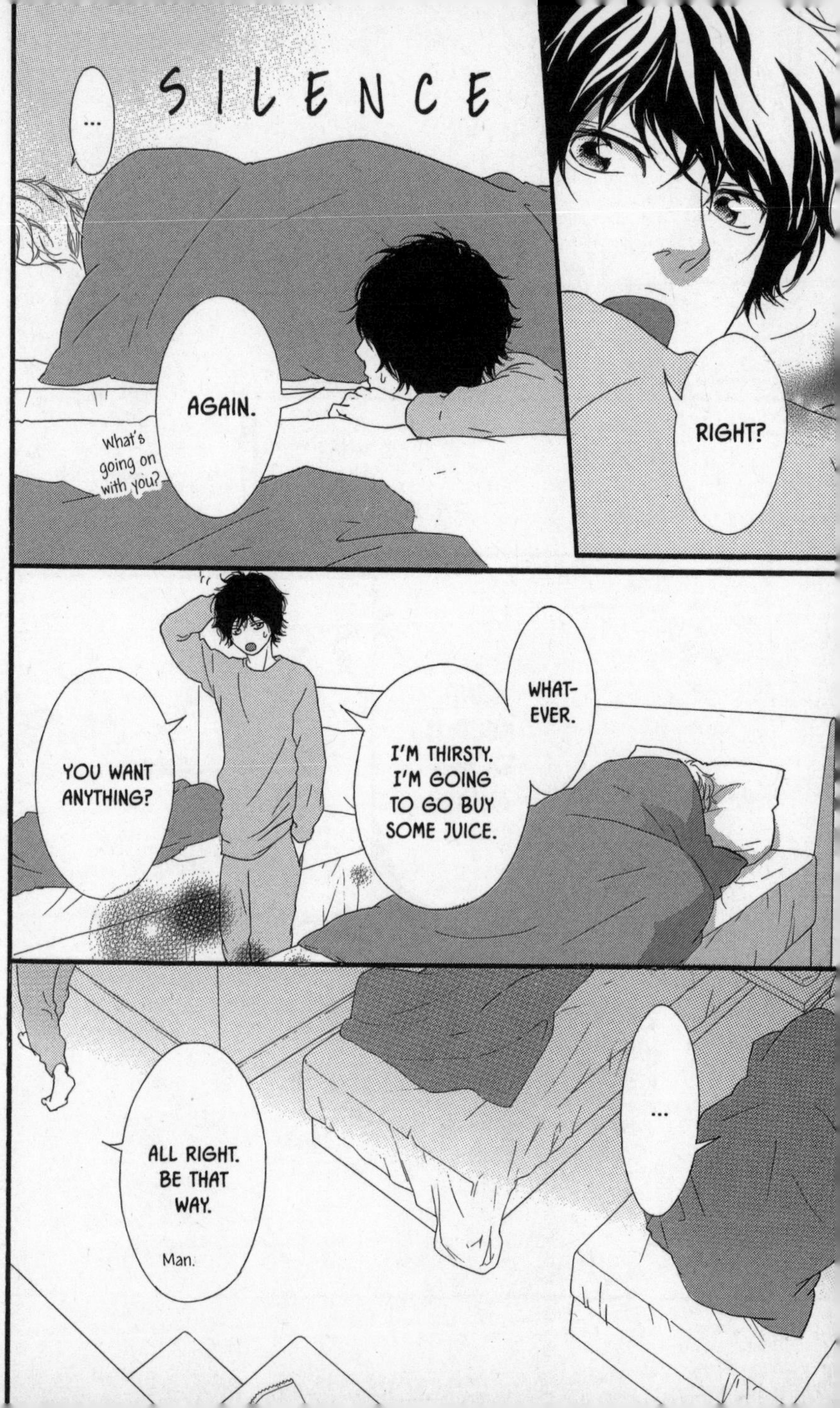
RIGHT?
SILENCE
...
AGAIN.
What's going on with you?
WHAT-EVER.
I'M THIRSTY. I'M GOING TO GO BUY SOME JUICE.
YOU WANT ANYTHING?
...
ALL RIGHT. BE THAT WAY.
Man.

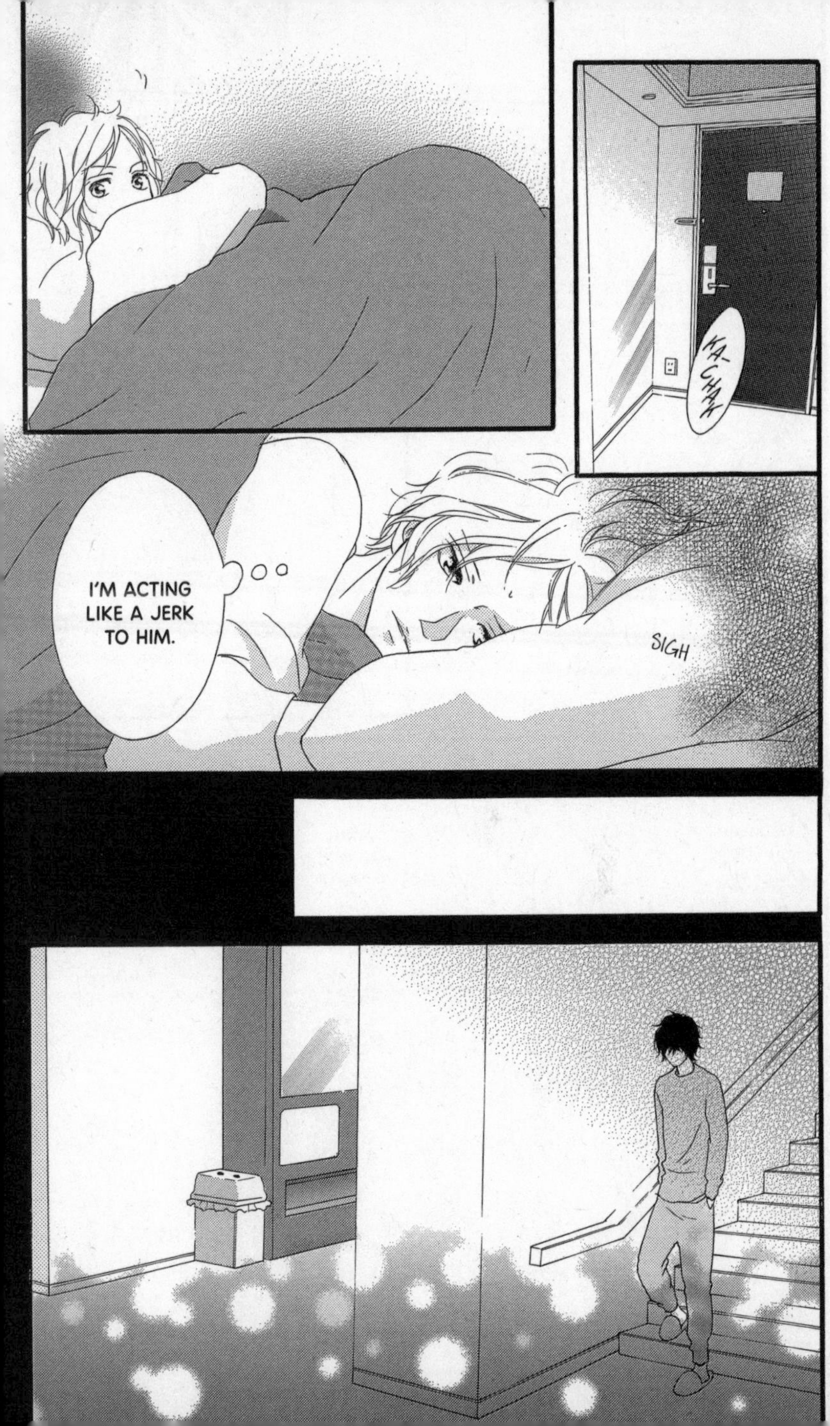
KA-CHAK
I'M ACTING LIKE A JERK TO HIM.
SIGH

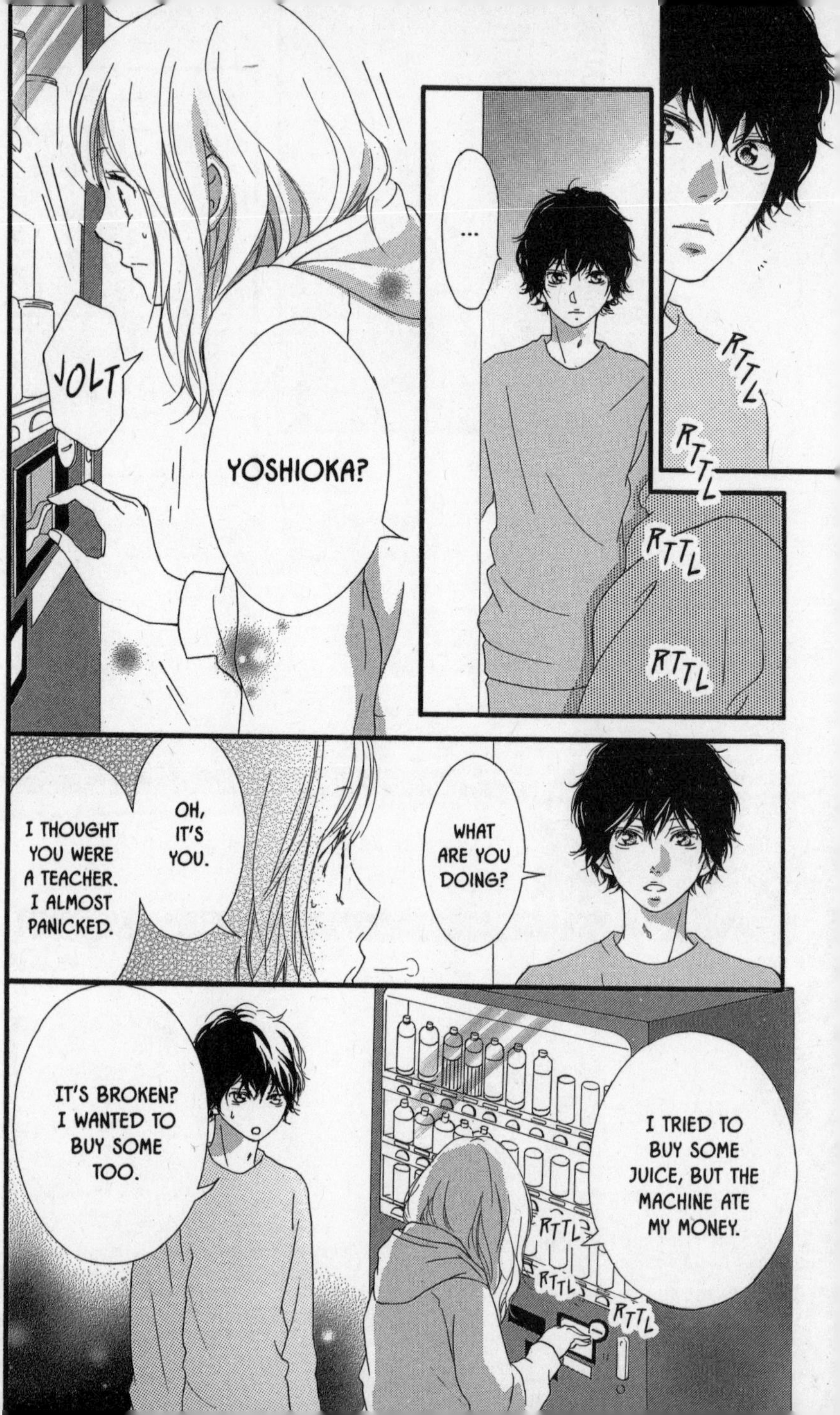
RTTL
RTTL
RTTL
RTTL
...
JOLT
YOSHIOKA?
WHAT ARE YOU DOING?
OH, IT'S YOU.
I THOUGHT YOU WERE A TEACHER. I ALMOST PANICKED.
I TRIED TO BUY SOME JUICE, BUT THE MACHINE ATE MY MONEY.
RTTL
RTTL
RTTL
IT'S BROKEN? I WANTED TO BUY SOME TOO.

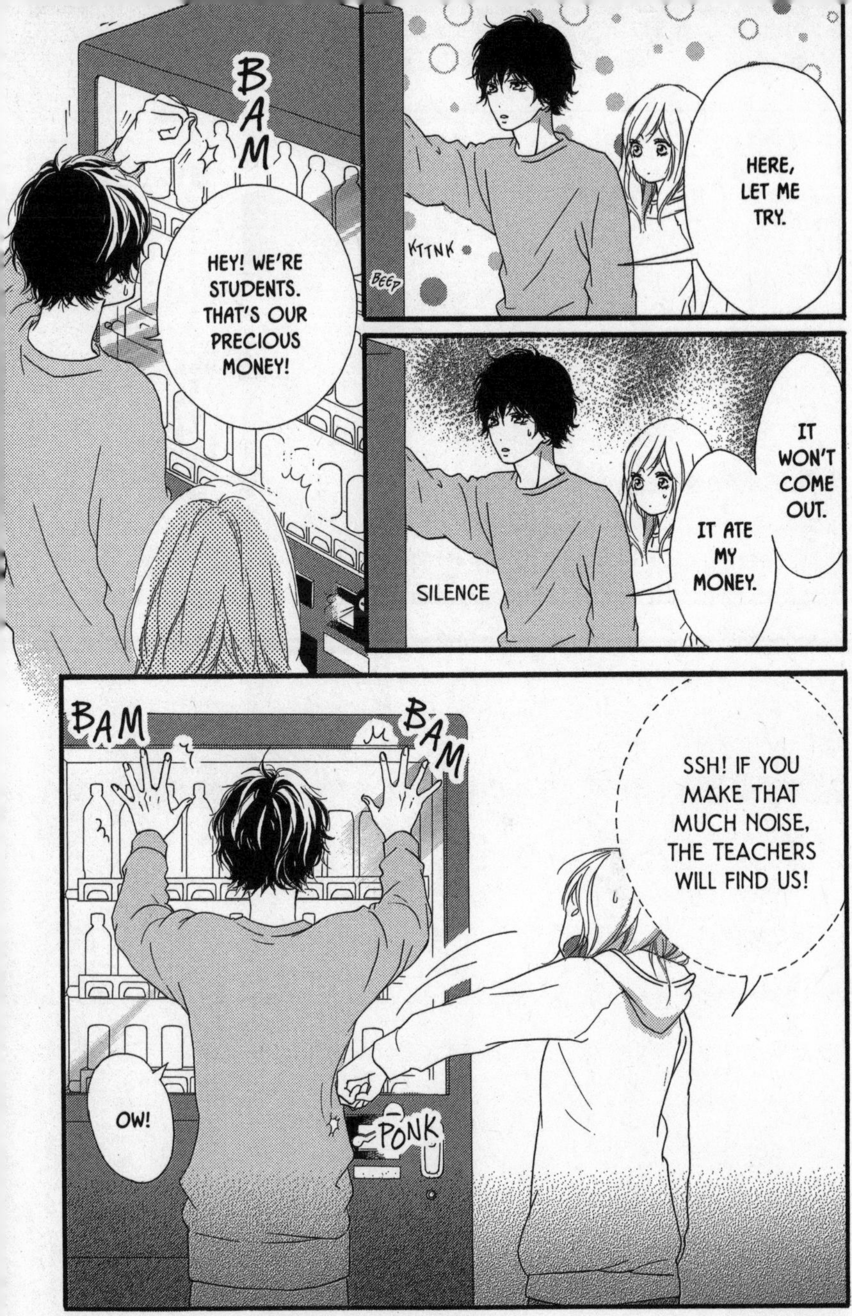
HERE, LET ME TRY.
KTTNK
BEEP
IT WON'T COME OUT.
IT ATE MY MONEY.
SILENCE
BAM
HEY! WE'RE STUDENTS. THAT'S OUR PRECIOUS MONEY!
SSH! IF YOU MAKE THAT MUCH NOISE, THE TEACHERS WILL FIND US!
BAM
BAM
OW!
PONK

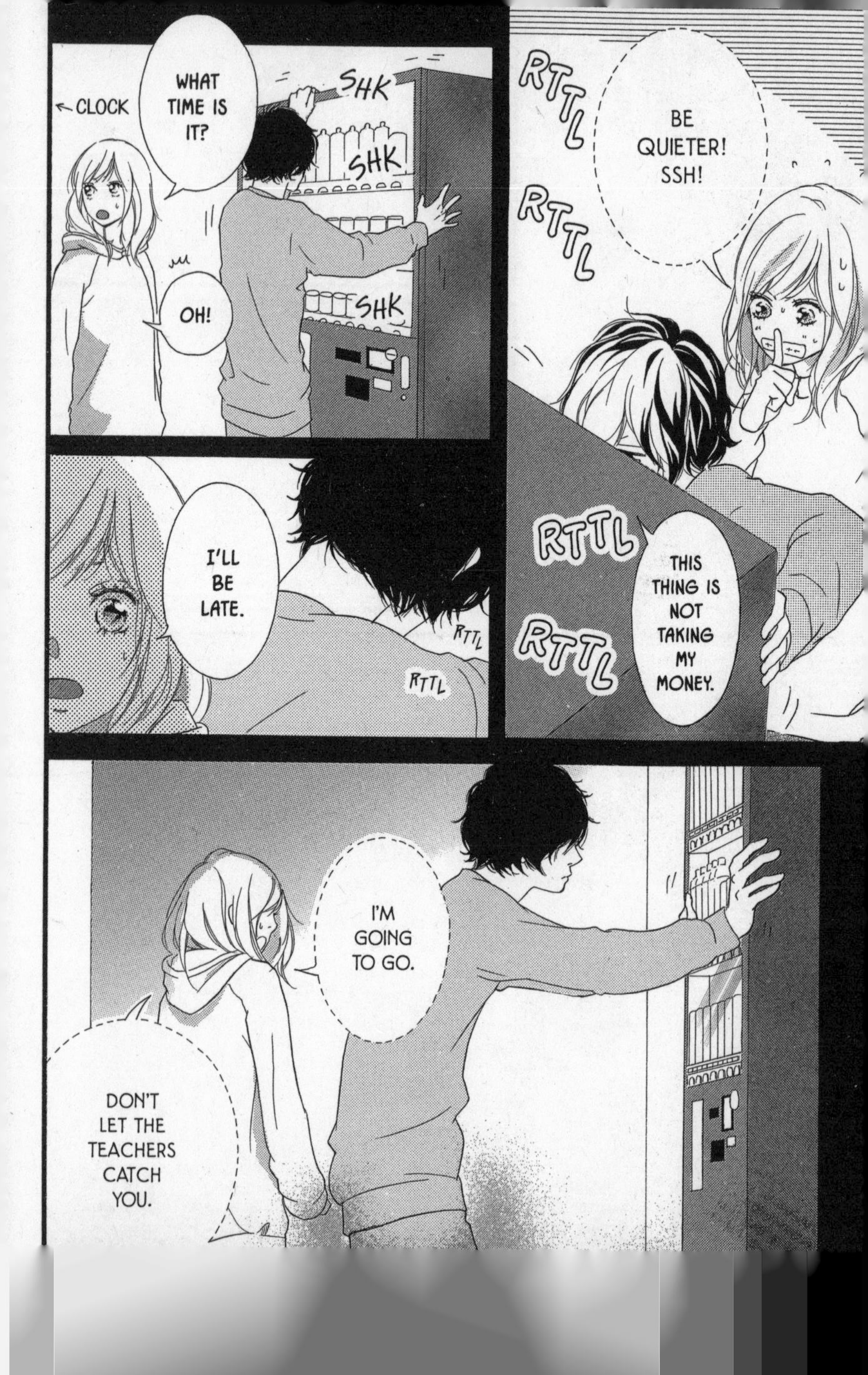
BE QUIETER! SSH!
RTTL
RTTL
THIS THING IS NOT TAKING MY MONEY.
RTTL
RTTL
SHK
WHAT TIME IS IT?
← CLOCK
SHK
OH!
SHK
I'LL BE LATE.
RTTL
RTTL
I'M GOING TO GO.
DON'T LET THE TEACHERS CATCH YOU.

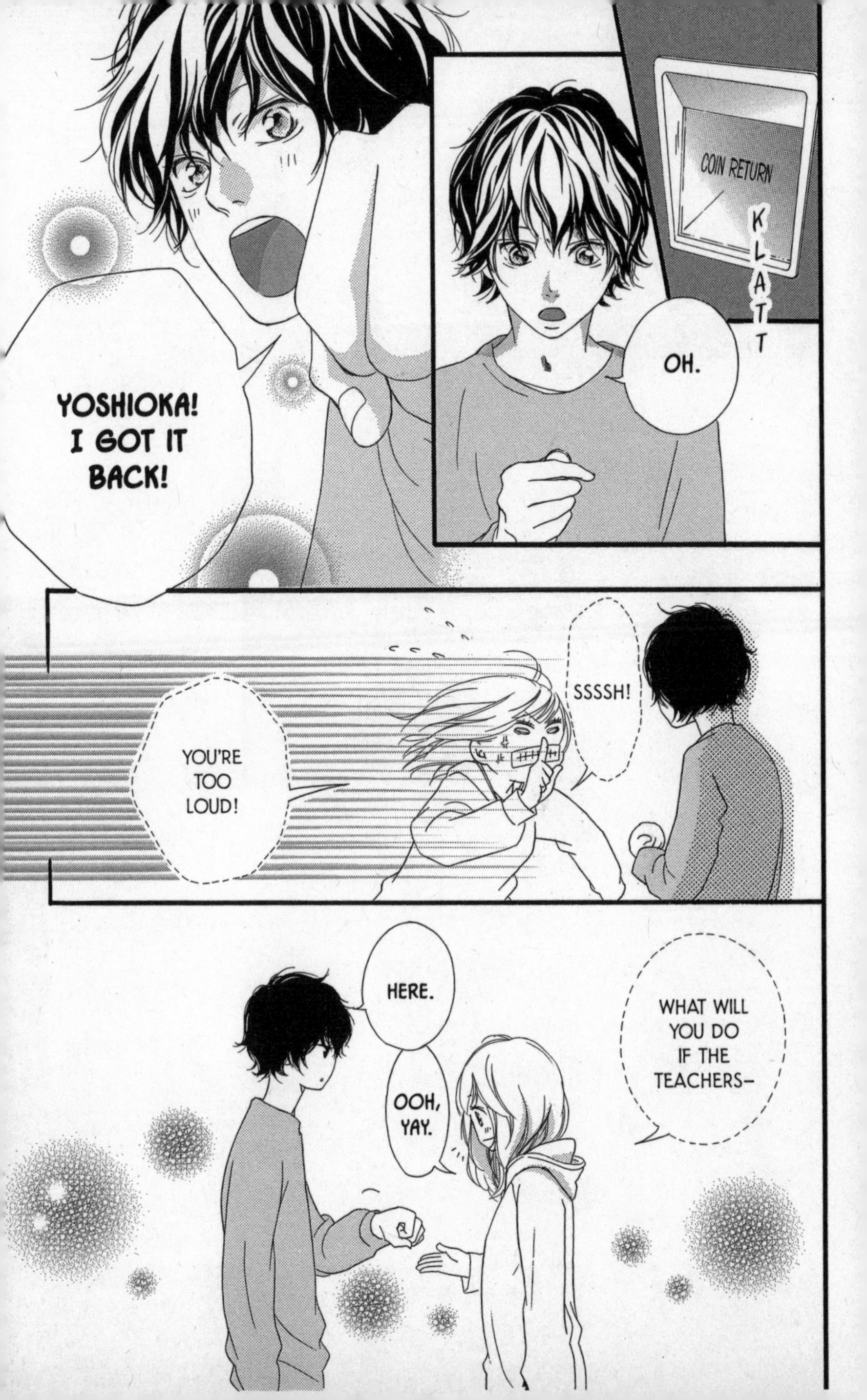
COIN RETURN
KLATT
OH.
YOSHIOKA! I GOT IT BACK!
SSSSH!
YOU'RE TOO LOUD!
WHAT WILL YOU DO IF THE TEACHERS—
HERE.
OOH, YAY.

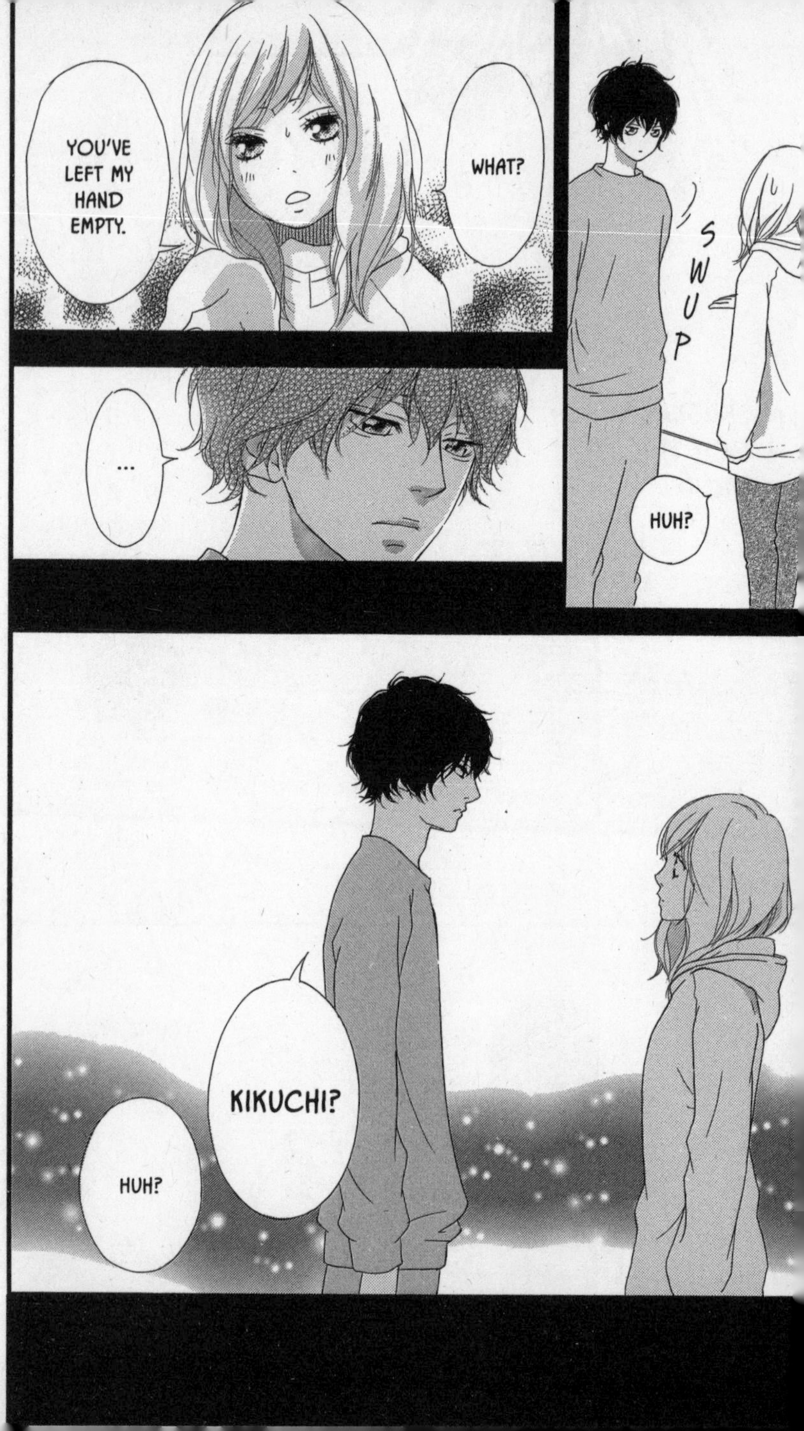
SWUP
HUH?
WHAT?
YOU'VE LEFT MY HAND EMPTY.
...
KIKUCHI?
HUH?

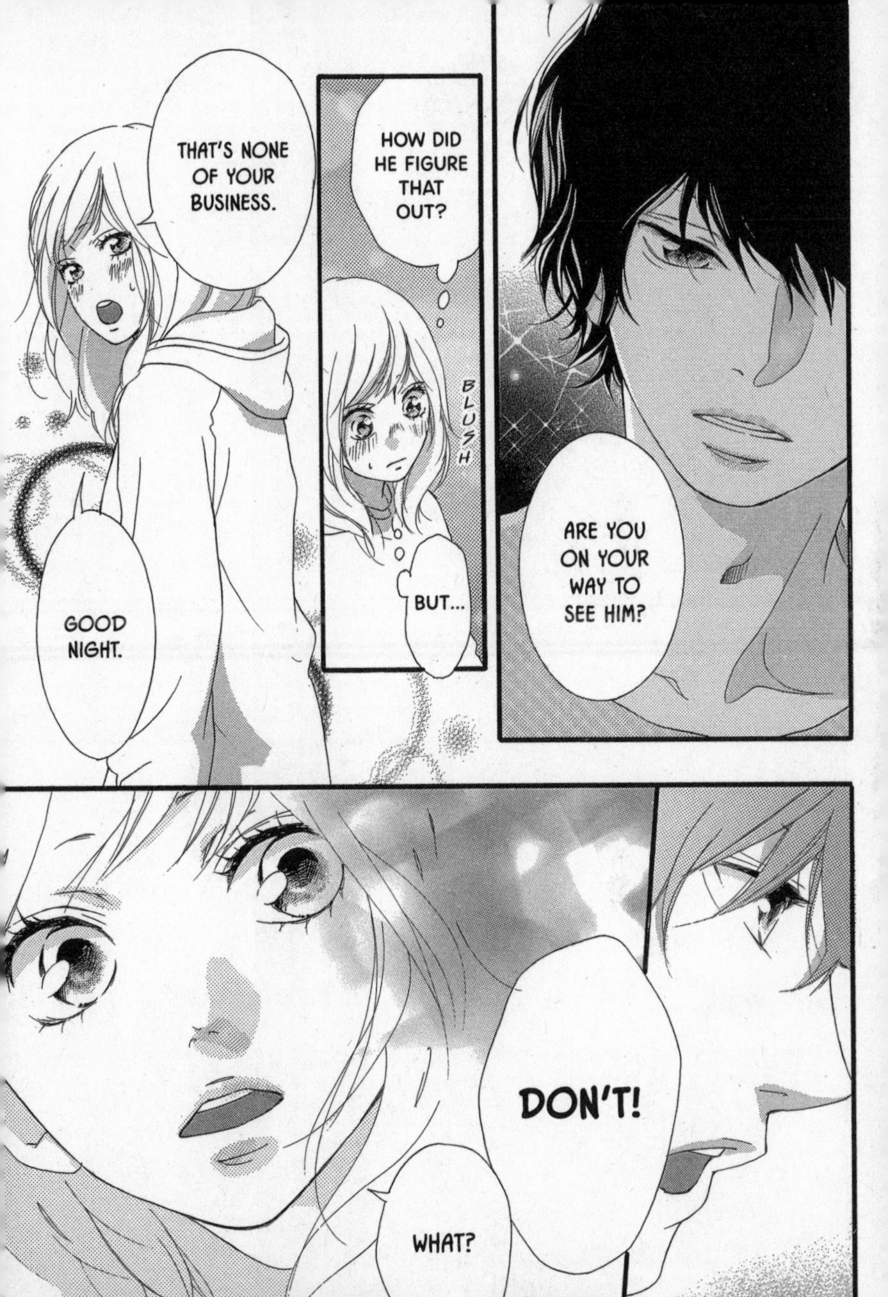
ARE YOU ON YOUR WAY TO SEE HIM?
HOW DID HE FIGURE THAT OUT?
BLUSH
BUT...
THAT'S NONE OF YOUR BUSINESS.
GOOD NIGHT.
DON'T!
WHAT?

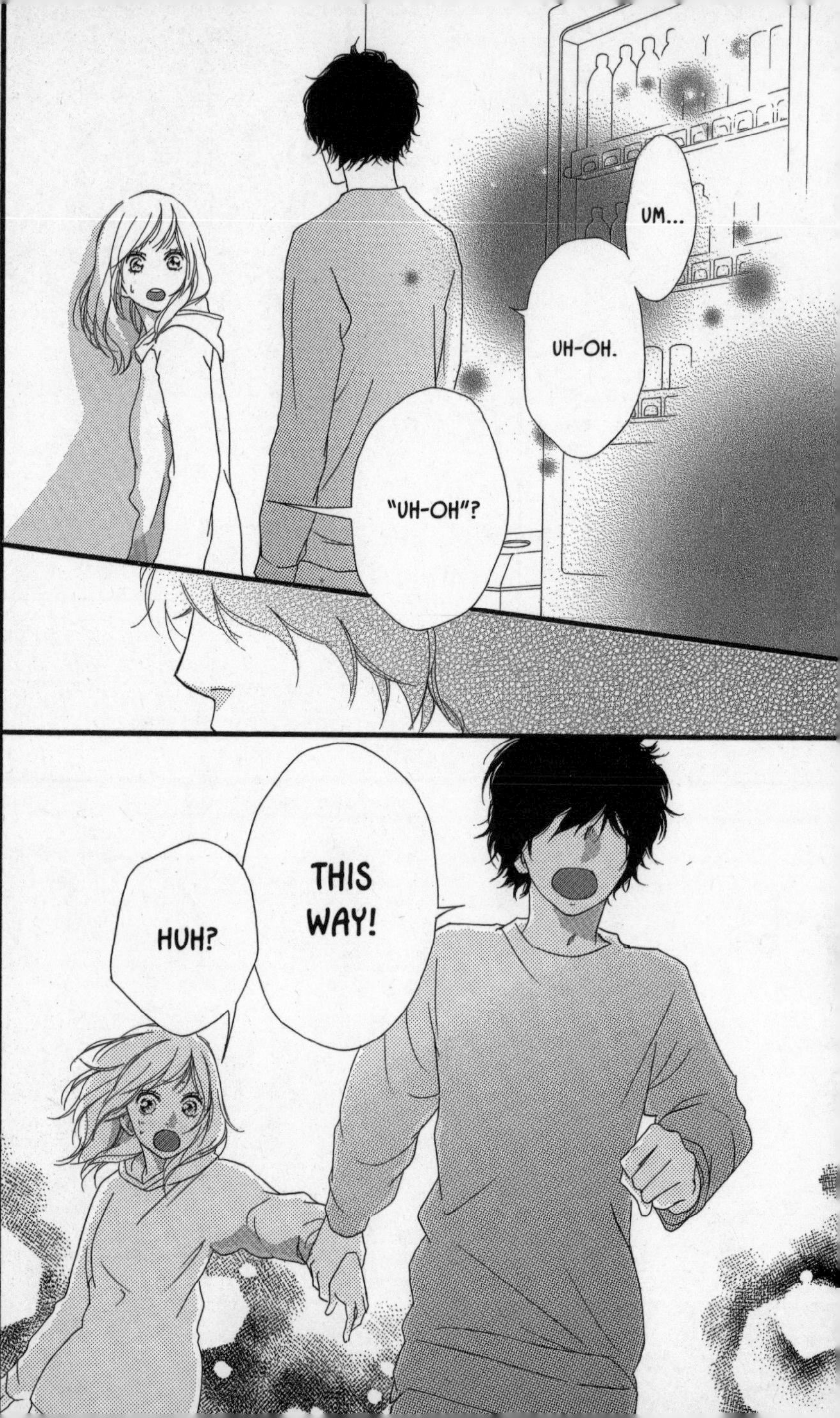
UM...
UH-OH.
"UH-OH"?
THIS WAY!
HUH?

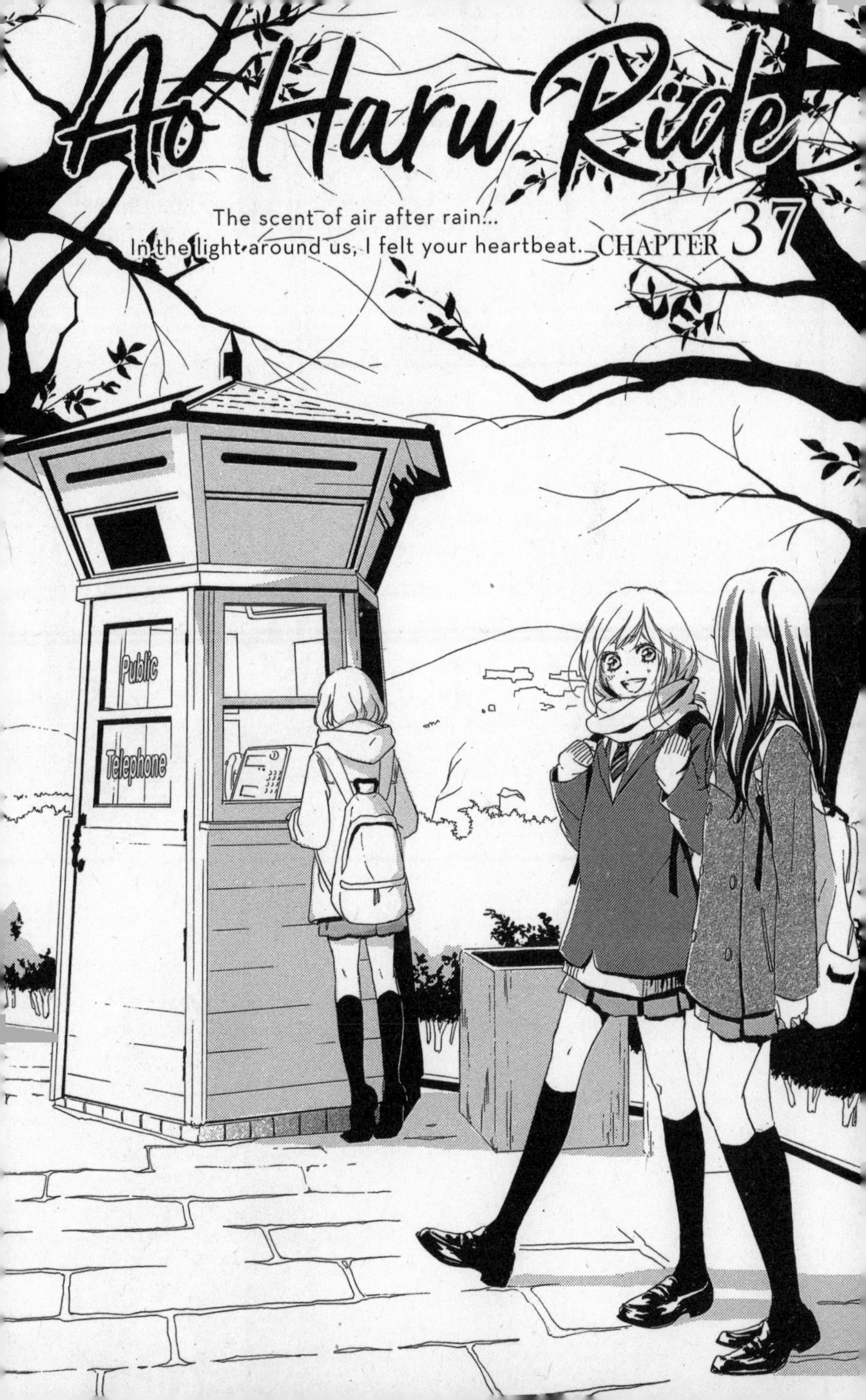
Ao Haru Ride
The scent of air after rain...
In the light around us, I felt your heartbeat.
CHAPTER 37
Public
Telephone

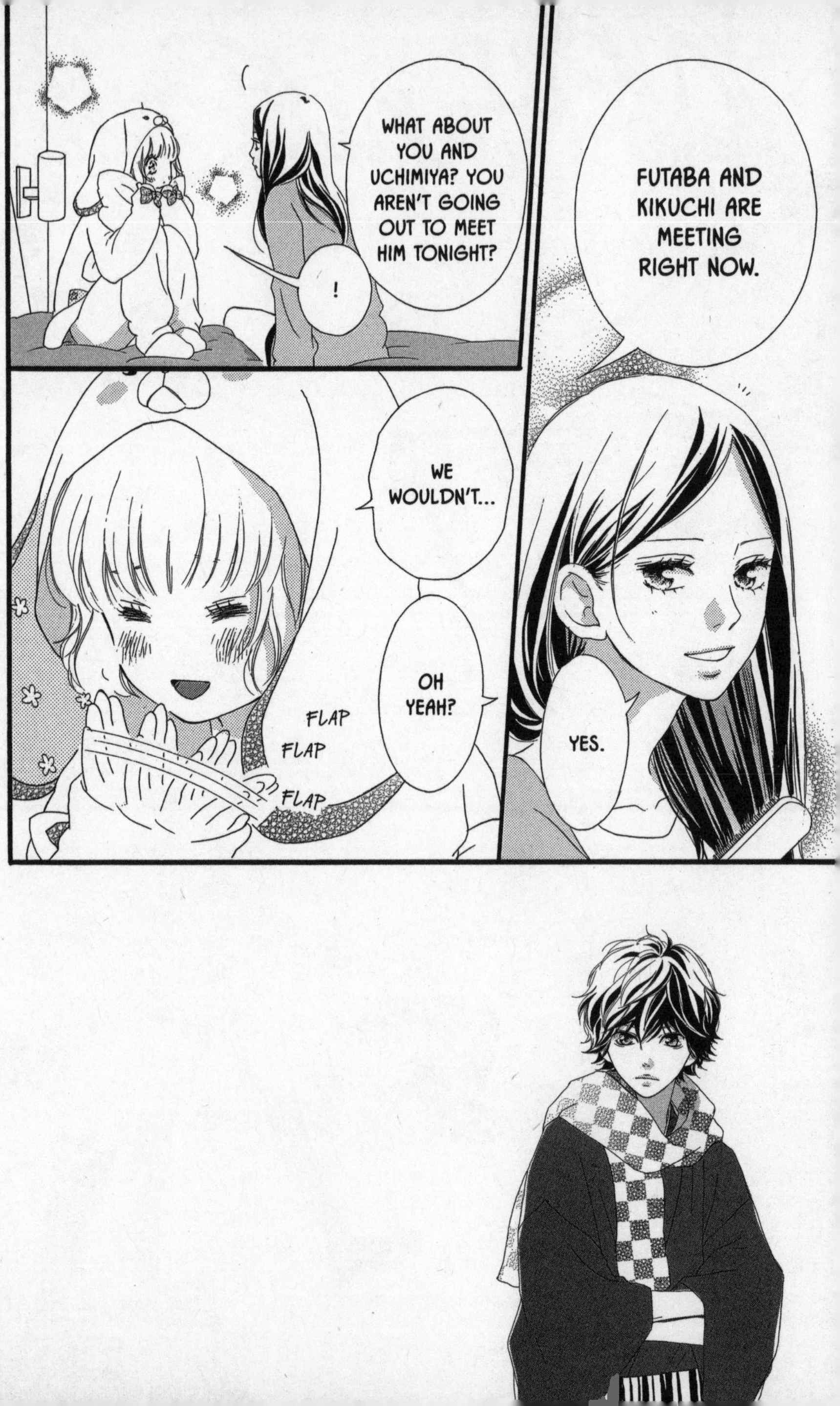
FUTABA AND KIKUCHI ARE MEETING RIGHT NOW.
YES.
WHAT ABOUT YOU AND UCHIMIYA? YOU AREN'T GOING OUT TO MEET HIM TONIGHT?
!
WE WOULDN'T...
OH YEAH?
FLAP
FLAP
FLAP

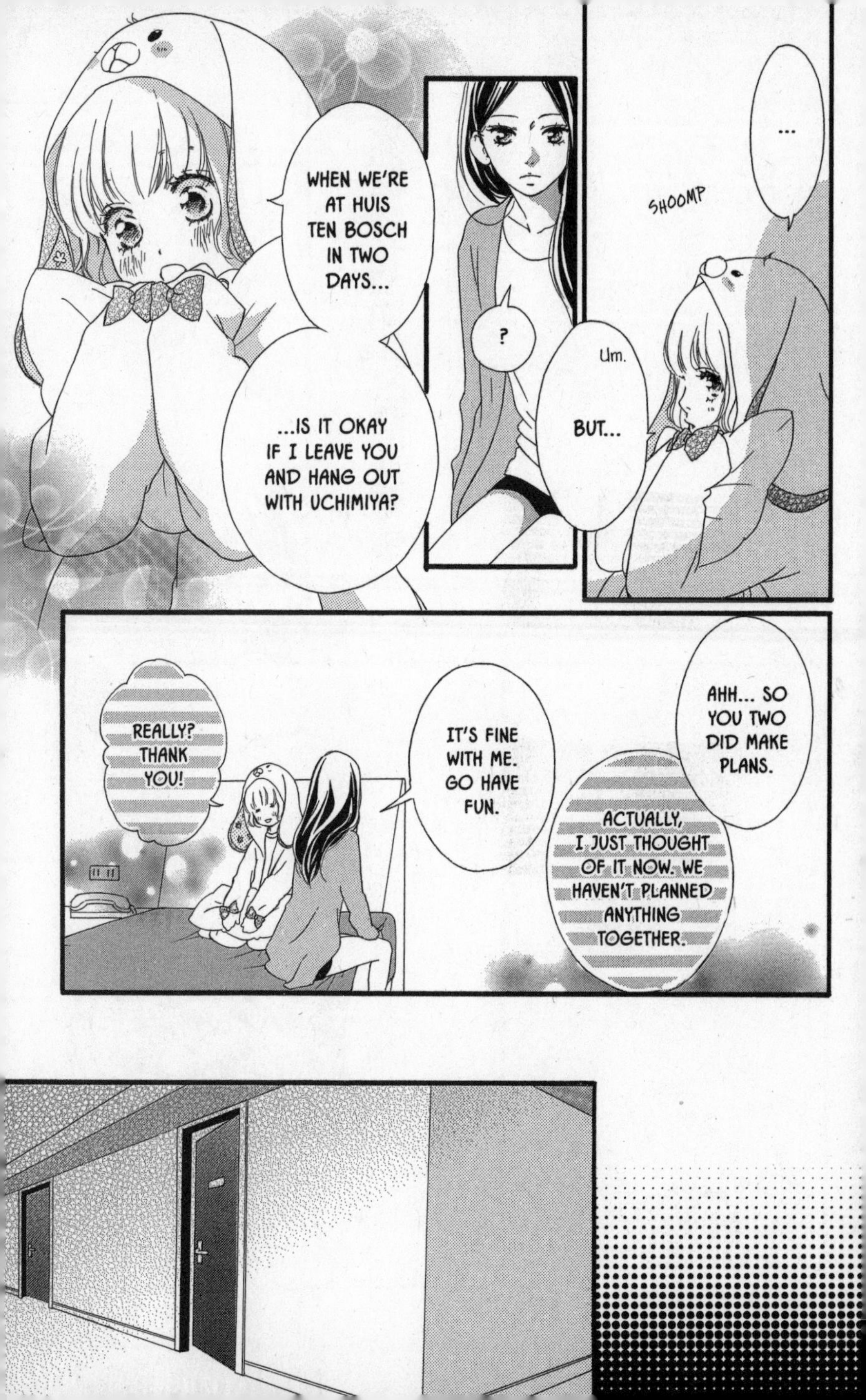
...
SHOOMP
Um.
BUT...
?
WHEN WE'RE AT HUIS TEN BOSCH IN TWO DAYS...
...IS IT OKAY IF I LEAVE YOU AND HANG OUT WITH UCHIMIYA?
AHH... SO YOU TWO DID MAKE PLANS.
ACTUALLY, I JUST THOUGHT OF IT NOW. WE HAVEN'T PLANNED ANYTHING TOGETHER.
IT'S FINE WITH ME. GO HAVE FUN.
REALLY? THANK YOU!

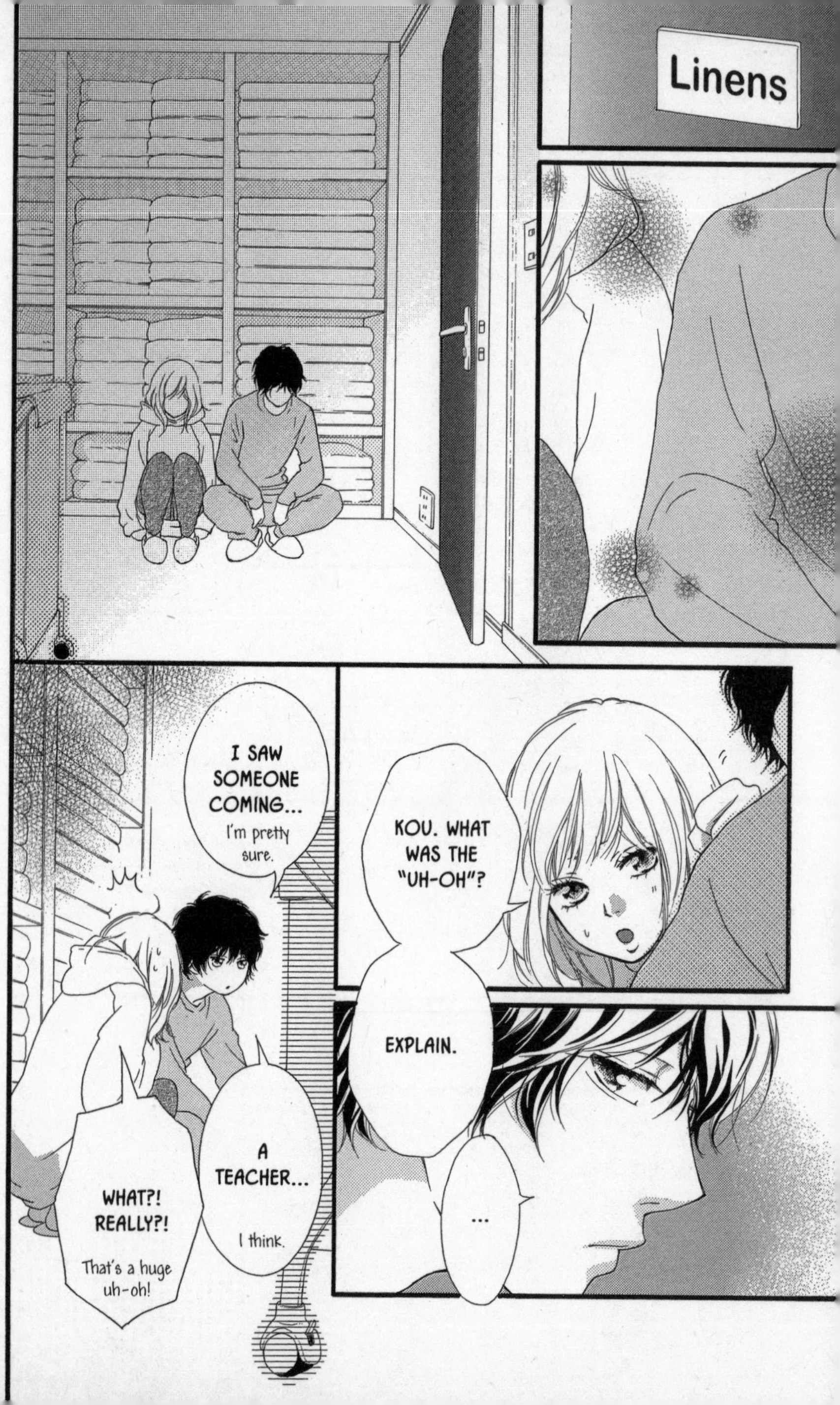
Linens
KOU. WHAT WAS THE "UH-OH"?
EXPLAIN.
...
I SAW SOMEONE COMING... I'm pretty sure.
A TEACHER... I think.
WHAT?! REALLY?! That's a huge uh-oh!

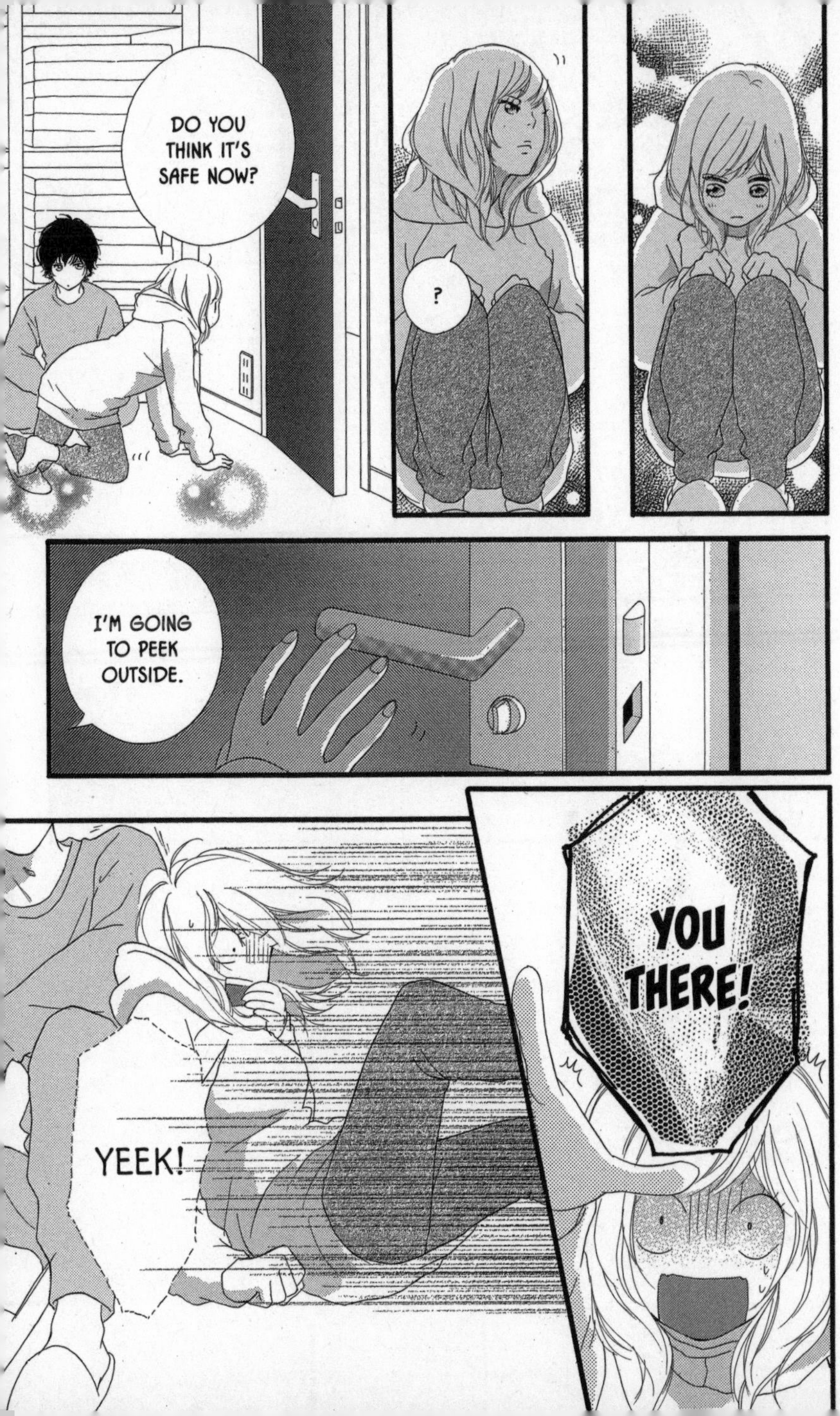
?
DO YOU THINK IT'S SAFE NOW?
I'M GOING TO PEEK OUTSIDE.
YOU THERE!
YEEK!

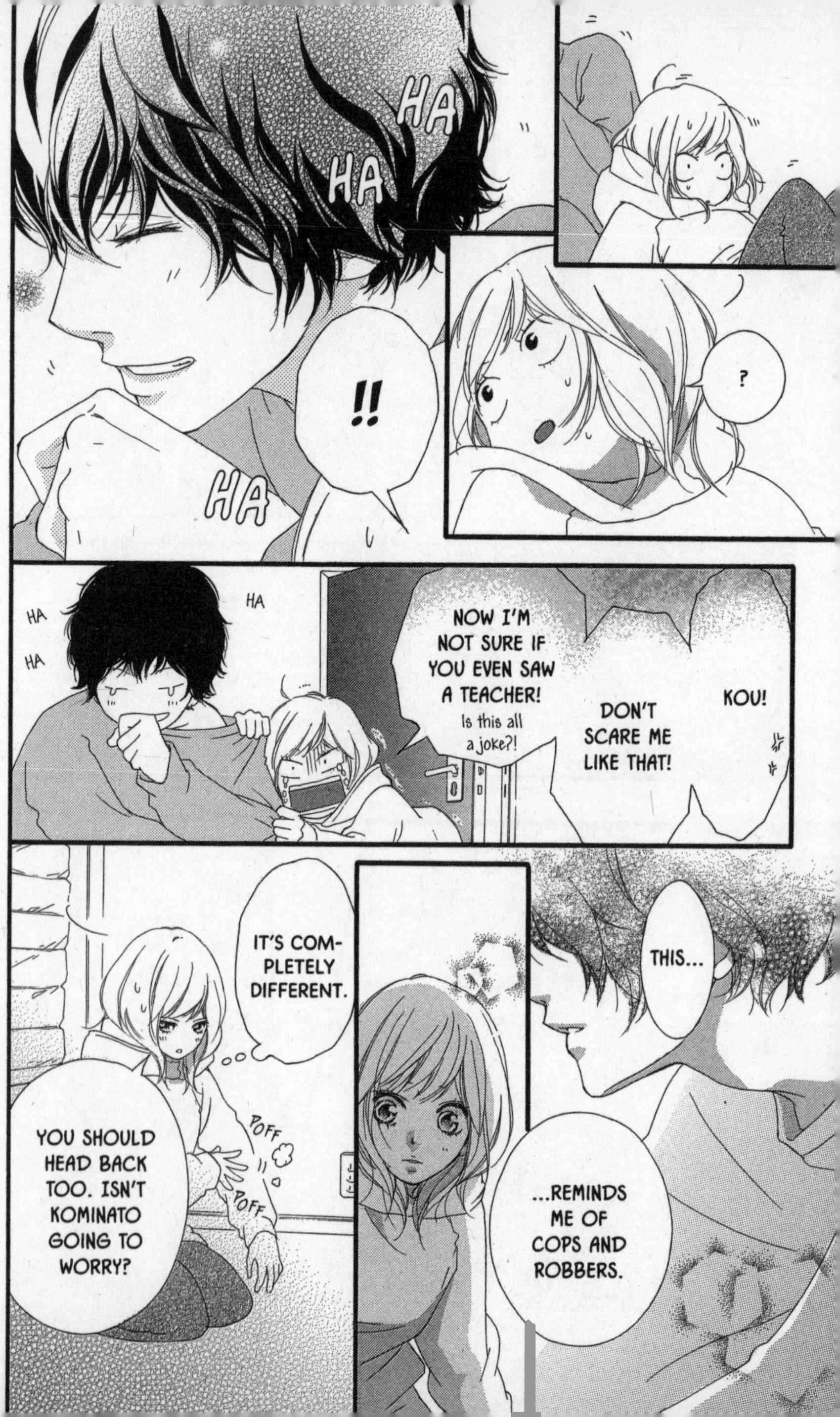
?
HA
HA
!!
HA
KOU!
DON'T SCARE ME LIKE THAT!
NOW I'M NOT SURE IF YOU EVEN SAW A TEACHER!
Is this all a joke?!
HA
HA
HA
THIS...
...REMINDS ME OF COPS AND ROBBERS.
IT'S COM-PLETELY DIFFERENT.
POFF
POFF
YOU SHOULD HEAD BACK TOO. ISN'T KOMINATO GOING TO WORRY?

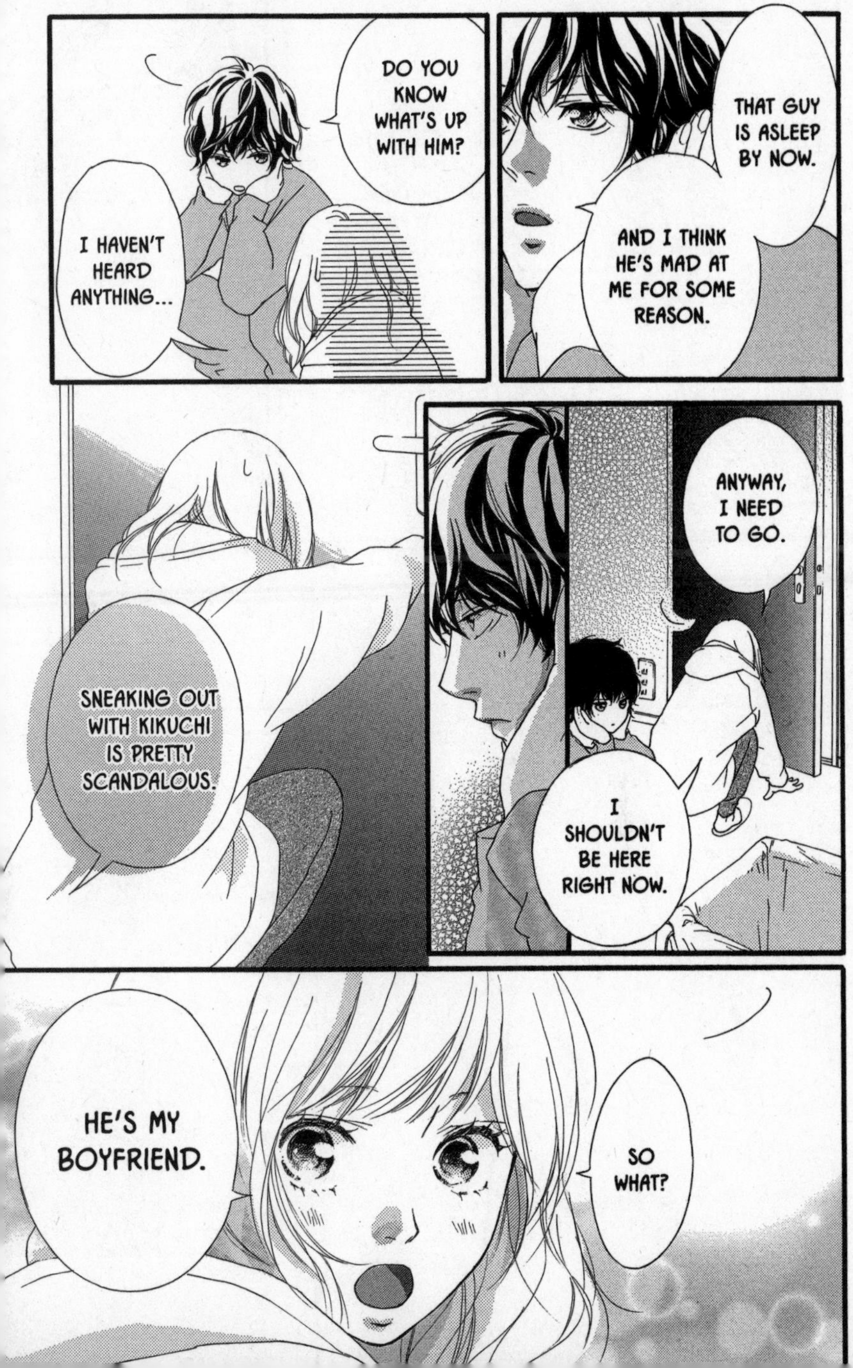
THAT GUY IS ASLEEP BY NOW.
AND I THINK HE'S MAD AT ME FOR SOME REASON.
DO YOU KNOW WHAT'S UP WITH HIM?
I HAVEN'T HEARD ANYTHING...
ANYWAY, I NEED TO GO.
I SHOULDN'T BE HERE RIGHT NOW.
SNEAKING OUT WITH KIKUCHI IS PRETTY SCANDALOUS.
SO WHAT?
HE'S MY BOYFRIEND.

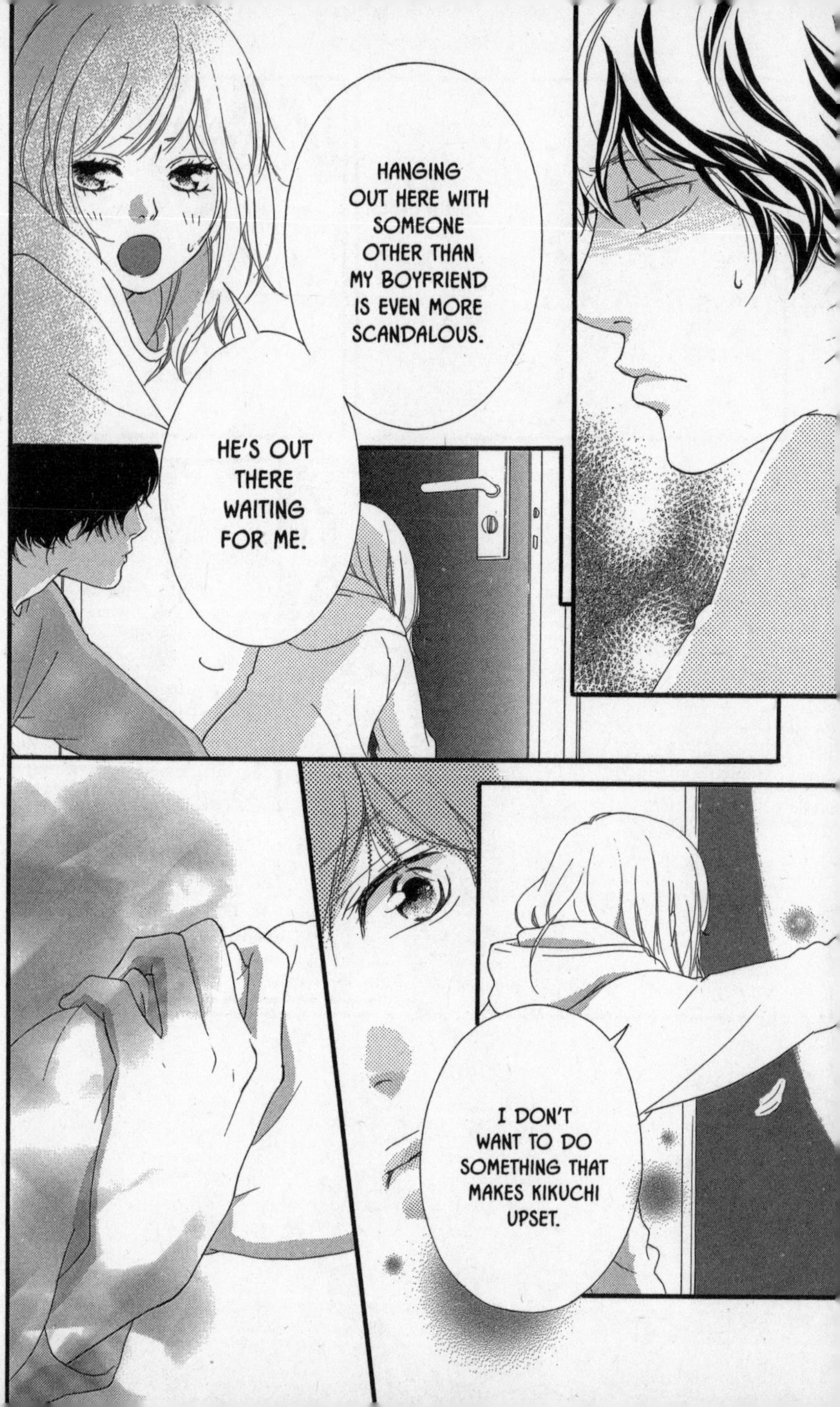
HANGING OUT HERE WITH SOMEONE OTHER THAN MY BOYFRIEND IS EVEN MORE SCANDALOUS.
HE'S OUT THERE WAITING FOR ME.
I DON'T WANT TO DO SOMETHING THAT MAKES KIKUCHI UPSET.

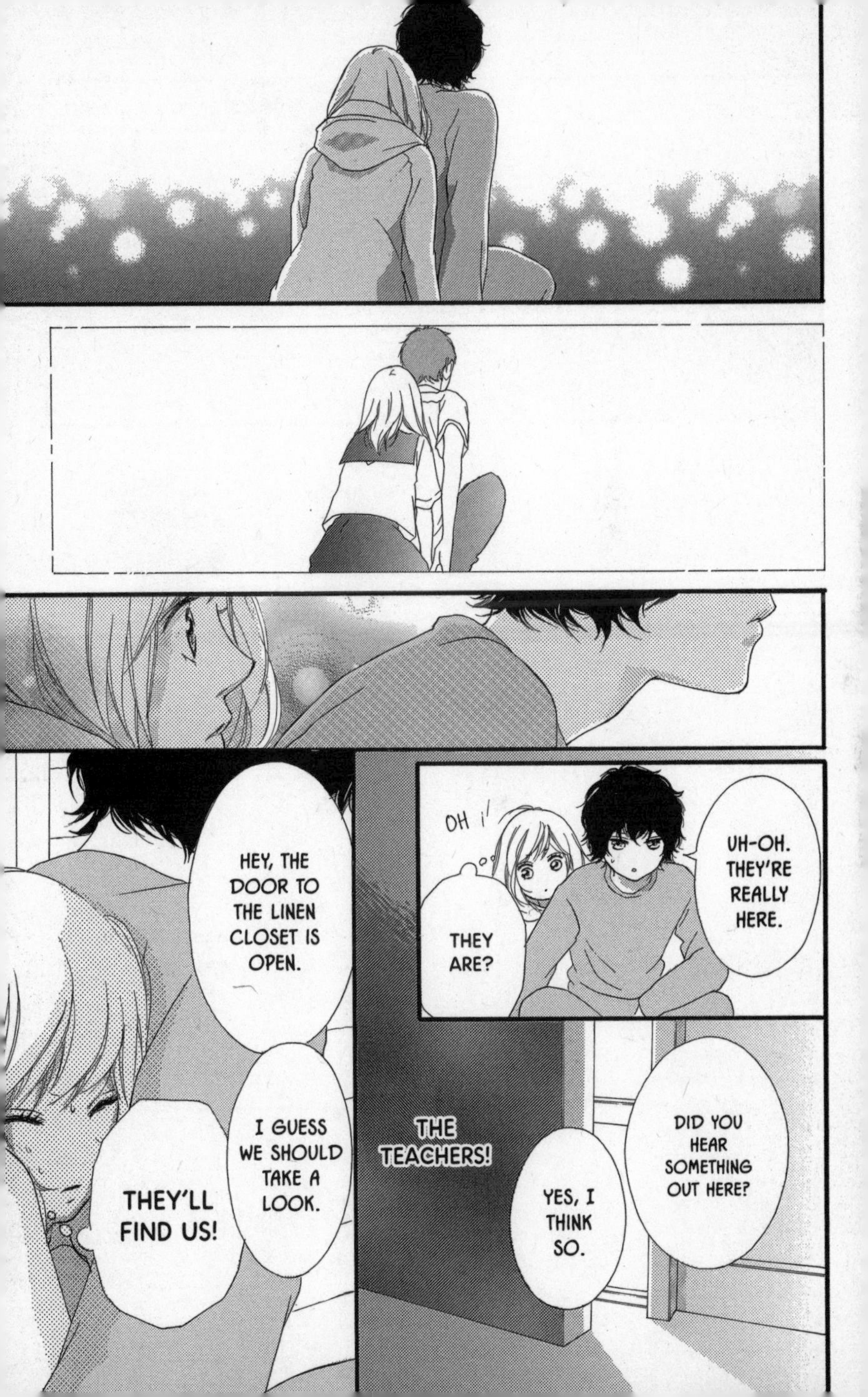
UH-OH. THEY'RE REALLY HERE.
OH!
THEY ARE?
DID YOU HEAR SOMETHING OUT HERE?
YES, I THINK SO.
THE TEACHERS!
HEY, THE DOOR TO THE LINEN CLOSET IS OPEN.
I GUESS WE SHOULD TAKE A LOOK.
THEY'LL FIND US!

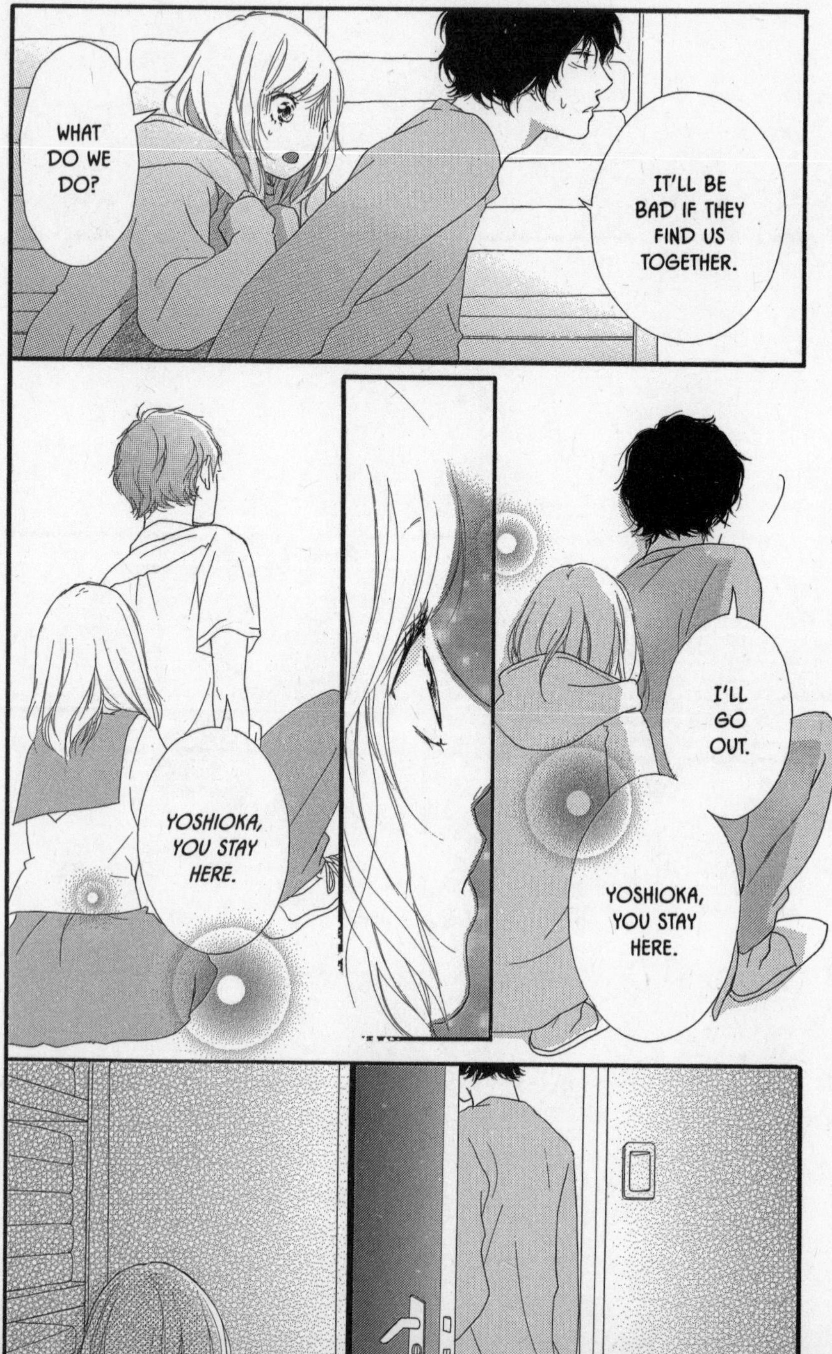
IT'LL BE BAD IF THEY FIND US TOGETHER.
WHAT DO WE DO?
I'LL GO OUT.
YOSHIOKA, YOU STAY HERE.
YOSHIOKA, YOU STAY HERE.

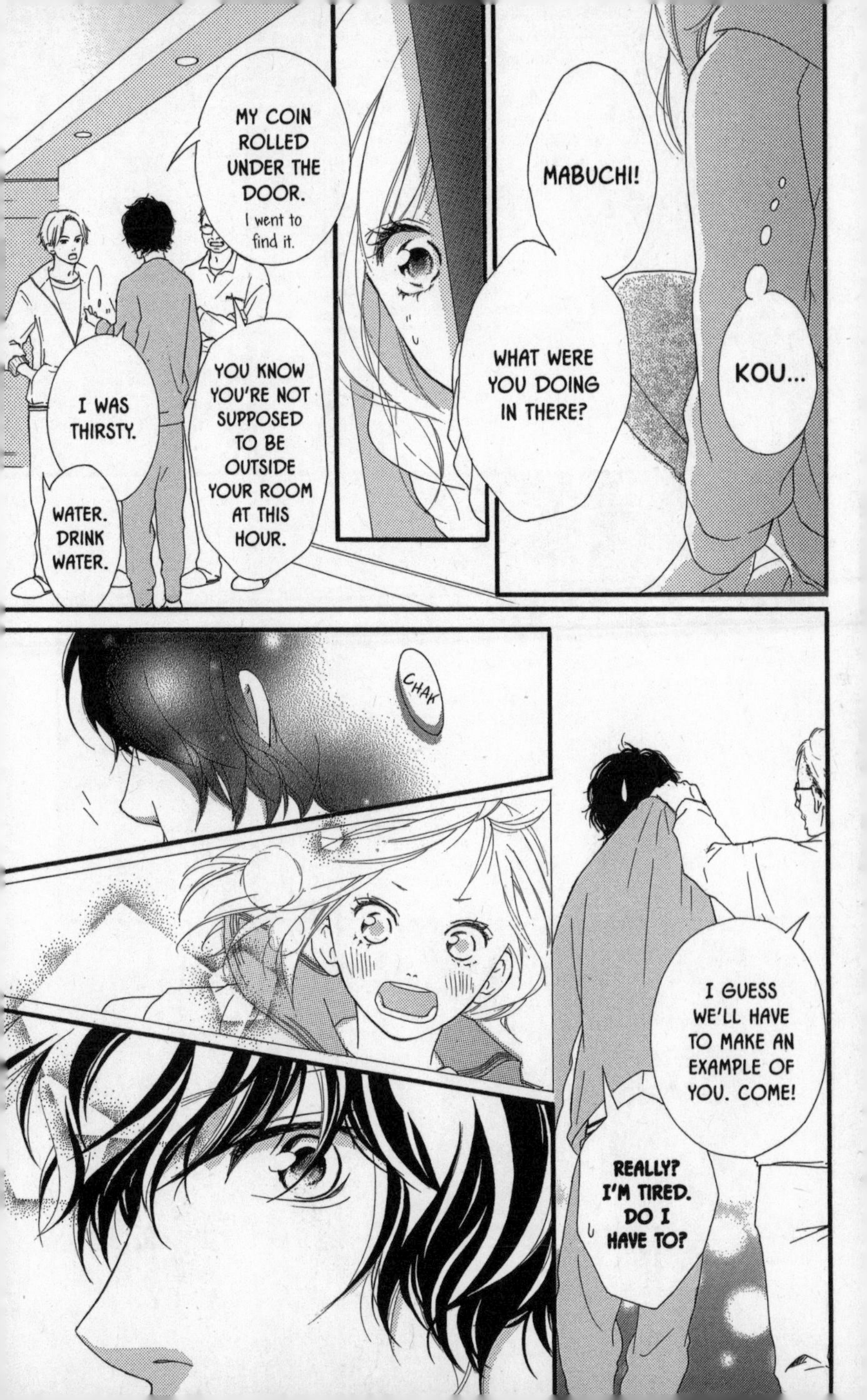
MABUCHI!
KOU...
WHAT WERE YOU DOING IN THERE?
MY COIN ROLLED UNDER THE DOOR. I went to find it.
YOU KNOW YOU'RE NOT SUPPOSED TO BE OUTSIDE YOUR ROOM AT THIS HOUR.
I WAS THIRSTY.
WATER. DRINK WATER.
I GUESS WE'LL HAVE TO MAKE AN EXAMPLE OF YOU. COME!
REALLY? I'M TIRED. DO I HAVE TO?
CHAK

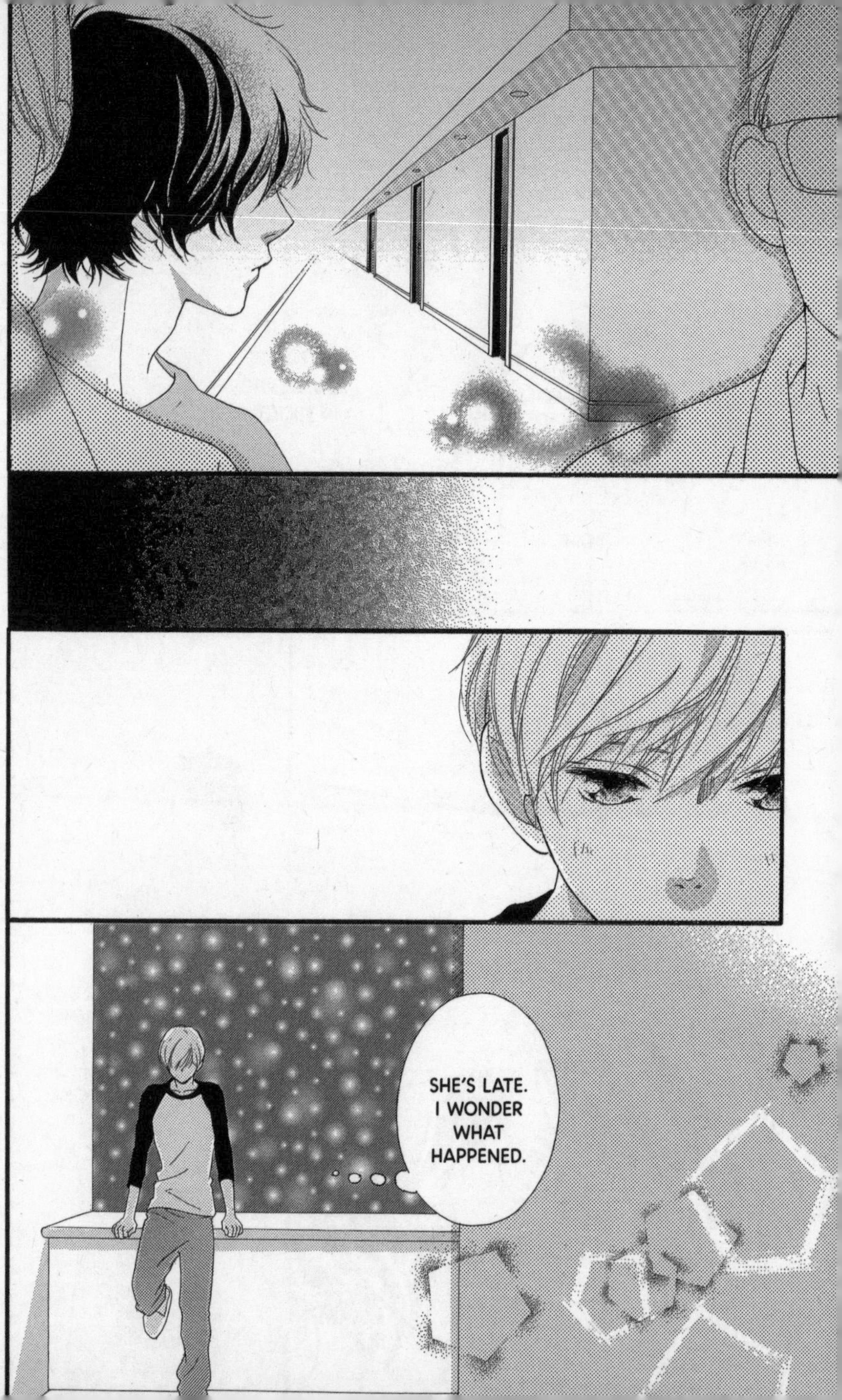
SHE'S LATE. I WONDER WHAT HAPPENED.

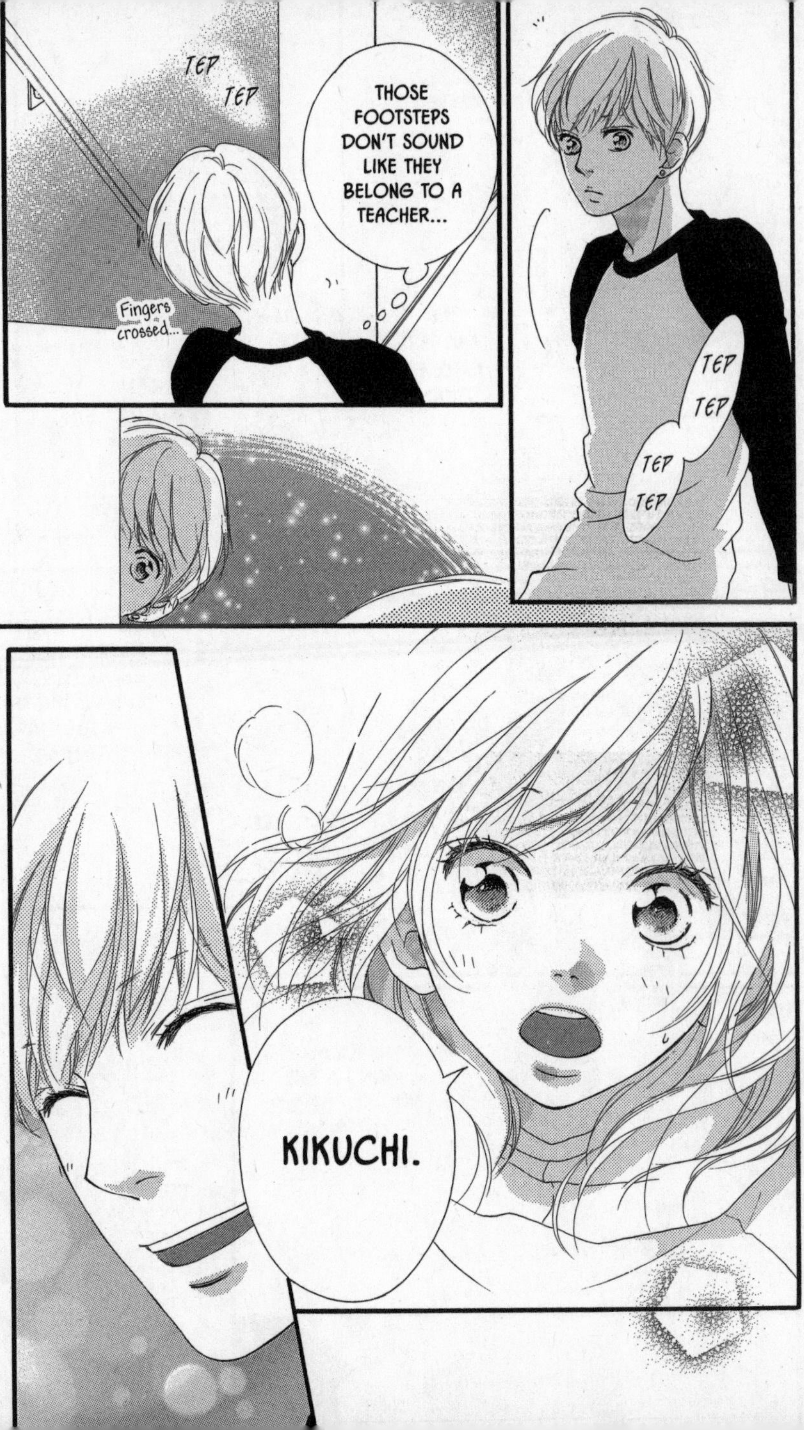
TEP
TEP
TEP
TEP
THOSE FOOTSTEPS DON'T SOUND LIKE THEY BELONG TO A TEACHER...
TEP
TEP
Fingers crossed...
KIKUCHI.

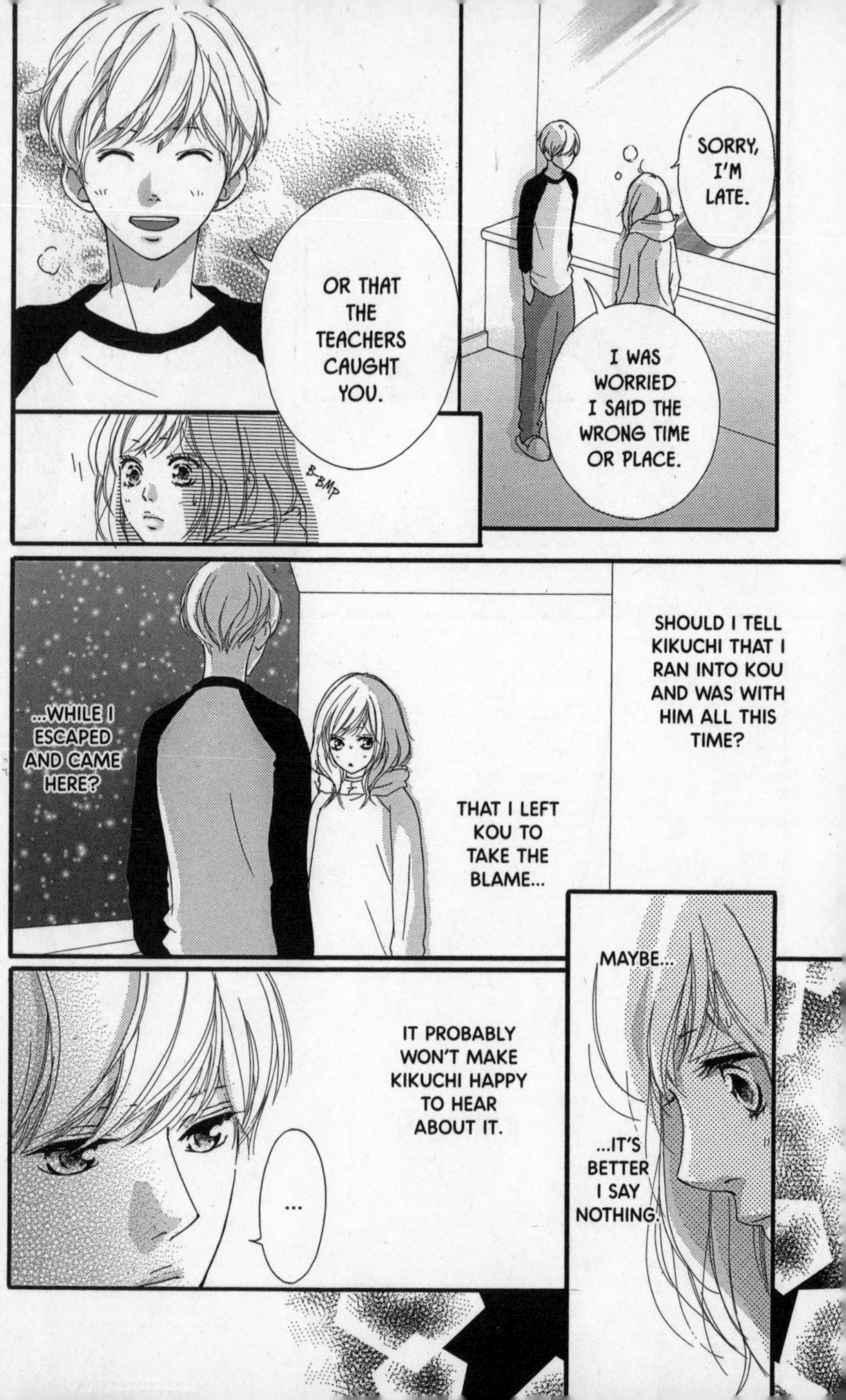
SORRY, I'M LATE.
I WAS WORRIED I SAID THE WRONG TIME OR PLACE.
OR THAT THE TEACHERS CAUGHT YOU.
B-BMP
SHOULD I TELL KIKUCHI THAT I RAN INTO KOU AND WAS WITH HIM ALL THIS TIME?
THAT I LEFT KOU TO TAKE THE BLAME...
...WHILE I ESCAPED AND CAME HERE?
MAYBE...
...IT'S BETTER I SAY NOTHING.
IT PROBABLY WON'T MAKE KIKUCHI HAPPY TO HEAR ABOUT IT.
...

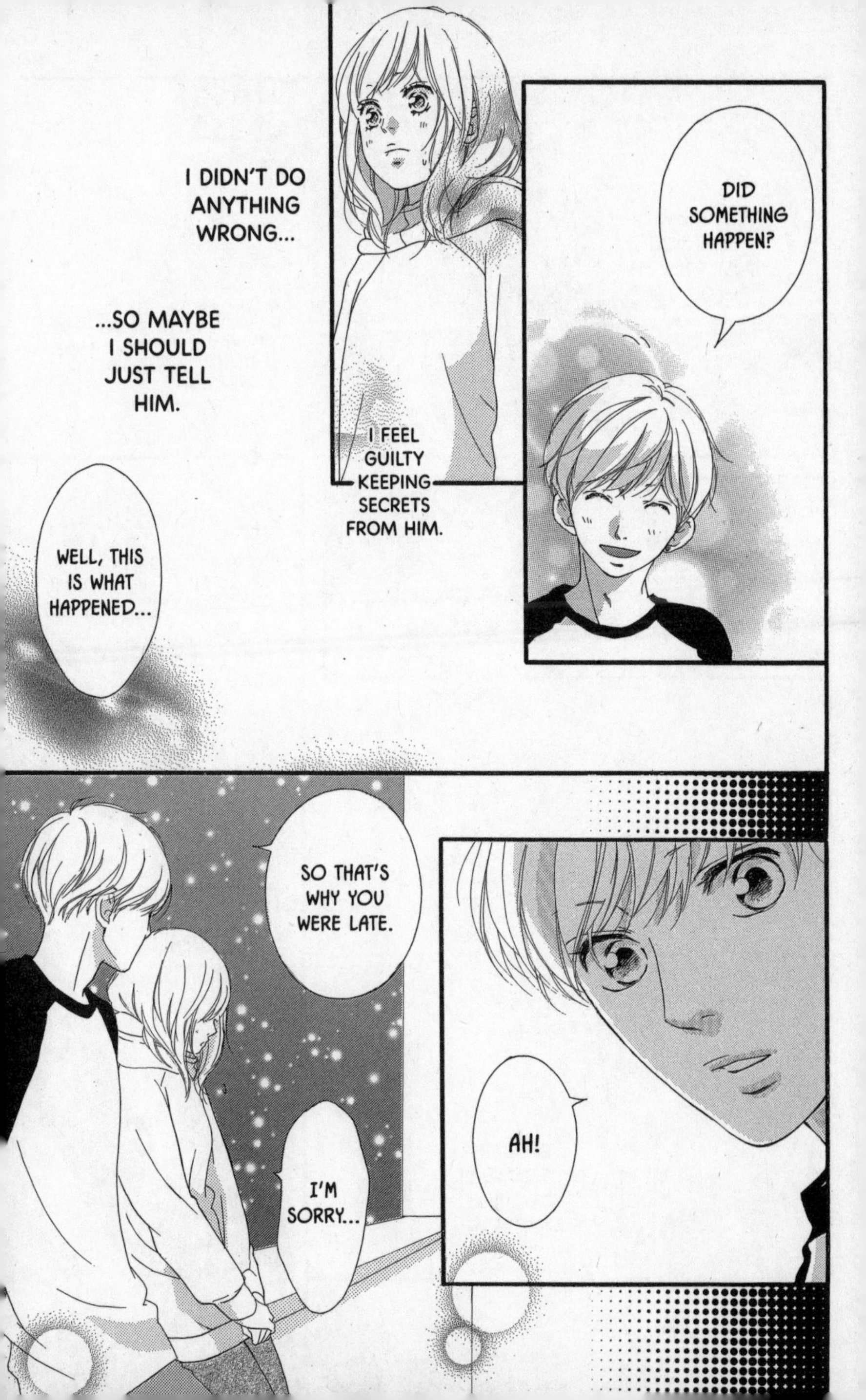
DID SOMETHING HAPPEN?
I FEEL GUILTY KEEPING SECRETS FROM HIM.
I DIDN'T DO ANYTHING WRONG...
...SO MAYBE I SHOULD JUST TELL HIM.
WELL, THIS IS WHAT HAPPENED...
AH!
SO THAT'S WHY YOU WERE LATE.
I'M SORRY...

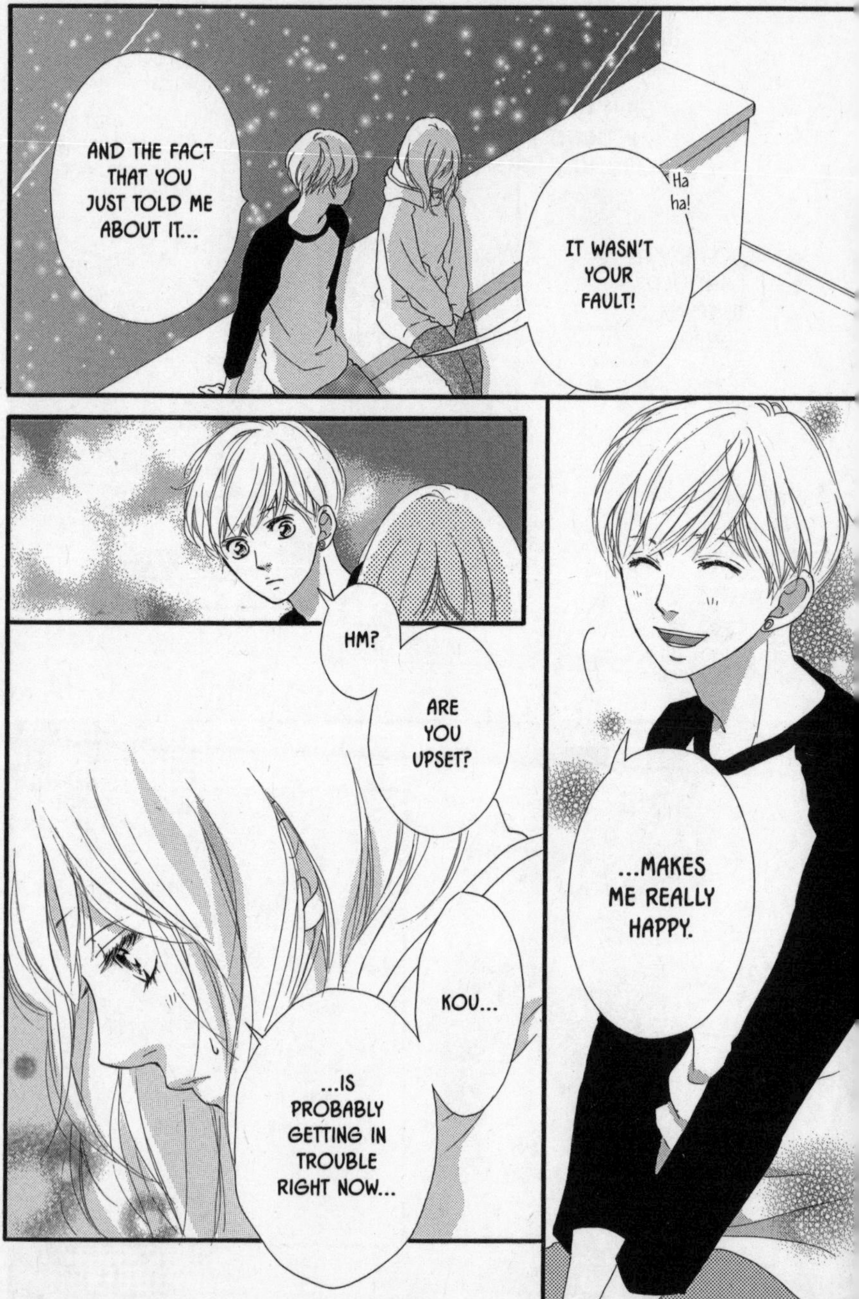
Ha ha!
IT WASN'T YOUR FAULT!
AND THE FACT THAT YOU JUST TOLD ME ABOUT IT...
...MAKES ME REALLY HAPPY.
HM?
ARE YOU UPSET?
KOU...
...IS PROBABLY GETTING IN TROUBLE RIGHT NOW...

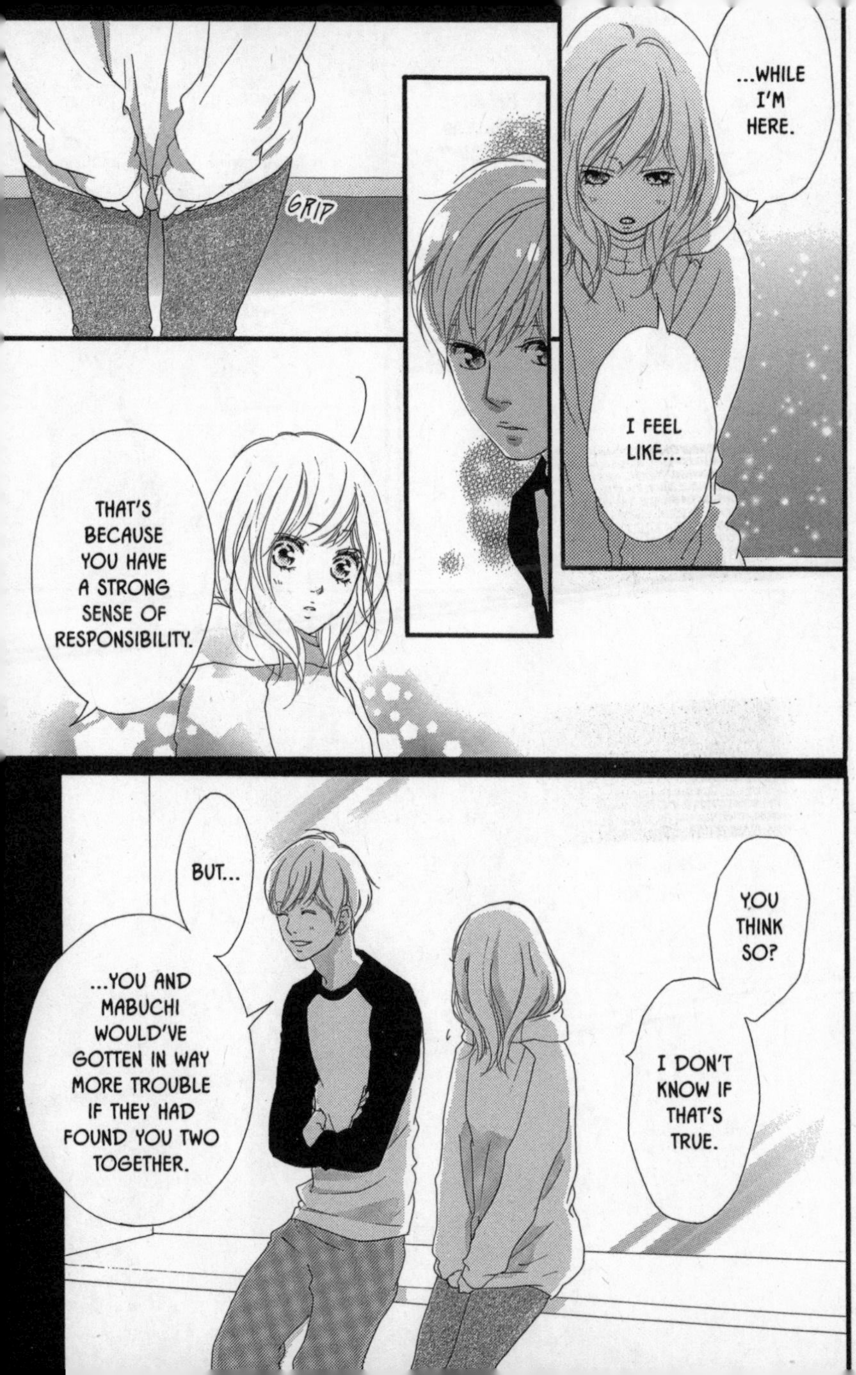
...WHILE I'M HERE.
I FEEL LIKE...
GRIP
THAT'S BECAUSE YOU HAVE A STRONG SENSE OF RESPONSIBILITY.
YOU THINK SO?
I DON'T KNOW IF THAT'S TRUE.
BUT...
...YOU AND MABUCHI WOULD'VE GOTTEN IN WAY MORE TROUBLE IF THEY HAD FOUND YOU TWO TOGETHER.

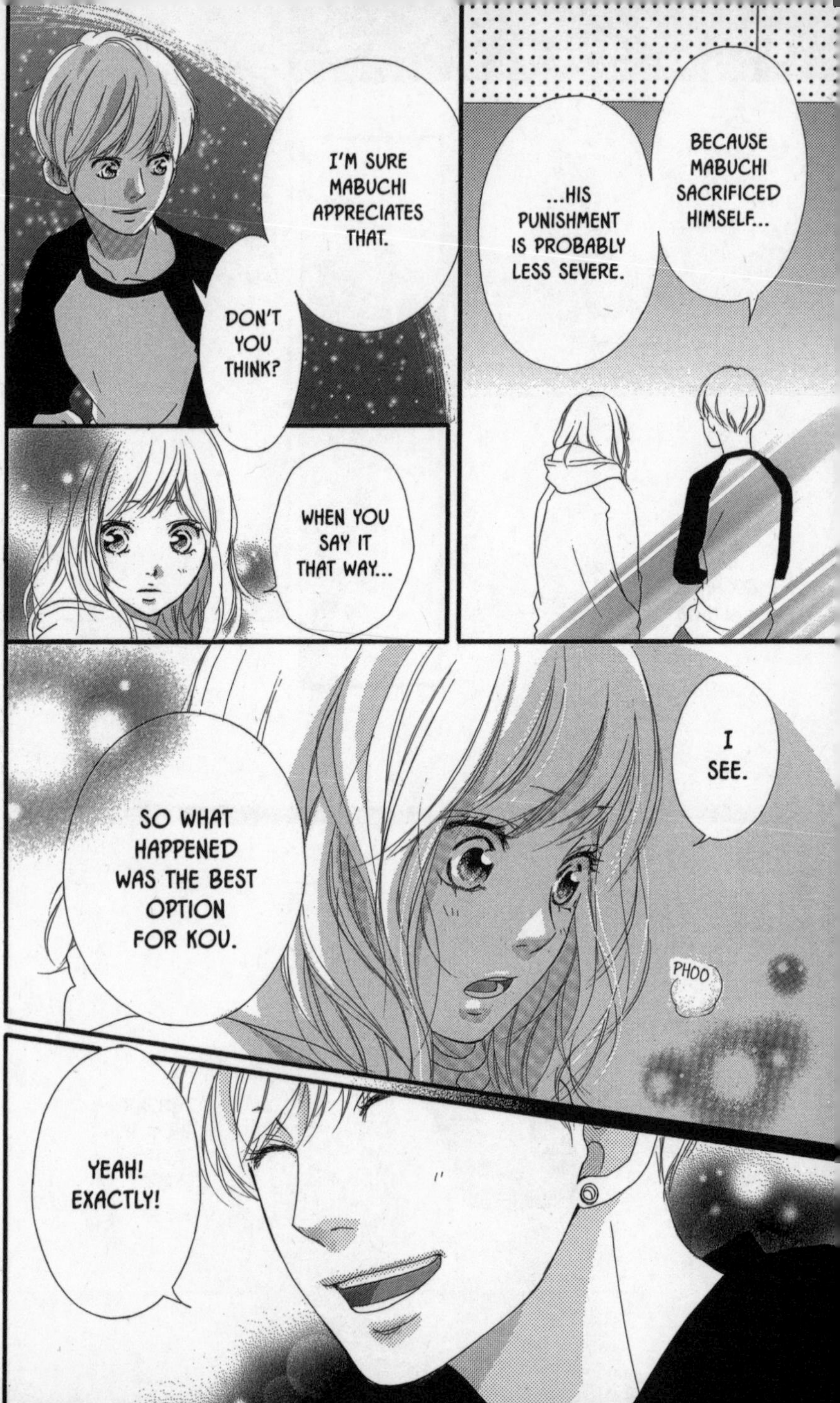
BECAUSE MABUCHI SACRIFICED HIMSELF...
...HIS PUNISHMENT IS PROBABLY LESS SEVERE.
I'M SURE MABUCHI APPRECIATES THAT.
DON'T YOU THINK?
WHEN YOU SAY IT THAT WAY...
I SEE.
SO WHAT HAPPENED WAS THE BEST OPTION FOR KOU.
PHOO
YEAH! EXACTLY!

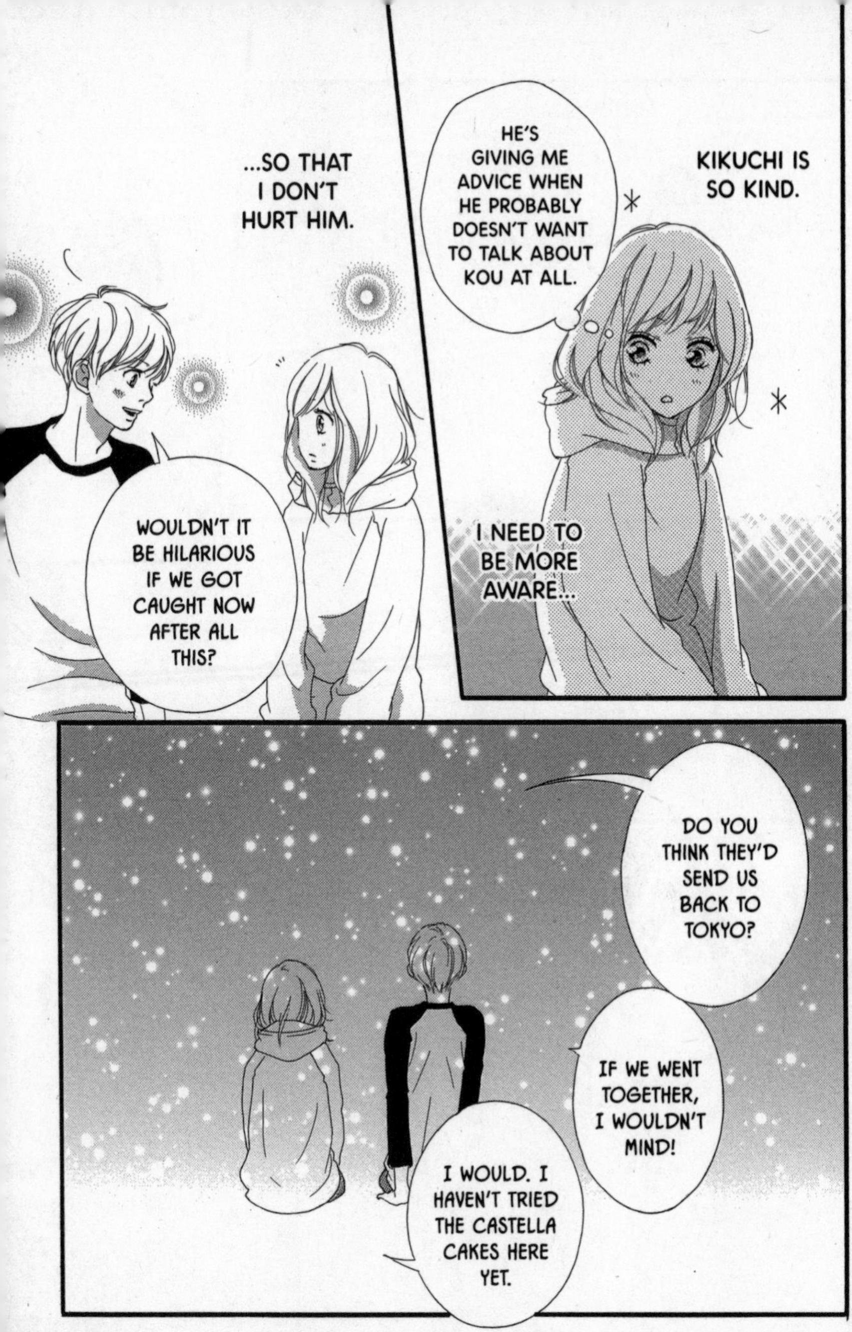
KIKUCHI IS SO KIND.
HE'S GIVING ME ADVICE WHEN HE PROBABLY DOESN'T WANT TO TALK ABOUT KOU AT ALL.
I NEED TO BE MORE AWARE...
...SO THAT I DON'T HURT HIM.
WOULDN'T IT BE HILARIOUS IF WE GOT CAUGHT NOW AFTER ALL THIS?
DO YOU THINK THEY'D SEND US BACK TO TOKYO?
IF WE WENT TOGETHER, I WOULDN'T MIND!
I WOULD. I HAVEN'T TRIED THE CASTELLA CAKES HERE YET.

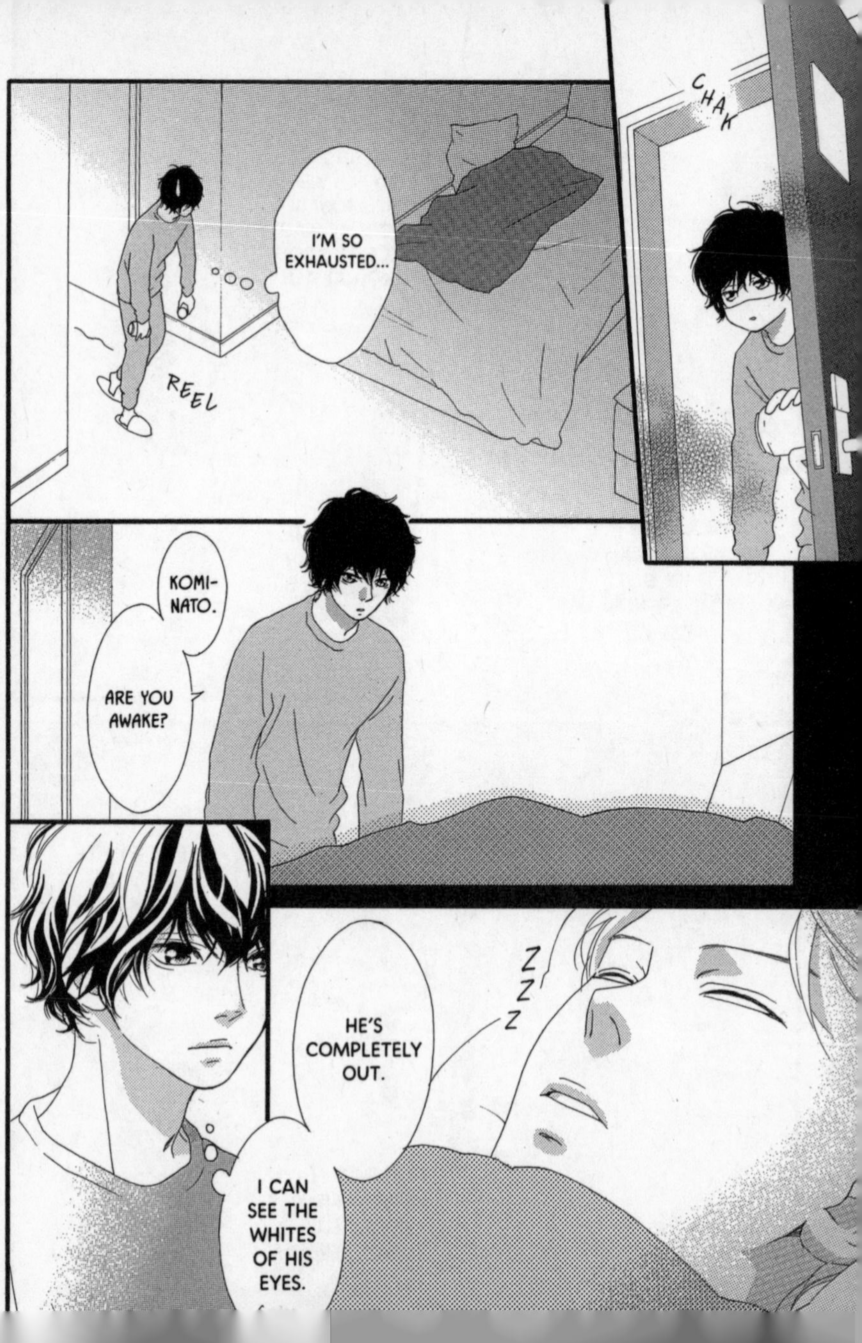
CHAK
REEL
I'M SO EXHAUSTED...
KOMI-NATO.
ARE YOU AWAKE?
ZZZ
HE'S COMPLETELY OUT.
I CAN SEE THE WHITES OF HIS EYES.

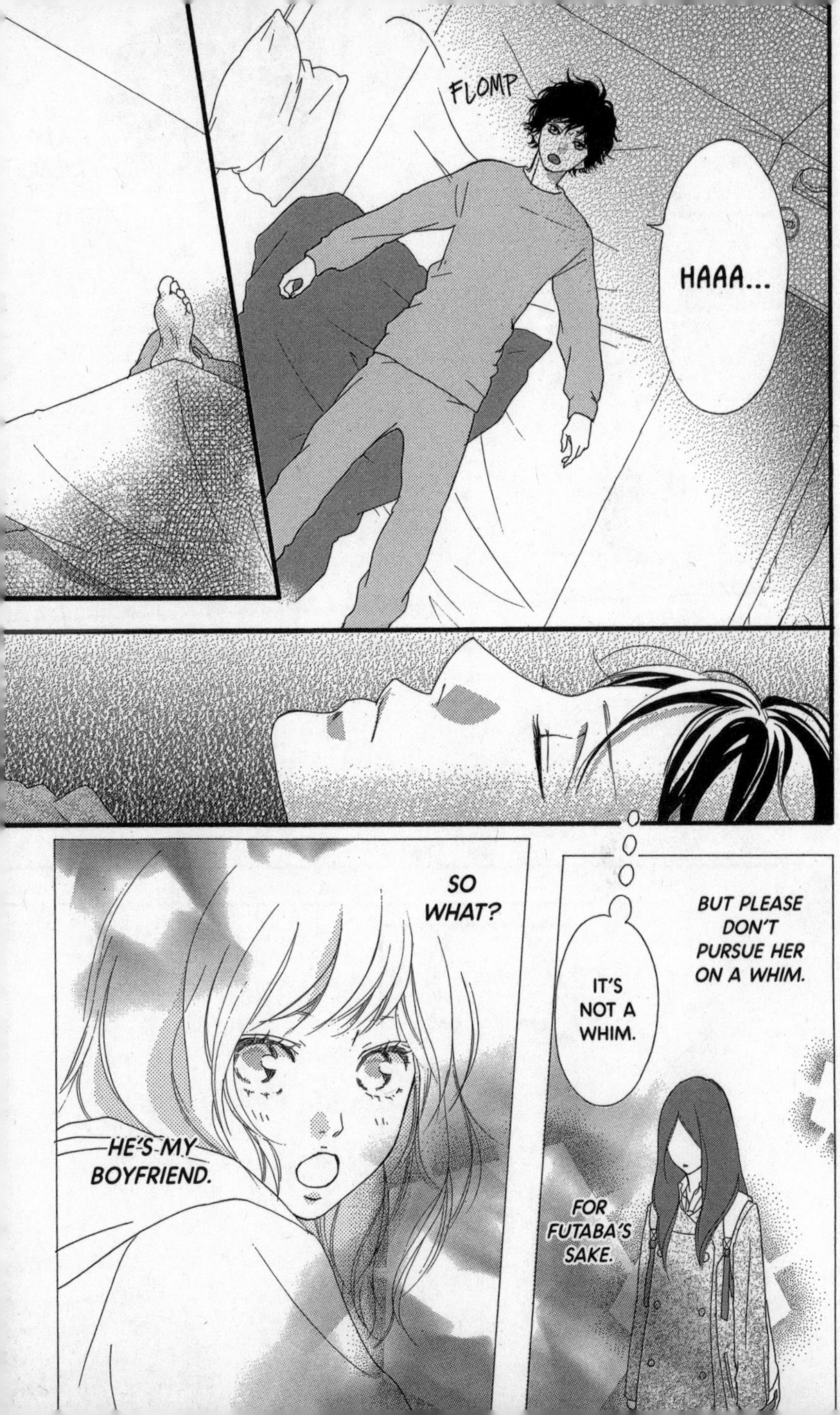
FLOMP
HAAA...
BUT PLEASE DON'T PURSUE HER ON A WHIM.
IT'S NOT A WHIM.
FOR FUTABA'S SAKE.
SO WHAT?
HE'S MY BOYFRIEND.

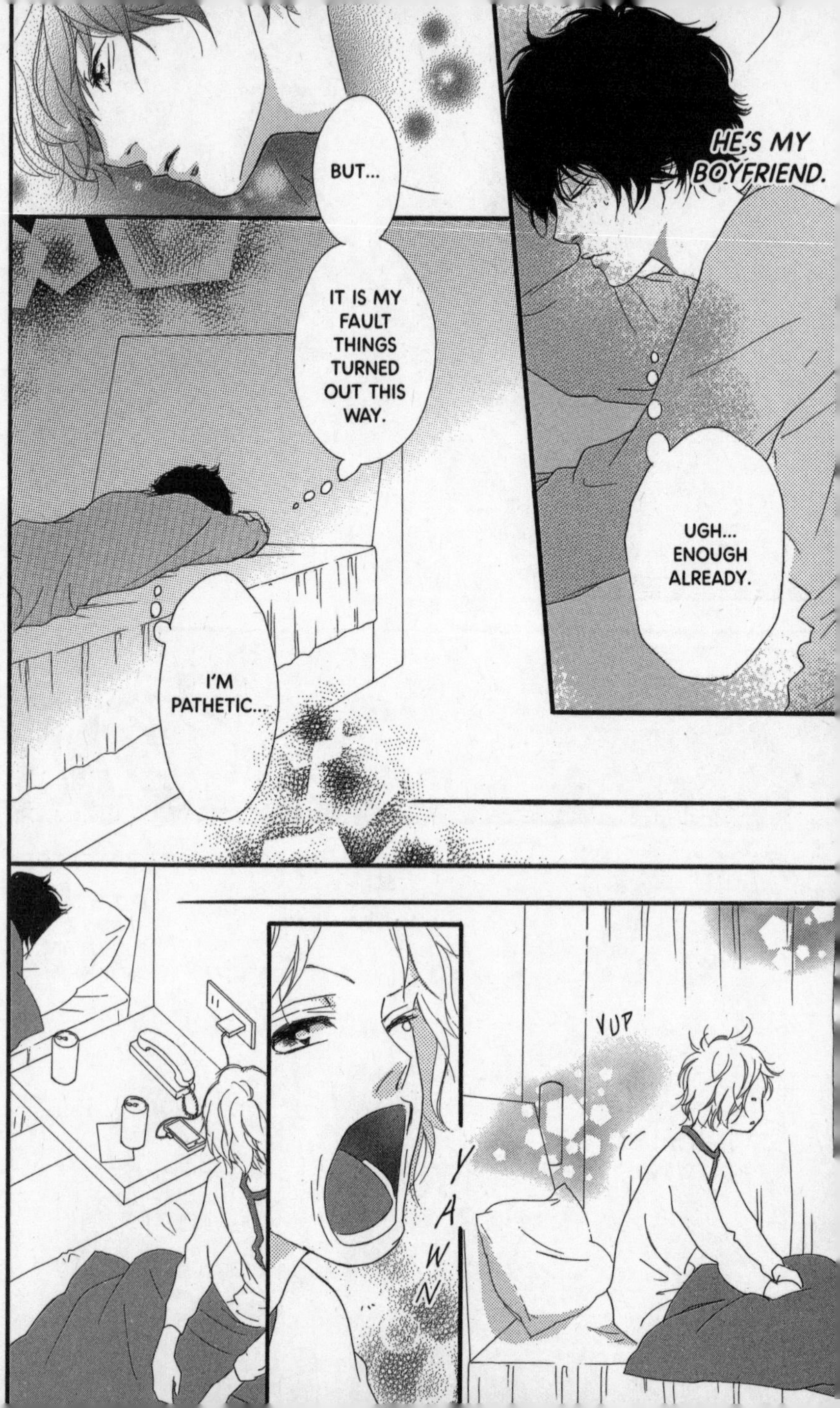
HE'S MY BOYFRIEND.
UGH... ENOUGH ALREADY.
BUT...
IT IS MY FAULT THINGS TURNED OUT THIS WAY.
I'M PATHETIC...
VUP
YAWN

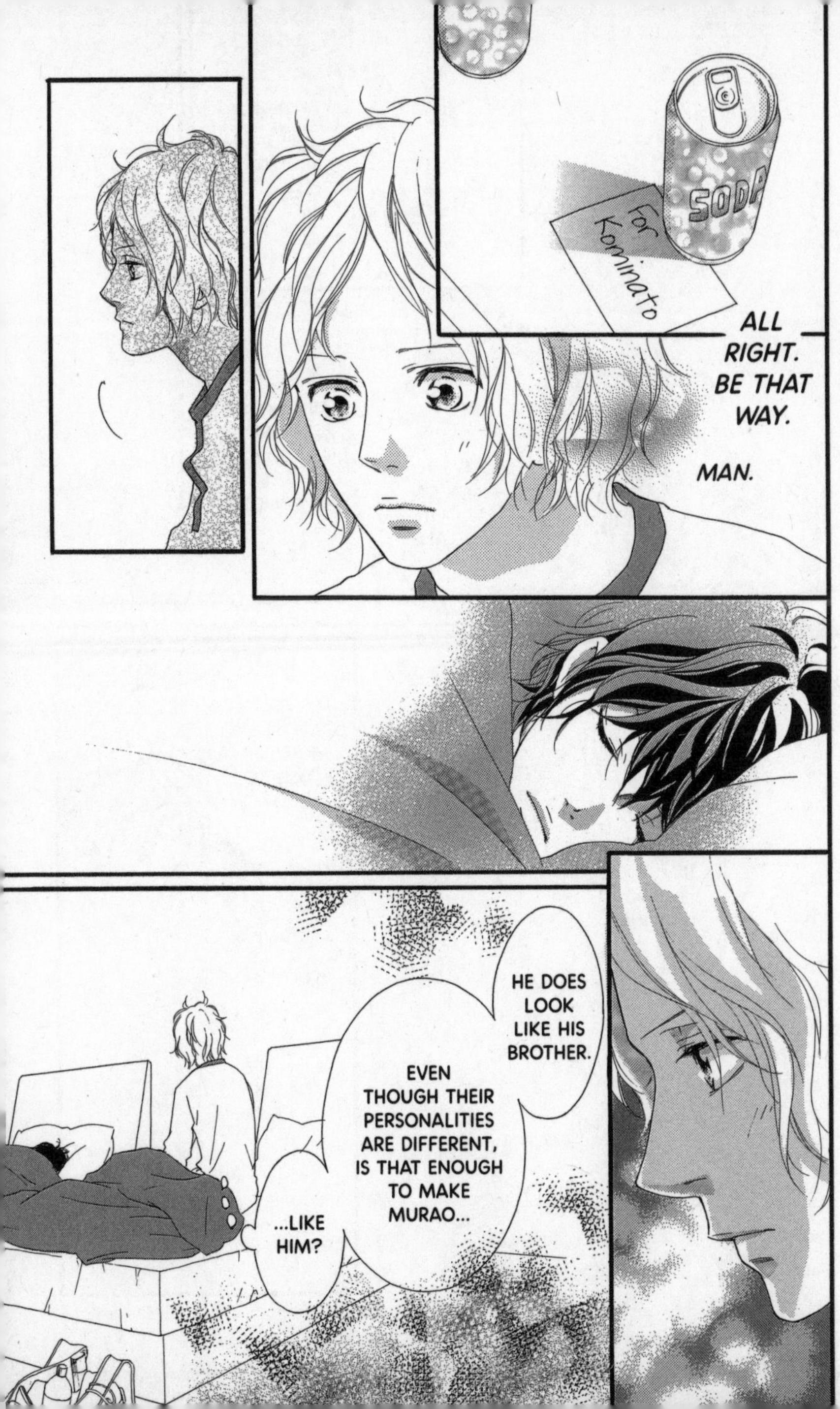
SODA
For Kominato
ALL RIGHT. BE THAT WAY.
MAN.
HE DOES LOOK LIKE HIS BROTHER.
EVEN THOUGH THEIR PERSONALITIES ARE DIFFERENT, IS THAT ENOUGH TO MAKE MURAO...
...LIKE HIM?

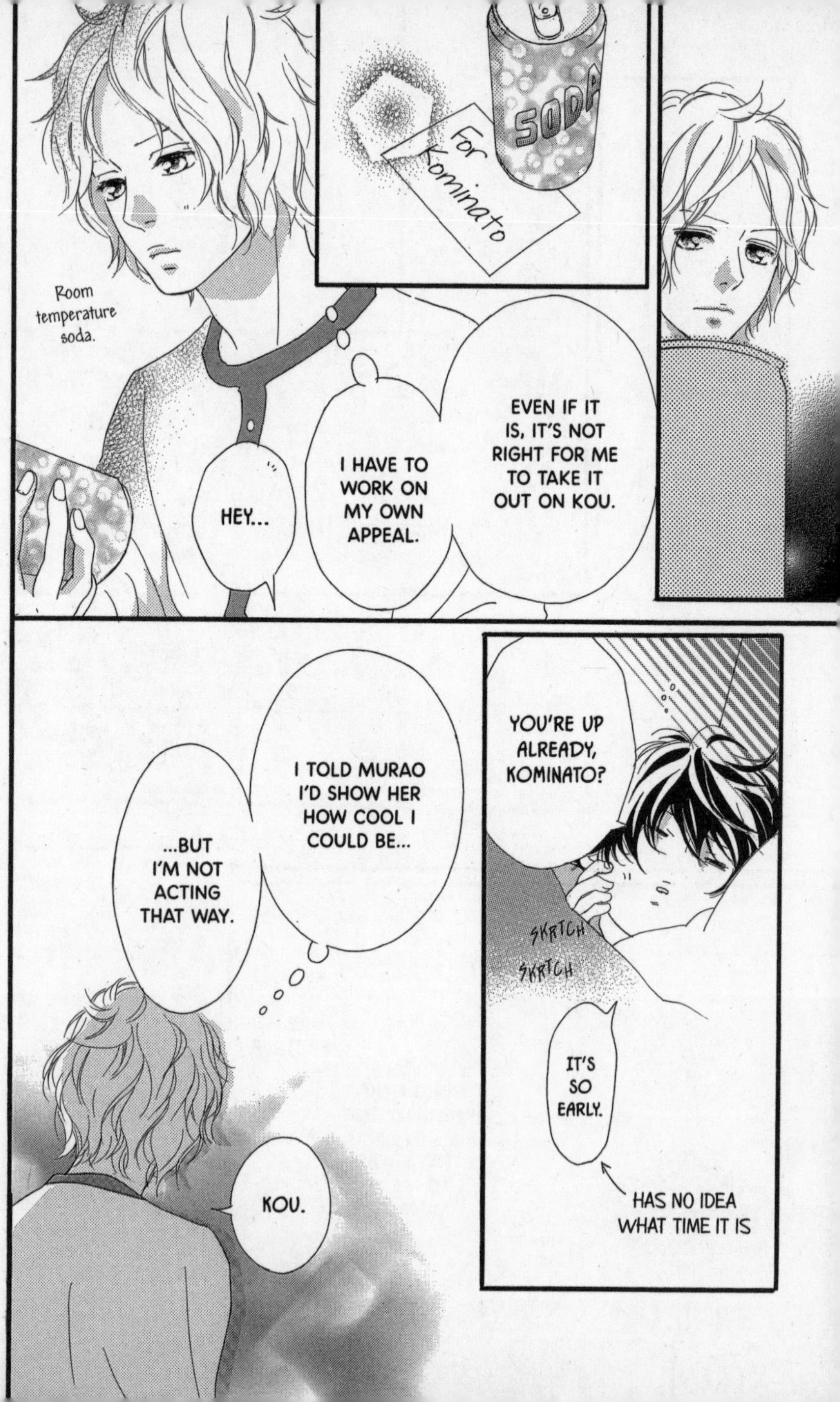
SODA
For Kominato
Room temperature soda.
EVEN IF IT IS, IT'S NOT RIGHT FOR ME TO TAKE IT OUT ON KOU.
I HAVE TO WORK ON MY OWN APPEAL.
HEY...
YOU'RE UP ALREADY, KOMINATO?
SKRTCH
SKRTCH
IT'S SO EARLY.
HAS NO IDEA WHAT TIME IT IS
I TOLD MURAO I'D SHOW HER HOW COOL I COULD BE...
...BUT I'M NOT ACTING THAT WAY.
KOU.

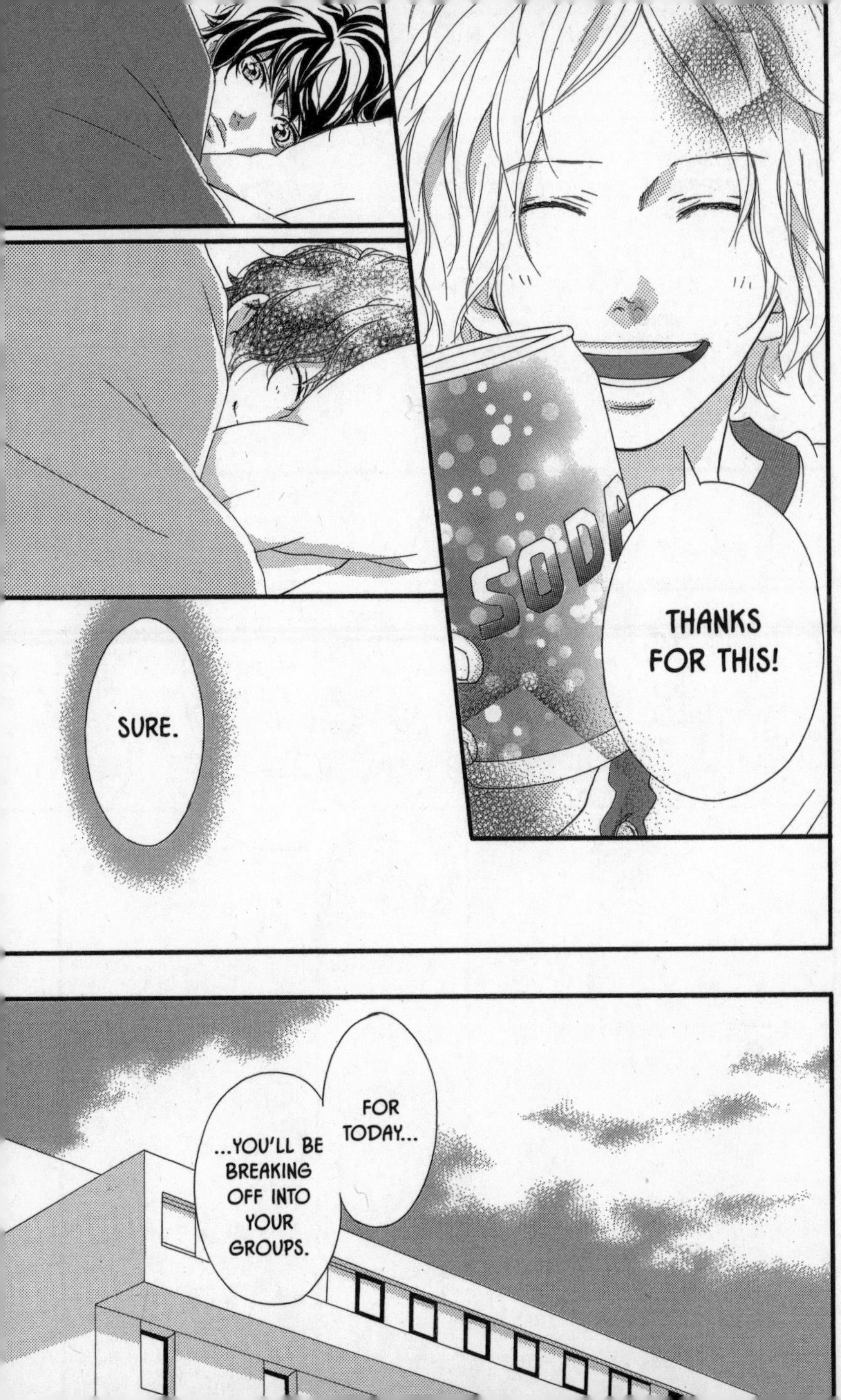
SODA
THANKS FOR THIS!
SURE.
FOR TODAY...
...YOU'LL BE BREAKING OFF INTO YOUR GROUPS.

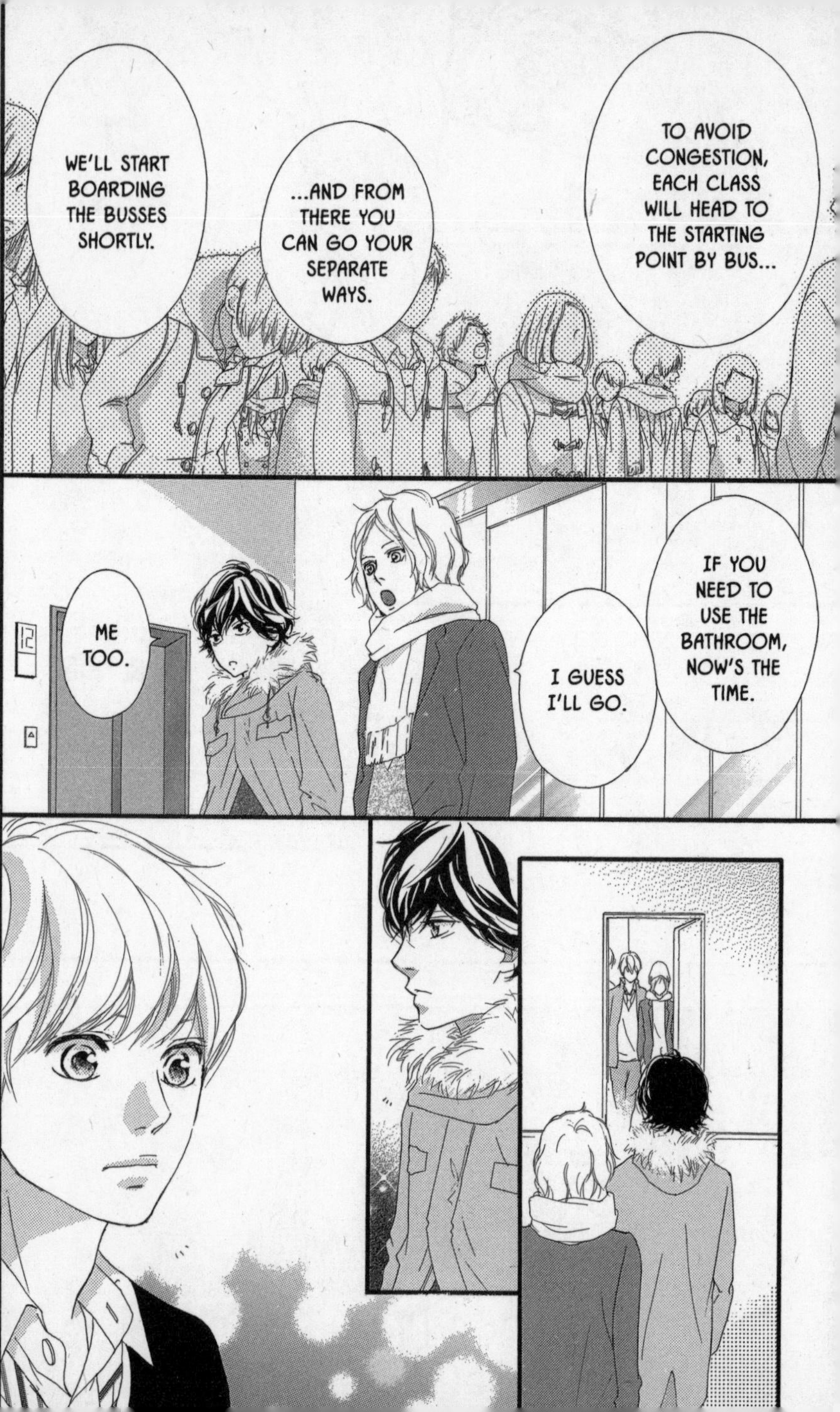
TO AVOID CONGESTION, EACH CLASS WILL HEAD TO THE STARTING POINT BY BUS...
...AND FROM THERE YOU CAN GO YOUR SEPARATE WAYS.
WE'LL START BOARDING THE BUSSES SHORTLY.
IF YOU NEED TO USE THE BATHROOM, NOW'S THE TIME.
I GUESS I'LL GO.
ME TOO.

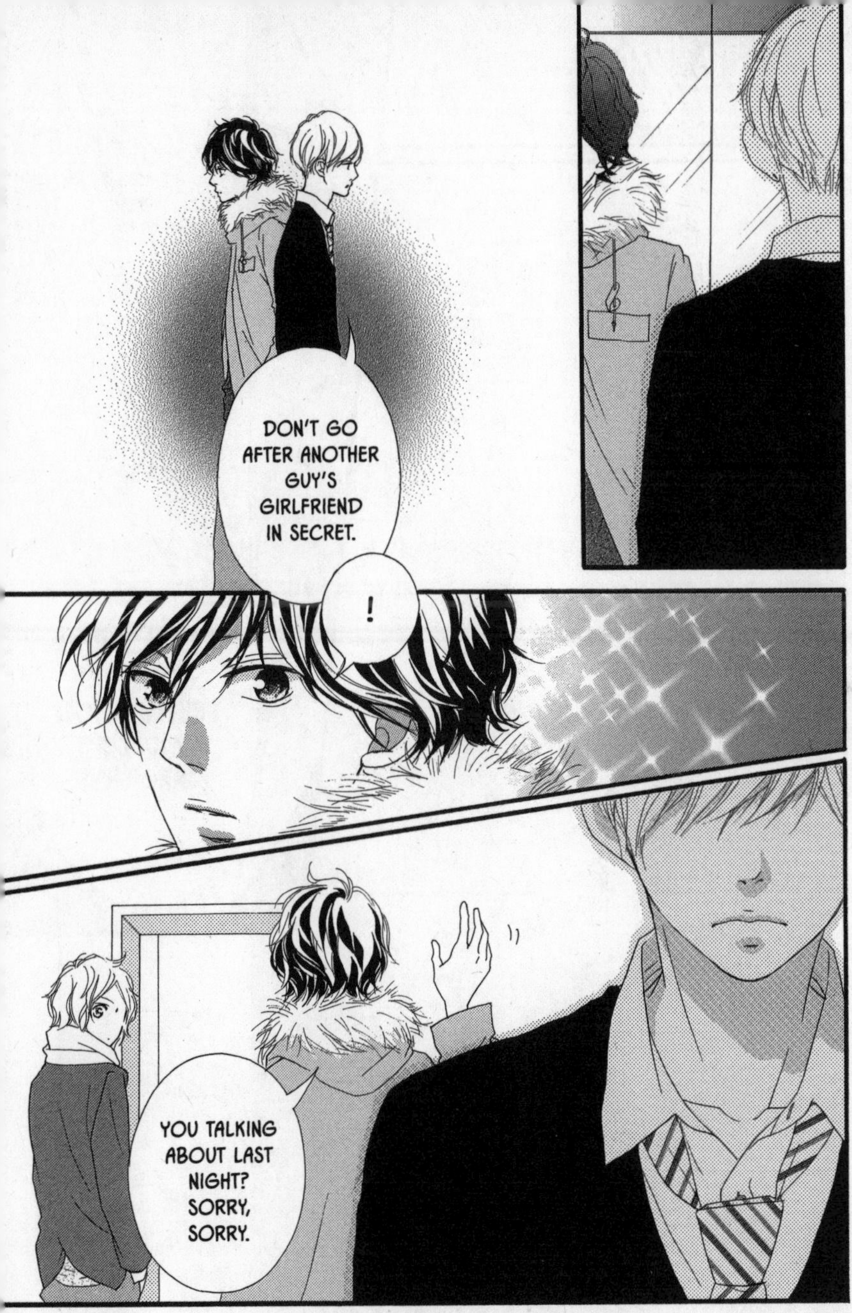
DON'T GO AFTER ANOTHER GUY'S GIRLFRIEND IN SECRET.
!
YOU TALKING ABOUT LAST NIGHT?
SORRY, SORRY.

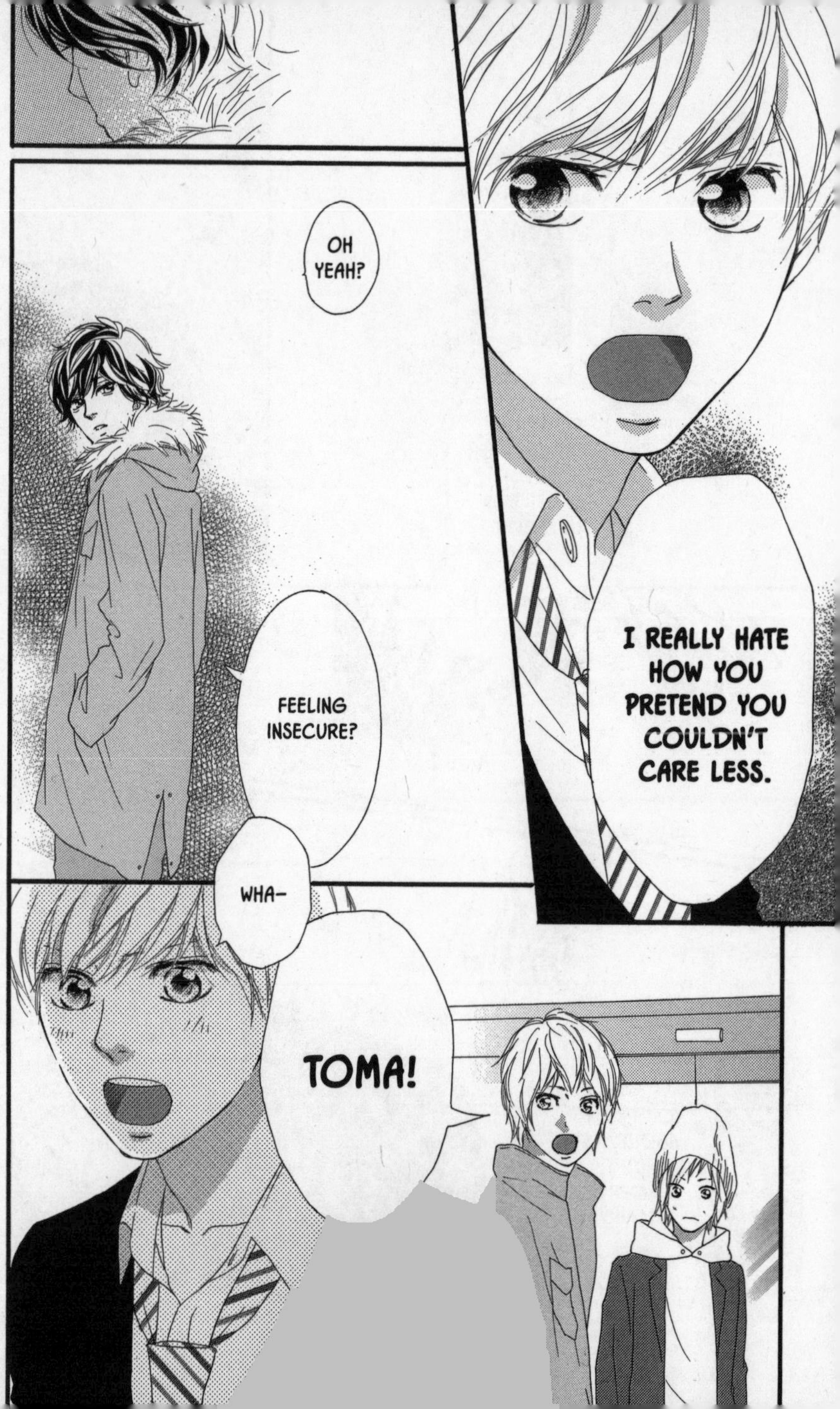
I REALLY HATE HOW YOU PRETEND YOU COULDN'T CARE LESS.
OH YEAH?
FEELING INSECURE?
WHA-
TOMA!

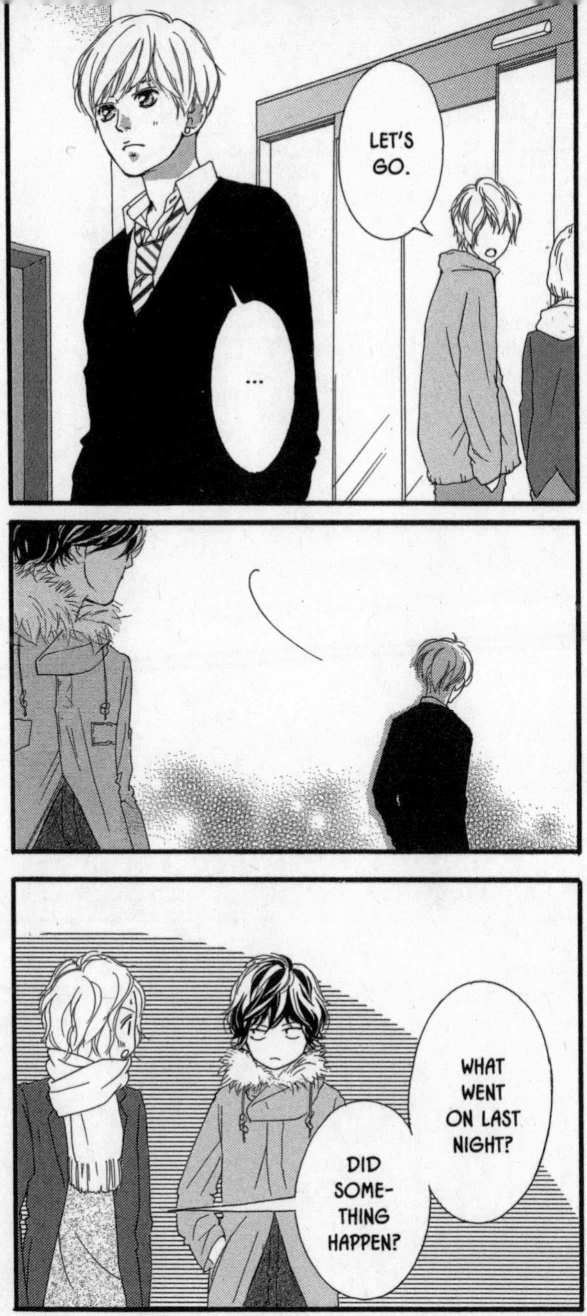
LET'S GO.
...
WHAT WENT ON LAST NIGHT?
DID SOME-THING HAPPEN?

I visited the editorial department to do some filming for a DVD bonus gift in *Betsuma* magazine. Aruko was in town filming that day too, and I was excited to see her for the first time in ages! After we finished, I didn't want to just say goodbye and leave, so I kept chatting with Aruko, and then we went out for drinks. I don't really remember what we talked about (not that I was drunk—I just don't think it was anything important), but we were having so much fun that we didn't want to go home. We ended up hanging out until morning. It made me think fondly of the days when we used to hang out regularly. We've known each other for over ten years now. I've always loved Aruko—she's so much fun.

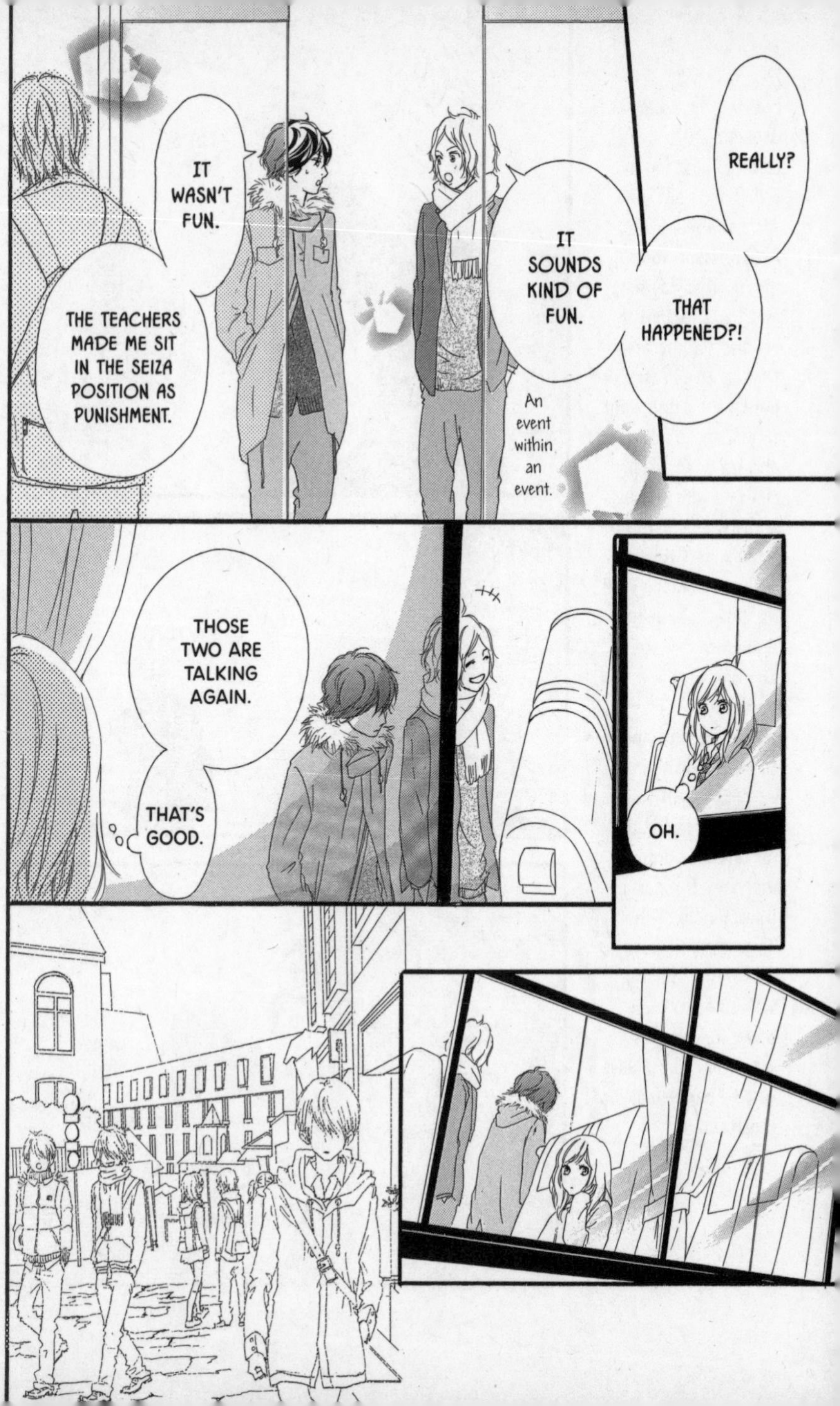
REALLY?
THAT HAPPENED?!
IT SOUNDS KIND OF FUN.
An event within an event.
IT WASN'T FUN.
THE TEACHERS MADE ME SIT IN THE SEIZA POSITION AS PUNISHMENT.
OH.
THOSE TWO ARE TALKING AGAIN.
THAT'S GOOD.

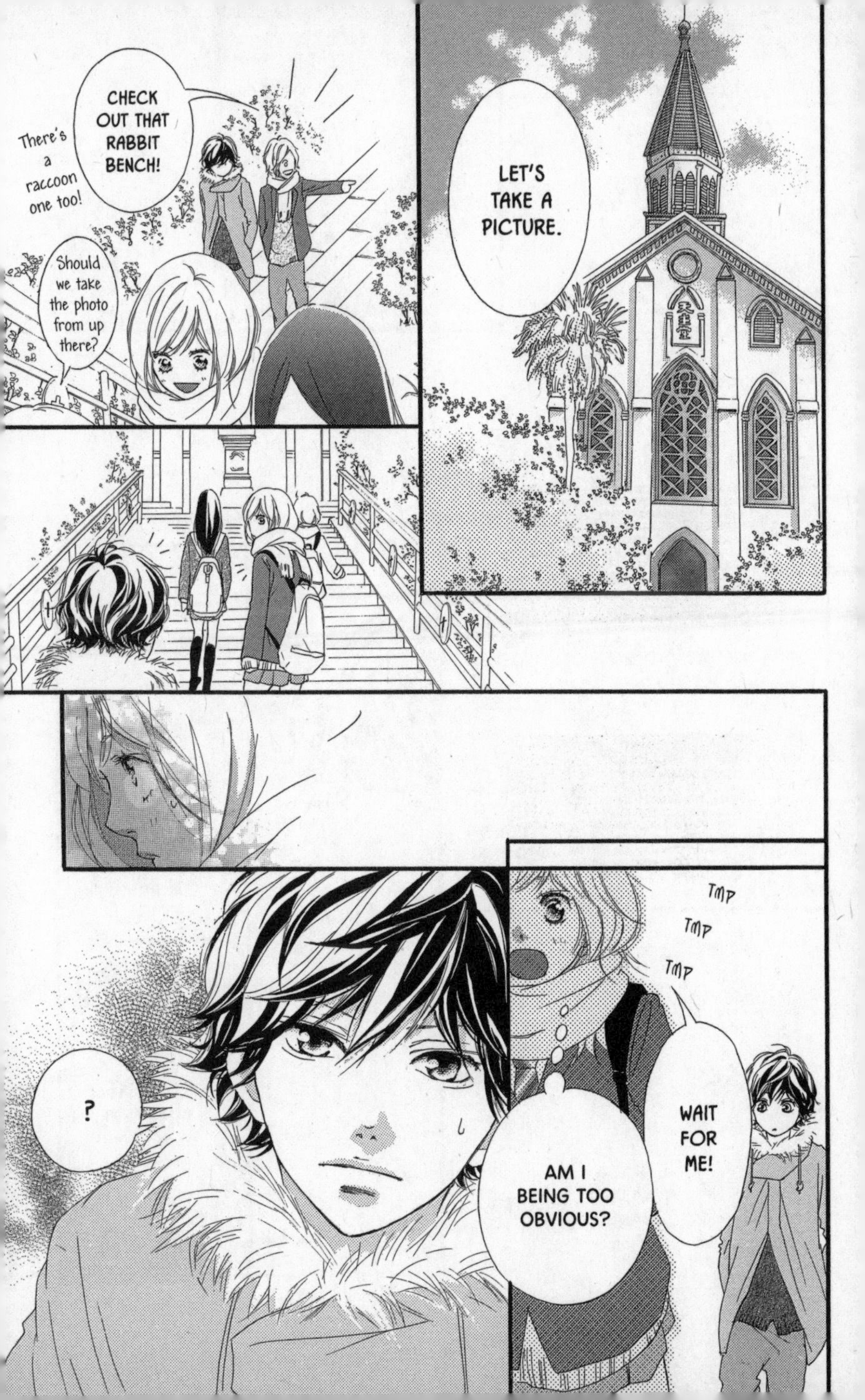
LET'S TAKE A PICTURE.
CHECK OUT THAT RABBIT BENCH!
There's a raccoon one too!
Should we take the photo from up there?
TMP
TMP
TMP
WAIT FOR ME!
AM I BEING TOO OBVIOUS?
?

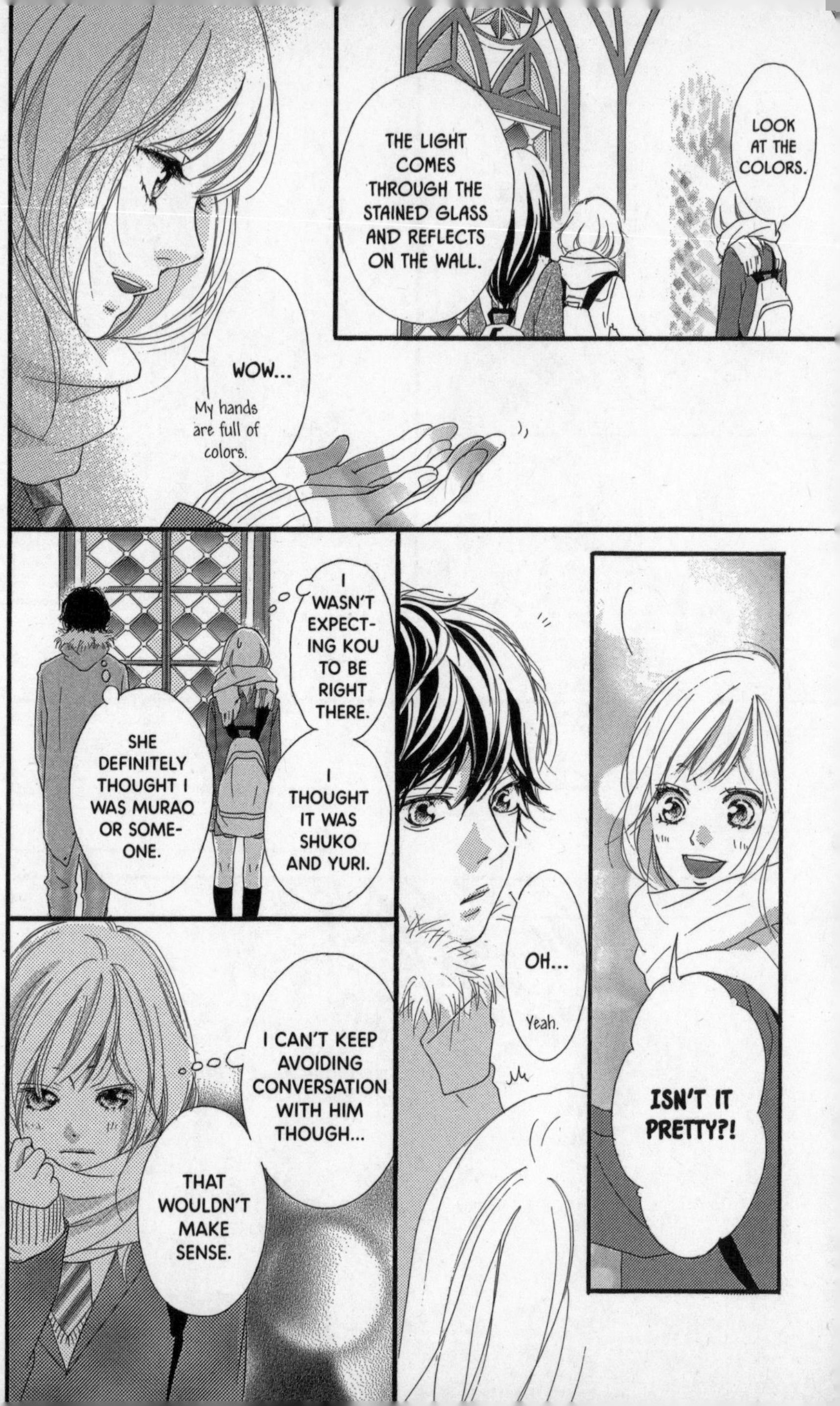
LOOK AT THE COLORS.
THE LIGHT COMES THROUGH THE STAINED GLASS AND REFLECTS ON THE WALL.
WOW...
My hands are full of colors.
ISN'T IT PRETTY?!
OH...
Yeah.
I WASN'T EXPECT-ING KOU TO BE RIGHT THERE.
I THOUGHT IT WAS SHUKO AND YURI.
SHE DEFINITELY THOUGHT I WAS MURAO OR SOME-ONE.
I CAN'T KEEP AVOIDING CONVERSATION WITH HIM THOUGH...
THAT WOULDN'T MAKE SENSE.

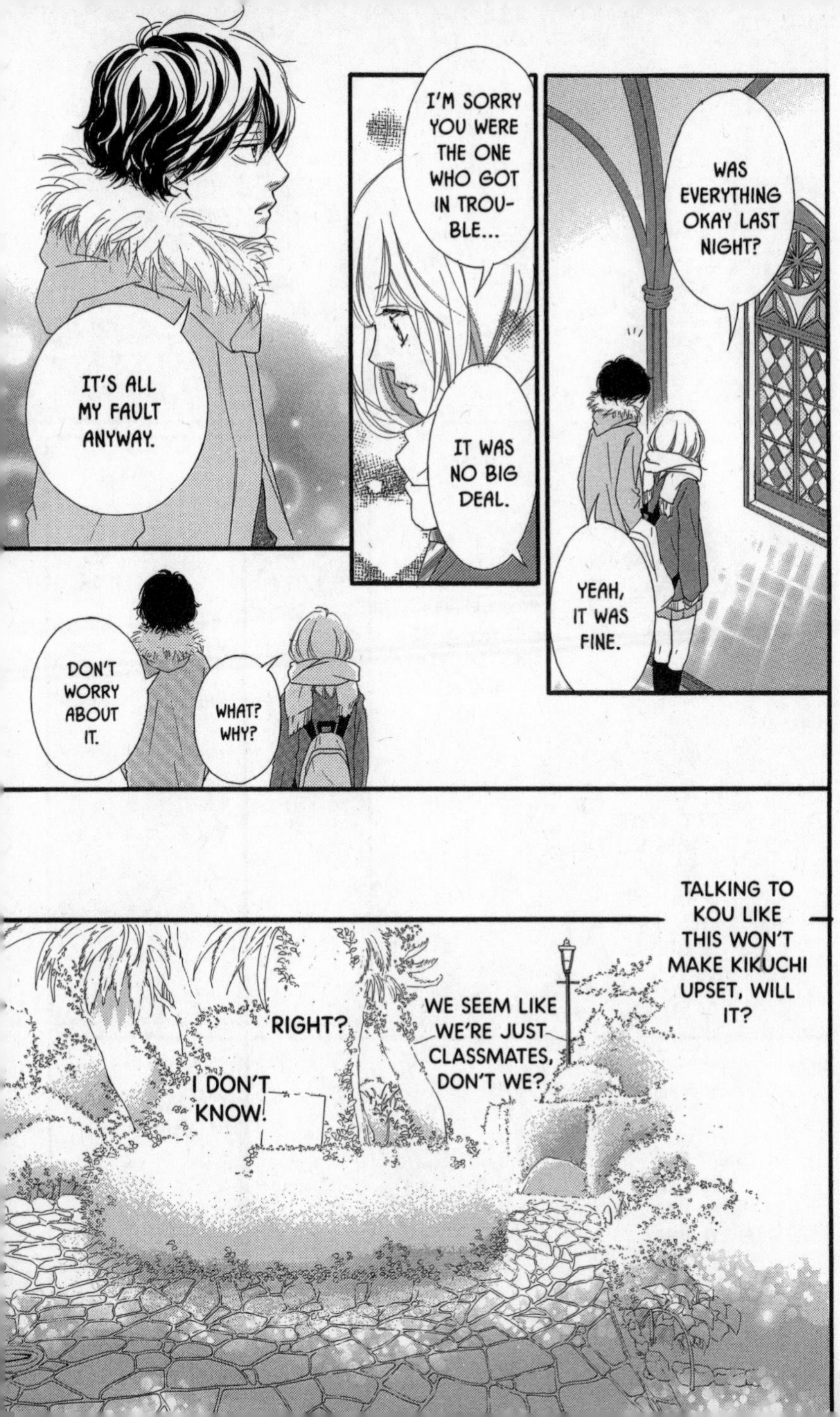
WAS EVERYTHING OKAY LAST NIGHT?
YEAH, IT WAS FINE.
I'M SORRY YOU WERE THE ONE WHO GOT IN TROU-BLE...
IT WAS NO BIG DEAL.
IT'S ALL MY FAULT ANYWAY.
WHAT? WHY?
DON'T WORRY ABOUT IT.
TALKING TO KOU LIKE THIS WON'T MAKE KIKUCHI UPSET, WILL IT?
WE SEEM LIKE WE'RE JUST CLASSMATES, DON'T WE?
RIGHT?
I DON'T KNOW.

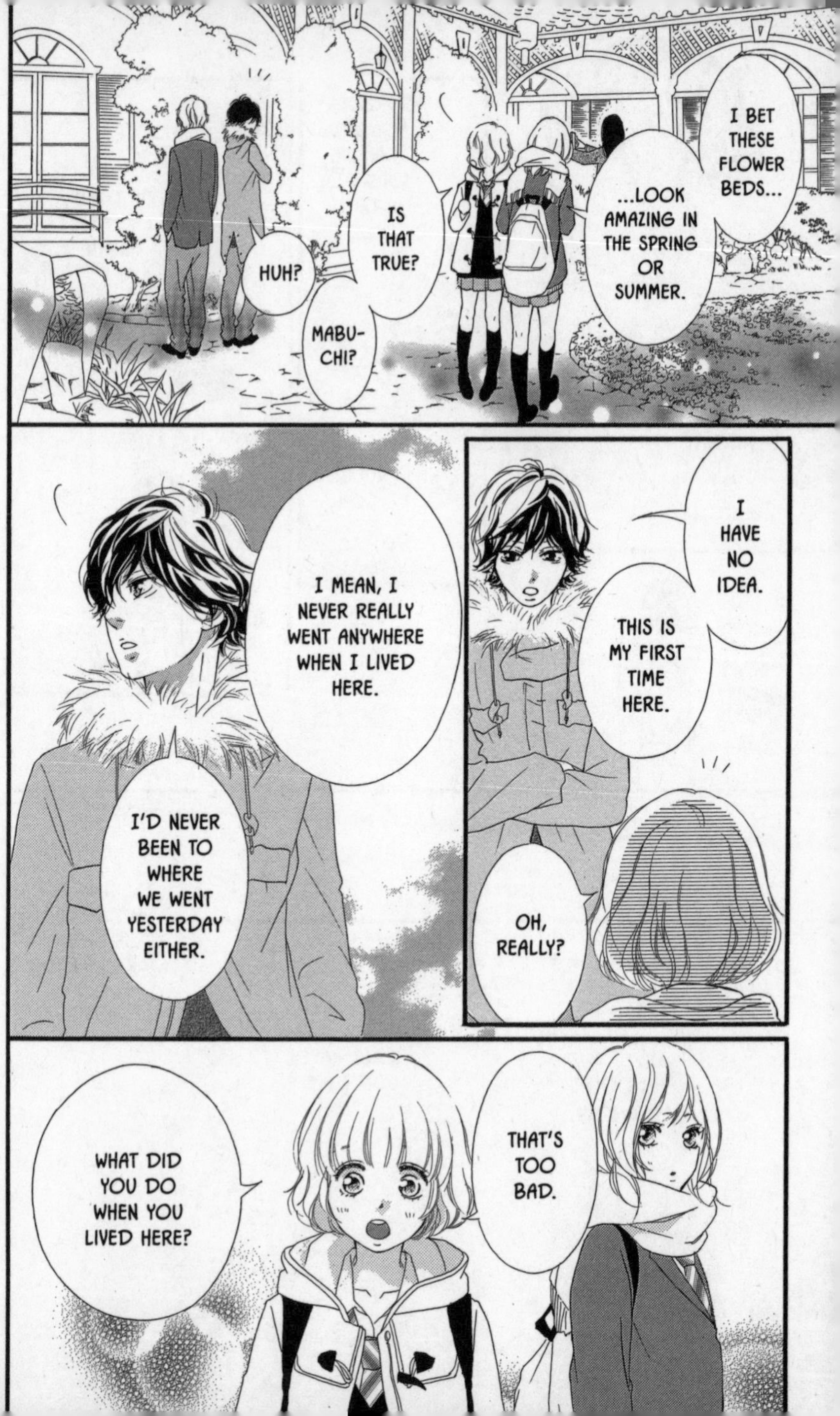
I BET THESE FLOWER BEDS...
...LOOK AMAZING IN THE SPRING OR SUMMER.
IS THAT TRUE?
MABU-CHI?
HUH?
I HAVE NO IDEA.
THIS IS MY FIRST TIME HERE.
OH, REALLY?
I MEAN, I NEVER REALLY WENT ANYWHERE WHEN I LIVED HERE.
I'D NEVER BEEN TO WHERE WE WENT YESTERDAY EITHER.
THAT'S TOO BAD.
WHAT DID YOU DO WHEN YOU LIVED HERE?

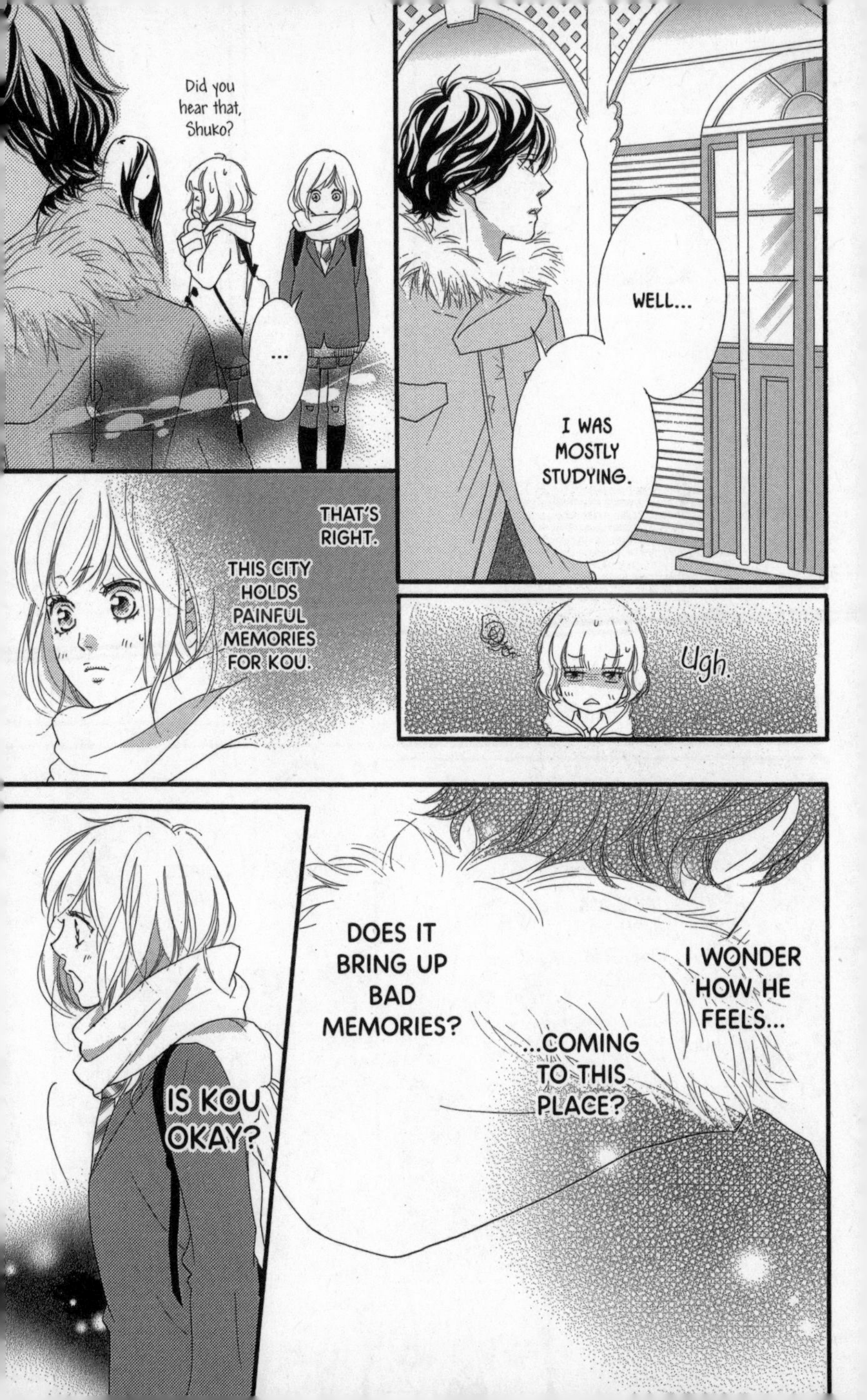
WELL...
I WAS MOSTLY STUDYING.
Did you hear that, Shuko?
...
Ugh.
THAT'S RIGHT.
THIS CITY HOLDS PAINFUL MEMORIES FOR KOU.
I WONDER HOW HE FEELS...
...COMING TO THIS PLACE?
DOES IT BRING UP BAD MEMORIES?
IS KOU OKAY?

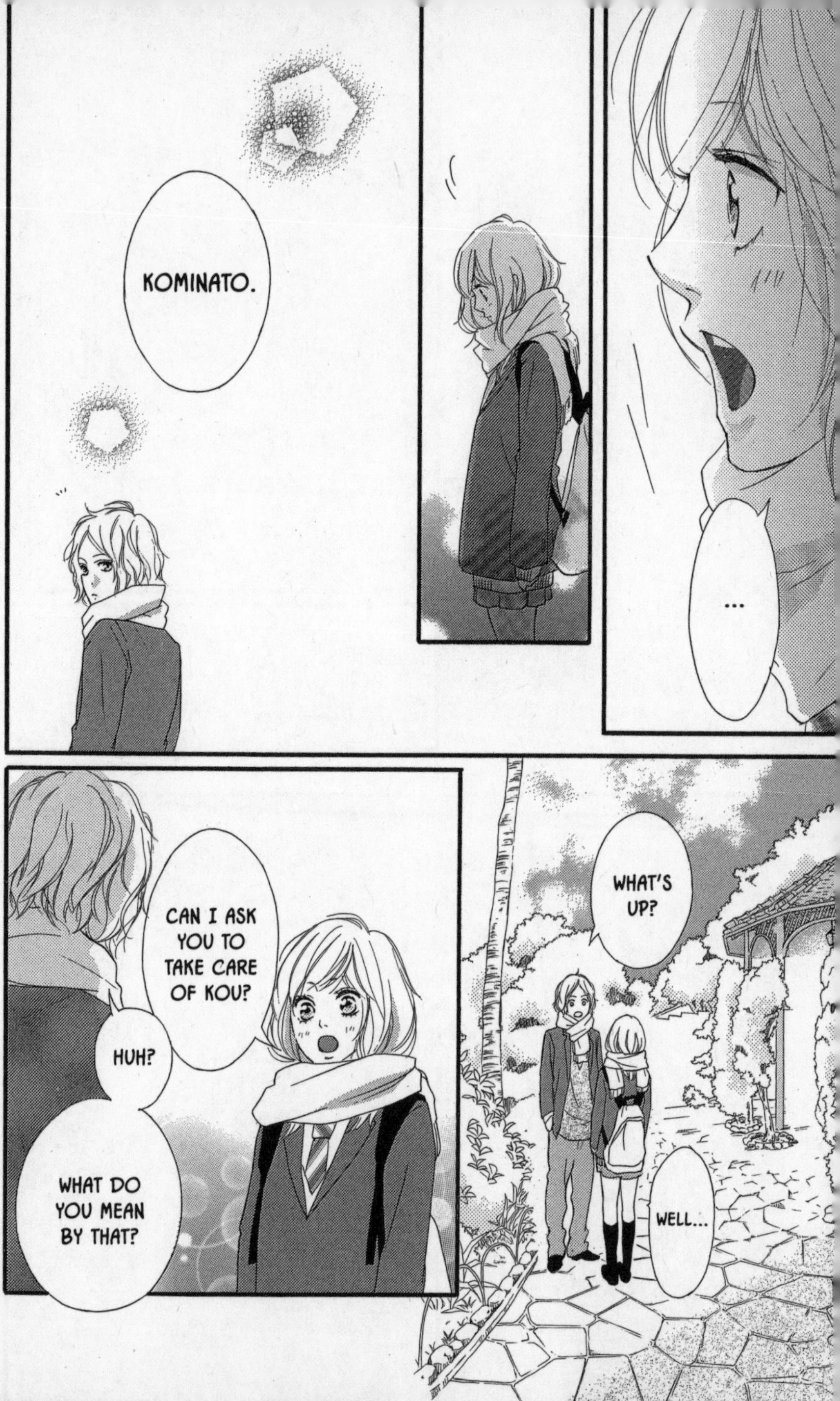
...
KOMINATO.
WHAT'S UP?
WELL...
CAN I ASK YOU TO TAKE CARE OF KOU?
HUH?
WHAT DO YOU MEAN BY THAT?

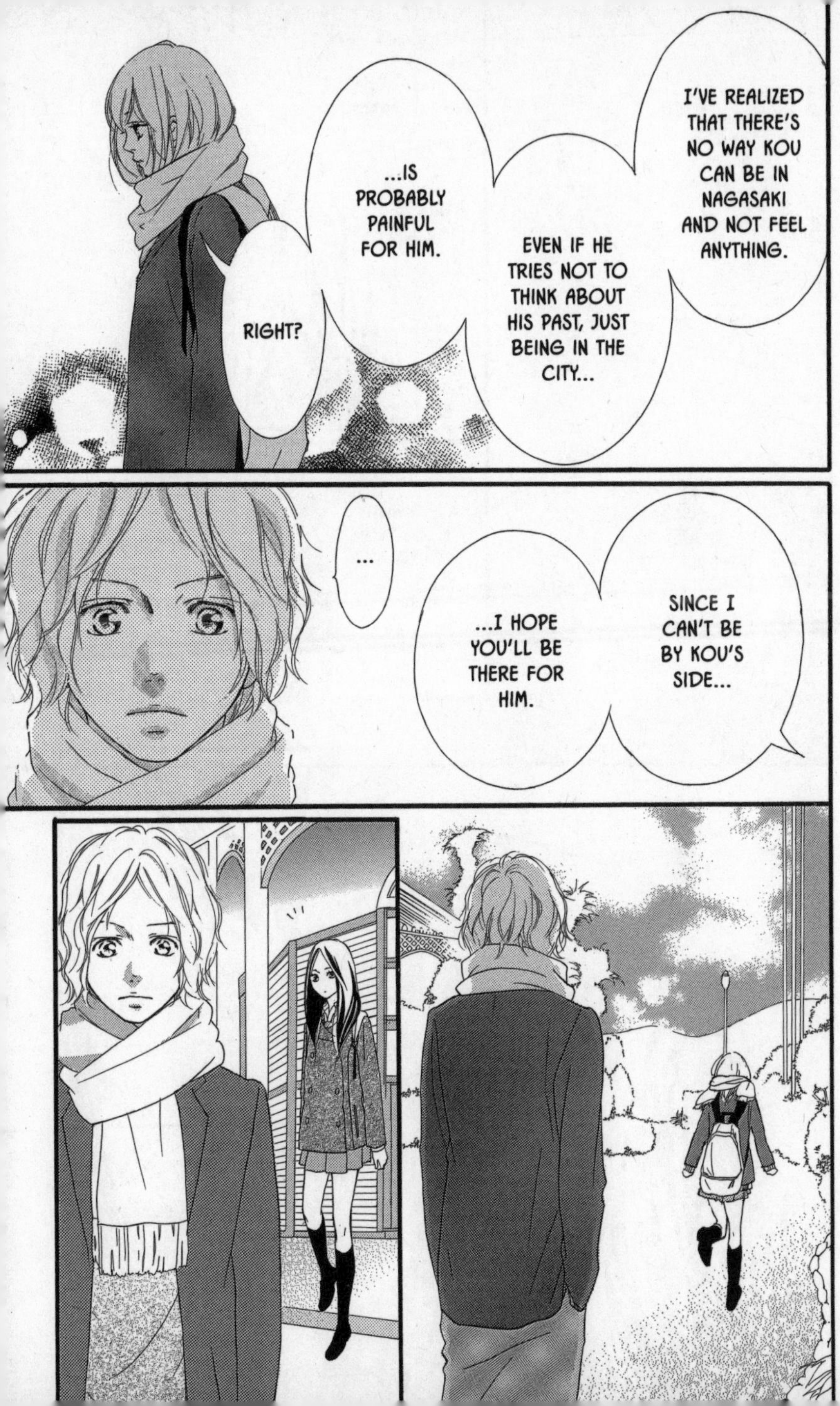
I'VE REALIZED THAT THERE'S NO WAY KOU CAN BE IN NAGASAKI AND NOT FEEL ANYTHING.
EVEN IF HE TRIES NOT TO THINK ABOUT HIS PAST, JUST BEING IN THE CITY...
...IS PROBABLY PAINFUL FOR HIM.
RIGHT?
SINCE I CAN'T BE BY KOU'S SIDE...
...I HOPE YOU'LL BE THERE FOR HIM.
...

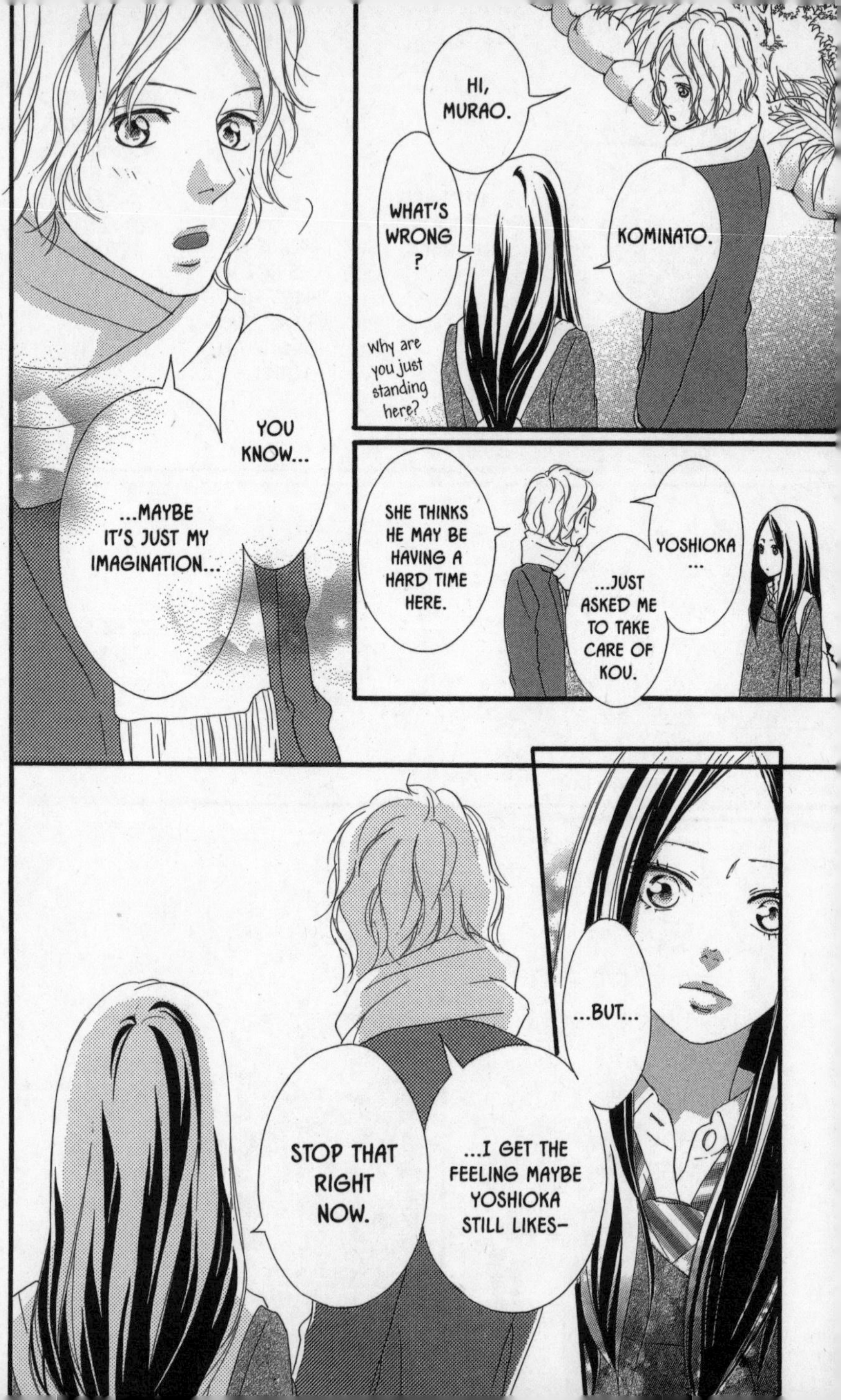
HI, MURAO.
KOMINATO.
WHAT'S WRONG?
Why are you just standing here?
YOSHIOKA...
...JUST ASKED ME TO TAKE CARE OF KOU.
SHE THINKS HE MAY BE HAVING A HARD TIME HERE.
YOU KNOW...
...MAYBE IT'S JUST MY IMAGINATION...
...BUT...
...I GET THE FEELING MAYBE YOSHIOKA STILL LIKES—
STOP THAT RIGHT NOW.

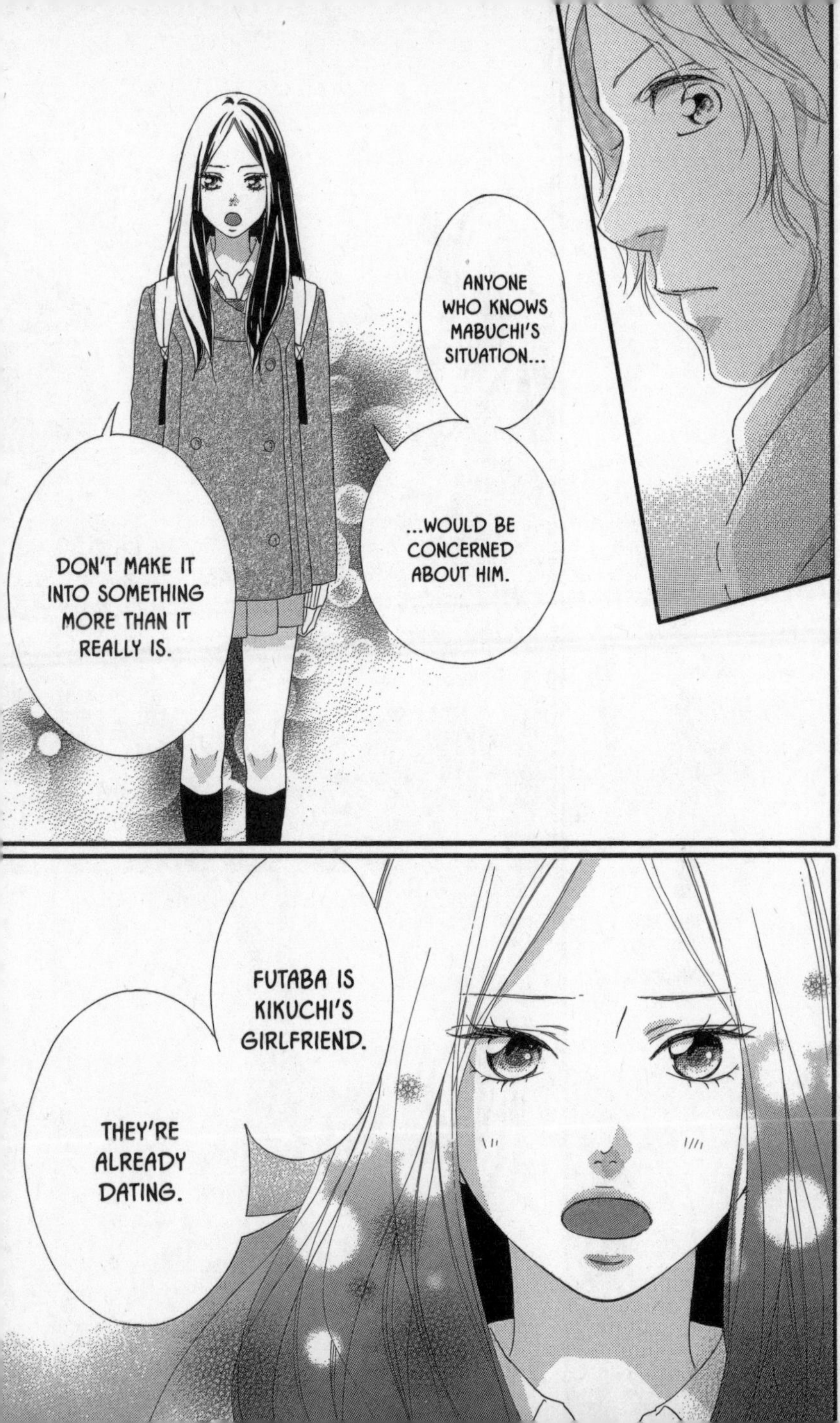
ANYONE WHO KNOWS MABUCHI'S SITUATION...
...WOULD BE CONCERNED ABOUT HIM.
DON'T MAKE IT INTO SOMETHING MORE THAN IT REALLY IS.
FUTABA IS KIKUCHI'S GIRLFRIEND.
THEY'RE ALREADY DATING.

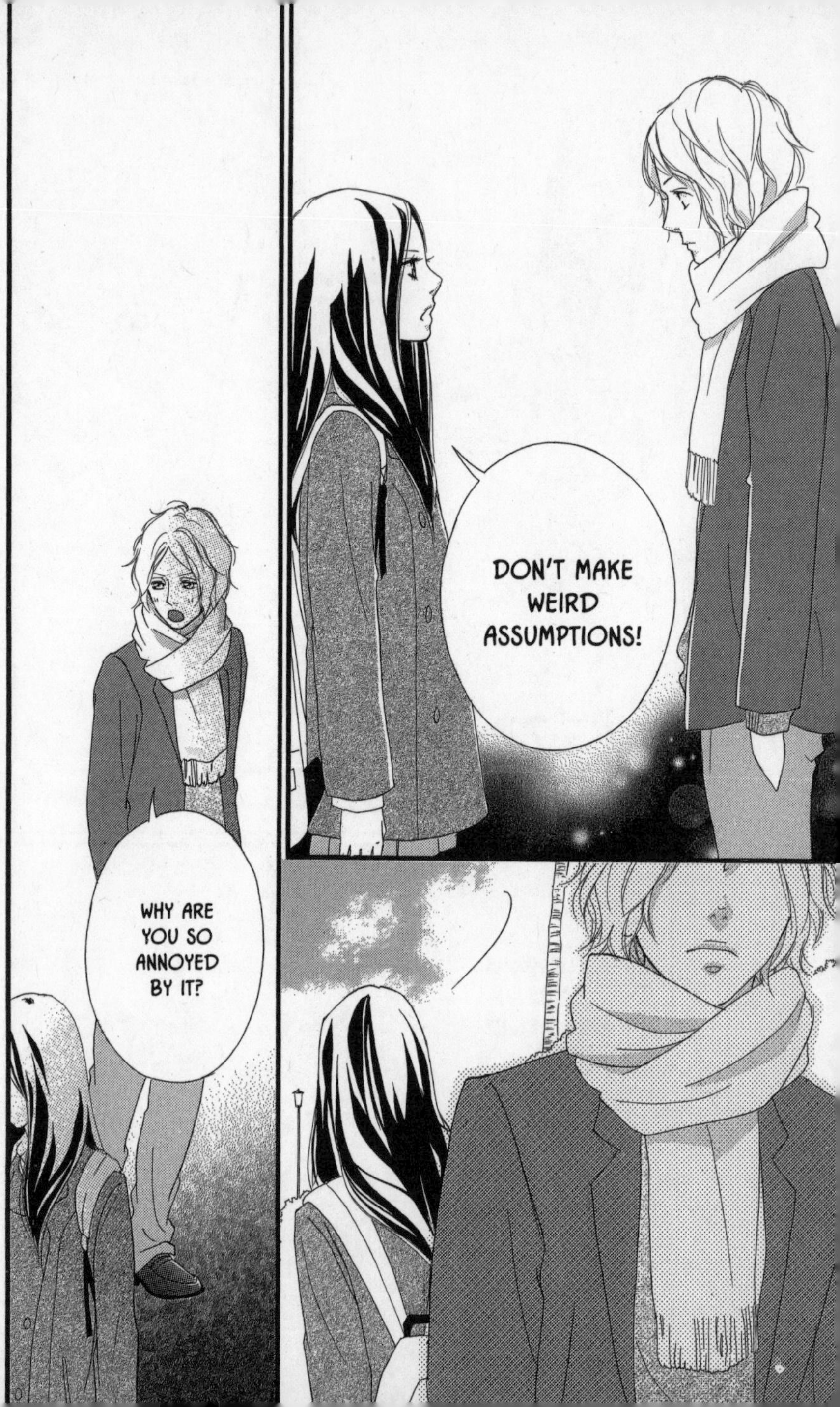
DON'T MAKE WEIRD ASSUMPTIONS!
WHY ARE YOU SO ANNOYED BY IT?

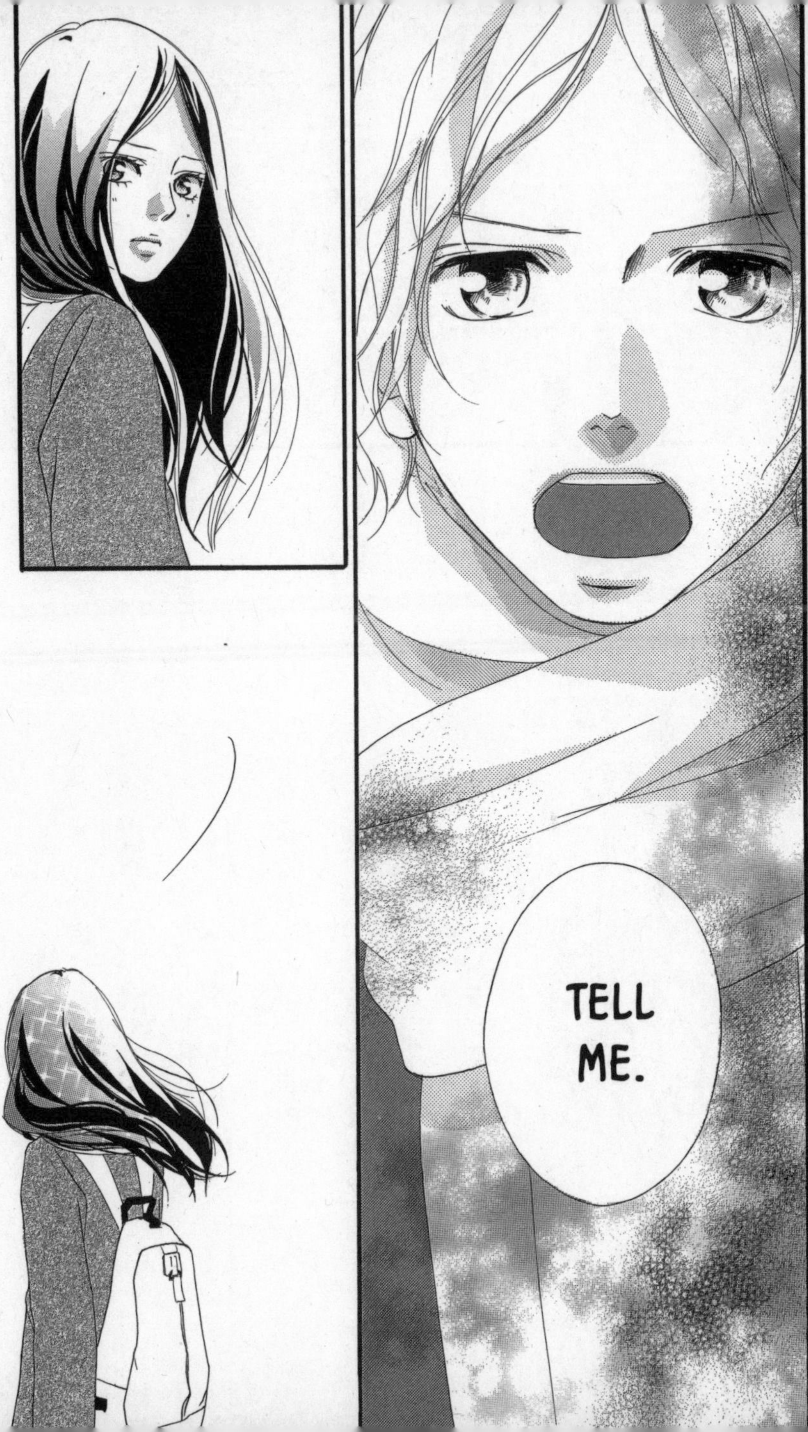
TELL ME.

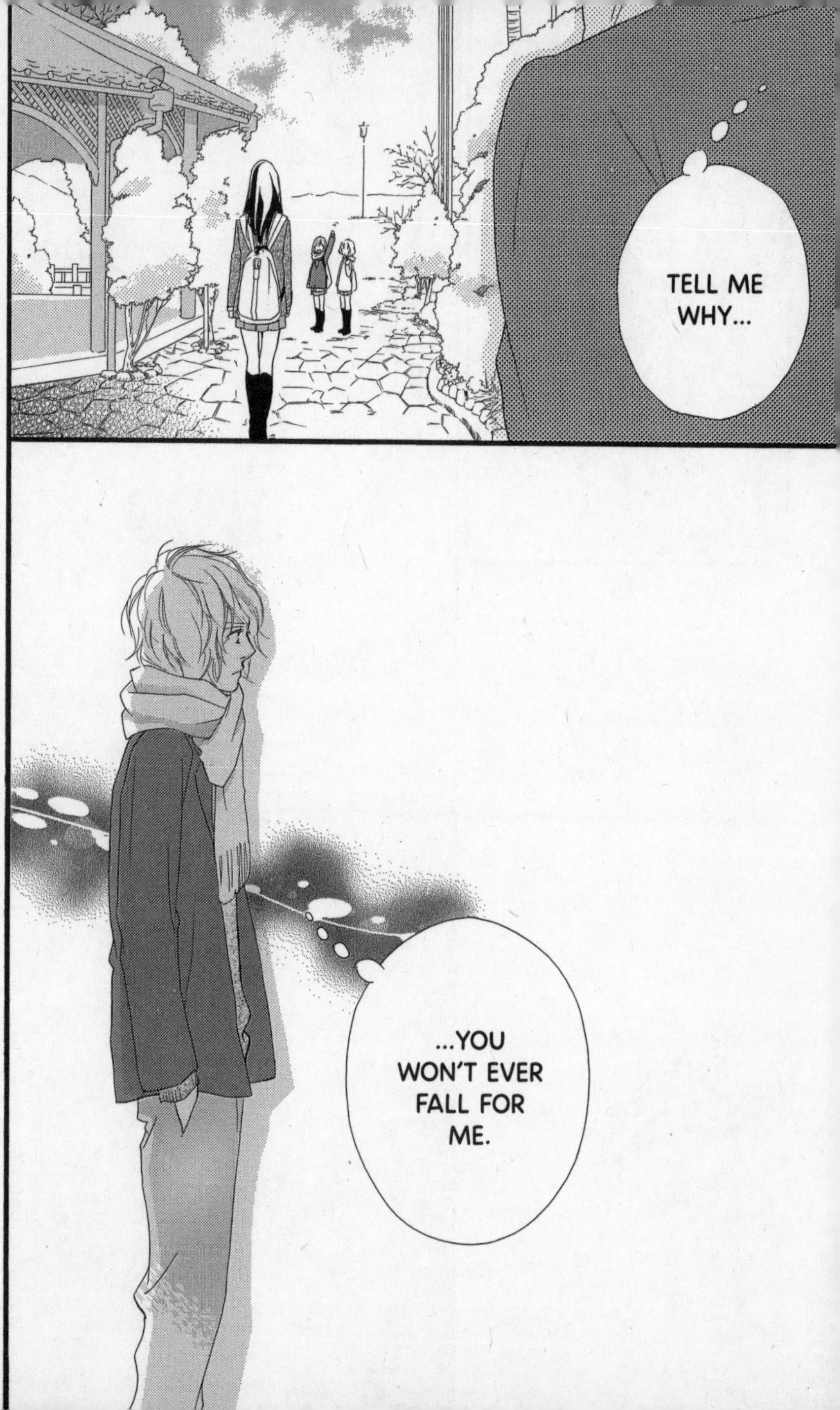
TELL ME WHY...
...YOU WON'T EVER FALL FOR ME.

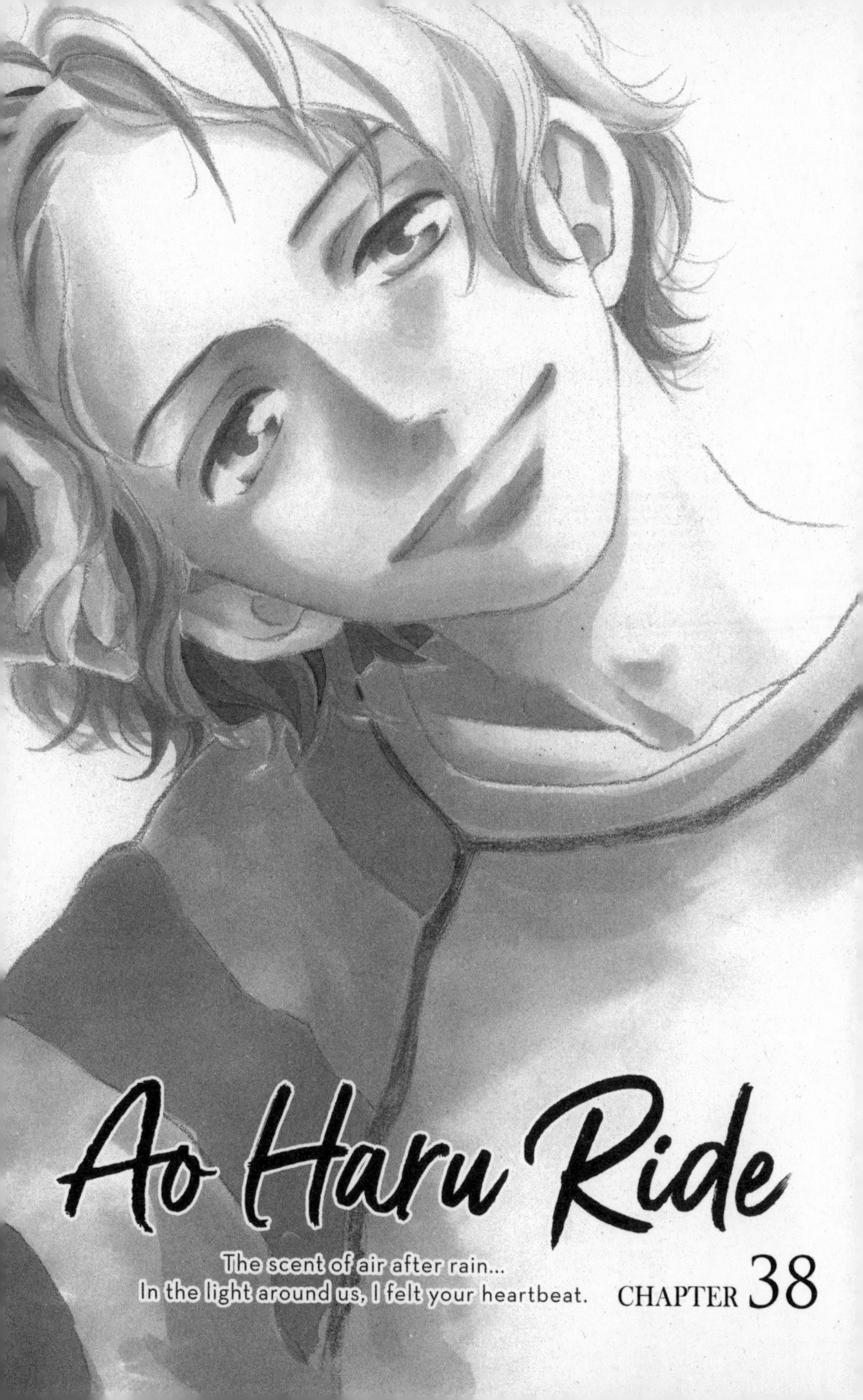
Ao Haru Ride
The scent of air after rain...
In the light around us, I felt your heartbeat.
CHAPTER 38

A while back (pretty far back), I asked readers to send in their ideas for Ramune swag. This was a long time ago.

I personally selected three ideas I thought were cute and fun. The plan was to include the three winning ideas in *Ao Haru Ride*. Of the three, one of them made it into the story pretty quickly and smoothly. I didn't forget about the other two, but the timing never felt right to draw them in, and I've felt guilty knowing I was probably keeping the winners waiting. Well, I am relieved to say that I was finally able to include the last two. To the final two winners, I apologize for the very long delay. I hope you're still following the story...

In case you're interested, these are the featured Ramune swag items: ① Ramune flower mirror (volume 5, chapter 17), ② Ramune hooded sweatshirt (volume 10, chapter 37), ③ Ramune strap (volume 10, chapter 38). I hope you'll look for them!

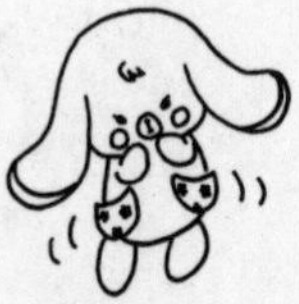

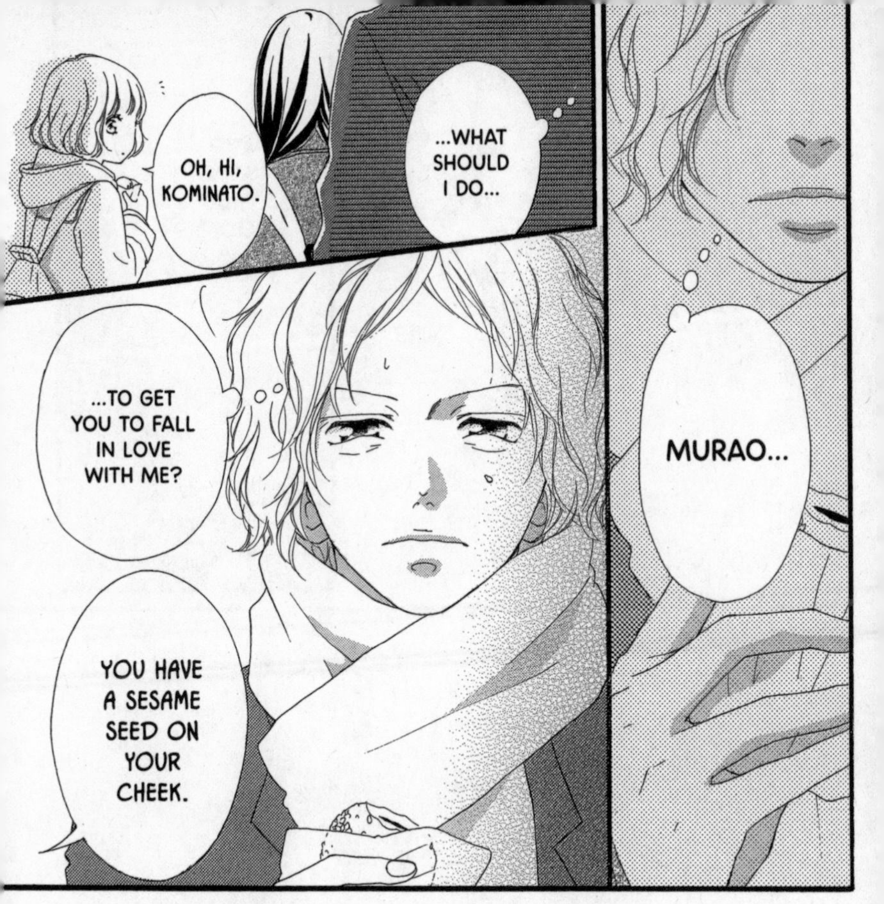
MURAO...
...WHAT SHOULD I DO...
OH, HI, KOMINATO.
...TO GET YOU TO FALL IN LOVE WITH ME?
YOU HAVE A SESAME SEED ON YOUR CHEEK.

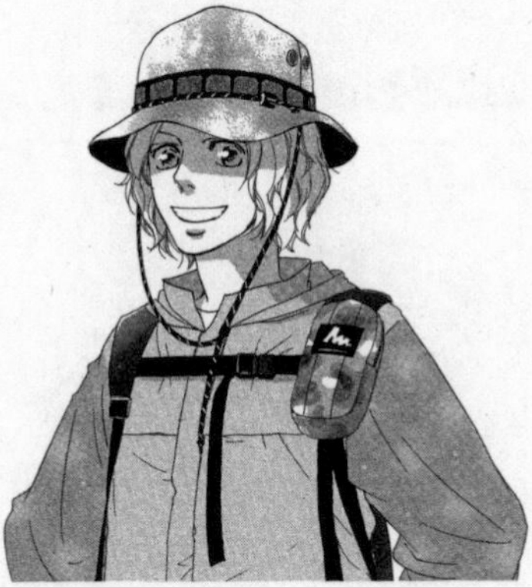

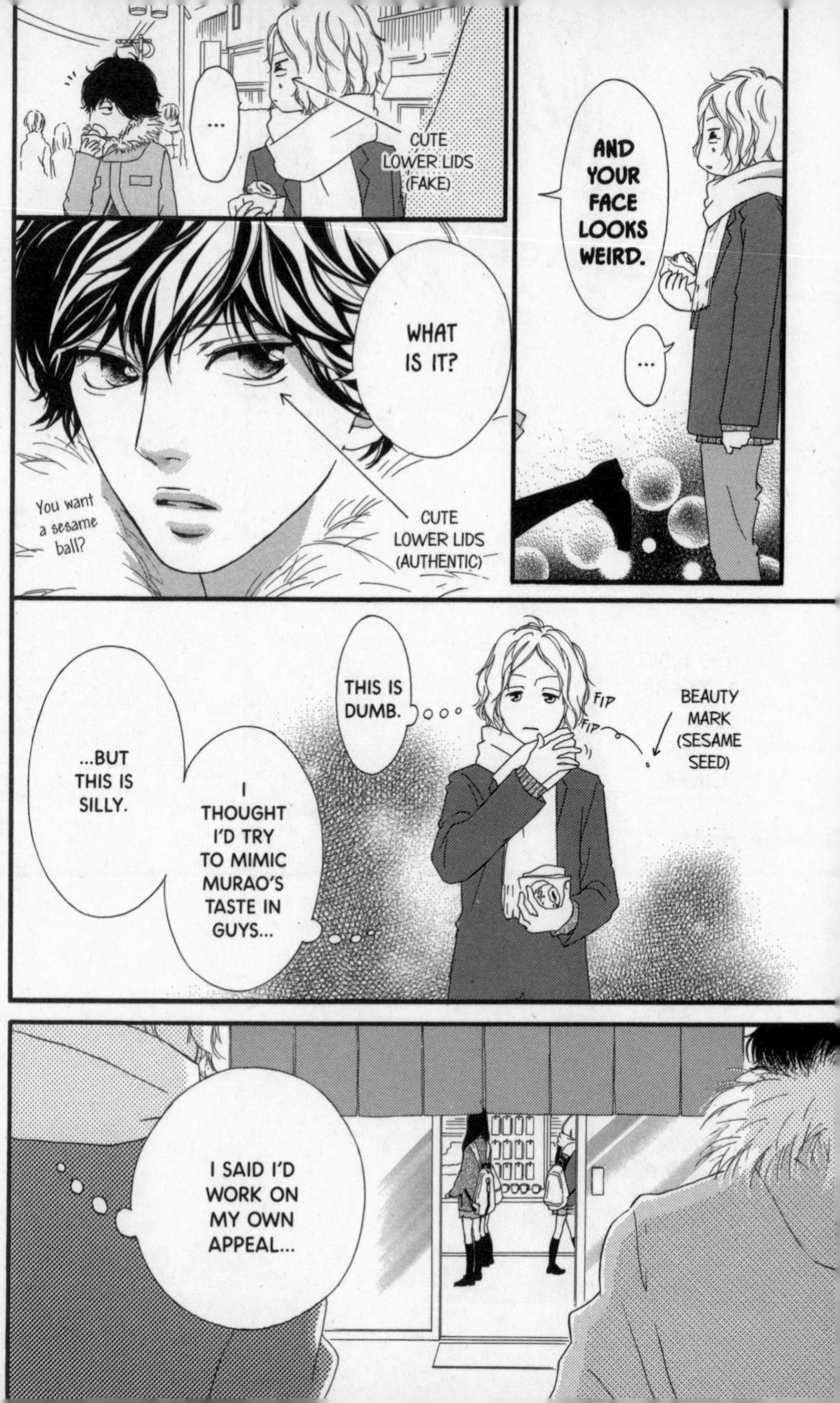
...
CUTE LOWER LIDS (FAKE)
WHAT IS IT?
CUTE LOWER LIDS (AUTHENTIC)
You want a sesame ball?
AND YOUR FACE LOOKS WEIRD.
...
BEAUTY MARK (SESAME SEED)
FIP
FIP
THIS IS DUMB.
I THOUGHT I'D TRY TO MIMIC MURAO'S TASTE IN GUYS...
...BUT THIS IS SILLY.
I SAID I'D WORK ON MY OWN APPEAL...

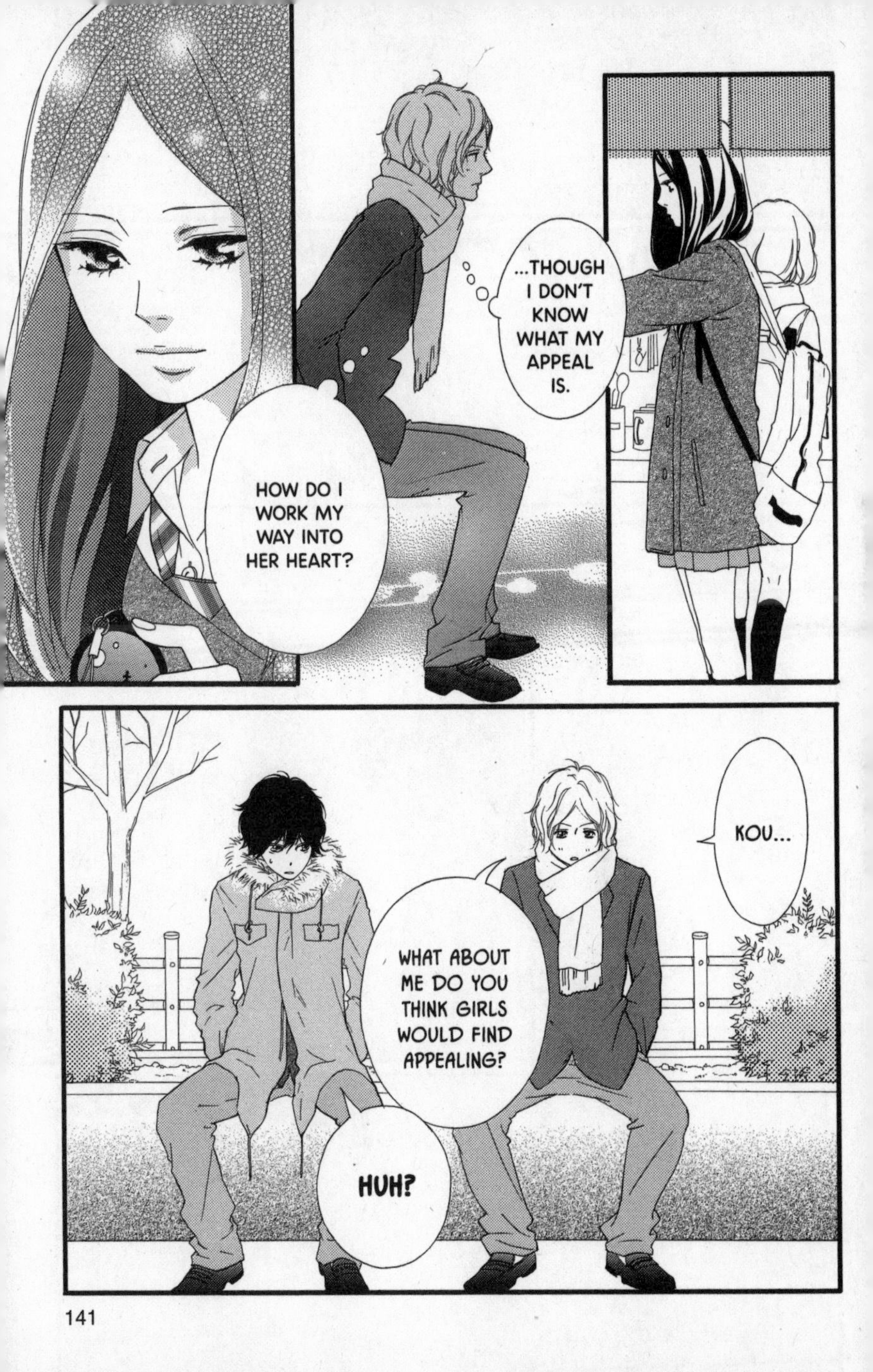

...THOUGH I DON'T KNOW WHAT MY APPEAL IS.
HOW DO I WORK MY WAY INTO HER HEART?
KOU...
WHAT ABOUT ME DO YOU THINK GIRLS WOULD FIND APPEALING?
HUH?

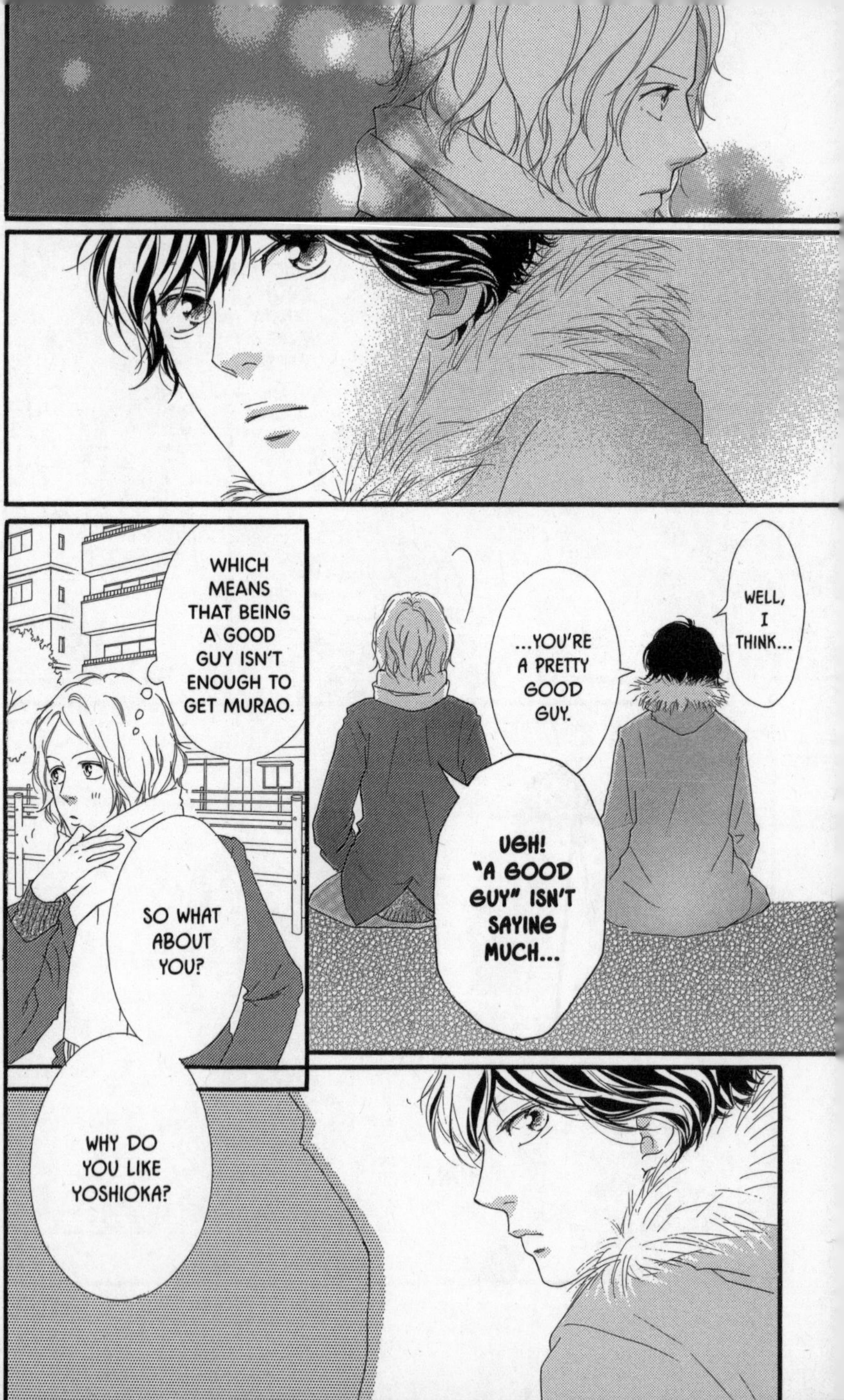
WELL, I THINK...
...YOU'RE A PRETTY GOOD GUY.
UGH! "A GOOD GUY" ISN'T SAYING MUCH...
WHICH MEANS THAT BEING A GOOD GUY ISN'T ENOUGH TO GET MURAO.
SO WHAT ABOUT YOU?
WHY DO YOU LIKE YOSHIOKA?

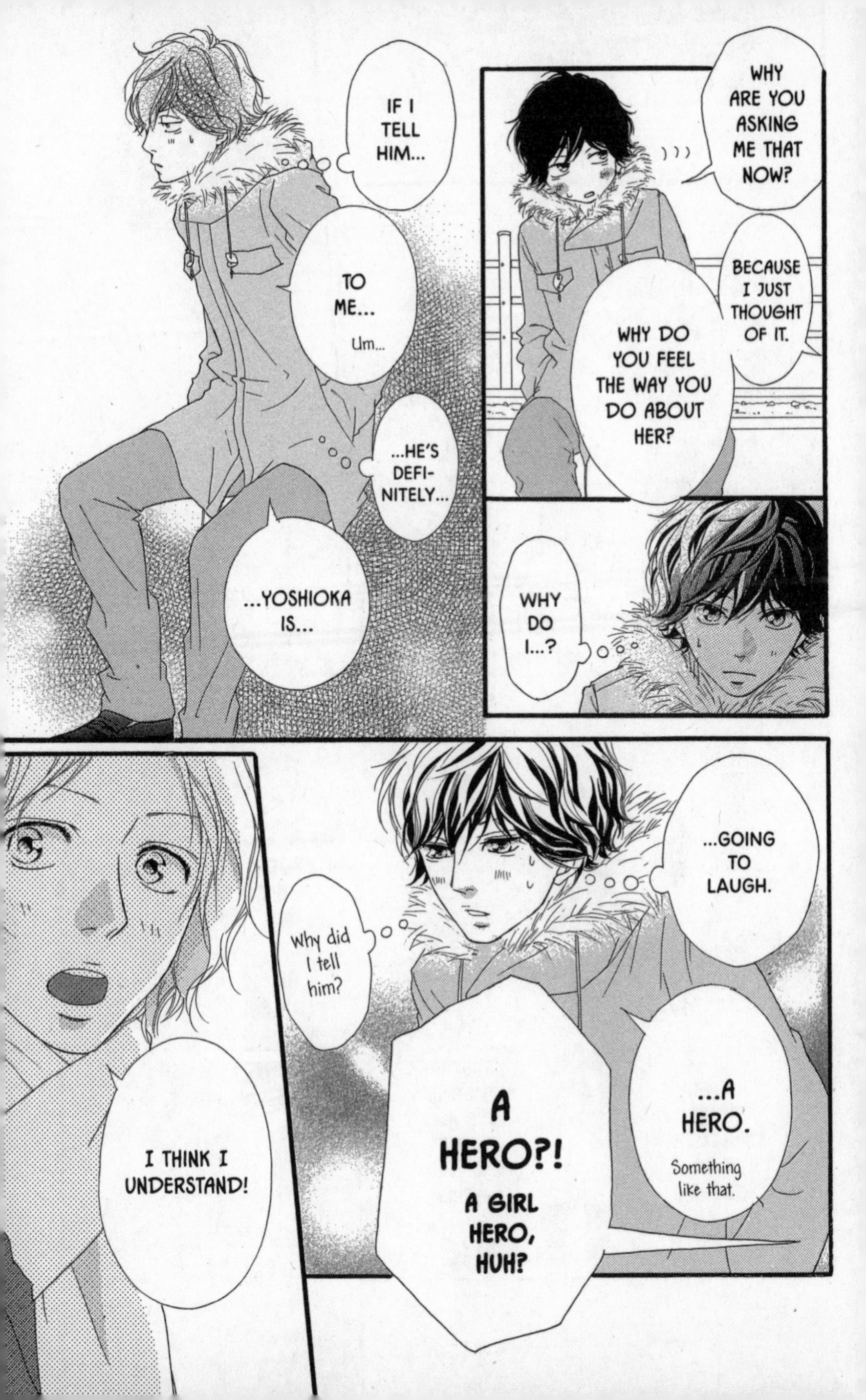
WHY ARE YOU ASKING ME THAT NOW?
BECAUSE I JUST THOUGHT OF IT.
WHY DO YOU FEEL THE WAY YOU DO ABOUT HER?
WHY DO I...?
IF I TELL HIM...
TO ME...
Um...
...HE'S DEFI-NITELY...
...YOSHIOKA IS...
...GOING TO LAUGH.
Why did I tell him?
...A HERO.
Something like that.
A HERO?!
A GIRL HERO, HUH?
I THINK I UNDERSTAND!

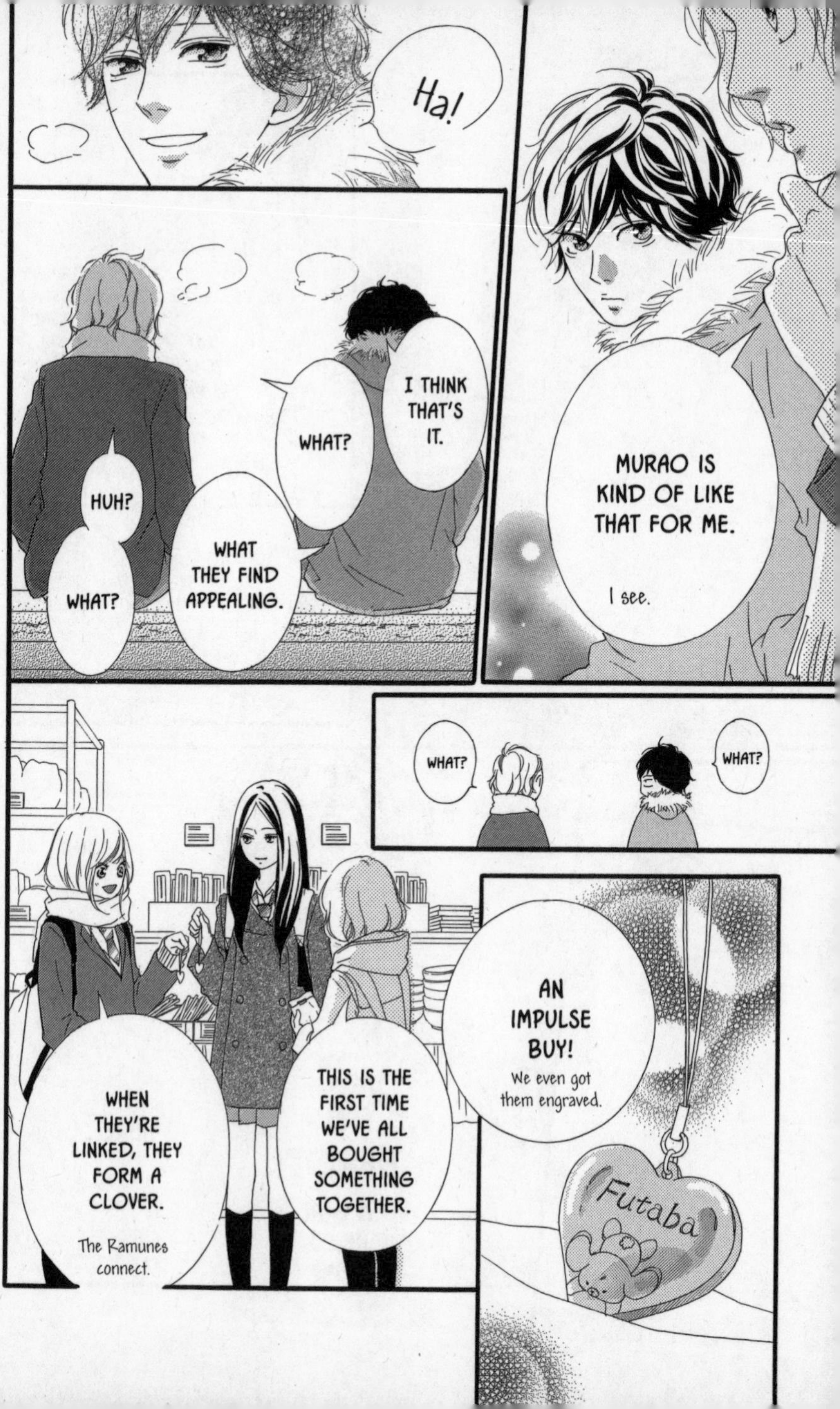
MURAO IS KIND OF LIKE THAT FOR ME.
I see.
Ha!
I THINK THAT'S IT.
WHAT?
WHAT THEY FIND APPEALING.
HUH?
WHAT?
WHAT?
WHAT?
AN IMPULSE BUY!
We even got them engraved.
Futaba
THIS IS THE FIRST TIME WE'VE ALL BOUGHT SOMETHING TOGETHER.
WHEN THEY'RE LINKED, THEY FORM A CLOVER.
The Ramunes connect.

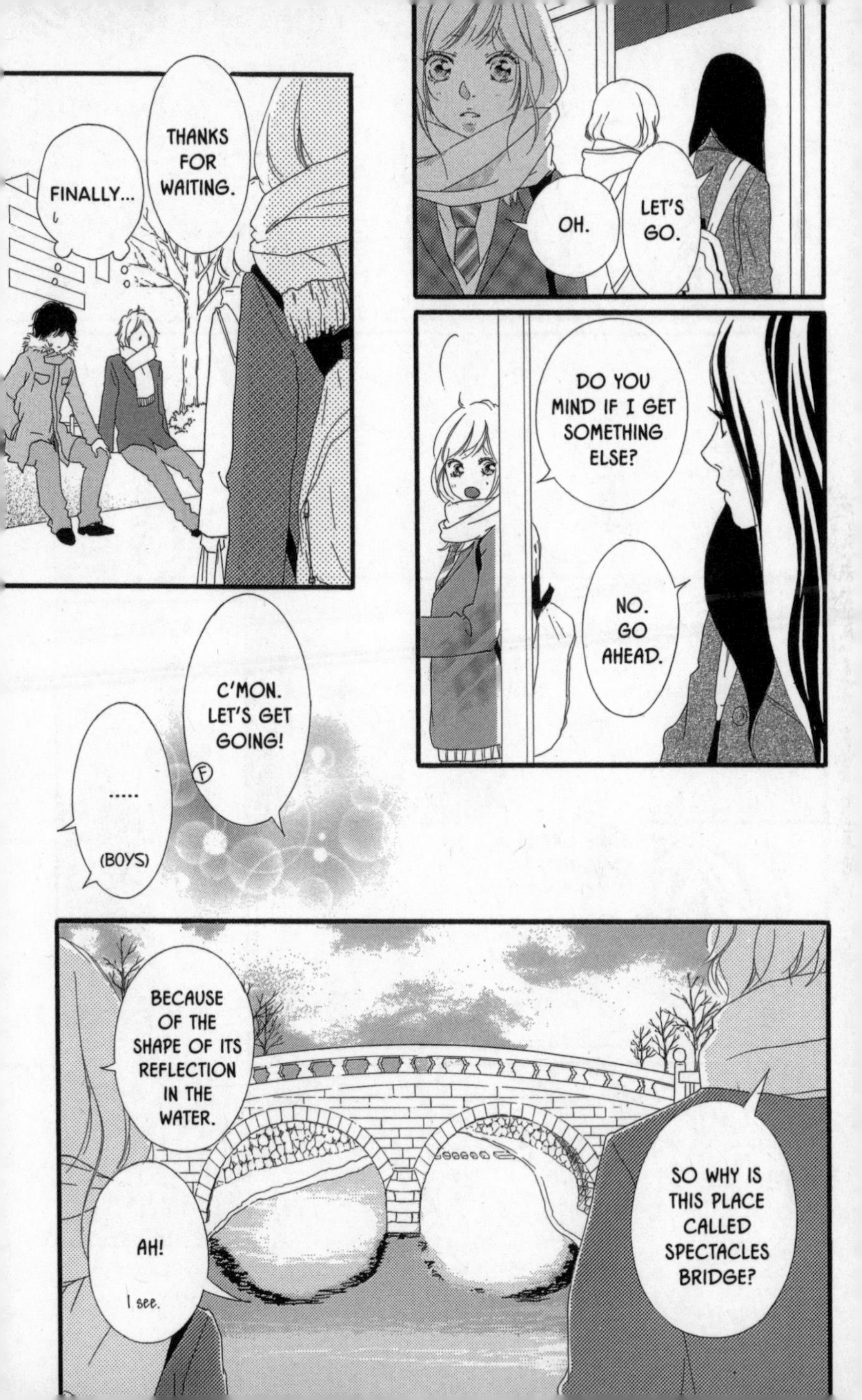
LET'S GO.
OH.
DO YOU MIND IF I GET SOMETHING ELSE?
NO. GO AHEAD.
THANKS FOR WAITING.
FINALLY...
C'MON. LET'S GET GOING!
F
.....
(BOYS)
SO WHY IS THIS PLACE CALLED SPECTACLES BRIDGE?
BECAUSE OF THE SHAPE OF ITS REFLECTION IN THE WATER.
AH!
I see.

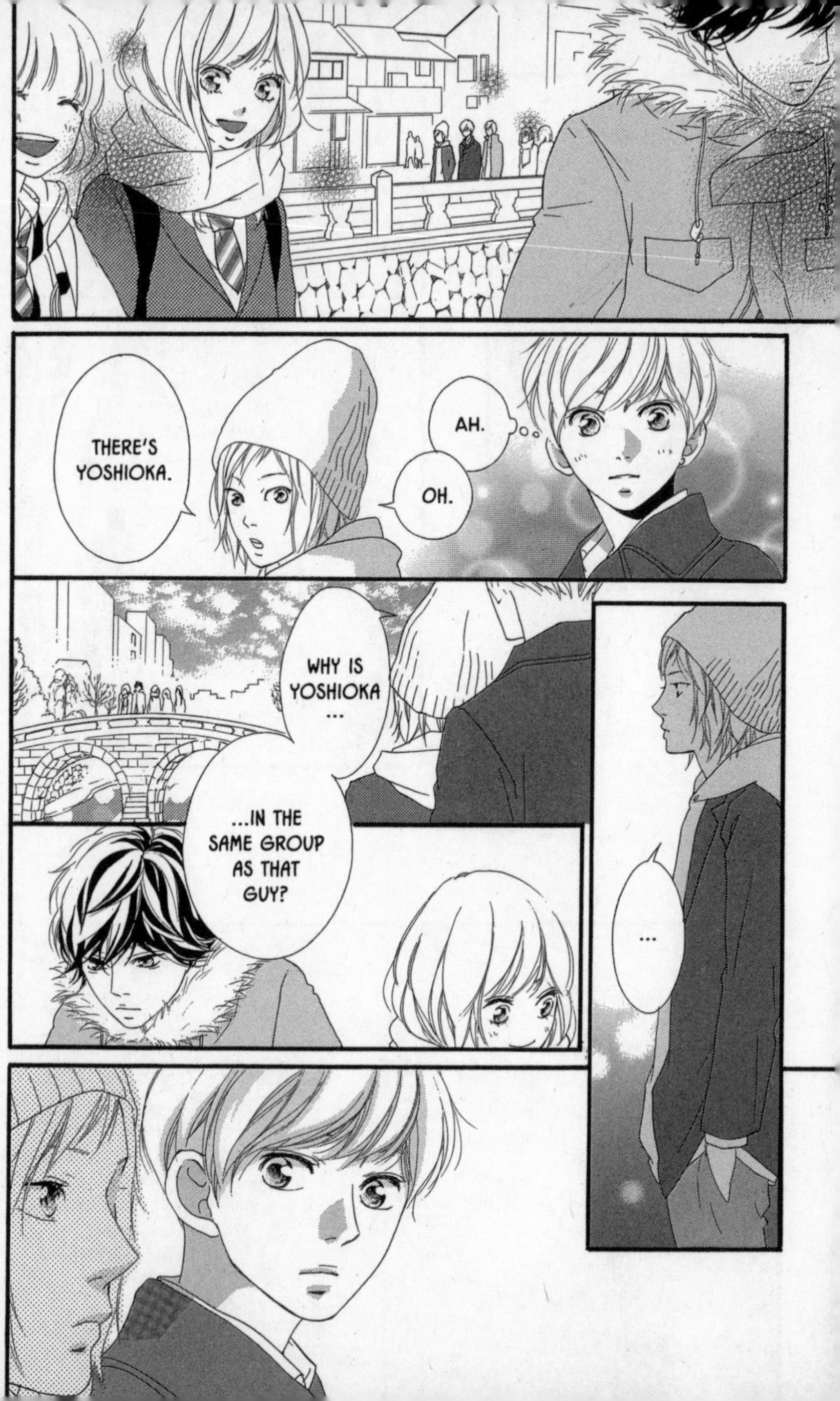
AH.
OH.
THERE'S YOSHIOKA.
...
WHY IS YOSHIOKA ...
...IN THE SAME GROUP AS THAT GUY?

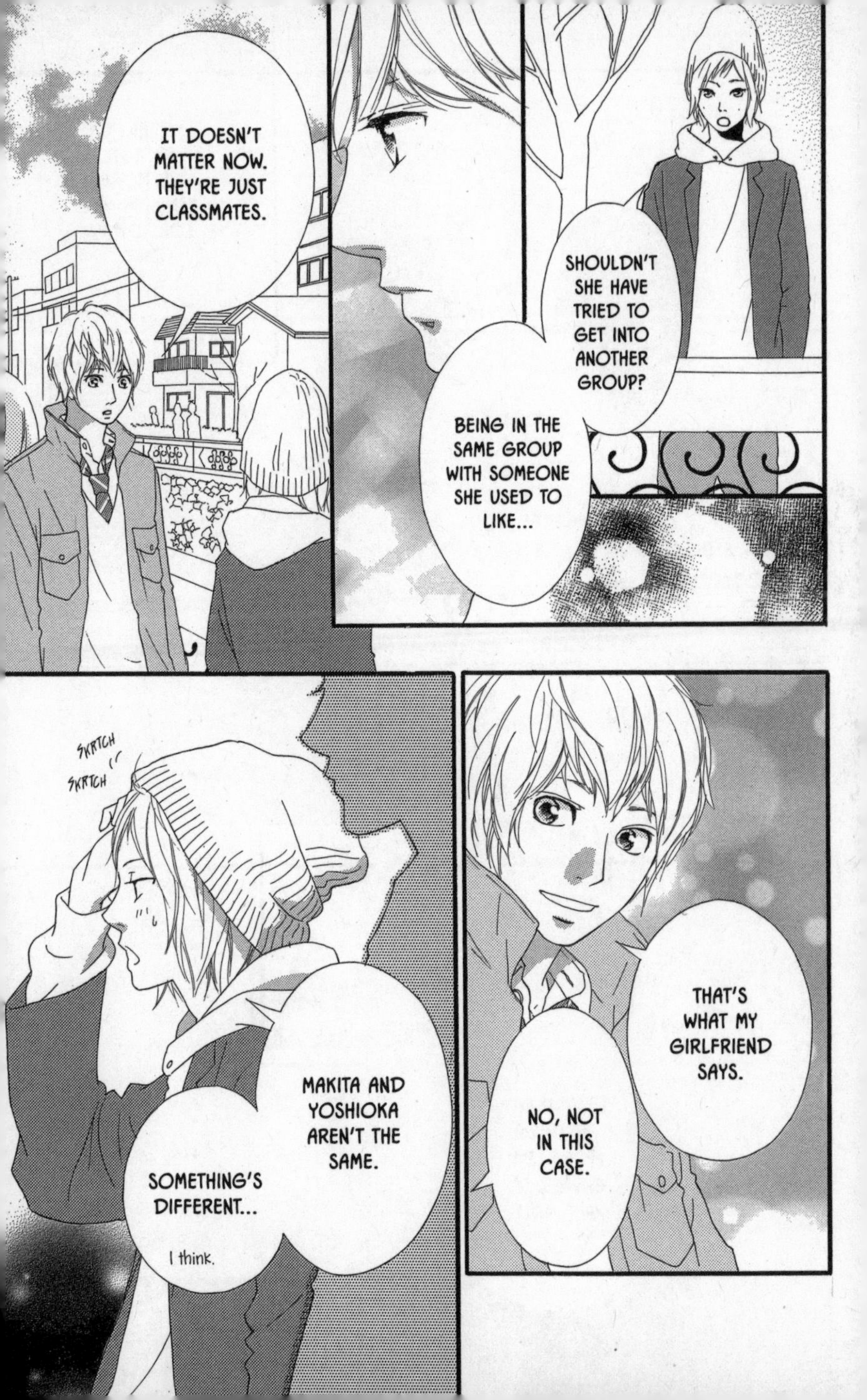
SHOULDN'T SHE HAVE TRIED TO GET INTO ANOTHER GROUP?
BEING IN THE SAME GROUP WITH SOMEONE SHE USED TO LIKE...
IT DOESN'T MATTER NOW. THEY'RE JUST CLASSMATES.
THAT'S WHAT MY GIRLFRIEND SAYS.
NO, NOT IN THIS CASE.
SKRTCH SKRTCH
MAKITA AND YOSHIOKA AREN'T THE SAME.
SOMETHING'S DIFFERENT...
I think.

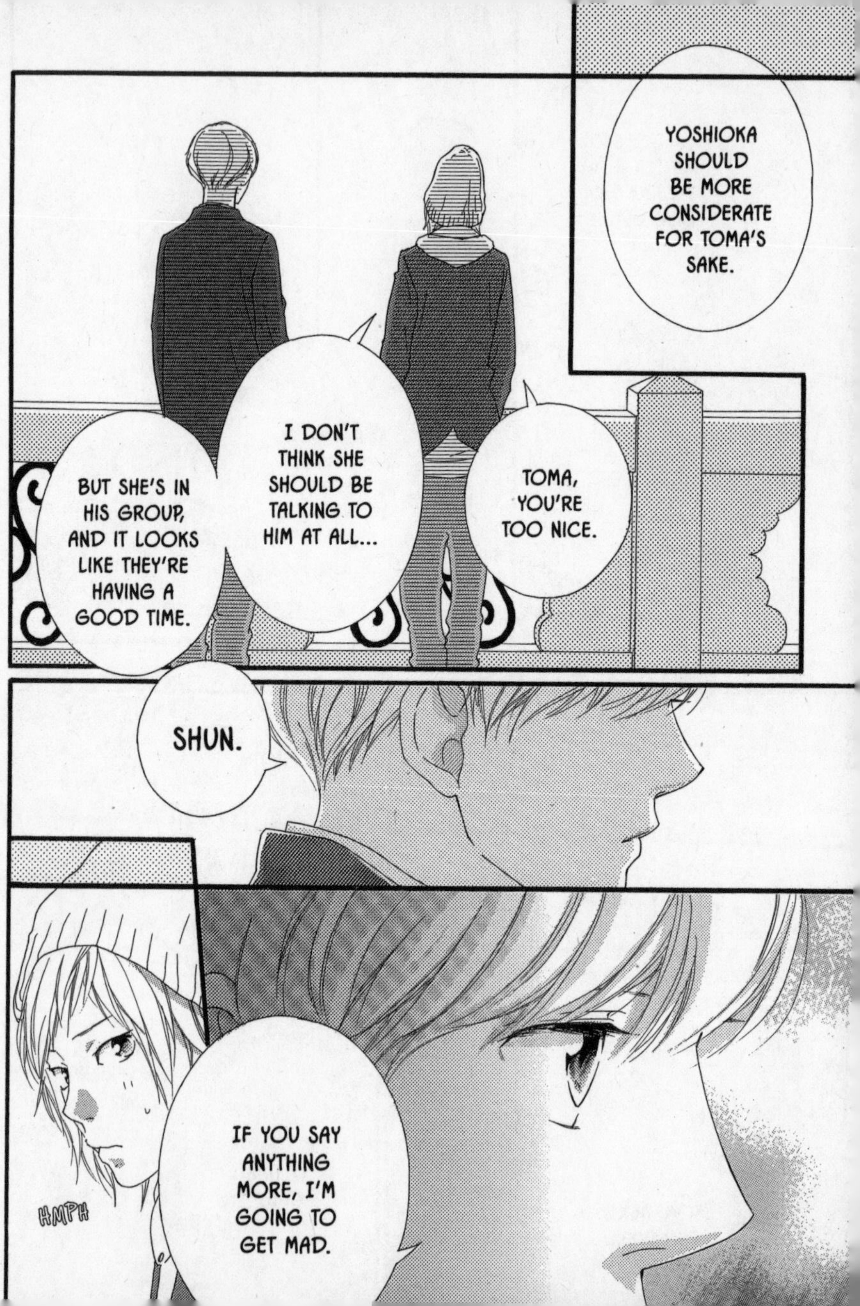
YOSHIOKA SHOULD BE MORE CONSIDERATE FOR TOMA'S SAKE.
TOMA, YOU'RE TOO NICE.
I DON'T THINK SHE SHOULD BE TALKING TO HIM AT ALL...
BUT SHE'S IN HIS GROUP, AND IT LOOKS LIKE THEY'RE HAVING A GOOD TIME.
SHUN.
IF YOU SAY ANYTHING MORE, I'M GOING TO GET MAD.
HMPH

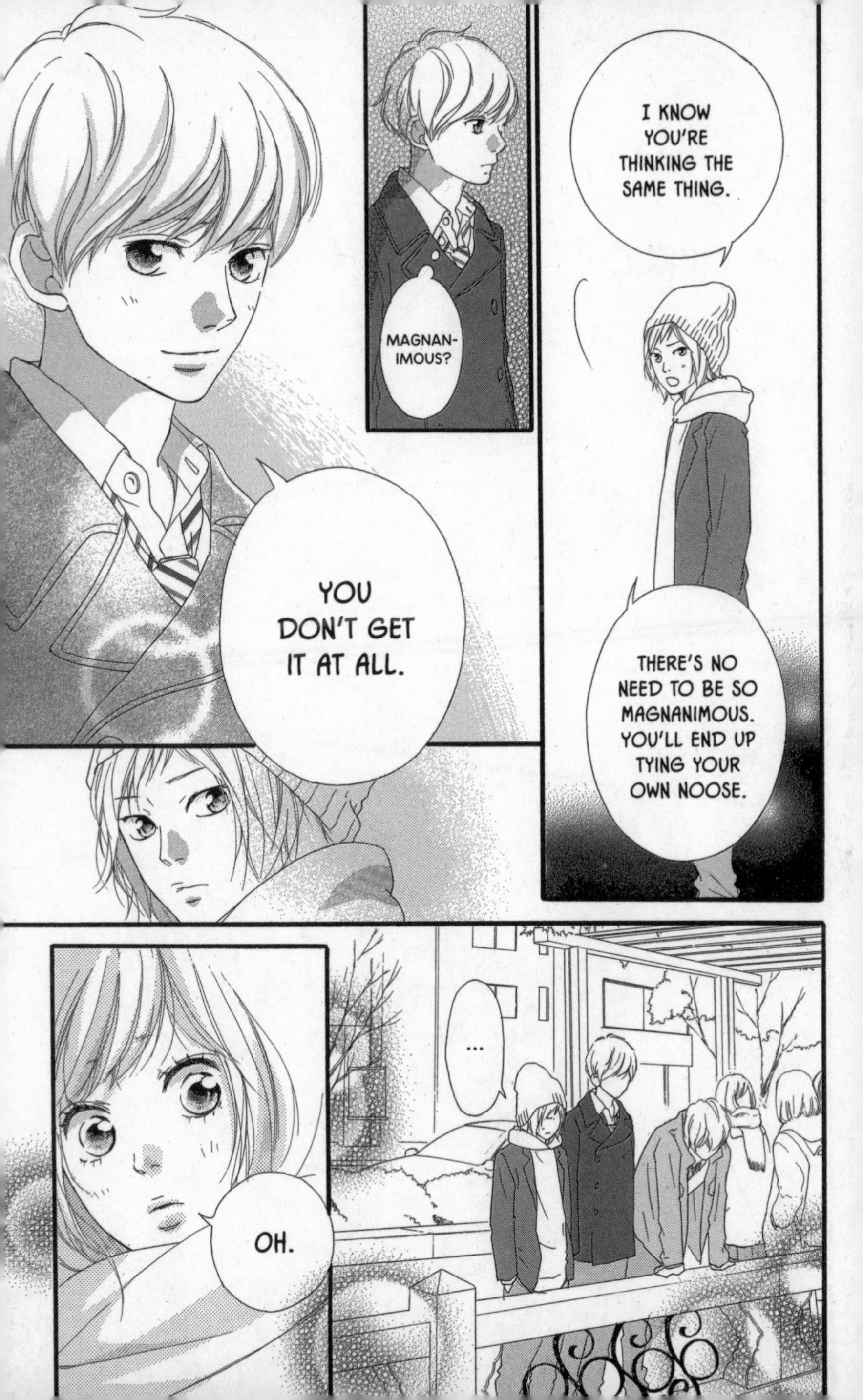
I KNOW YOU'RE THINKING THE SAME THING.
THERE'S NO NEED TO BE SO MAGNANIMOUS. YOU'LL END UP TYING YOUR OWN NOOSE.
MAGNAN-IMOUS?
YOU DON'T GET IT AT ALL.
...
OH.

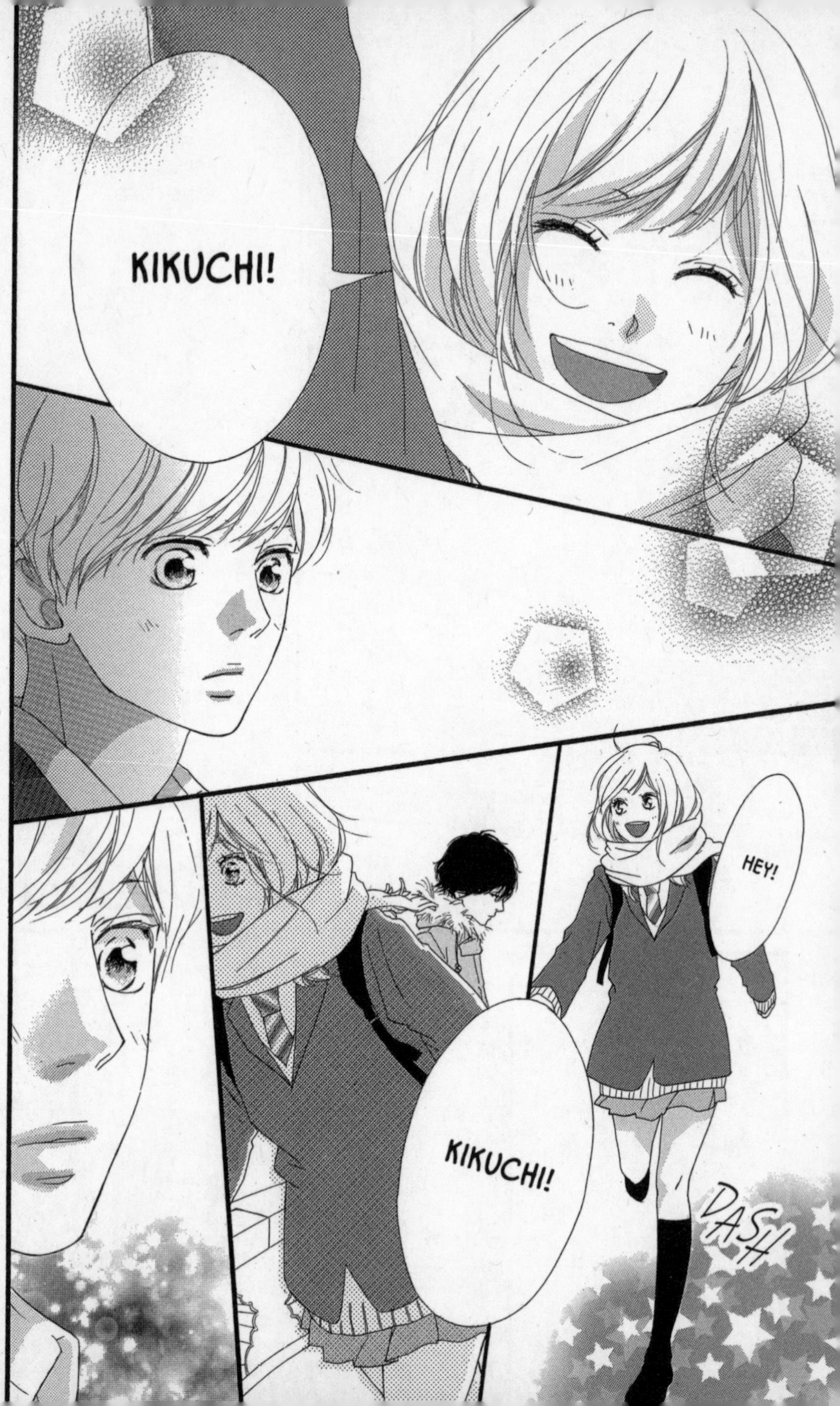
KIKUCHI!
HEY!
KIKUCHI!
DASH

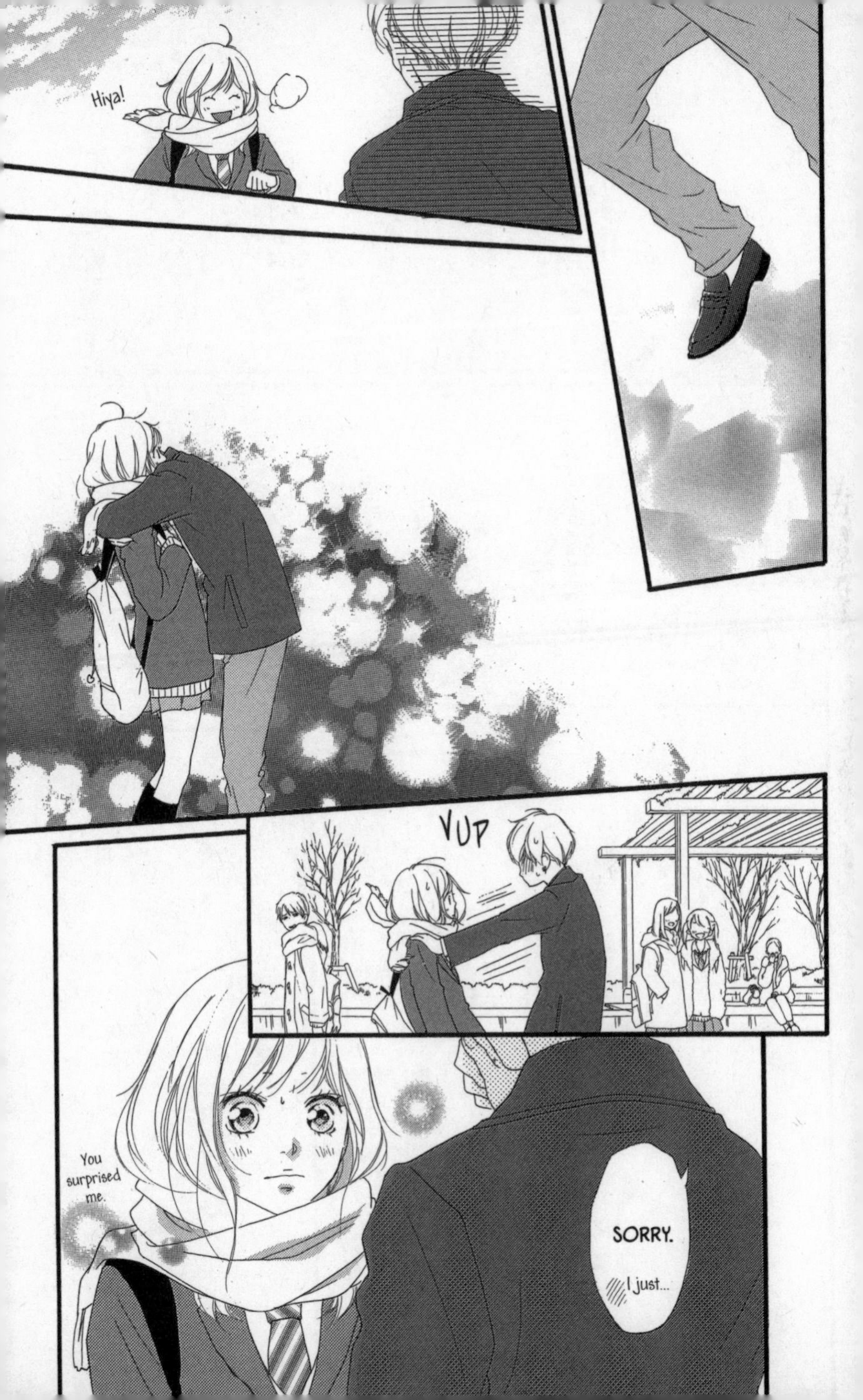

Hiya!
VUP
SORRY.
I just...
You surprised me.

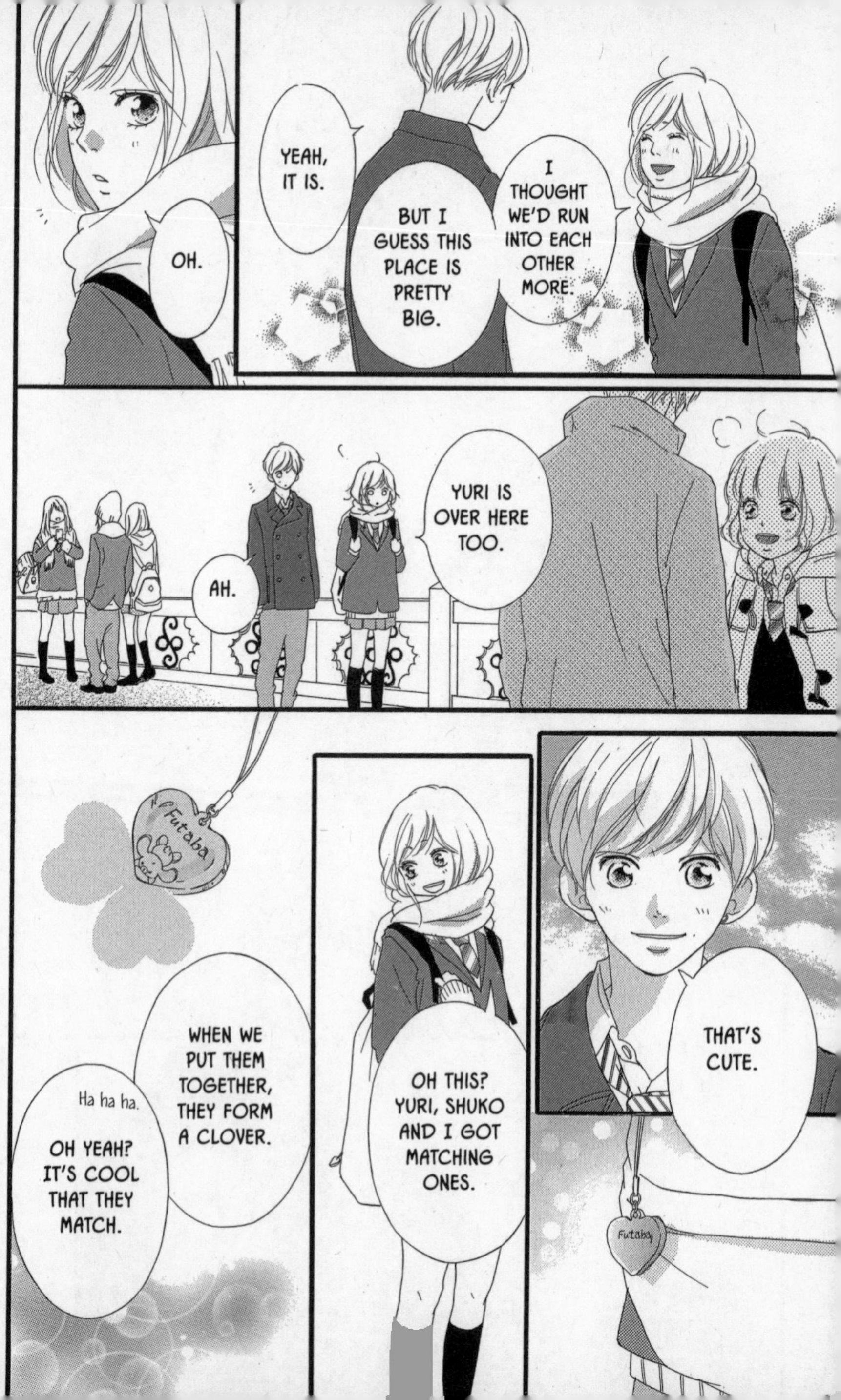
I THOUGHT WE'D RUN INTO EACH OTHER MORE.
YEAH, IT IS.
BUT I GUESS THIS PLACE IS PRETTY BIG.
OH.
YURI IS OVER HERE TOO.
AH.
THAT'S CUTE.
Futaba
OH THIS? YURI, SHUKO AND I GOT MATCHING ONES.
WHEN WE PUT THEM TOGETHER, THEY FORM A CLOVER.
Futaba
Ha ha ha.
OH YEAH? IT'S COOL THAT THEY MATCH.

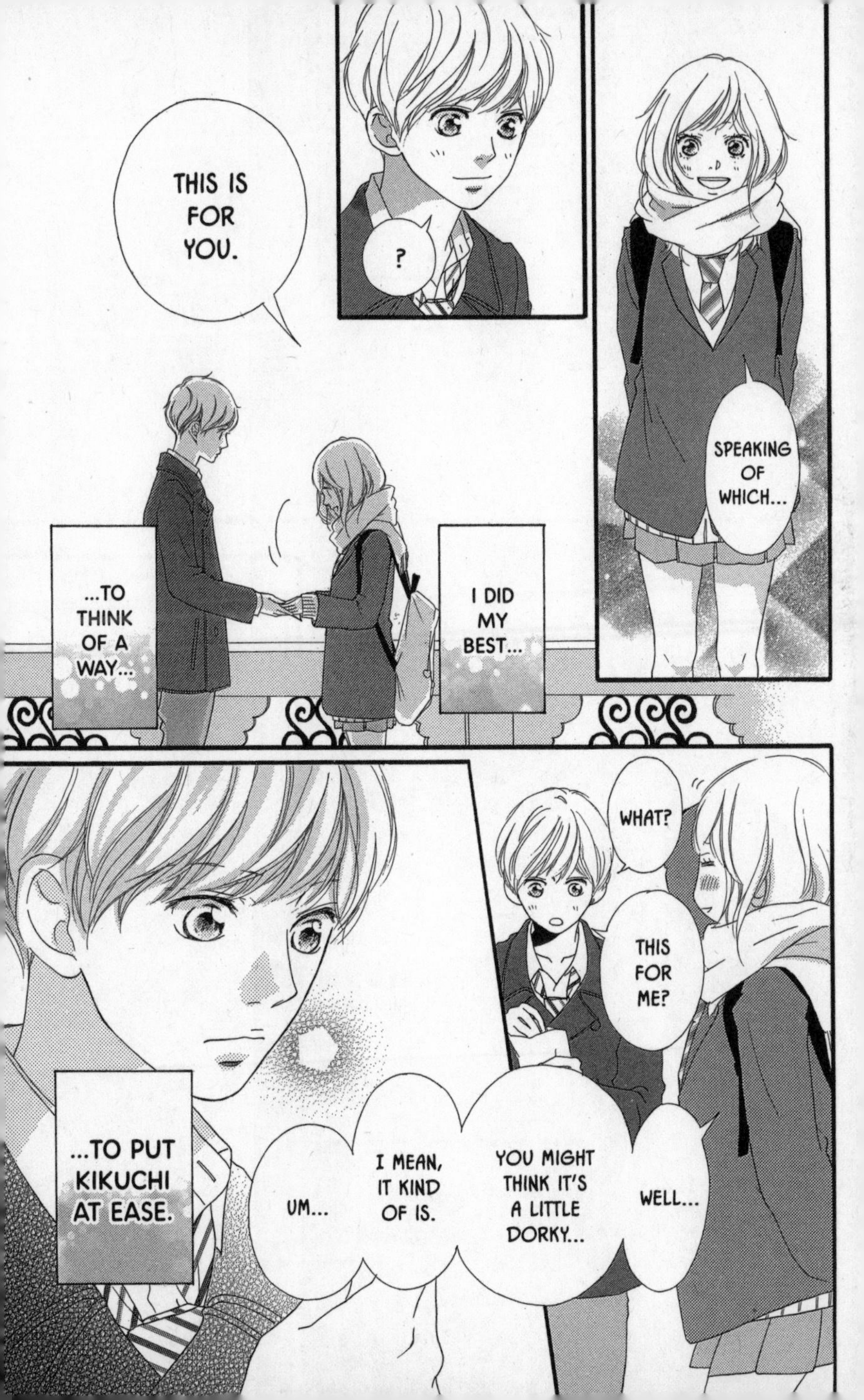
SPEAKING OF WHICH...
?
THIS IS FOR YOU.
I DID MY BEST...
...TO THINK OF A WAY...
WHAT?
THIS FOR ME?
WELL...
YOU MIGHT THINK IT'S A LITTLE DORKY...
I MEAN, IT KIND OF IS.
UM...
...TO PUT KIKUCHI AT EASE.

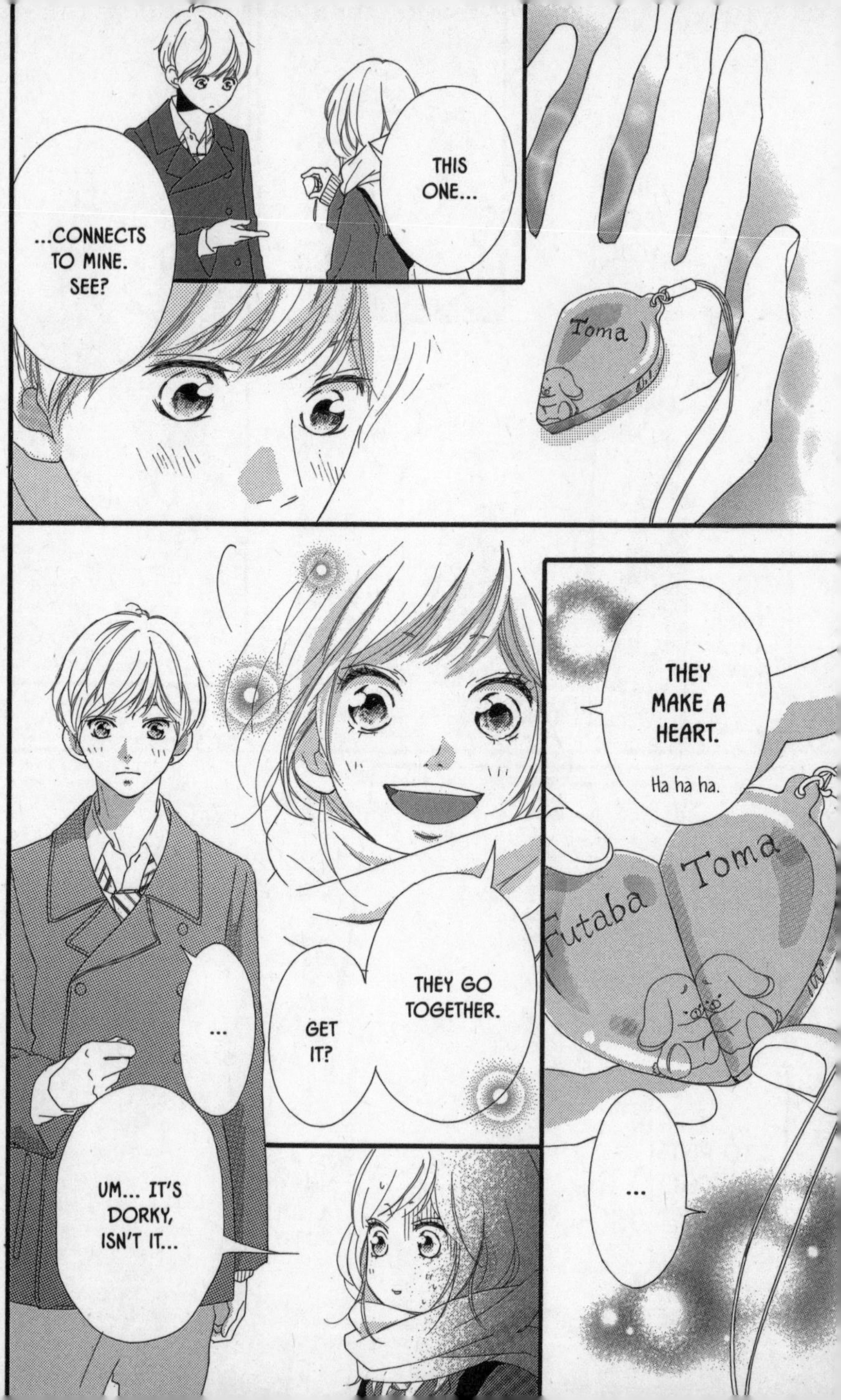
THIS ONE...
...CONNECTS TO MINE. SEE?
Toma
THEY MAKE A HEART.
Ha ha ha.
Futaba
Toma
...
THEY GO TOGETHER.
GET IT?
...
UM... IT'S DORKY, ISN'T IT...

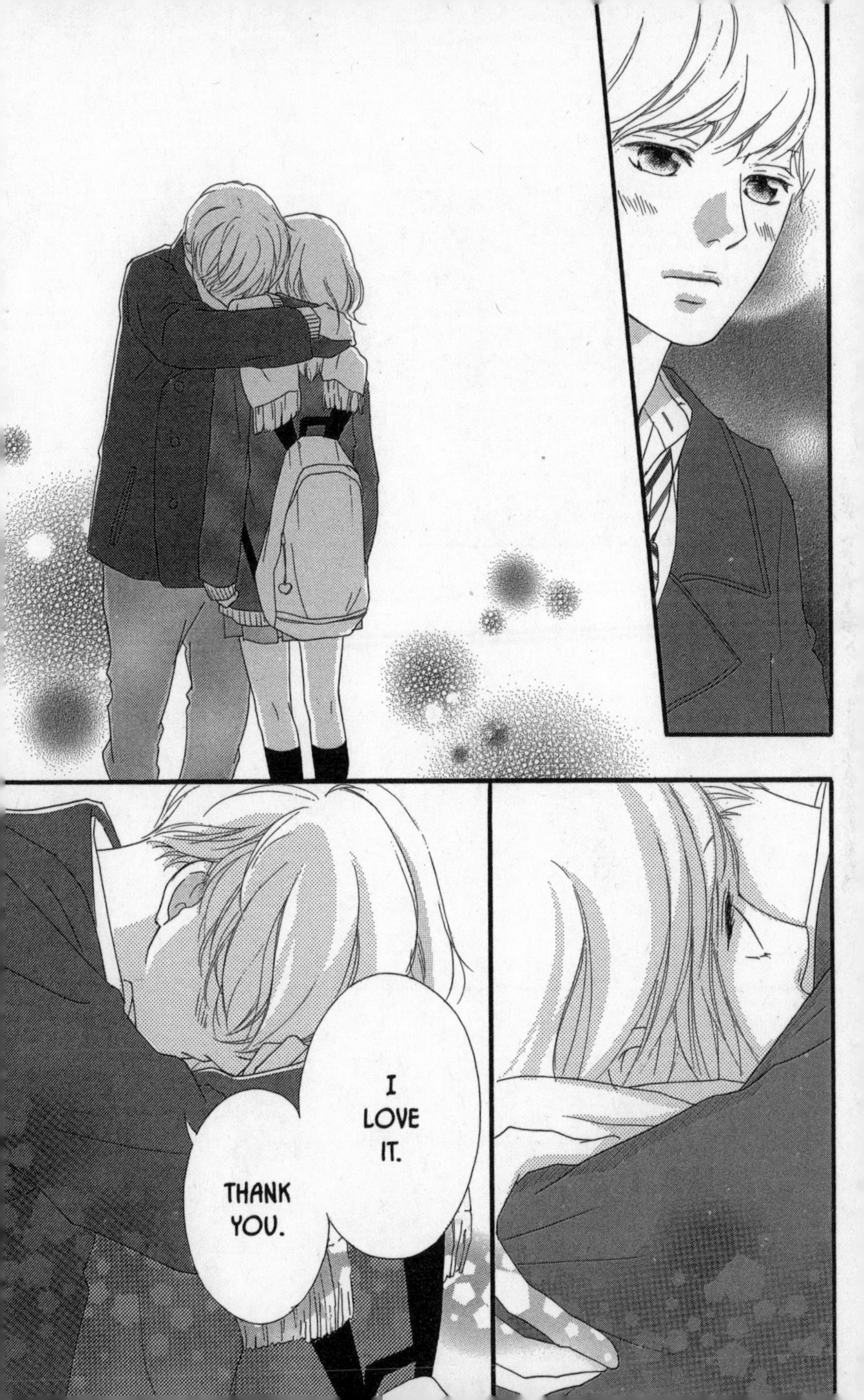
I LOVE IT.
THANK YOU.

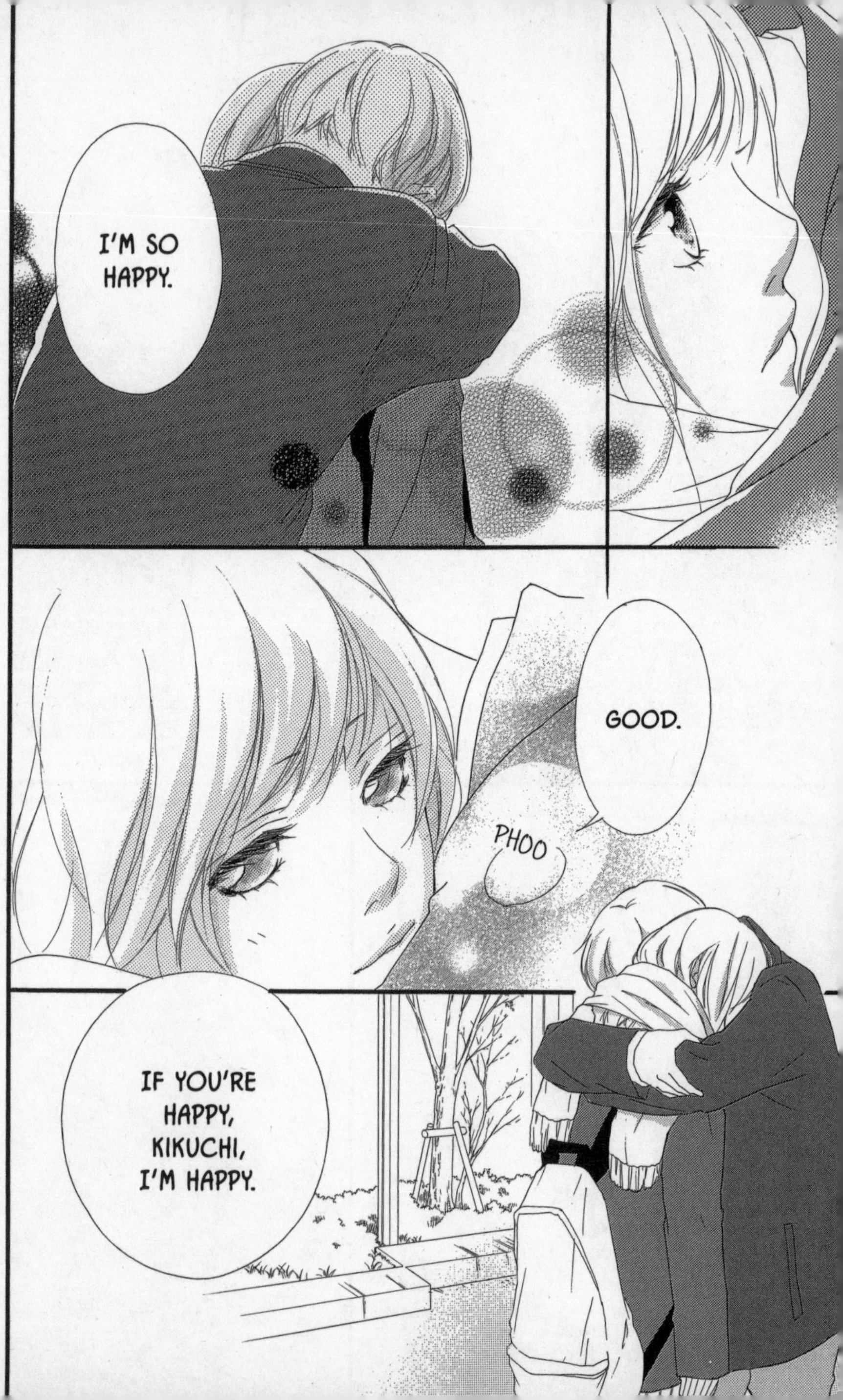
I'M SO HAPPY.
GOOD.
PHOO
IF YOU'RE HAPPY, KIKUCHI, I'M HAPPY.

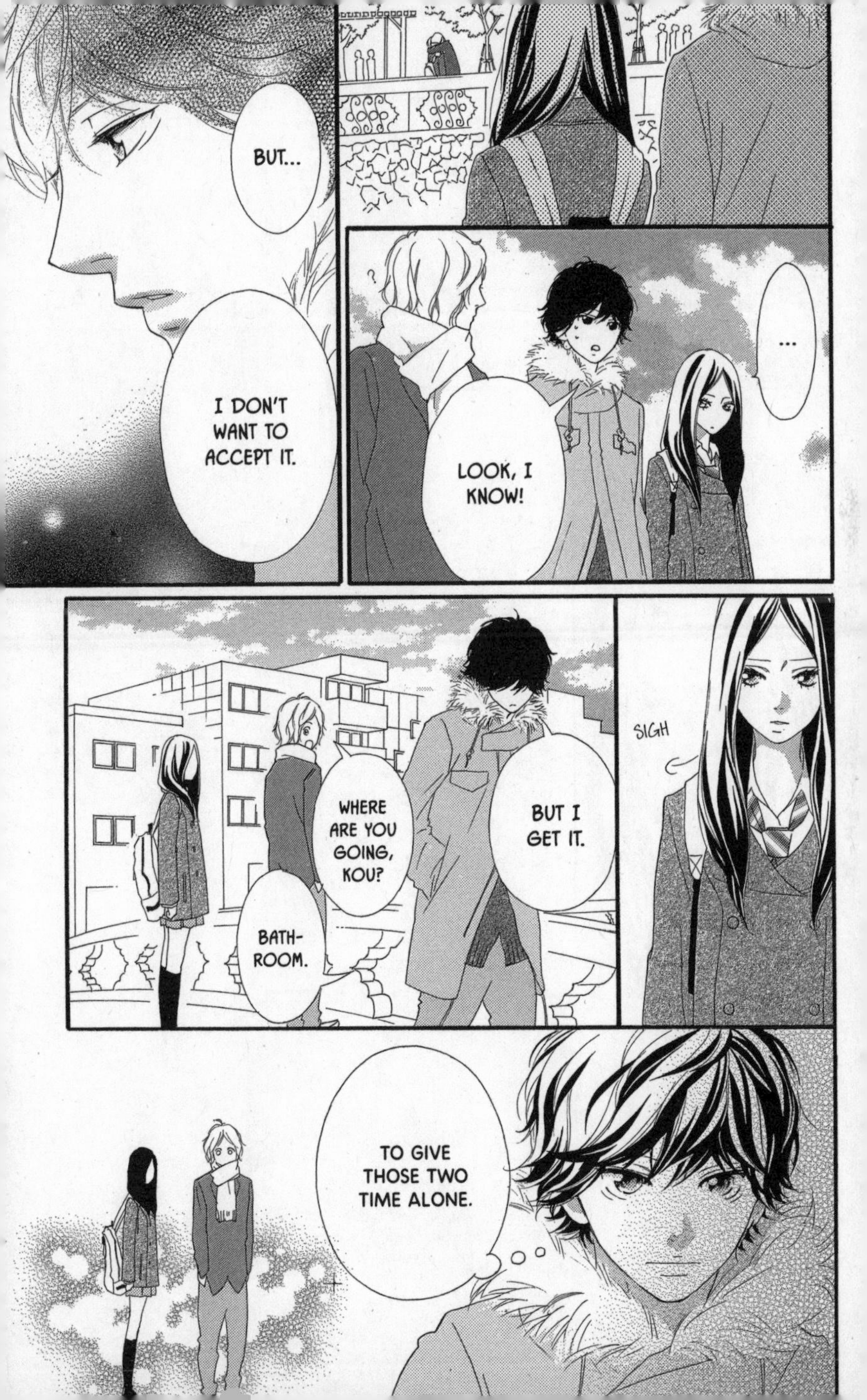
...
LOOK, I KNOW!
BUT...
I DON'T WANT TO ACCEPT IT.
SIGH
BUT I GET IT.
WHERE ARE YOU GOING, KOU?
BATH-ROOM.
TO GIVE THOSE TWO TIME ALONE.

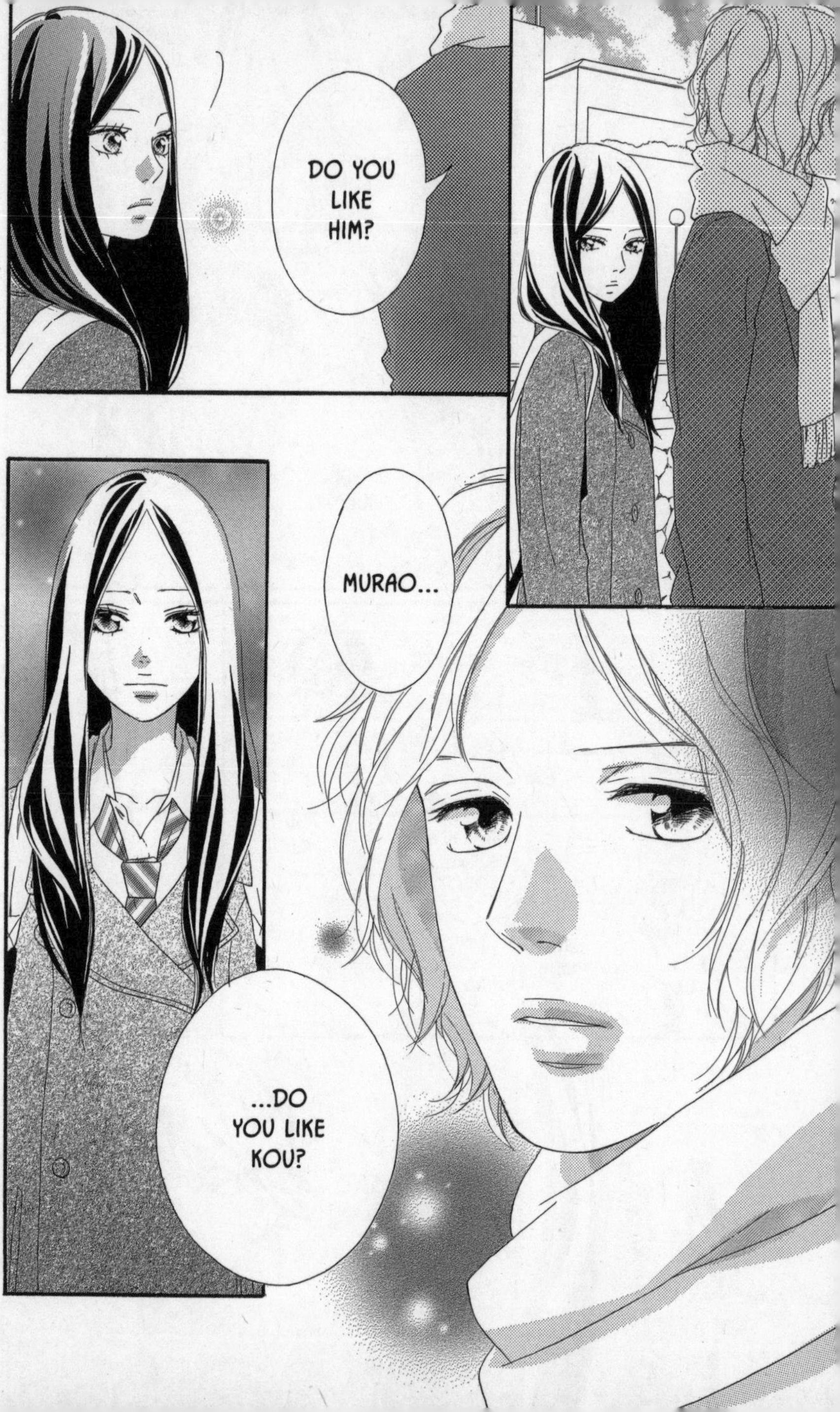
DO YOU LIKE HIM?
MURAO...
...DO YOU LIKE KOU?

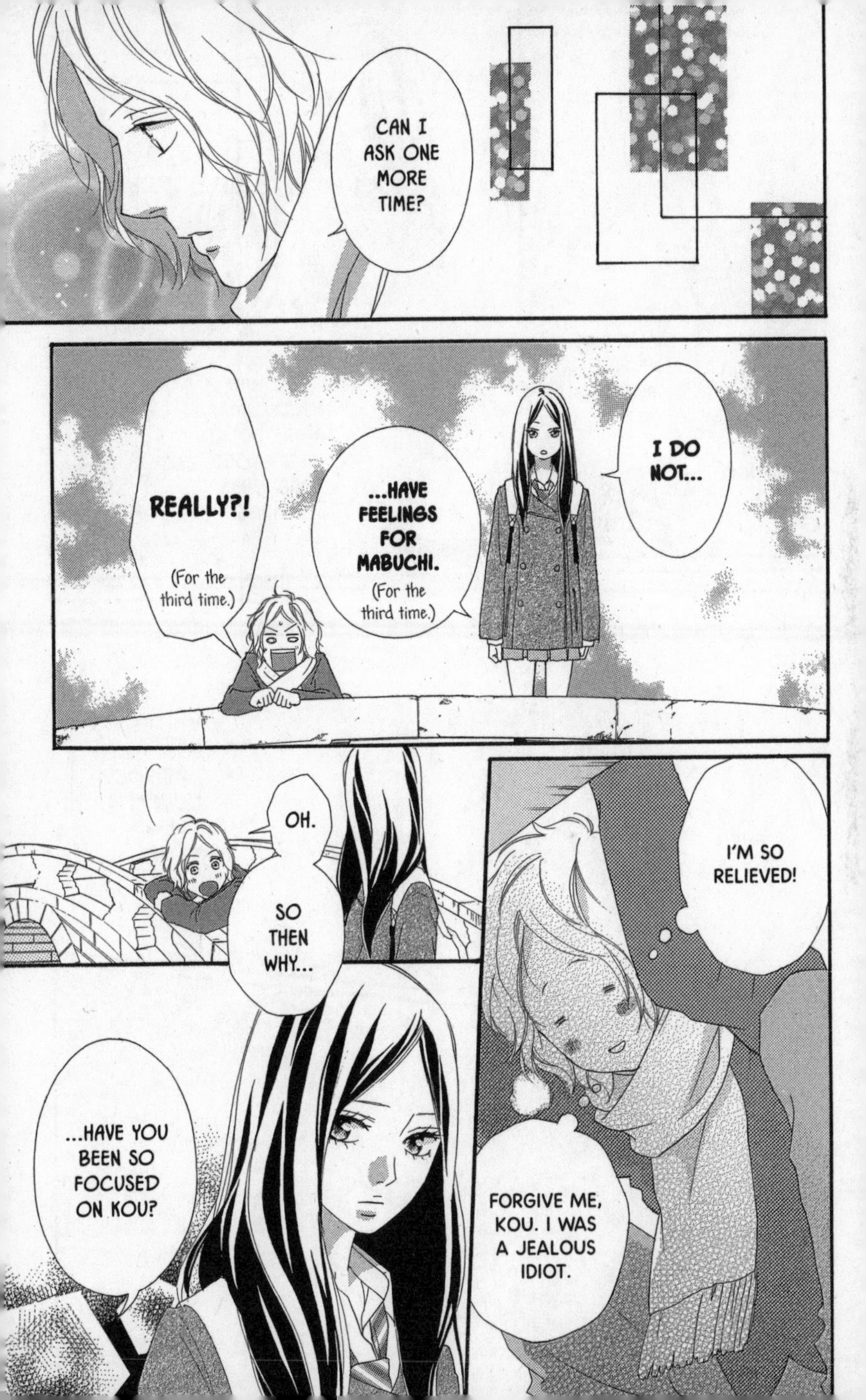
CAN I ASK ONE MORE TIME?
I DO NOT...
...HAVE FEELINGS FOR MABUCHI.
(For the third time.)
REALLY?!
(For the third time.)
I'M SO RELIEVED!
FORGIVE ME, KOU. I WAS A JEALOUS IDIOT.
OH.
SO THEN WHY...
...HAVE YOU BEEN SO FOCUSED ON KOU?

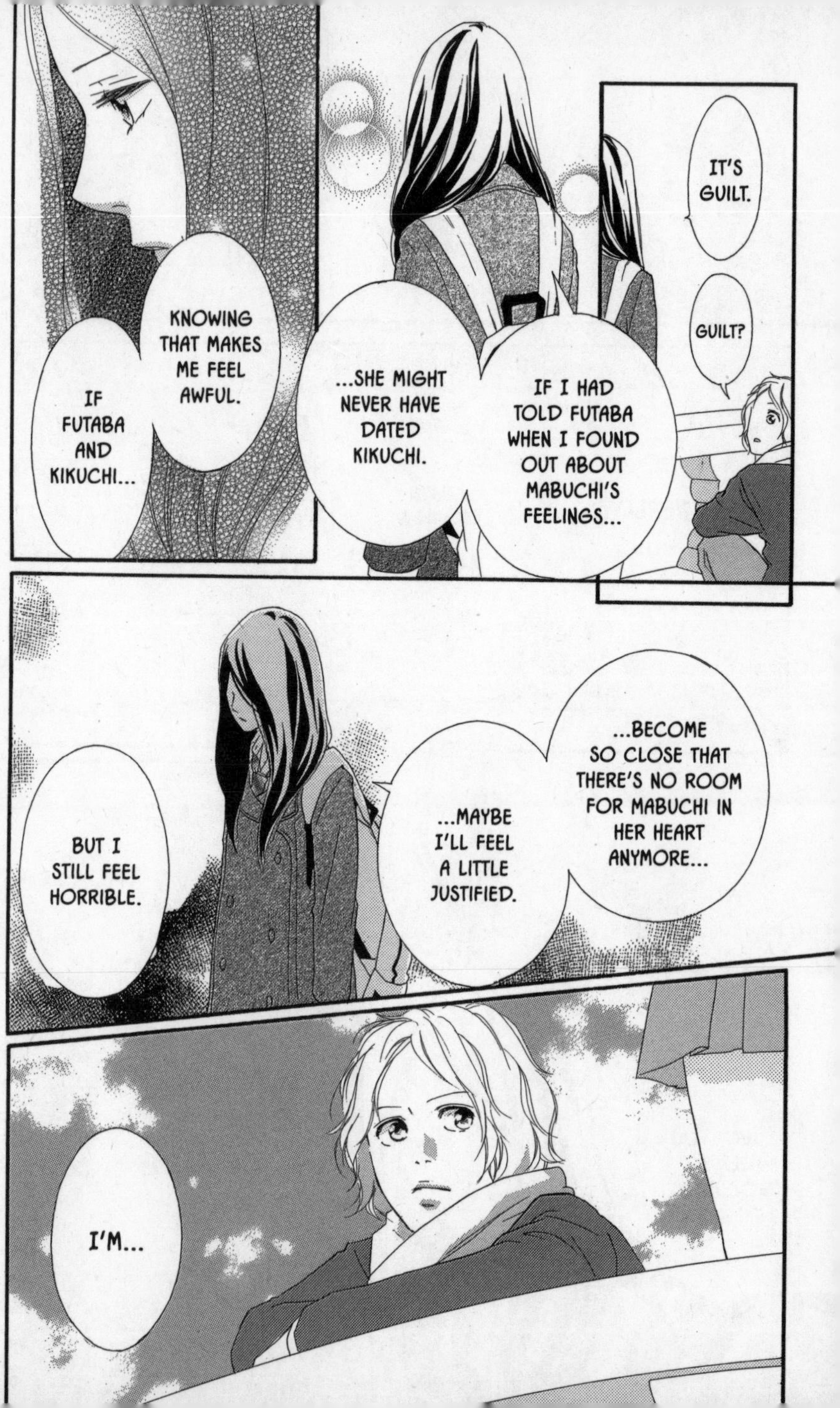
IT'S GUILT.
GUILT?
IF I HAD TOLD FUTABA WHEN I FOUND OUT ABOUT MABUCHI'S FEELINGS...
...SHE MIGHT NEVER HAVE DATED KIKUCHI.
KNOWING THAT MAKES ME FEEL AWFUL.
IF FUTABA AND KIKUCHI...
...BECOME SO CLOSE THAT THERE'S NO ROOM FOR MABUCHI IN HER HEART ANYMORE...
...MAYBE I'LL FEEL A LITTLE JUSTIFIED.
BUT I STILL FEEL HORRIBLE.
I'M...

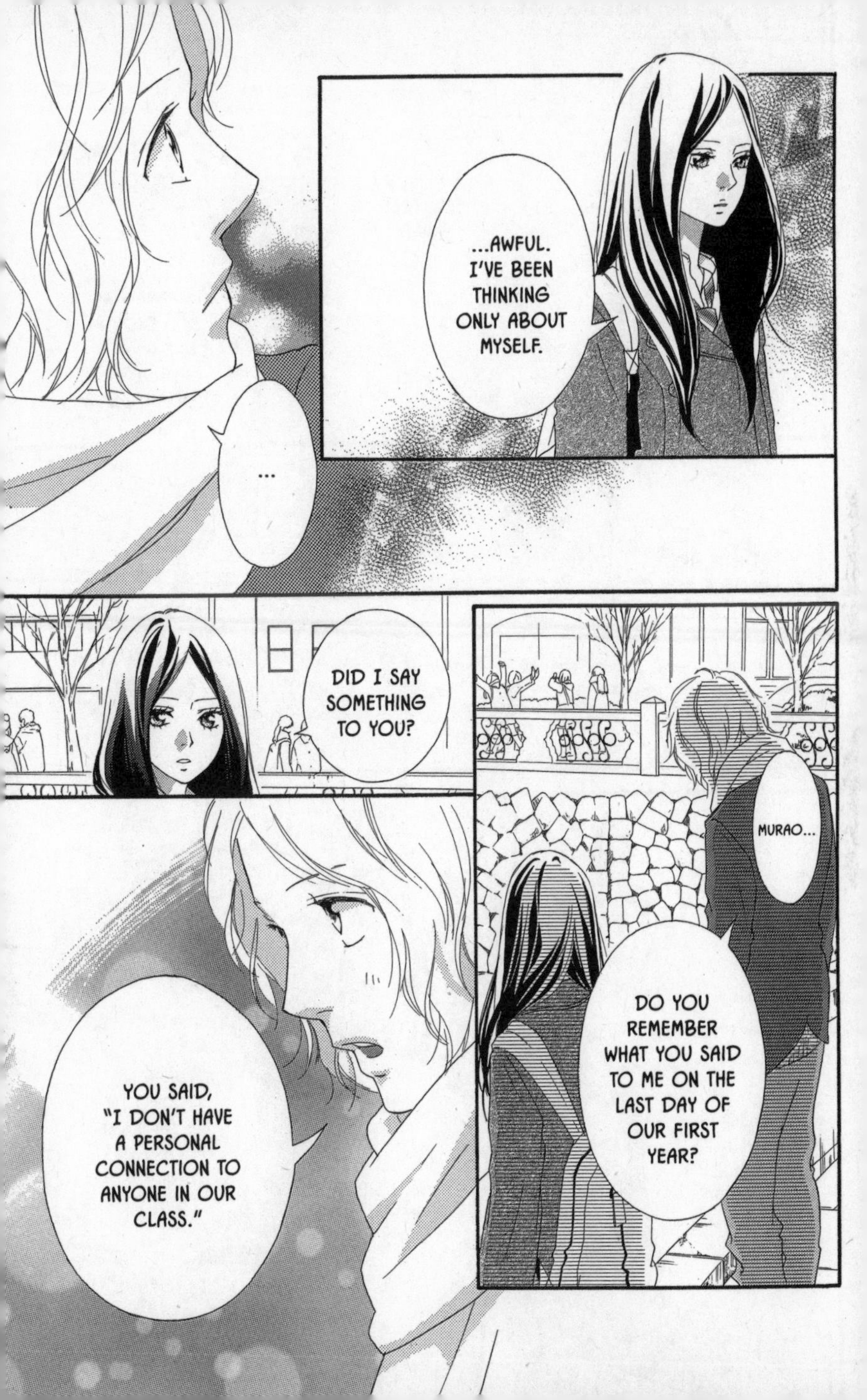
...AWFUL. I'VE BEEN THINKING ONLY ABOUT MYSELF.
...
MURAO...
DO YOU REMEMBER WHAT YOU SAID TO ME ON THE LAST DAY OF OUR FIRST YEAR?
DID I SAY SOMETHING TO YOU?
YOU SAID, "I DON'T HAVE A PERSONAL CONNECTION TO ANYONE IN OUR CLASS."

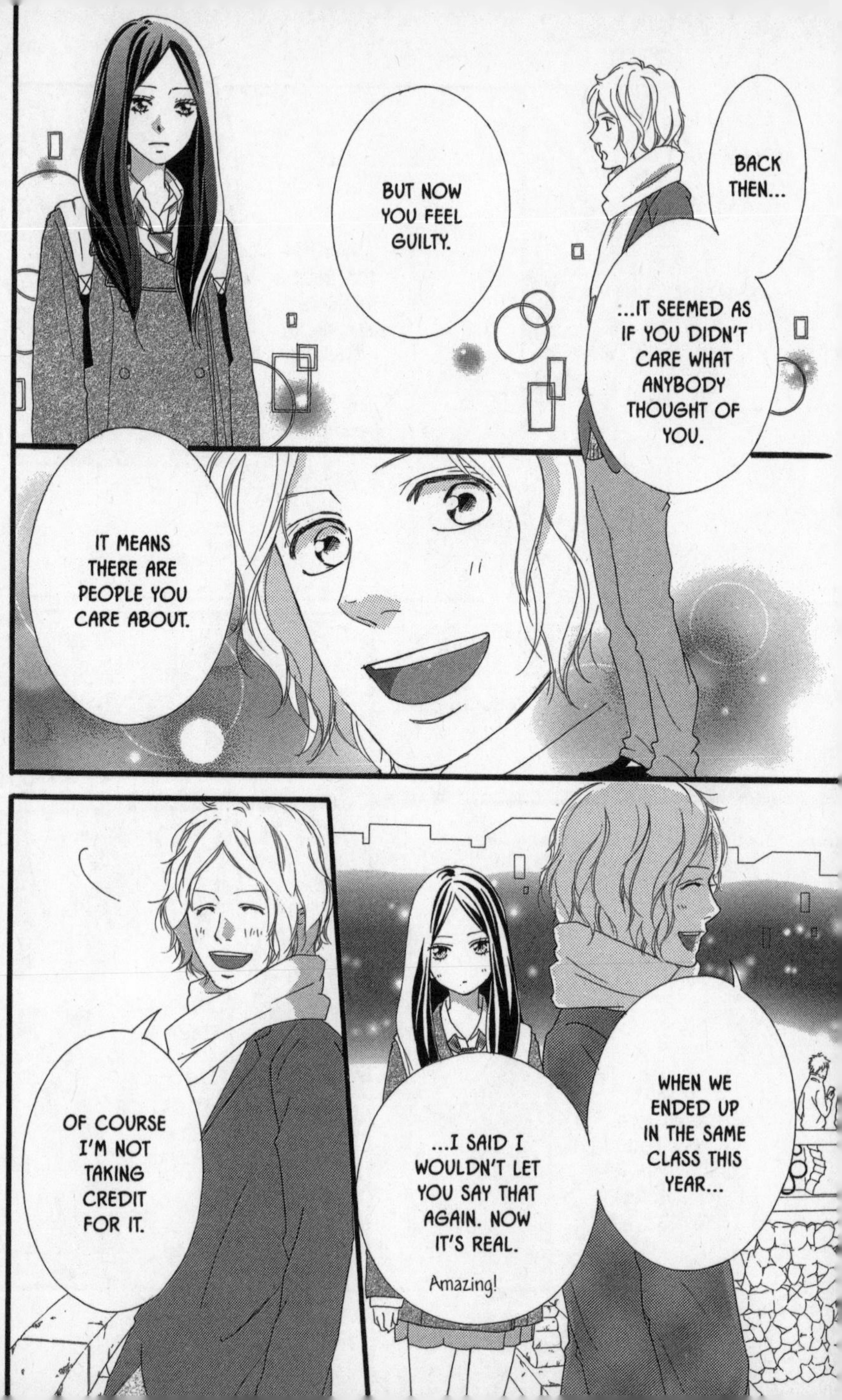
BACK THEN...
...IT SEEMED AS IF YOU DIDN'T CARE WHAT ANYBODY THOUGHT OF YOU.
BUT NOW YOU FEEL GUILTY.
IT MEANS THERE ARE PEOPLE YOU CARE ABOUT.
WHEN WE ENDED UP IN THE SAME CLASS THIS YEAR...
...I SAID I WOULDN'T LET YOU SAY THAT AGAIN. NOW IT'S REAL.
Amazing!
OF COURSE I'M NOT TAKING CREDIT FOR IT.

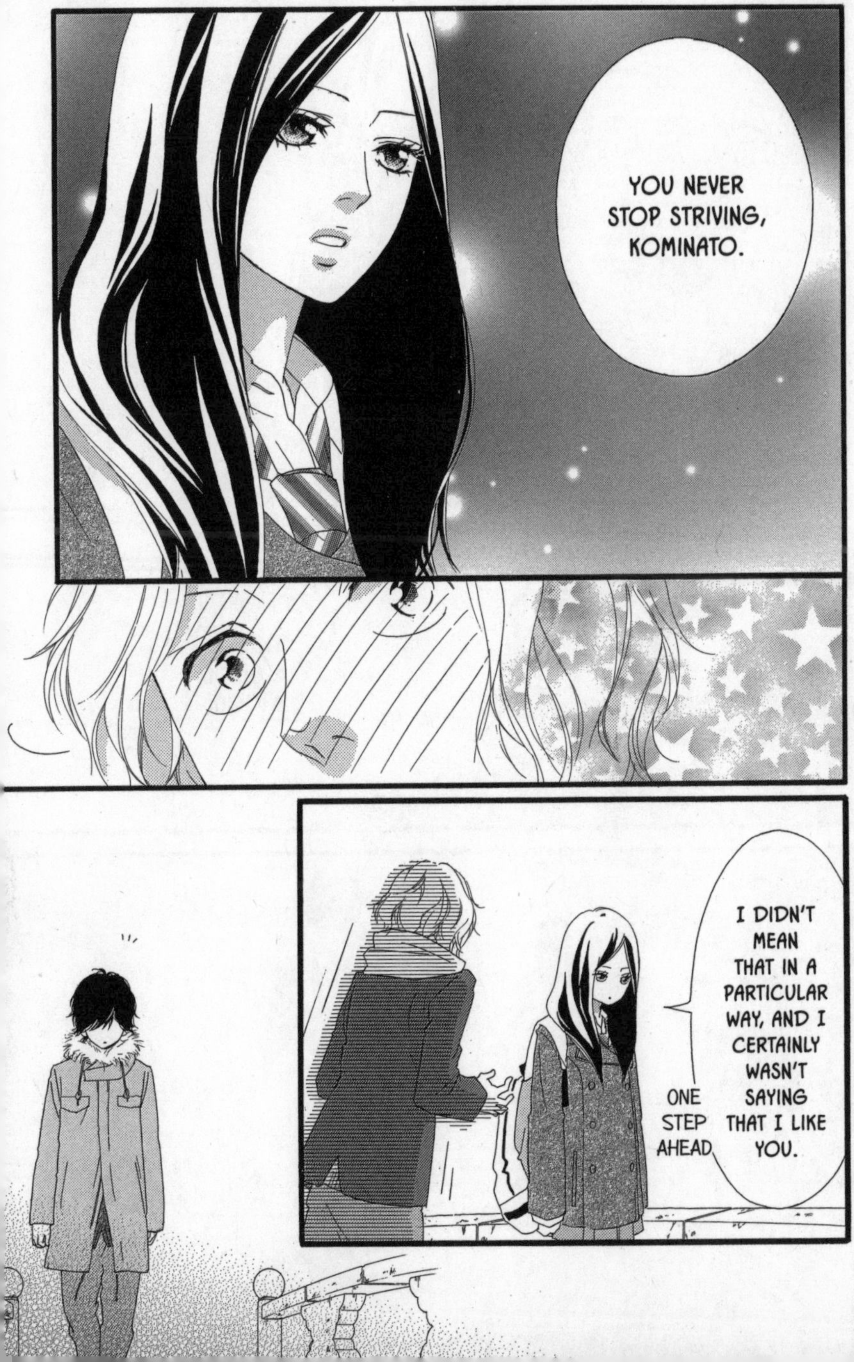
YOU NEVER STOP STRIVING, KOMINATO.
I DIDN'T MEAN THAT IN A PARTICULAR WAY, AND I CERTAINLY WASN'T SAYING THAT I LIKE YOU.
ONE STEP AHEAD

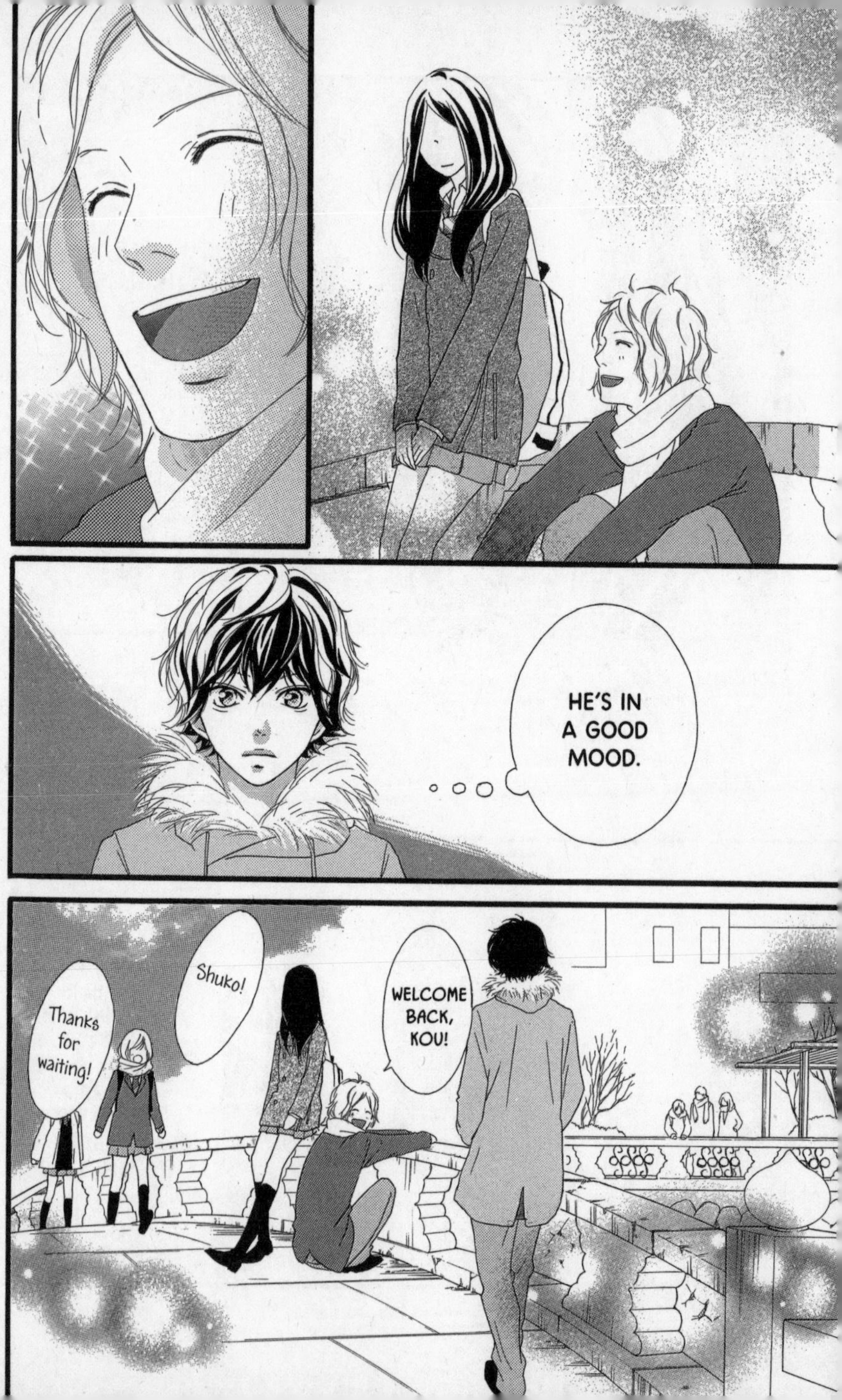
HE'S IN A GOOD MOOD.
WELCOME BACK, KOU!
Shuko!
Thanks for waiting!

Why is it so embarrassing when someone else hears your stomach rumble? When it happens, I'll say "excuse me," but I wonder why I need to. It's not like I'm emitting a strange object or substance... I often have this discussion with my assistants. Even though I've worked with them for many years, I'm still a little embarrassed when they hear my stomach. I have a feeling that my stomach rumbles more than the average person. And as a stomach-rumbler, I tend to get very uneasy in places that are especially quiet. I'm always in a place I least want to be heard when my stomach goes RRRMBL! I had someone show me the pressure points to prevent stomach rumbling, and I will grind them so hard that they hurt. Still, RRRMBL! I pray for the day when it's declared that stomach rumbling is not anything to be ashamed of.

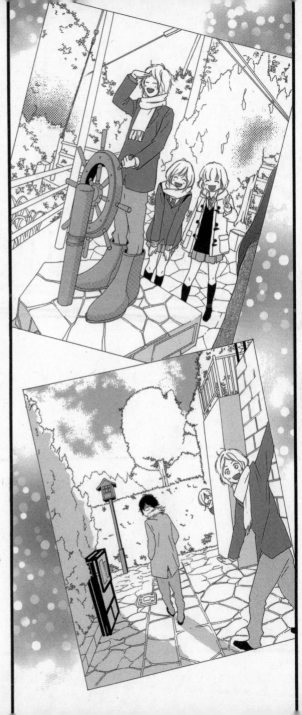

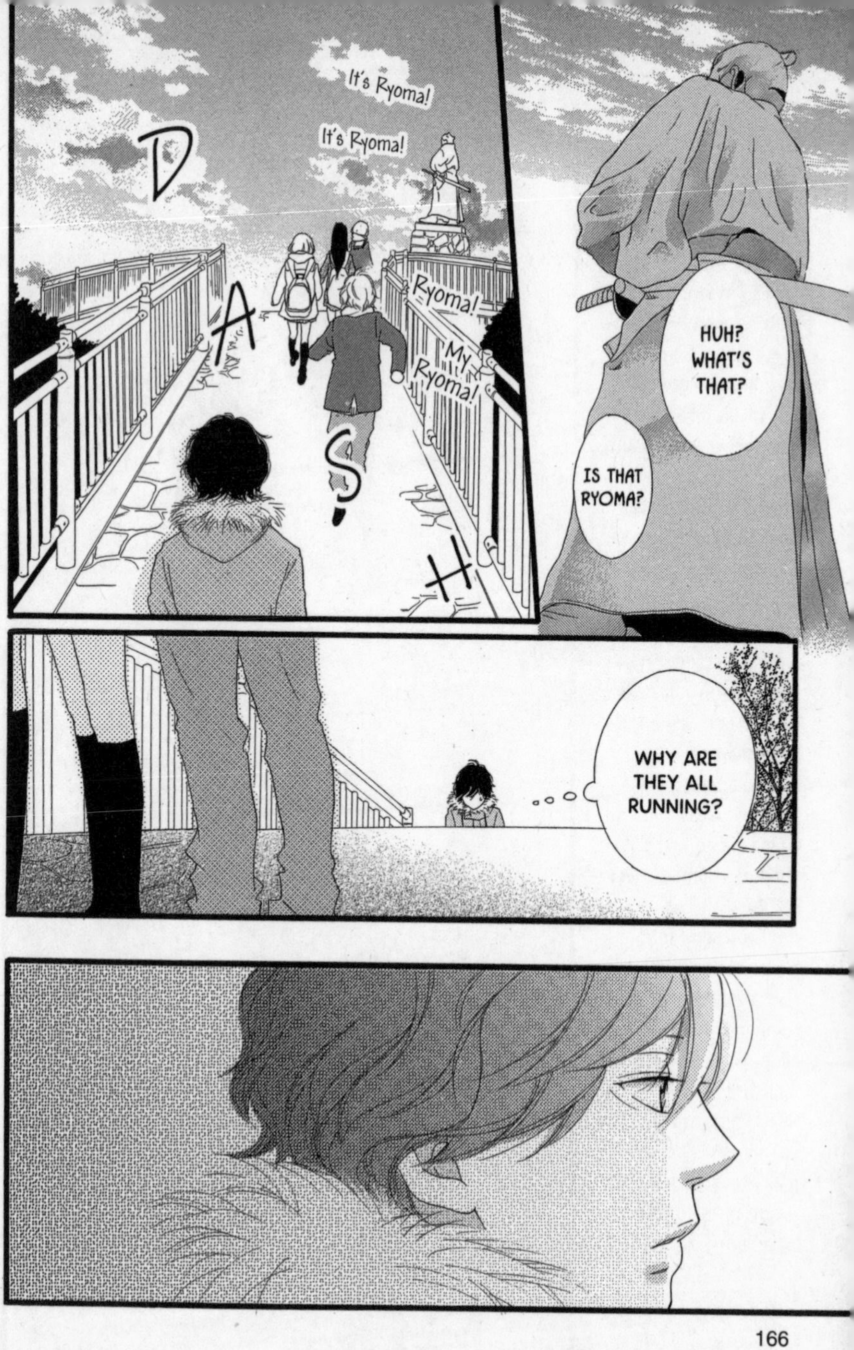
HUH? WHAT'S THAT?
IS THAT RYOMA?
It's Ryoma!
It's Ryoma!
Ryoma!
My Ryoma!
DASH
WHY ARE THEY ALL RUNNING?

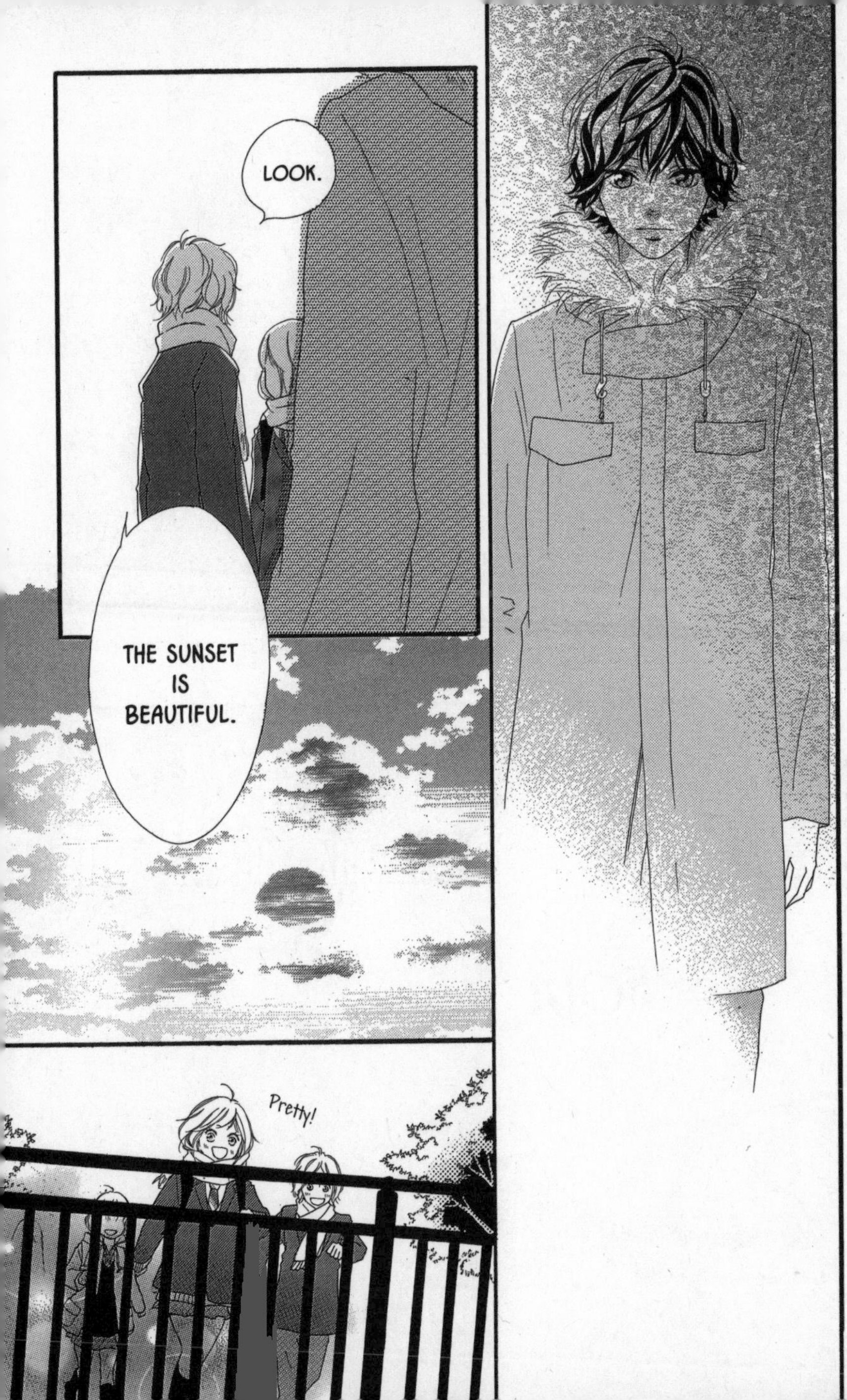
LOOK.
THE SUNSET IS BEAUTIFUL.
Pretty!

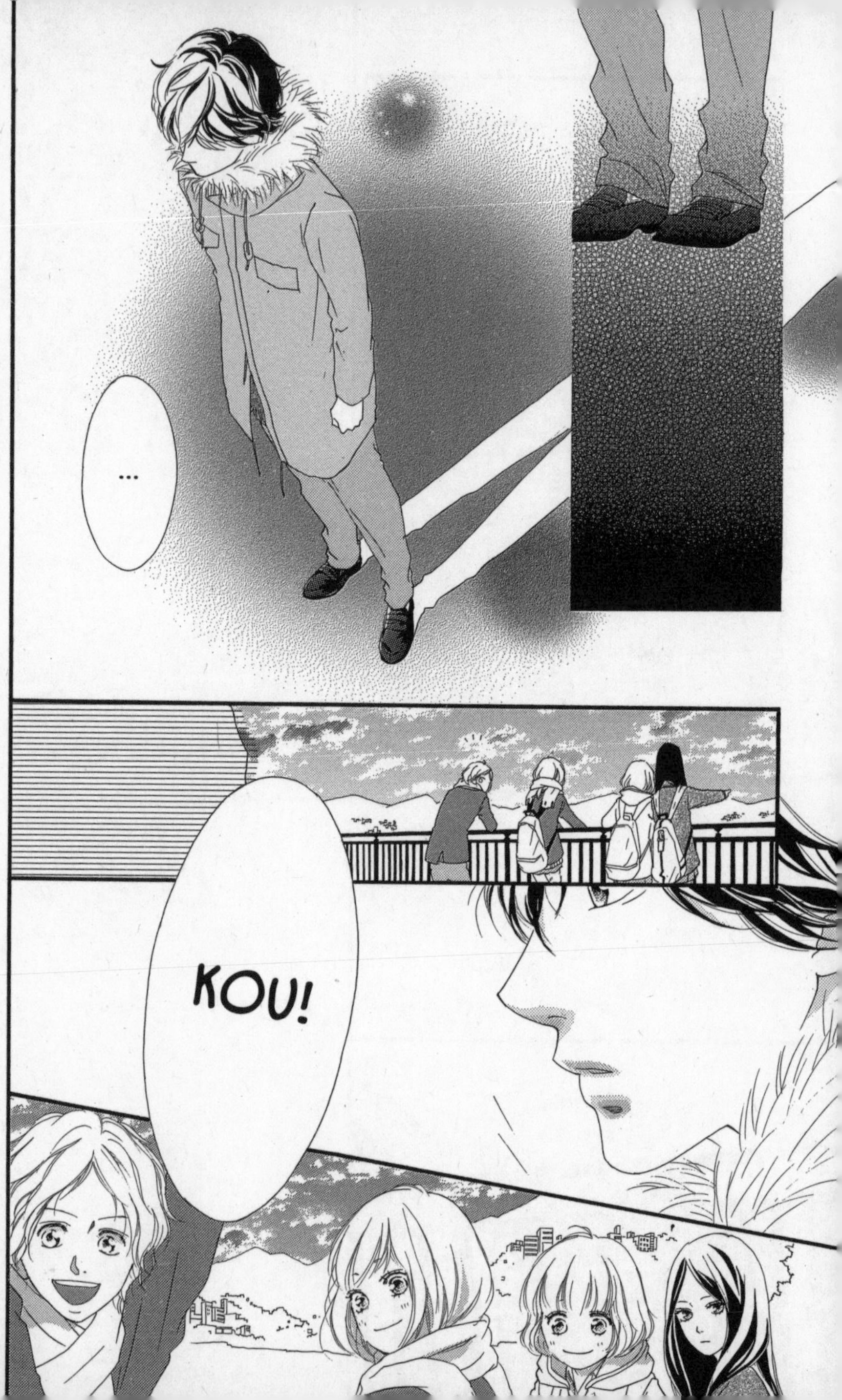
...
KOU!

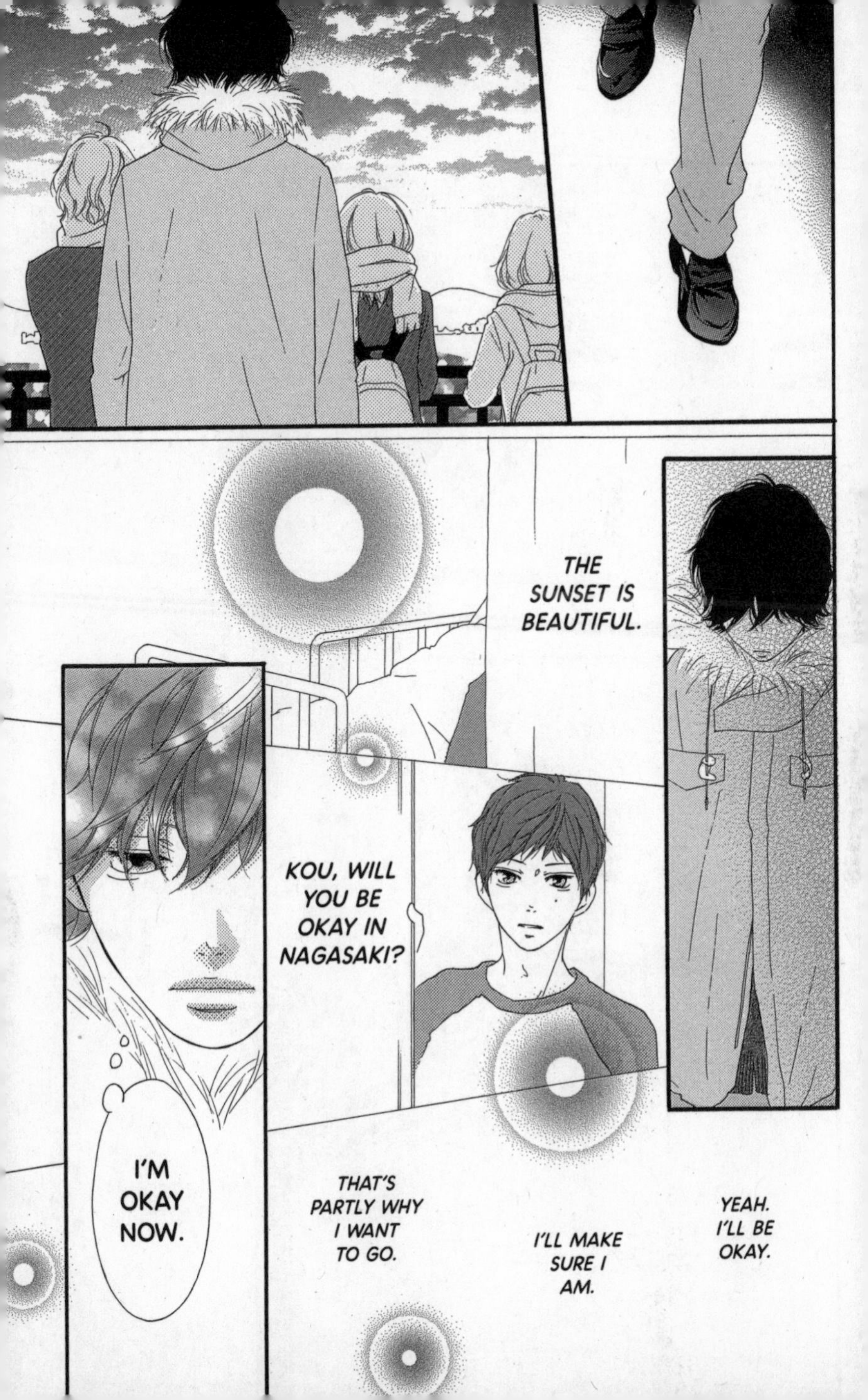
THE SUNSET IS BEAUTIFUL.
KOU, WILL YOU BE OKAY IN NAGASAKI?
YEAH. I'LL BE OKAY.
I'LL MAKE SURE I AM.
THAT'S PARTLY WHY I WANT TO GO.
I'M OKAY NOW.

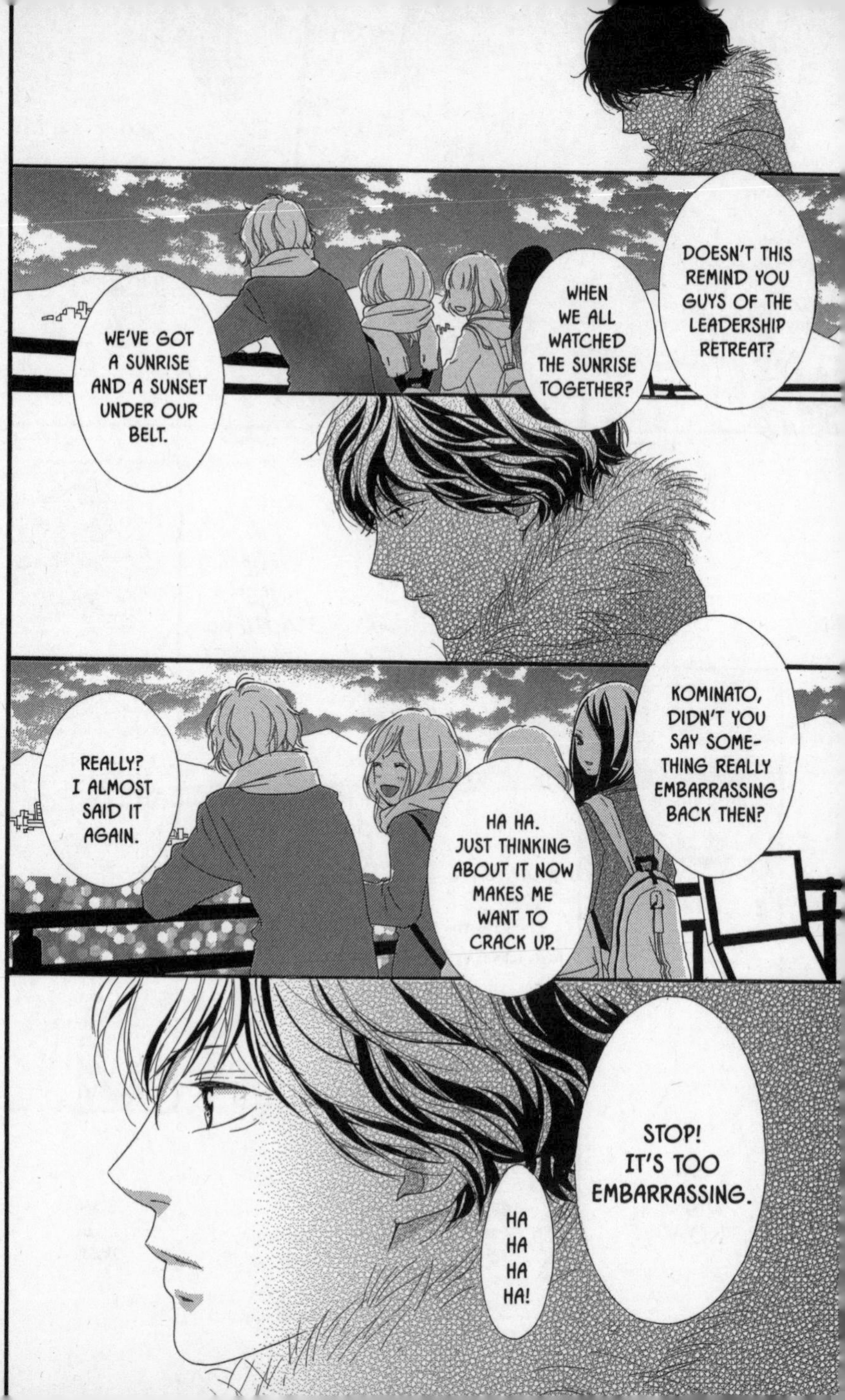
DOESN'T THIS REMIND YOU GUYS OF THE LEADERSHIP RETREAT?
WHEN WE ALL WATCHED THE SUNRISE TOGETHER?
WE'VE GOT A SUNRISE AND A SUNSET UNDER OUR BELT.
KOMINATO, DIDN'T YOU SAY SOME-THING REALLY EMBARRASSING BACK THEN?
HA HA. JUST THINKING ABOUT IT NOW MAKES ME WANT TO CRACK UP.
REALLY? I ALMOST SAID IT AGAIN.
STOP! IT'S TOO EMBARRASSING.
HA HA HA HA!

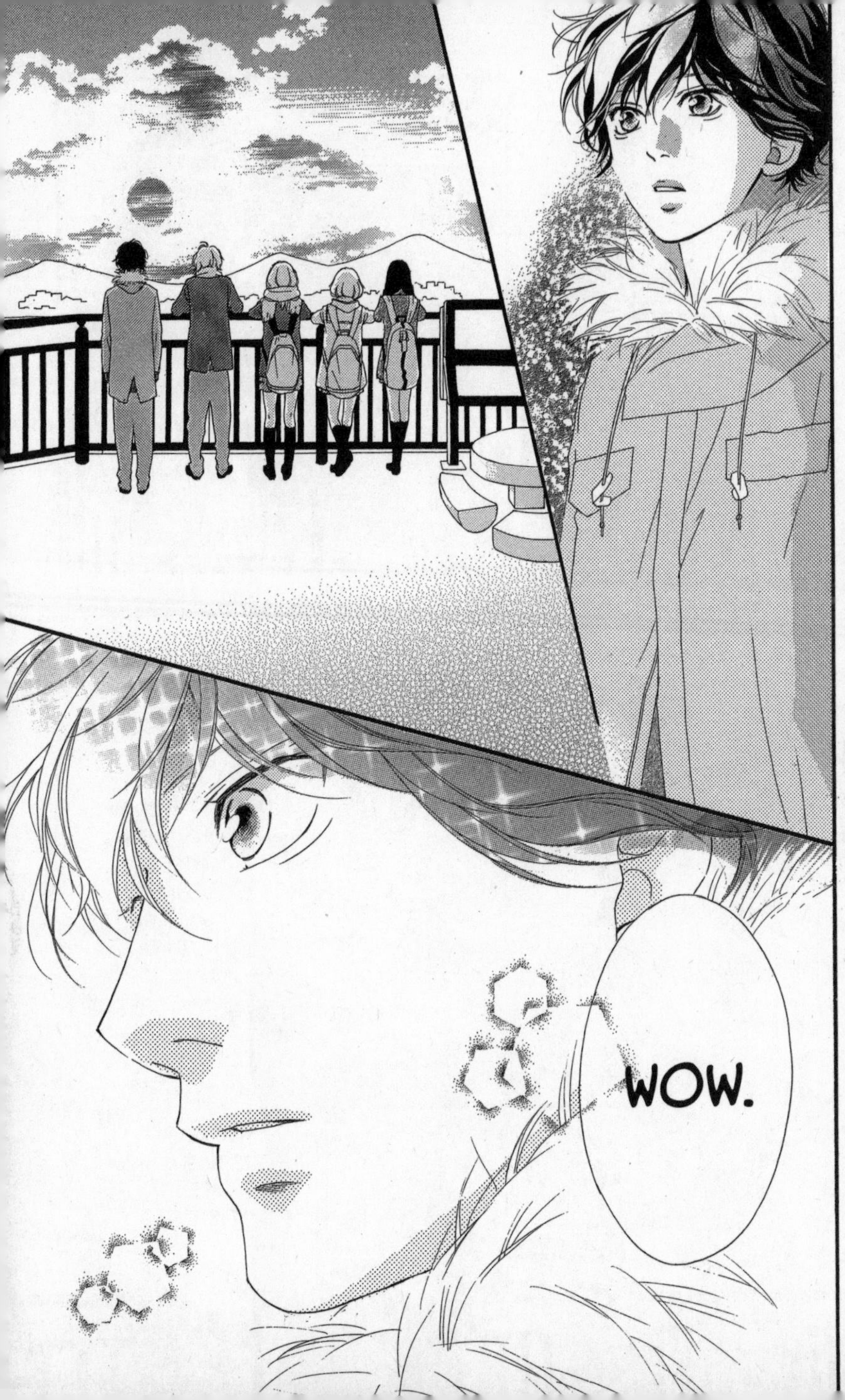
WOW.

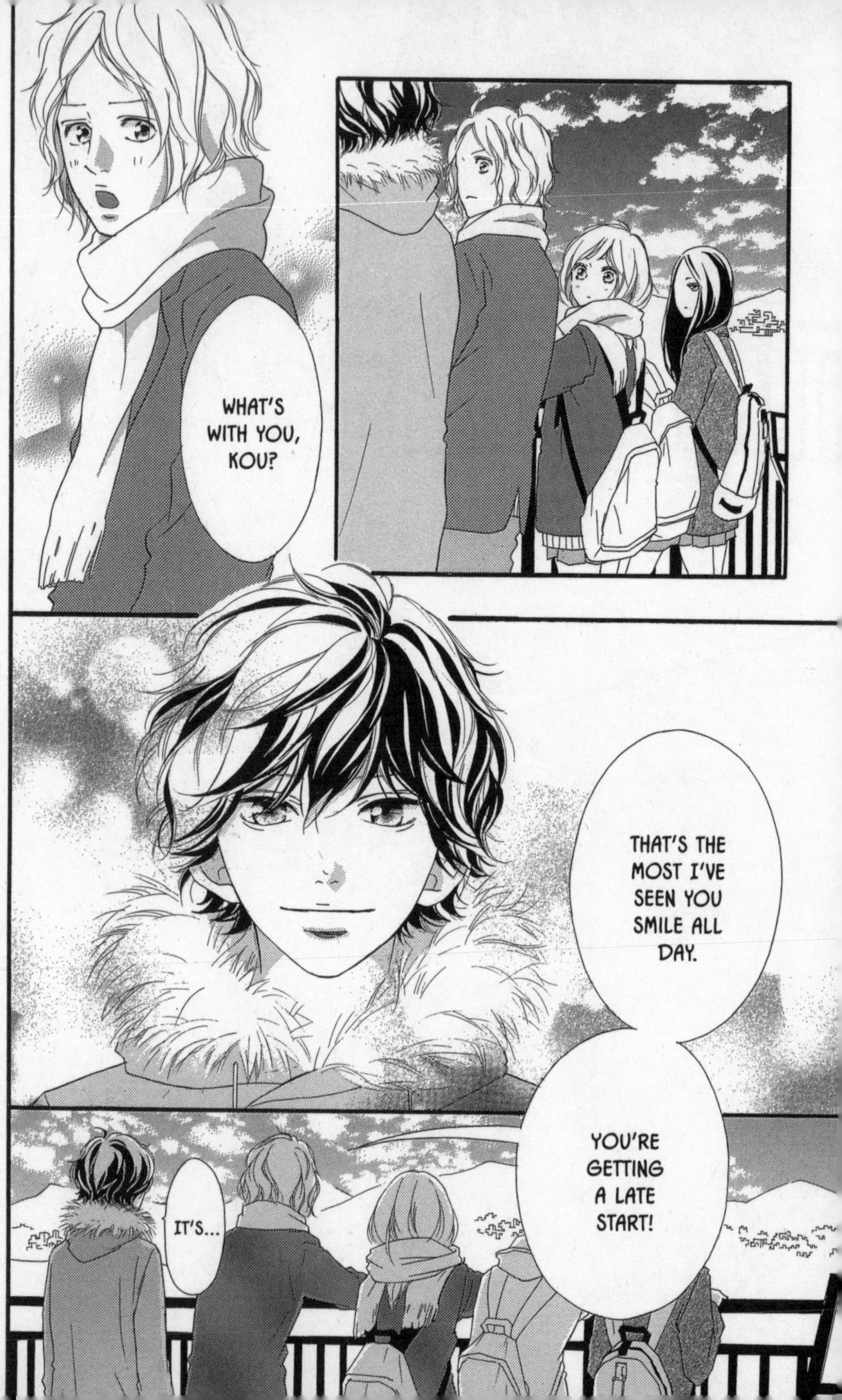
WHAT'S WITH YOU, KOU?
THAT'S THE MOST I'VE SEEN YOU SMILE ALL DAY.
YOU'RE GETTING A LATE START!
IT'S...

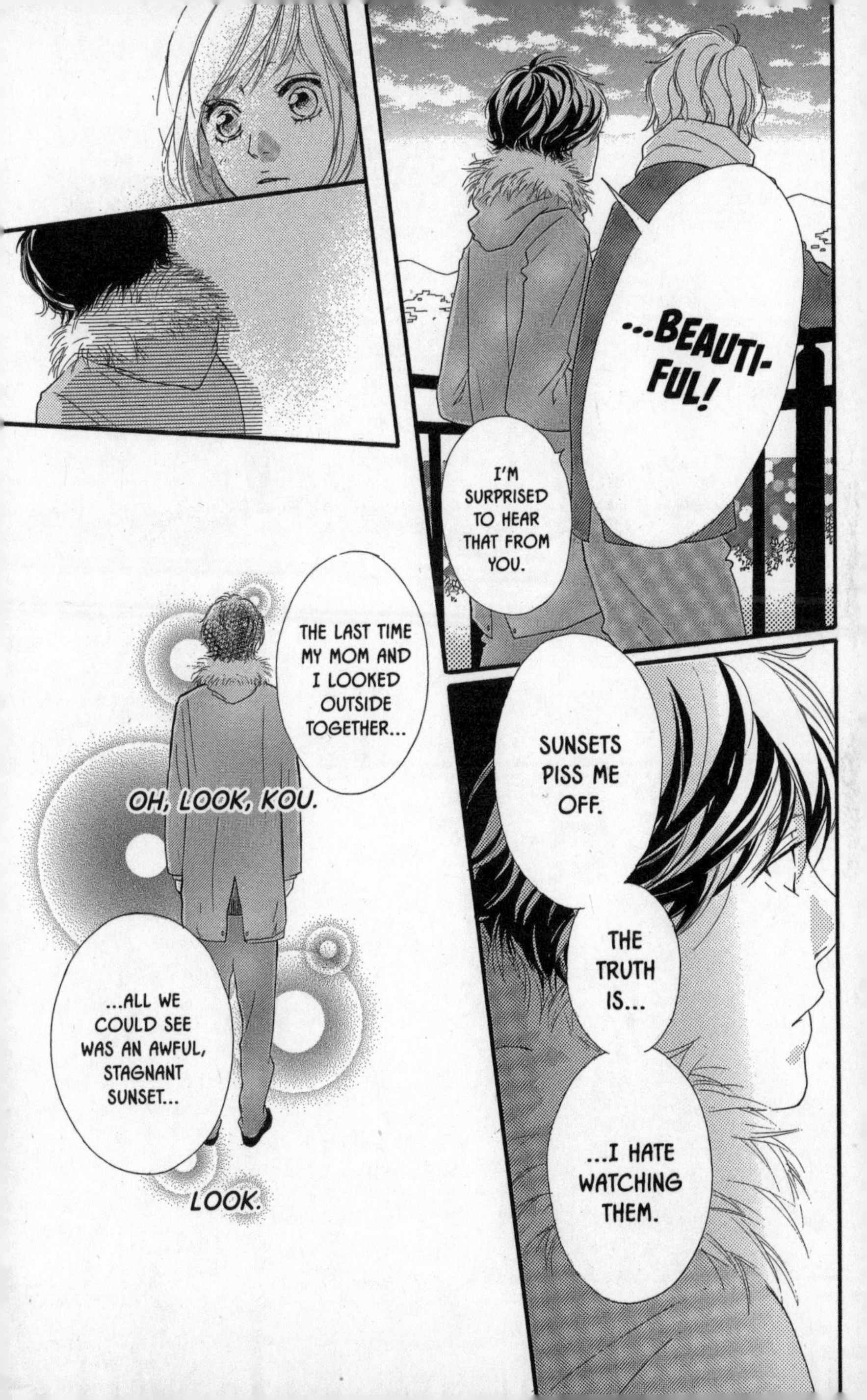
...BEAUTI-FUL!
I'M SURPRISED TO HEAR THAT FROM YOU.
SUNSETS PISS ME OFF.
THE TRUTH IS...
...I HATE WATCHING THEM.
THE LAST TIME MY MOM AND I LOOKED OUTSIDE TOGETHER...
OH, LOOK, KOU.
...ALL WE COULD SEE WAS AN AWFUL, STAGNANT SUNSET...
LOOK.

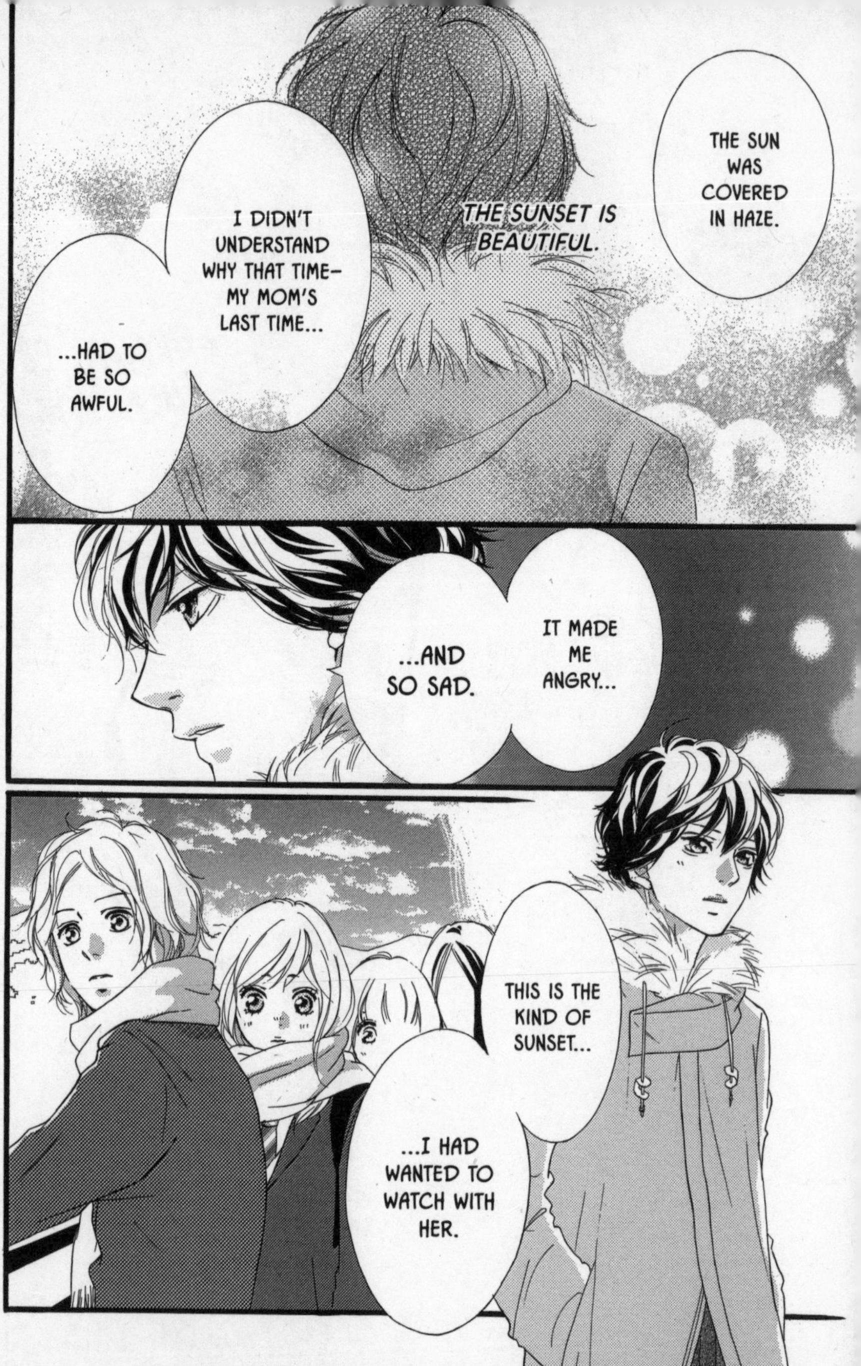
THE SUN WAS COVERED IN HAZE.
THE SUNSET IS BEAUTIFUL.
I DIDN'T UNDERSTAND WHY THAT TIME— MY MOM'S LAST TIME...
...HAD TO BE SO AWFUL.
IT MADE ME ANGRY...
...AND SO SAD.
THIS IS THE KIND OF SUNSET...
...I HAD WANTED TO WATCH WITH HER.

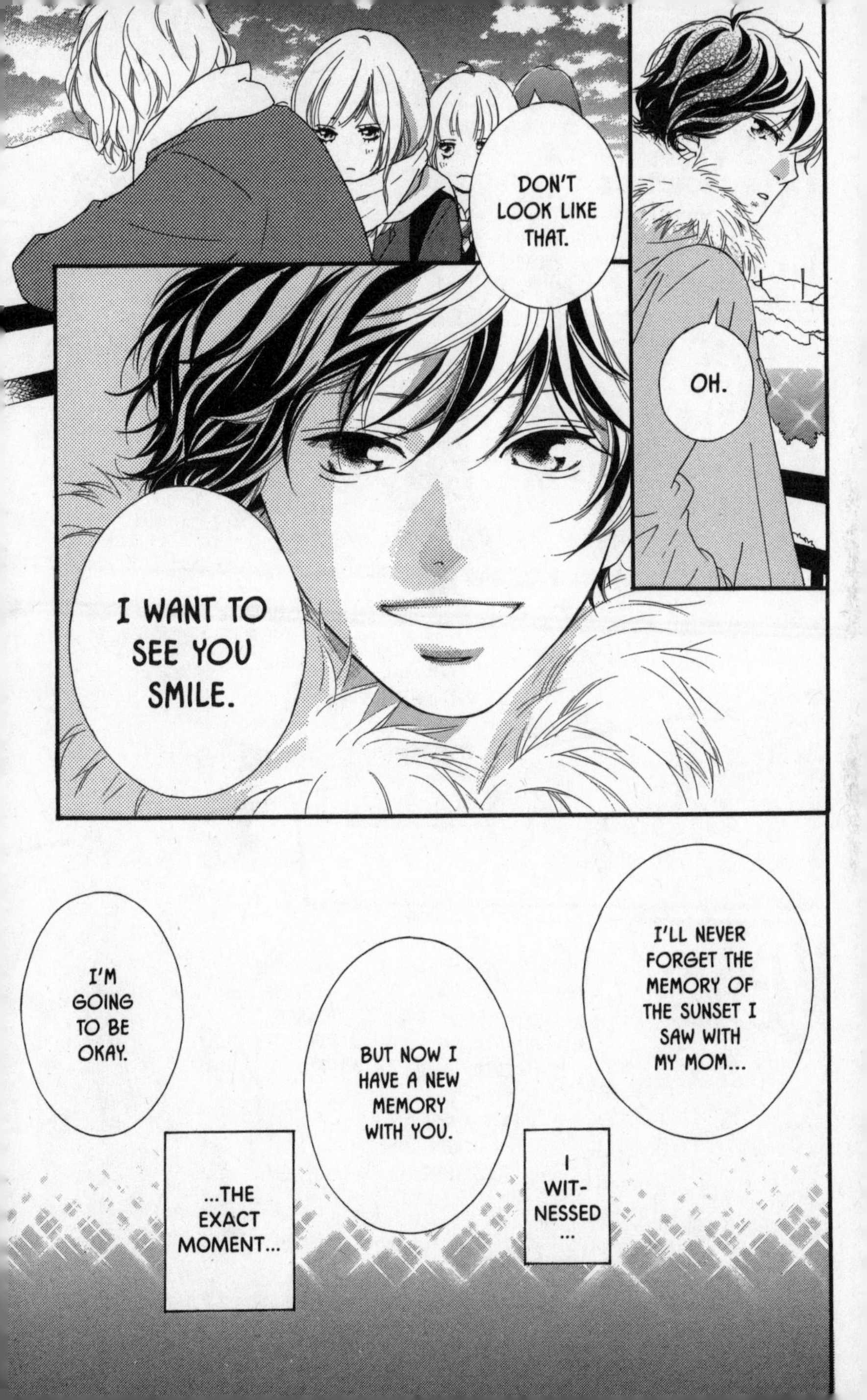
DON'T LOOK LIKE THAT.
OH.
I WANT TO SEE YOU SMILE.
I'LL NEVER FORGET THE MEMORY OF THE SUNSET I SAW WITH MY MOM...
I WIT-NESSED ...
BUT NOW I HAVE A NEW MEMORY WITH YOU.
...THE EXACT MOMENT...
I'M GOING TO BE OKAY.

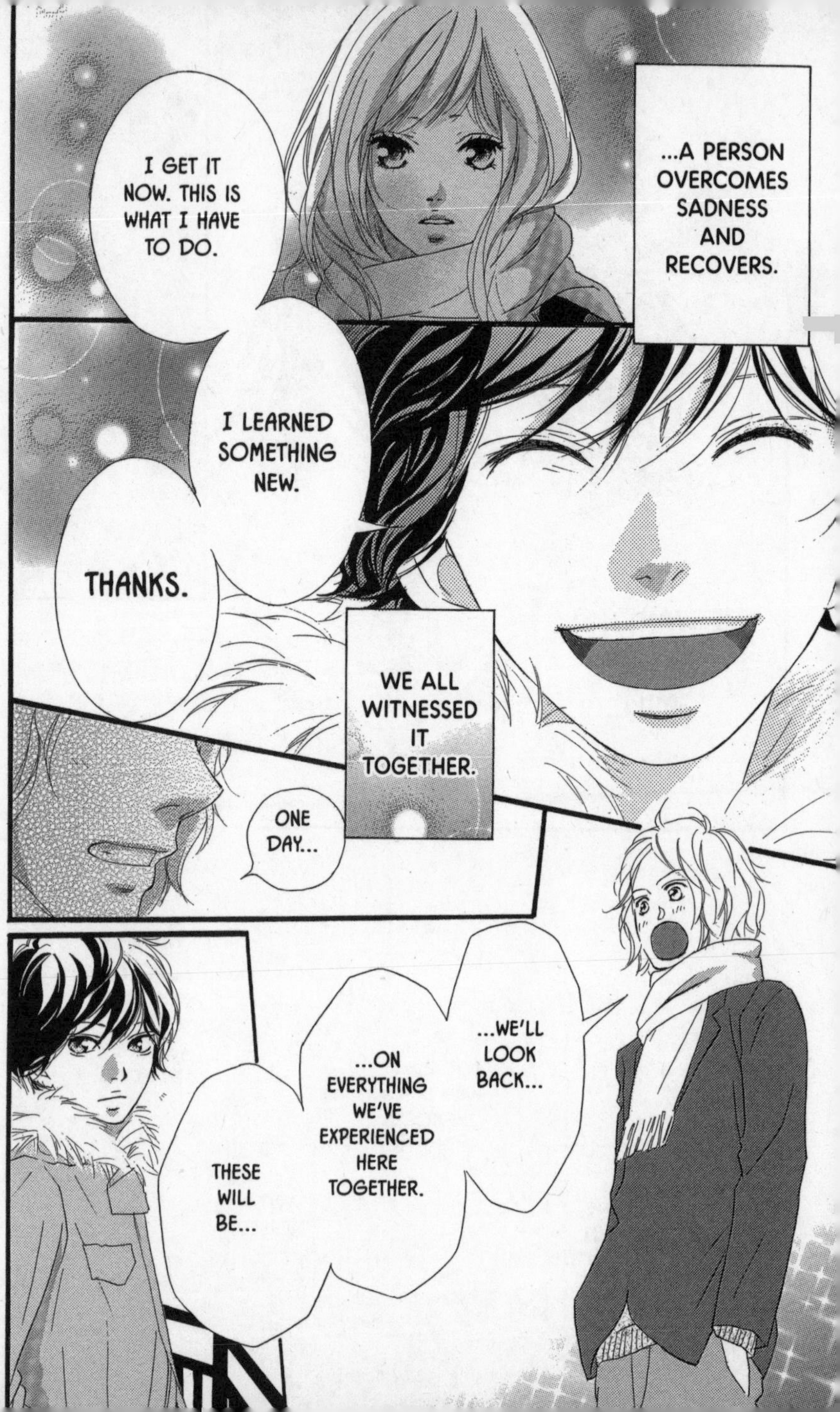

...A PERSON OVERCOMES SADNESS AND RECOVERS.
I GET IT NOW. THIS IS WHAT I HAVE TO DO.
I LEARNED SOMETHING NEW.
THANKS.
WE ALL WITNESSED IT TOGETHER.
ONE DAY...
...WE'LL LOOK BACK...
...ON EVERYTHING WE'VE EXPERIENCED HERE TOGETHER.
THESE WILL BE...

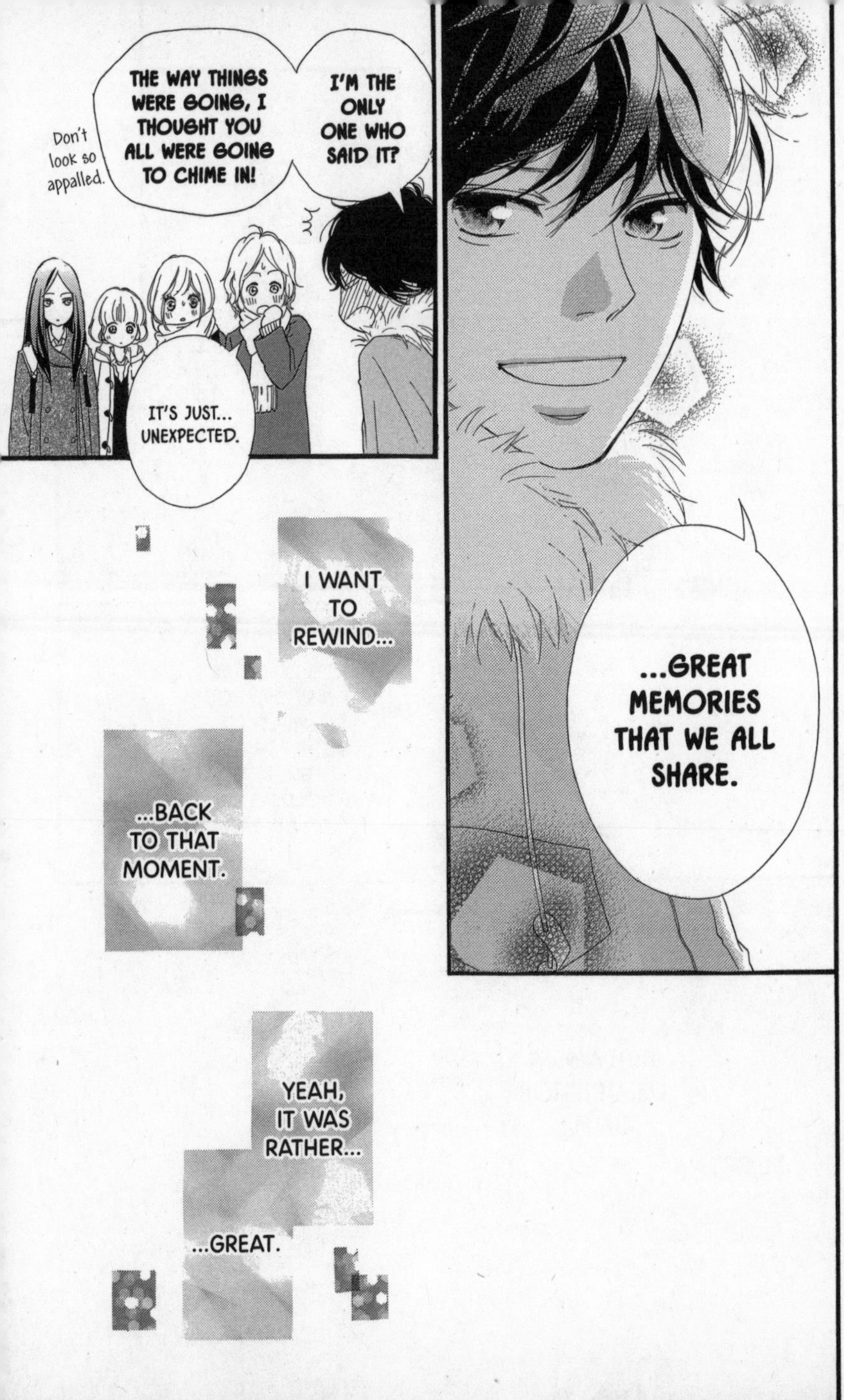
...GREAT MEMORIES THAT WE ALL SHARE.
I'M THE ONLY ONE WHO SAID IT?
THE WAY THINGS WERE GOING, I THOUGHT YOU ALL WERE GOING TO CHIME IN!
Don't look so appalled.
IT'S JUST... UNEXPECTED.
I WANT TO REWIND...
...BACK TO THAT MOMENT.
YEAH, IT WAS RATHER...
...GREAT.

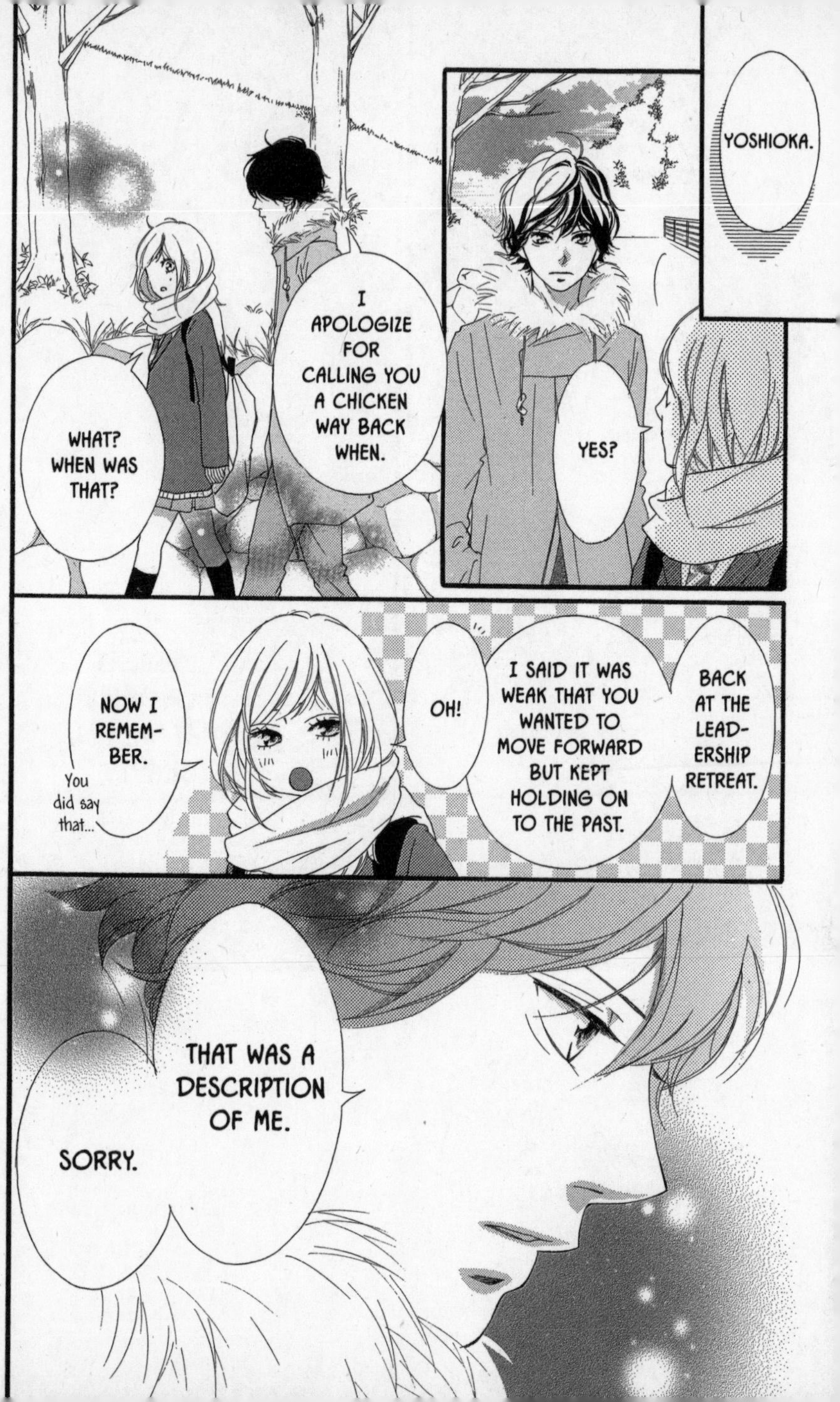
YOSHIOKA.
YES?
I APOLOGIZE FOR CALLING YOU A CHICKEN WAY BACK WHEN.
WHAT? WHEN WAS THAT?
BACK AT THE LEAD-ERSHIP RETREAT.
I SAID IT WAS WEAK THAT YOU WANTED TO MOVE FORWARD BUT KEPT HOLDING ON TO THE PAST.
OH!
NOW I REMEM-BER.
You did say that...
THAT WAS A DESCRIPTION OF ME.
SORRY.

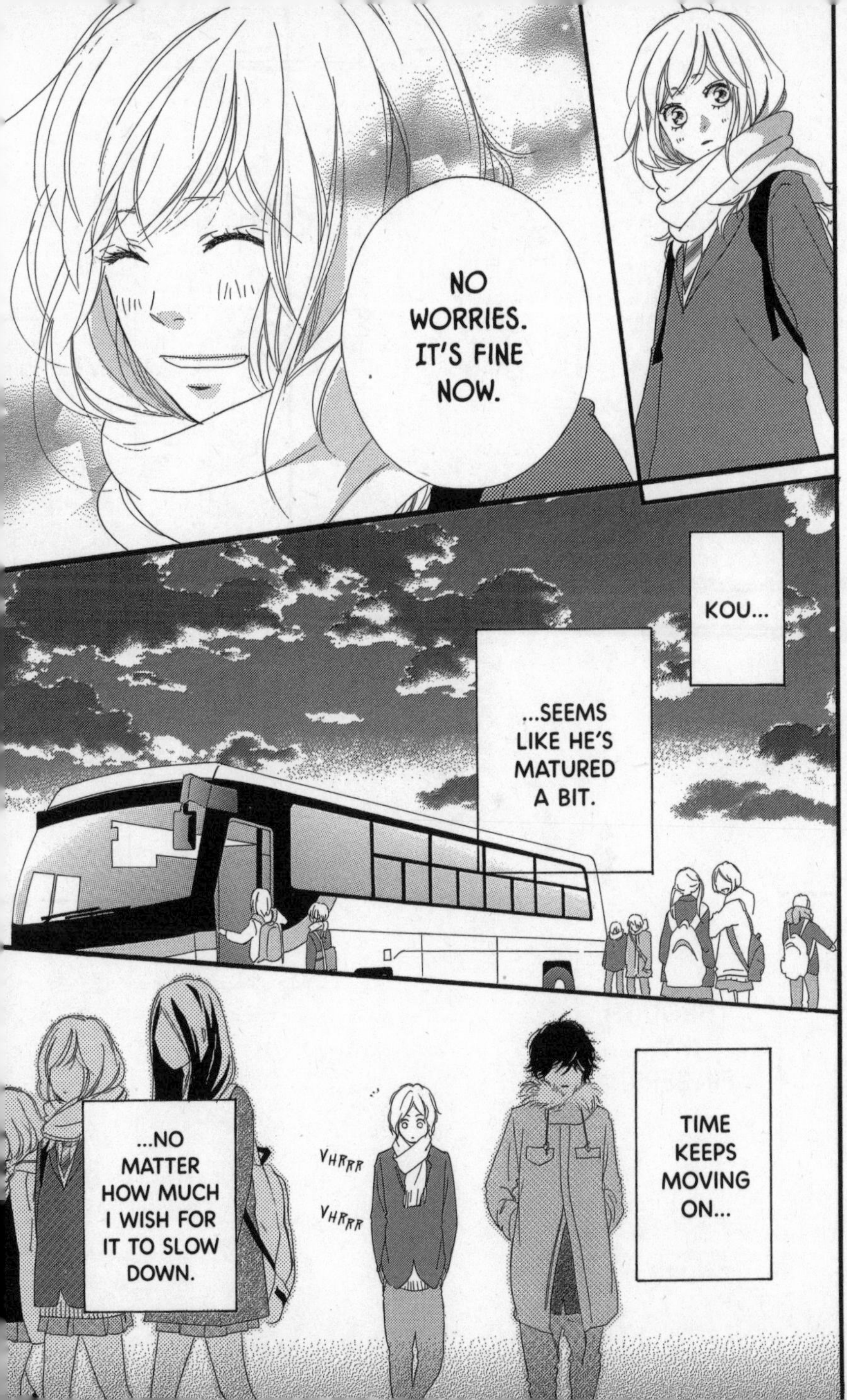
NO WORRIES. IT'S FINE NOW.
KOU...
...SEEMS LIKE HE'S MATURED A BIT.
TIME KEEPS MOVING ON...
VHRRR
VHRRR
...NO MATTER HOW MUCH I WISH FOR IT TO SLOW DOWN.

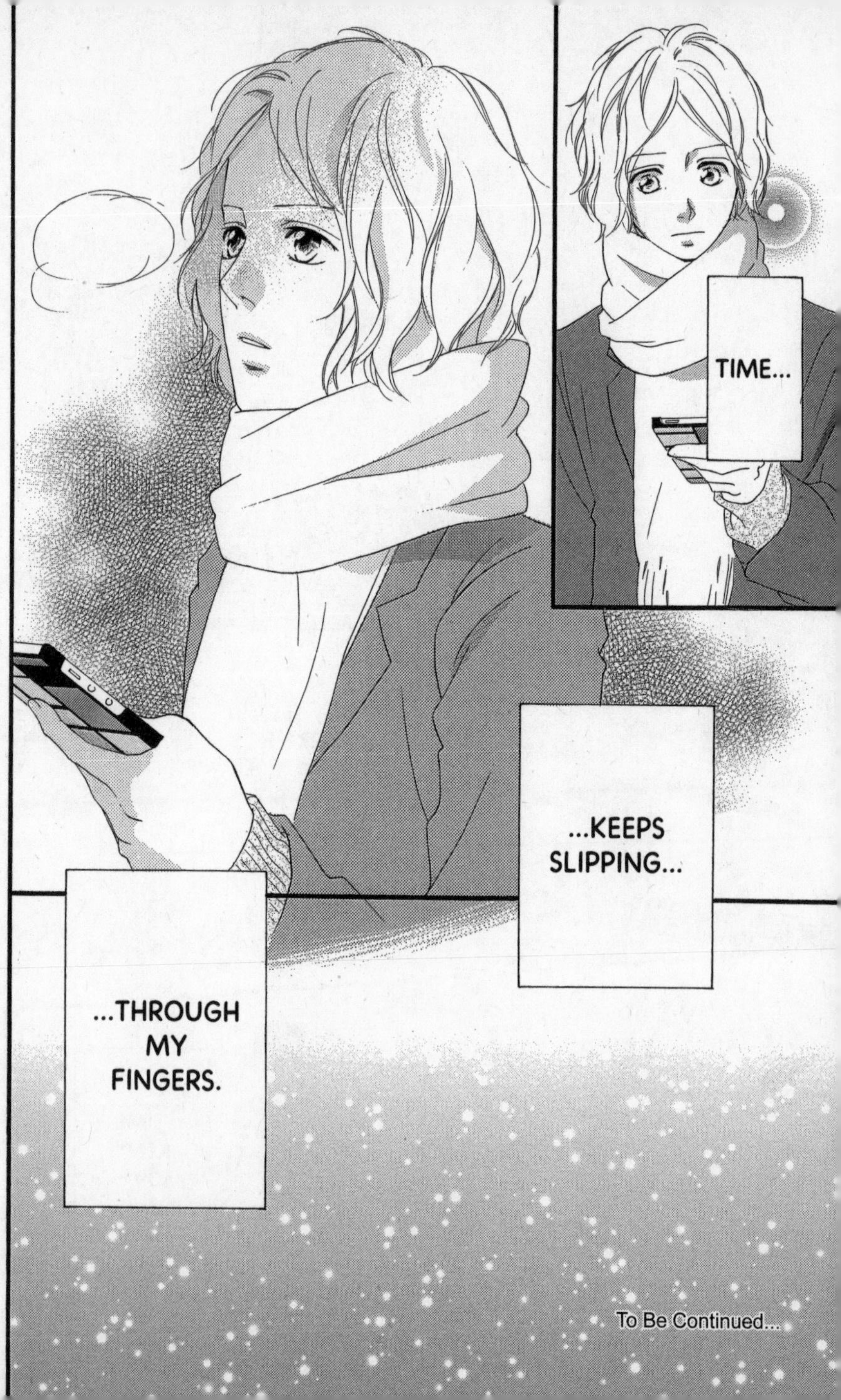
TIME...
...KEEPS SLIPPING...
...THROUGH MY FINGERS.
To Be Continued...

AFTERWORD

Thank you for reading through to the end!

I finally got myself a smartphone at the beginning of this year. People told me that if I played around with it, I would get used to it right away. I was looking forward to doing just that, but I really haven't used it much since I bought it, and I'm still unfamiliar with it. That makes sense. But when I have free time, I'm never in the mood to fiddle around with my phone. I'd much rather read a book, go see a movie or watch *Criminal Minds*... I know that I could find it useful, but I'm just not that interested... Somebody, please tell me how I can love my phone. What do I have to do to love it? I do want to love it.

This didn't end up being much of an afterword. And with that, with my head cocked a little to the side, I would like to end this volume.

See you all in the next volume!

 Io Sakisaka

Last time I wrote about my hair salon, and since I still haven't moved, I've been going there and acting as if nothing ever happened. It makes me wonder what that grand farewell was all about.

More importantly, I really want to move! Finding a new home is all about luck and timing!

IO SAKISAKA

Born on June 8, Io Sakisaka made her debut as a manga creator with *Sakura, Chiru*. Her works include *Call My Name*, *Gate of Planet* and *Blue*. *Strobe Edge*, her previous work, is also published by VIZ Media's Shojo Beat imprint. *Ao Haru Ride* was adapted into an anime series in 2014. In her spare time, Sakisaka likes to paint things and sleep.

Ao Haru Ride

VOLUME 10
SHOJO BEAT EDITION

STORY AND ART BY **IO SAKISAKA**

TRANSLATION **Emi Louie-Nishikawa**
TOUCH-UP ART + LETTERING **Inori Fukuda Trant**
DESIGN **Shawn Carrico**
EDITOR **Nancy Thistlethwaite**

First published in Japan in 2011 by SHUEISHA Inc., Tokyo.
English translation rights arranged by SHUEISHA Inc.

Printed in the U.S.A.

Published by VIZ Media, LLC
P.O. Box 77010
San Francisco, CA 94107

10 9 8 7 6 5 4 3 2 1
First printing, April 2020

ratings.viz.com RATED T TEEN

PARENTAL ADVISORY
AO HARU RIDE is rated T for Teen and is recommended for ages 13 and up. This volume contains the wanderlust of youth.

VIZ MEDIA
viz.com

Shojo Beat
shojobeat.com

STOP!

YOU MAY BE READING THE WRONG WAY.

In keeping with the original Japanese comic format, this book reads from right to left—so action, sound effects and word balloons are completely reversed to preserve the orientation of the original artwork.